"Readers will be swept off their feet by [ ] ment of the Sedgwick County Chronicles. *The Songs That Could Have Been* takes readers on a stunning journey of loss, love, and yearning for the things that could have been. Within these pages, Wen masterfully handles difficult themes like addiction and racism with authenticity, grace, and hope. Past and present are deftly woven together in this dual-timeline narrative that will leave readers flying through the pages. *The Songs That Could Have Been* is the 'can't miss' book of the year."

—AMANDA COX, author of the 2021 Christy Book of the Year, *The Edge of Belonging*

"Amanda Wen is a fresh new voice in the Christian fiction arena! Blending well-researched historical events with modern-day, relatable characters, she crafts tales within tales that are guaranteed to delight and inspire readers. I highly recommend this inspiring writer."

—KIM VOGEL SAWYER, best-selling author of *Freedom's Song*

"There are so many brilliant moments in *The Songs That Could Have Been*. Amanda Wen took risks that paid off with a treasure trove of themes which will resonate in my heart for a very long time. Peppered with struggle and yearning, the journeys of Carter and Lauren, Rosie and Ephraim, will ultimately fill you with deep hope and joy. Have tissues ready, but know they will be mostly for happy tears."

—DEBORAH RANEY, author of *Bridges* and the Chandler Sisters series

"As poignant as it is intricately crafted, *The Songs That Could Have Been* takes readers on a journey spanning decades and linking the stories of two couples who find themselves drawn together in unexpected and beautiful ways. This is a reading experience both heartfelt and heart-tugging, a timeless exploration of young and enduring love and the grace found in second chances. Amanda Wen is a rare and remarkable storyteller, and this is a novel I will not soon forget."

—AMANDA BARRATT, Christy Award–winning author of *The White Rose Resists*

the

SONGS

THAT COULD HAVE BEEN

Sedgwick County Chronicles

AMANDA WEN

KREGEL
PUBLICATIONS

Library of Congress Cataloging-in-Publication Data
Names: Wen, Amanda, 1979- author.
Title: The songs that could have been / Amanda Wen.
Description: Grand Rapids, MI : Kregel Publications, [2022] | Series:
  Sedgwick County chronicles ; 2
Identifiers: LCCN 2021062956 (print) | LCCN 2021062957 (ebook) | ISBN
  9780825447693 (paperback) | ISBN 9780825476983 (epub)
Subjects: LCGFT: Novels.
Classification: LCC PS3623.E524 S66 2022 (print) | LCC PS3623.E524
  (ebook) | DDC 813/.6--dc23/eng/20220104
LC record available at https://lccn.loc.gov/2021062956
LC ebook record available at https://lccn.loc.gov/2021062957

ISBN 978-0-8254-4769-3, print
ISBN 978-0-8254-7698-3, epub
ISBN 978-0-8254-6940-4, Kindle

Printed in the United States of America
22 23 24 25 26 27 28 29 30 31 / 5 4 3 2 1

To the glory of God
in honor of the Lees, Millers, Petersons, and Wens.
Thank you for welcoming our marriage.

CHAPTER ONE

CARTER DOUGLAS HATED running out of makeup.

Nearly eight years in the broadcast business, eight years of coating his face with foundation before going on air, had taught him to always keep a backup bottle on hand. But July in Wichita meant summer vacations, screwed-up schedules, and squall lines that kept him watching radar in the weather center long past his usual bedtime. This combo platter of too much work and not enough shut-eye meant many things had fallen by the wayside. So here he sat, half an hour before the Saturday 6:00 p.m. newscast, tilting, tapping, and turning the little bottle, pleading with those last clinging drops of creamy beige to slide out onto the sponge and let him smear them on his skin.

"No luck, huh?" Melanie Powell, on set in the anchor's chair, glanced up from her tablet. Like Carter, she routinely clocked in at three every weekday morning to help guide Kansans through school bus stops and rush-hour commutes. And, like Carter, she was pulling extra shifts to cover someone else's summer travels. The thick coating of cosmetics she'd already applied didn't quite hide the resulting blue-tinged bags beneath her eyes, but Carter knew better than to call attention to that.

Her observation forced him to face the truth. This bottle had nothing left. Zip. Zilch. Nada.

"Nope." Pushing his rolling office chair back from the desk, he tossed the makeup bottle, free-throw style, toward the metal wastebasket on the opposite side of the weather center. It hit the empty can with a satisfying clang. *And the crowd goes wild.*

"I'd let you use mine." His colleague's voice held a smile. "But I'm pretty sure you'd look like a vampire."

Carter chuckled. Mel's pale-as-a-bathroom-sink foundation combined with his deep-brown hair and slight widow's peak . . . that might not be too far off. All he'd need was a cape and some fangs.

"Help me remember that for the Halloween show, all right?" Tossing her a grin, he rose from the chair and retrieved his wallet from the desk drawer. "I'm off for more spackle. Get you anything?"

Mel tucked a lock of platinum-blonde hair behind her ear and looked up with a tired smile. "Coffee. Please. The stronger the better."

"One extra-strength rocket fuel comin' right up." Carter slid his wallet into the pocket of his dress pants and pushed open the wooden door to the studio.

A moment later he stepped through the lobby's double glass doors and into the wavy heat of the Channel Five parking lot. The contrast from freeze-dried indoor air to an outdoors as hot and damp as a dog's breath never ceased to amaze him. In the arid southwestern corner of Kansas, that endless sweep of horizon where he'd grown up, humidity was a non-issue. But here, even a two-minute walk across the parking lot made him break a sweat.

At least it was a relatively easy forecast.

The glass doors of Dylan's slid wide and beckoned Carter into the grocery store's air-conditioned bliss. Its location next to the studio made it the source of countless last-minute grocery runs and quick carryout meals—disappointing Mexican, decent Chinese, a beer fridge he avoided at all cost—and coffee so strong it practically required a fork, a longtime Channel Five favorite. He'd grab Mel's coffee just as soon as he picked up another bottle of foundation. He hung a quick left, strode down the cosmetics aisle to the section in the middle where his favorite brand could be found, and . . .

Well, crap.

The racks of foundation were nicely filled except the one that contained his perfect shade. The one he'd used for years. The only one that didn't make him look like a spray-tan experiment gone horribly wrong. Teeth clenched, he pawed through the bottles, praying one had been misplaced somehow, but no luck. His shade, the catchily named B385, was nowhere to be seen.

Guess he wasn't the only one who sometimes forgot to plan ahead.

><

Lauren Anderson welcomed the blast of cold air that awaited her on the other side of Dylan's sliding glass doors. Peeling damp strands of hair off her neck, she gave quiet voice to uncharitable thoughts about the couple who'd insisted on an outdoor wedding despite triple-digit temperatures and humidity that made it feel even worse. While outdoor weddings led to some of the most gorgeous photos she'd ever taken, if she ever walked down the aisle herself? Indoors all the way.

At least the reception was inside, providing Lauren a few minutes en route to restock her coconut water. But as heavenly as the chilled beverage sounded, she ducked first into the ladies' room to assess her appearance. Ugh. Like a moron, she'd forgotten to wear waterproof mascara, and two hours of snapping photos under the relentless sun made her look more than a little like a demented raccoon.

A wet paper towel undid some of the damage, but not enough. With a sigh, she tossed the paper towel into the trash and jetted out of the bathroom. This was a job for makeup remover.

At just before six on a Saturday evening, she hadn't expected to encounter anyone in the cosmetics aisle, but tonight a dark-haired man stood there in a crisp white dress shirt and black slacks, frowning at rows of foundation as though they contained the secret formula for turning Diet Coke into plutonium. She suppressed a laugh at the man's obvious confusion. Was he making an emergency date-night makeup run for a wife or girlfriend? Contemplating a future as a drag queen?

But then she caught a glimpse of his profile, and her smile slid off and crashed to the floor. That strong, straight nose. Square jaw. Eyelashes that went on for miles.

This wasn't just any man.

It was Carter Douglas. Right here. In the flesh.

Lauren tore her attention away as if burned and tried to calm her queasy stomach and racing heart. She'd known since last spring he was here in Wichita. And in case she could've forgotten, that enormous *Mornings with Carter and Mel* billboard beaming down on the expressway stood as a reminder of the face that had haunted her since high school.

He'd been lanky and teen-idol cute back then, with gleaming dark eyes and a devil-may-care grin. But now, now that broad shoulders filled out every inch of that dress shirt in the best possible way, now that faint smile lines bracketed his mouth and his formerly unruly hair was cut and styled to perfection . . . now, he was positively *smoldering*.

He glanced her way, and her cheeks heated despite the air-conditioning. She fixed her gaze forward on the fluorescently lit shelves, pretending to be deeply interested in . . .

Zit cream.

Great. Just when it couldn't get any more thirteen years ago.

"Excuse me." His tenor voice, deeper and more sonorous with age, jerked her attention to her right. A self-deprecating grin curved his lips, and deep-brown eyes held a touch of puppy-dog pleading.

Her stomach knotted. "Yes?"

"I'm not trying to be sexist, promise, so please don't take this the wrong way, but I go on air in a few minutes, and I could use another pair of eyes." He held up two bottles of foundation, one on each side of his face. "Which one's a better match? They're out of my usual."

Lauren stared. Not at the ludicrous sight of her ex-boyfriend trying to decide on makeup shades—although that would doubtless be funny later—but because he didn't recognize her. Not even a flicker of remembrance crossed those sculpted features.

How many times had she dreamed of this moment? Carter Douglas tumbling back into her life unexpectedly and not recognizing her because she was thin and gorgeous.

Okay. After an afternoon under the Kansas broiler, she wasn't gorgeous. Not right now.

But she was thin.

That, she'd made sure of.

Suppressing a smile of triumph, she glanced at the two bottles he held. Neither was ideal, but another brand one rack over held the perfect match.

"This one." She grabbed it and held it out to him.

"You sure?" He shifted both bottles to his right hand and took the new one.

"Mm-hm. Those others are too warm for your undertones. They'll make you look kinda orangey."

"Thank you. Truly. You may have just saved my job." Bottles clinked together as he returned the unwanted makeup to the rack. "So are you an artist of some kind? You sure seem to know a lot about undertones."

Was he . . . flirting with her? The playfulness in his voice indicated he might be, and the suggestive wiggle of his eyebrows confirmed it. Then he flashed a smile, one almost bright enough to produce a cartoonlike *ping*.

He still had no idea. She could walk out of here right now and he'd never be the wiser. That would probably be the smart, responsible, adult-y thing to do.

But all those empty promises, those pretty but meaningless words, had left deep wounds. Wounds that had taken years to recover from. And her battle-scarred heart wouldn't let her walk away without Carter Douglas knowing beyond a doubt just exactly who had picked out the perfect shade of makeup for him.

"I'm a photographer, yeah." Stepping to her left, she reached for the makeup-remover wipes and grabbed two packages. She tucked one under her arm, then gently thumped the other one into the center of Carter's chest. "That stuff's waterproof, by the way. You'll need these."

He replaced her hand on the package, his expression bewildered. "Thanks."

"Now you have everything." Mic dropped to perfection, she walked past him, humming a song she and Carter had performed under those summer-theater spotlights here in Wichita all those years ago. She'd played Hodel, her blonde curls hidden beneath a dark wig and colorful kerchief, while Carter stood tall and proud, a beret on his head and a rakish grin on his lips, *Fiddler on the Roof*'s perfect Perchik. Her steps were slow enough, though, and quiet enough, to hear the shuffle of his shoes, the crinkle of the plastic package still cradled against his chest.

"*Lauren?*"

There it was.

She stopped. Turned.

Carter stood in the middle of the aisle, makeup in one hand, package of wipes in the other. His mouth hung open, and a vertical line formed between furrowed dark brows.

The victorious smile she'd been fighting finally burst forth.

"Hello, Carter."

Chapter Two

Lauren Anderson. After all this time.

The stunning truth must've made him stare a beat too long, if her slightly raised eyebrow was any indication. And the smile tugging at her lips, the one that deepened an adorable dimple on the right side of her mouth, shot him back to that sweet summer. Ten magical weeks, too perfect to last.

"Wow, Lauren. It's great to see you." He didn't want to stare, but he couldn't help it. She looked so different. The round, apple-cheeked face he remembered now featured high cheekbones and a defined jaw. Delicate collarbones peeked from beneath the straps of her sundress, and one slender arm wrapped around a midsection much smaller than it used to be. Even her hair was different. A deeper, more golden hue than the bleached blonde she'd had in high school, and she'd ditched her tight, carefully curled ringlets for a riot of tousled waves atop her head. Sun-kissed, wind-blown strands escaped to dance around her long neck and freckled shoulders.

But her bottomless blue eyes, ringed with green in the center and fringed with long dark lashes . . . those hadn't changed. They'd peered at him with such love, those eyes had, and that image had haunted him for the last thirteen years. Served to remind him all that his train wreck of a life had cost them both.

Her tilted head told him he'd been staring again, and he summoned his best camera-ready smile. "Sorry. It's just . . . you look so different. The years have been good to you."

She laughed. The same silvery Lauren laugh, but it held an edge he hadn't heard before. "Thank you."

Had he hit a nerve somehow? She'd been sensitive about her weight that summer. A couple thoughtless comments from the director had brought her near tears and burned his heart with rage on her behalf. Over and over he'd tried to help her see herself the way he saw her.

To him, she'd always been beautiful.

"So what brings you to Wichita?" Tucking the package of makeup-remover wipes beneath his arm, Carter dusted off the boxes in his memory bank. "Your grandparents live here, right?"

"Grandma does. Grandpa passed away a couple years back, right when Grandma's Alzheimer's started to get bad. I moved in with her to help, and it worked okay for a while, but . . ." She paused, the story she wasn't telling him filled in by the warbling of a country singer on the store's sound system. "We had to move her to a home last year. She likes it, though, and she still remembers me most of the time, so it could be worse."

His heart ached at the one-two punch Lauren had suffered. Warmed at her compassion. "I'm so sorry." Without thinking, he reached out and gave her shoulder a gentle squeeze. The muscles beneath his fingertips tensed, but she didn't jerk away. He'd consider that a hopeful sign.

"What about you?" Her chin lifted, and the arm around her midsection tightened. "I mean, I guess you live here now too, what with Channel Five and all . . ."

"And all the perks that come with that." He jiggled the bottle of foundation. "But yeah. Been doing weather there a little over a year."

"Weather, huh?" She looked him up and down. "Last time I checked, you were dead set on the anchor's chair at CNN."

Carter stuffed his free hand into his pocket. "Yeah, well. Life has a way of not going quite the way you planned."

"If it's any comfort, my career ambition as the next Taylor Swift didn't exactly pan out either."

Moonlit memories swam to the surface. Memories of that little spot by the creek on her grandparents' farm. Of Lauren, her hair whispering against her cheek as she bent over the neck of that beat-up guitar.

That was the night that had changed everything.

He cleared his throat. "So you're a photographer now?"

"I am." Her shoulders lowered, and the grip of her arm around her midsection eased. "Weddings, newborns, my food blog . . ."

He blinked. "Food blog?"

A spark lit her eyes, albeit a guarded one. "Health food mostly."

That probably explained her weight loss.

"I do a lot of plant-based, organic, that kind of thing. I want people to know how delicious and fun it is to cook and eat the food God intended."

He grinned. "I'm mostly on the Drive-Thru Diet, so I'll have to take your word for it."

"You'd swear off that drive-thru junk if you made my Bananarama Pancakes." She poked her index finger at him. "Three ingredients, super easy, and way yummier than a McFat-and-Calories Deluxe."

"I'll have to pop the batteries out of my smoke detector before I start, then."

Lauren's laugh made him feel like he'd just swished a three-pointer. "Seriously, anyone can make this." Bracelets clinked as she pawed through a colorful woven bag and pulled out a business card. "Here. The pancakes were last Thursday's post."

He took the card from her outstretched fingertips, but his eyes skated right over the web address to the little picture of her on the right. Graceful cupped hands overflowed with berries and leafy greens, loose golden waves tumbled over her shoulders, and her smile was the same one that had made his heart thump all those years ago.

It thumped now too.

He pretended not to notice.

"Listen, Carter, I've got to run. But it was good seeing you again." She paused, opened her mouth, then shut it with a slight shake of her head, whatever she'd been about to say destined to remain a mystery. "You take care, okay?"

"Yeah." His voice didn't sound like his own. "You too, Lauren."

She retreated down the cosmetics aisle, her sandals slapping softly against the tile floor in an odd rhythm with the final strains of the song.

A sharp buzz in his pocket jolted him, and he pulled out his phone. Mel.

"Let me guess. You want iced coffee, not hot?"

"Forget the coffee, dill weed." Mel's favorite insult knifed his left ear. "Did you forget you've got a show tonight? We're on air in twelve minutes."

His stomach dropped. As a matter of fact, he had forgotten.

Lauren Anderson had made him forget everything.

Just like she always did.

→←

The next afternoon Lauren's red Jeep responded with a cheerful horn chirp as she pressed the lock button, then slipped her keys into her purse and crossed the sunbaked parking lot to the entrance of Plaza de Paz for her traditional Sunday visit. Garrett had been right about this place, blast him. Though Rosie Spencer still had plenty of bad days as her Alzheimer's proceeded down its predictably tragic path, the care and company of staff and residents alike meant that, more often than not, she was still the spunky, vibrant woman Lauren had always known. Even if she rarely remembered Lauren's name.

It had taken Grandma wandering off during a tornado—one that passed within yards of the family farm—for Lauren to see what her brother had been trying to tell her for weeks: Grandma wasn't safe in her home any longer. Goose bumps pricked along Lauren's arms, despite triple-digit temperatures, at the memory of that close call last spring. The dissonant moan of the siren. The panicked desperation when she returned to the kitchen and found Grandma's chair empty. And the meteorologist on TV, his voice strained with impassioned urgency. Her first glimpse of Carter in thirteen years. In fact, he'd—

"Lauren. Hey."

Her brother's greeting mercifully jerked her out of the past, and she glanced across the posh lobby to see him step off the elevator.

"Garrett." She crossed the room for a quick embrace. "I didn't know you were coming today."

They started toward the reception desk, and Garrett's dimple deepened. "Me neither, but Sloane's been going through more boxes."

Grinning, Lauren scribbled her name on the sign-in sheet, then handed the pen to Garrett. "What'd she find this time?" Since purchasing the Spencers' farmhouse and moving in last summer, her history-geek future sister-in-law had taken great joy in digging through a century-and-a-half's worth of family artifacts.

"An old Bible. Black, with red trim on the pages and Grandma's maiden name on the front." He glanced over his shoulder at her. "I'd never seen it before. Does it ring any bells for you?"

"Don't think so, no."

Garrett turned back to the sign-out sheet. "Anyway, I thought I'd drop it by. See if she remembered it."

"Did she?"

"Hard to say. She took it from me and looked through it, but I don't know if it registered." He stashed the pen and swiveled toward Lauren. "So how are you?"

"I'm good." She tightened her grip on the strap of her purse. "I, uh . . . ran into Carter yesterday."

"Yeah?" Garrett leaned against the reception desk. "Couldn't avoid that forever, I suppose. How'd it go?"

"Okay, I think. He didn't recognize me." That moment still ranked as one of her life's most unassailable triumphs. She'd pictured a thousand different versions of Stunned Carter, but even her wildest imaginings paled in comparison to the real thing.

"Well, you've grown up a lot, Lo."

"So's he." And that was where the triumph ended. Because her heart—covered in the scars his knife had inflicted—had still done backflips at the sight of those depthless dark eyes. At that sweet tenor voice. At the warmth of his hand on her shoulder during that brief second of reassurance.

Garrett studied her with the same attention to detail he gave his clients' investment portfolios. "So . . . are you all right?"

"Sure. Fine. I mean, it's always a little awkward, seeing your ex. But we're both adults. We exchanged hellos, caught up for a couple minutes, and went our separate ways. And it's over now. Never have to see him again." Except for that stupid billboard . . .

"Okay." Garrett quirked a brow, his almost-infallible Sibling Crap Detector giving off a nearly audible beep.

"Okay. I'm gonna go see Grandma." Lauren pressed the elevator button, and it lit beneath her touch. "You and Sloane are still on for dinner tomorrow night, right?"

"Long as you make something with gluten in it, we're golden."

The ding of the elevator was perfectly timed with the raspberry she blew him, and he tossed a cheerful wave as she stepped between the sliding steel doors.

→←

Moments later Lauren rounded the corner of a bright-blue hallway and arrived at her grandmother's suite, an entrance decorated with columns and a white picket fence in an effort to make Plaza de Paz as homey as possible. A small touch, perhaps, but one Lauren appreciated.

"Grandma?" She tapped with the brass knocker. "It's me, Lauren."

The resulting silence wasn't unusual, since Grandma sometimes napped during the day. Maybe the visit with Garrett had tuckered her out.

"I'm coming in, okay?" Lauren crept in, and sure enough, Grandma's familiar snowy curls peeked up over the top of her much-loved blue recliner.

"Grandma?" Lauren peered around the chair.

The pale-blue eyes behind Grandma's gilt-framed glasses were wide and filled with tears. Her thin lips trembled. Open on her lap was a softly worn Bible.

Lauren fell to her knees in front of Grandma's chair and sought the unseeing gaze. "Grandma." She laid a hand over the wrinkled one on the Bible. "Grandma, it's okay. You're safe. It's me, Lauren. Barbara's daughter. Your granddaughter."

But a tear spilled down the weathered cheek. "I can't . . . can't . . ." With her free hand, she tapped the Bible.

Lauren glanced at the red-edged white pages in her grandmother's lap. The print was smaller than the Bible Grandma usually read, the one that always sat on the little table beside the recliner. Her vision was still sharp, especially given her age, but that font was pretty small.

"Would you like me to read to you? Is that it?" Relieved at having uncovered the source of frustration, Lauren eased the Bible from her grandmother's shaky grasp.

Genesis 48? Lauren's forehead creased. Usually her grandmother found her comfort and encouragement in the Psalms or the letters of Paul.

"Grandma, is this where you want me to start? In Genesis?"

Taking her grandmother's silence as assent, Lauren sank into the chair beside hers, the faithful companion recliner that had belonged to Grandpa. Orrin Spencer had been gone nearly two years now, but the plush blue velvet still gave off a faint comforting whiff of musky aftershave and pipe smoke.

She adjusted the Bible on her lap. "And it came to pass after these things, that one told Joseph, Behold, thy father is sick: and he took with him his two sons, Manasseh and Ephraim—" A choked sob cut her off. Grandma held a wrinkled fist to trembling lips.

"Grandma?" Lauren leaned in. "Please tell me what's wrong."

"Ephraim," came the guttural response. "He should've been here by now. We were supposed to meet . . . Can someone tell me please . . . what's happened to Ephraim?"

Chapter Three

"Grandma?" Kneeling, Lauren sought her grandmother's frantic gaze and tried to still the aged, trembling hands. "Who's Ephraim?"

"He's never this late." Beneath Lauren's gentle grasp, one cold hand clenched and loosed, clenched and loosed. "Where *is* he? Has something happened?"

Lauren grabbed the remote and switched off the TV. "Grandma, it's all right. We'll find Ephraim." The unfamiliar name rolled around her tongue. "But . . . let's get some help, okay?" Reaching for the speaker on the wall behind the couch, she yanked its cord and kept her voice as calm as she could. "Hello? Hi. Hi. Can we get some help please? Rosie Spencer, room 621."

"I'll have someone right there," came the fuzzy reply.

"Thank you." Lauren turned from the intercom to her grandmother. "Grandma, help's on the way. Do you want me to call Garrett?"

Grandma stared at Lauren, jaw slack. "Who?"

Lauren could have face-palmed. The last year and a half or so, Grandma had mistaken Garrett for her late husband, whom Garrett strongly favored. "I meant Orrin. Could I call Orrin to come help you?"

Grandma drew back, shaking her head. "N-n-no, not . . . I don't know any . . . I'm supposed to meet *Ephraim*."

"Okay, okay." Lauren placed her hands on the thin, stooped shoulders. "It's okay. We'll find—"

"Get your hands off me." Grandma twisted free, venom in her eyes. "Don't *touch* me."

Lauren stood, eyes stinging, her own limbs trembling. Before Alzheimer's, Rosie Spencer had been the perfect blend of sugar and spice. But her brain's ravenous, unwanted guest sometimes turned her into an entirely new person.

Lauren knew to expect it. But she never knew how to make it not hurt.

The door opened, and a heavyset blonde nurse clad in green scrubs walked in. *Marsha*, her name tag read. "You called for some help?"

"Thank you, Jesus," Lauren whispered, and dove for her phone to text Garrett.

Marsha took over, and after a few moments, Grandma was subdued but weeping quietly. Taking refuge in the bedroom, Lauren pressed a fist to her mouth to stifle her own sobs. Her heart broke over and over and over again at her grandmother's misery. At the relentless horror of this awful disease.

Garrett burst through the door. "I came back as quick as I could. What's going on?"

"Grandma was already upset when I got here, and I think I made it worse." Lauren yanked a tissue from the box on the nightstand. "She didn't know who I was or where she was. She just kept talking about someone named Ephraim."

Brow knit, Garrett looped his arm around Lauren's shoulders while she blew her nose.

"Ephraim?" he asked. "Does she even know someone named Ephraim?"

"I don't think so. She was reading that Bible you gave her, the part of Genesis where Jacob blesses Joseph's sons. One of them had that name." Lauren balled up the damp tissues and tossed them into the trash can, then sank onto the bed. "But I don't remember that story meaning anything special to her, and she kept looking around, saying Ephraim was supposed to meet her, and it wasn't like him to be this late." She glanced up, hoping against hope her know-it-all big brother would have a ready answer. "What in the world could that mean?"

But her confusion reflected on Garrett's face, and he spread his hands. "No idea."

A quiet knock came from the door, and Marsha beckoned them into the living room, stethoscope draped around her neck and laptop in her arms. "I think the worst of it is past. I went ahead and gave her the Namenda and a touch of Ativan to calm her down." Blue, heavily lined eyes flitted from Lauren to Garrett and back again. "Do you two have any idea what might've upset her?"

"The only thing I can think of is that old Bible I brought earlier," Garrett said. "We found it in some stuff from her old house."

"And when I got here, she had it open and was crying and asking about someone named Ephraim." Lauren twisted the ring she wore on her middle finger. "We've got no idea who that is."

"Well, here's the Bible." Marsha retrieved it from where she'd placed it on Grandpa's chair. "Maybe put it away for now, yeah?"

Nodding, Garrett took it and slid it onto a high bookshelf. "She had it open to a passage that referred to an Ephraim. Could that have triggered a memory?"

"It's possible." Marsha's pager beeped. She pulled it from the pocket of her scrubs, gave it a glance, and replaced it. "Sometimes seemingly random things can remind them of another era of life, or even make them think they're living in that era. Remember, these patients perceive time much differently than we do."

"Right." Lauren's mind flitted back to after Grandpa had died, when Garrett wore suits for months because letting Grandma believe he was her husband seemed easier than breaking her heart every day with the news of his death. She didn't make that mistake as often anymore, which was a comparative mercy. But beneath the mercy was sadness. She didn't recognize Garrett much at all these days.

"In any case, it's triggering something powerful. Something locked deep inside," Marsha explained. "It's surfacing—or trying to—but she can't quite access it."

Garrett tilted his head. "So she remembers enough to know she should remember, but not enough to actually remember."

Marsha closed her laptop with a sad smile. "Basically, yeah."

"So what now?" Lauren's gaze traveled to Grandma.

"She should be fine." Marsha started for the door. "But maybe try to find out who Ephraim is. And why he seems to mean so much to her."

><

Where is it? Where's that book?

That handsome young man who visits often, the one who my heart knows but my mind can't remember, brought me a book today. And something about it upset me.

That's probably why I can't find it. The lady in green, who's always smiling and cheerful and gives me my medications every afternoon, probably told them to hide it from me so I wouldn't get upset.

They're so protective, all these people in green. Handsome is too, and the girl who looks just like him. They want to protect me from everything. Keep me safe. They love me. They say that often, and my heart knows it's true.

But sometimes all this protectiveness, all this thinking they know what's best for me, doesn't feel like love.

There it is. On that top shelf. Handsome put it up there. He's much taller than I, but if I stretch up . . . just a little more . . .

There. Got it.

Holy Bible.

The Bible's what got me all stirred up?

That can't be right. I've found such comfort in these pages over the years. Such encouragement. Such wisdom.

But this isn't the Bible I usually read. This one is small. Black cover. White pages. Red edges.

Black. White. Red.

Ephraim.

The name socks me a good one.

But that's all I can remember.

Not his face, or how I knew him, or anything other than his name . . . and that he was supposed to meet me.

Meet me . . . where? And why?

He's running late. Oh, that's not unusual, not for him, not with things being the way they are. But even he's never this late. Where is he? Did something happen? Something must've happened.

Could I answer these questions once upon a time? Have the shadows in my mind eaten them like they have so much else? Or have the answers always been a mystery?

One thing I know for sure. He must've meant the world to me. I know that by the sting in my eyes. The ache in my heart.

But . . . who was he?

So much I don't remember.

And so much I'd give anything to be able to.

Chapter Four

Carter tapped the open doorframe of the news director's office moments after finishing the Monday noon newscast. "You wanted to see me?"

"Carter. Come in. Have a seat." Kathleen Weaver's fleshy fiftysomething face curved in a smile. Her beringed hands motioned to the padded chair opposite the large oak desk. "Can I get you a drink?"

He sank into the chair and loosened his tie. "Water would be great."

"You sure?" Kathleen slid a small bottle of Crown from the top drawer of her desk. "You're off the clock, and we've got something to celebrate."

Carter offered a tight smile to cover the shock and tamped down the churning in his gut that started up every time he saw alcohol. Smelled it. Thought about it. What it had done to his dad. To him. To nearly everyone he cared about.

Lauren Anderson included.

"Still gotta drive home, though." He tried to keep his tone light. "So water it is."

"Suit yourself." She retrieved a Dasani from the little refrigerator behind her desk and handed it to him, then doctored her travel mug. His shoulders tightened as the sharp smell poked at the flimsy cover he kept over his memories and messy emotions.

"You said we're celebrating?" He focused his gaze on his boss's face and not her drink.

"That we are. The latest ratings." Kathleen squeezed behind her desk and turned her computer screen.

Carter leaned in for a closer look. No, he wasn't seeing things. They really were a solid number two in the Wichita market for the first time since his arrival.

"Nice." He lifted his water bottle in a toast.

Kathleen clinked her coffee mug against it, cackling with glee. "Those cupcakes over at Channel Nine can choke on it."

They were still light-years behind Channel Fourteen, but Carter wasn't about to point that out.

Kathleen tore her gaze from the screen and feasted her eyes on him. "And it's all thanks to you."

Carter drew back. "Me?" Nearly a year and a half working the morning show, and he still couldn't believe they'd hired him. There he was, green as anything, attempting to convince the powers that be that his first job in weather should be in a place where lives would depend on his forecast. Even he didn't buy his sales pitch. Never in a million years would he have gone for it if not for the quiet yet relentless encouragement of his friend and mentor, Chief Meteorologist Jim Ford.

"Ratings are up across the board, but look where the highest jump is." Kathleen's long navy-blue fingernail pointed to a few lines in the report. "Monday through Friday mornings. Your shift."

Carter's eyes widened. "Really?"

"And it's not just TV either. Our YouTube channel gets thousands of hits, and our app use has tripled since you came on board."

"Wow. Thanks for telling me." His smile widened, and satisfaction filled his chest. Okay. So maybe he hadn't been immersed in weather since birth like most other meteorologists. Maybe he didn't have that bright, shiny University of Oklahoma meteorology degree beaming from the wall of the weather center like his colleagues did. Maybe his degree had come via online school instead, with study time stolen in fits and starts while holding down a job as a beat reporter in Alabama.

But maybe that didn't matter. Because it looked like he was finally getting the credit all his hard work deserved.

"It was a risk, hiring someone so inexperienced." Kathleen leaned back in her chair with a smile. "But it's paid off. We're attracting more viewers —younger viewers—than we have in years. Heck, even some older ones can't get enough of you." Her gaze slid over his face. "Helps that you're so easy on the eyes."

His balloon of professional pride deflated, zooming around the small office with an almost audible *pbbbbttthththt*. So he was just eye candy to his boss. Even after all this, she still didn't take him seriously.

Ah, well. He knew why he was here. And Jim believed in him. That had to count for something.

He slapped on the smile Kathleen doubtless expected. "Happy to help. Always am."

She beamed. "That's the kind of can-do spirit we like here at K-KAN. And that's why I think you'll be *thrilled* with our new noon segment: 'In the Kitchen with Carter.'"

His brows shot up. "I'm sorry?"

"You're always joking about how you don't cook, so what better way to add some pizzazz to the noon show than to showcase some local chefs? Let them show off some recipes live on air, and let our resident non-cook learn how to slice and dice."

Cooking lessons.

On air.

All those all-nighters he'd pulled striving for that meteorology degree couldn't possibly have prepared him for this.

He jiggled the half-empty water bottle. "So you're going to bring in real chefs, and they're giving me cooking lessons. On live TV."

"Precisely," Kathleen replied. "They'll get some exposure, a boost in business. You'll get more airtime . . ."

"And we'll get higher ratings."

"Gotta strike while the iron's hot, my friend."

Carter bought time with a hefty gulp of water. This whole thing reminded him of high school basketball, when he'd made varsity as a freshman but didn't get the minutes he wanted or the assignments he thought he deserved. "Just do your job, Douglas," was Coach Bell's only response.

It paid off, though. He did his job, his teammates did theirs, and they made the state playoffs all four years. They'd even taken home the state title when he was a junior.

So a cooking segment? Like it or not, it was his job. So he'd do it.

He lowered the bottle. "Yeah. Sounds like fun."

"Fantastic." Kathleen clapped her hands, bracelets jingling. "We're hoping to get this off the ground in time for sweeps. We've already got calls in to a bunch of local restaurants—Mottola's, Patrick's, the new vegan place on the east side . . ."

Kathleen prattled on in that throaty, chain-smoker voice of hers, but Carter's focus had slid off the road and into the ditch.

Vegan place. Health food.

Lauren.

"What about a food blogger?" The question hopped out before he could consider its merit.

Kathleen paused, her mug halfway to her mouth. "Do you know one?"

"Yeah. She does a lot of gluten-free, plant-based, keto, all that."

Kathleen's eyes lit. "Hmm. I hadn't considered that, but the gluten-free demographic is an important segment of the population." She took a sip. "Think she'd be good on camera?"

Hmm. Lauren was doubtless good behind a camera, if she was a professional photographer. But in front of one? With him?

She'd always had great stage presence, though. And talking about her blog was the only time she'd let her guard down with him the other day. The only time those blue eyes had taken on even a hint of the sparkle that had once been a regular feature. And if it went well, it could boost her blog traffic. Be a good opportunity for her.

A good opportunity for him as well. To extend the olive branch and begin to atone for the sins of his past. He couldn't hope a simple TV appearance could make up for everything he'd done.

But it was at least a start.

Leaning to one side, he retrieved his wallet, fished out her business card, and handed it to Kathleen. "I think she'd do great."

"You're brilliant, Carter. Brilliant."

Brilliant wasn't the term he'd use at this moment, now that Lauren's thousand-watt smile and hands full of berries were in the talons of his boss. Completely idiotic might be more accurate.

But Jim had always counseled him that God had a plan, and even man's stupidity couldn't thwart that plan. So if it wasn't meant to be, then

Lauren probably wouldn't be interested. A polite *thanks but no thanks* to the producer, and that would be that.

But an enthusiastic *are you kidding? I'd love to* also loomed as a distinct possibility.

And Carter had no idea which option terrified him most.

>←

Lauren's thumbs danced over the screen of her phone as she tapped out a text in reply to her future sister-in-law, Sloane.

OK, thanks! Just let us know if you see the name Ephraim in any of Gma's stuff.

She added a few emojis, then hit Send. A moment later, her phone buzzed with the reply.

Will do. See you tomorrow.

Lauren pinged back a thumbs-up emoji, then set the phone on the counter and returned to the Mediterranean sea bass sizzling on the stove. The first fillet had been a touch too done for photography, but not for her two cats, Alton and Nigella, who crouched before their bowls, happily devouring the rejects. Thanks to her text-related distraction, this fillet might meet the same fate.

Sliding her spatula beneath the fish, she flipped it to reveal—*yes!*—a perfect golden brown and delicious sear. This was her winner. She pictured it piled high with crimson grape tomatoes, deep-green lacinato kale, and a slice of lemon. Both the image and the aroma made her mouth water.

Her ringtone jangled, and she slid the fillet onto a plate to rest, then grabbed the phone.

"Hi, is this Lauren Anderson from Dollop of Delicious?"

"Speaking."

"This is Morgan Segars from—"

The caller kept talking, but Alton, the three-legged orange tabby, chose that moment to leap onto the counter, perilously close to the fish. With a yelp, Lauren lunged for her cat.

"Everything all right?" Morgan asked.

"Sure. Fine. Just some minor cat problems." Lauren slid a hand beneath

Alton's ample belly and deposited him onto the floor. He eyed her with cool disdain, then turned his attention to grooming his tail.

Morgan laughed. "I've got a pair of Siamese myself, so I get it, believe me. Anyway, I'm calling because your name came up for a new cooking segment we're doing on our noon newscast. I've taken a peek at your blog, and it looks incredible. I just went gluten-free a couple weeks ago, and I cannot *wait* to try those Bananarama Pancakes."

Her heart warmed at the praise. "Thank you."

"Our segment is looking for local food talent to appear on our show, cooking alongside one of our most popular news personalities. We'd like to schedule you for an appearance soon, if you're up for it."

Lauren gulped. Appearing on television wasn't exactly in her comfort zone. They always said the camera added a few pounds, but any time she saw herself on video, "a few" seemed a drastic understatement.

But that was Old Lauren. Fat, Insecure Lauren. This was New Lauren. Thin, Healthy, Confident Lauren. And every literary agent she'd queried in her efforts to secure a cookbook deal had told her she needed to boost her platform numbers. One had even suggested reaching out to local media and scheduling a TV appearance. And now here was the local media on the other end of the phone, offering a TV appearance, without her having had to lift a finger. Was this God's provision or what?

"Absolutely, Morgan, I'd love to, and I'm grateful for the opportunity." She glanced at the Van Gogh calendar on her wall. "When were you thinking?"

"How's next Thursday, the seventeenth? Around eleven, so we can get everything set up?"

"Perfect." She reached for a pencil. "I'm sorry—what station did you say you were with?"

"Channel Five."

She paused, pencil hovering over the calendar square and her stomach twisting into knots. Channel Five. That wasn't . . . was it?

"Can I ask how you found out about me?"

"Our news director had your card. She said she got it from our morning meteorologist. I guess you guys know each other? Anyway, he's the one you'll be cooking with. Our segment's called 'In the Kitchen with Carter.'"

AMANDA WEN

In the kitchen.

With *Carter.*

Her pencil clattered to the floor.

"Are you still there, Lauren?"

She bent to retrieve the pencil. "Yeah. I'm still here."

"Just to confirm, next Thursday the seventeenth. Does that work for you?"

No. It doesn't. Because Carter Douglas was out of my life, and I liked it that way.

But she needed an opportunity like this. She'd been praying for one. So what if it came with a side dish of discomfort? She was over Carter. Had been for years. She was Thin, Healthy, Confident Lauren. She could handle this.

Couldn't she?

"Yep, that works." It would have to.

In the kitchen.

With Carter.

The scrawl of her pencil on the calendar square confirmed it.

What in the world had she just gotten herself into?

CHAPTER FIVE

THE K-KAN STUDIO now contained a kitchen.

A kitchen on rollers, off to the side of the anchor desk. One with a stove, a sink, and a set of cookware so shiny Carter could check his hair in the coppery surfaces. A freshly painted backdrop hovered to the rear, its fumes mingling with the subtle electronics-and-coffee scent of the artificially chilled studio.

A kitchen. Where he'd doubtless be making a fool of himself in less than an hour. Live. On air.

With Lauren.

Just do your job, Douglas.

Carter's dress shoes broke the silence as he strolled closer. An array of brightly colored ingredients covered the countertop, waiting for Lauren's expert touch. He picked up a package of some strange, tiny round grain. Quinoa? God help him if he had to pronounce that on air. He'd have to double-check with her before the cameras started rolling.

Tomatoes and onions were easy enough to identify. That funny-shaped green pepper looked suspiciously like the poblanos his mother had roasted and stuffed during her Mexican cooking kick. And that bunch of leafy bright-green herbs . . . that had to be the cilantro she used to grow in the sunny windowsill of her kitchen. He plucked a sprig from the bunch, inhaled its fragrance to be sure, and was instantly transported back to childhood. The good parts. The parts where his sisters roped him into playing Barbies or letting them paint his toenails. The parts when he escaped all the estrogen for pickup basketball or soccer games with the boys on his block.

The parts without the stench of booze. Without the angry shouts and plaintive sobs and shattered dishes.

The step-slap, step-slap of a pair of flip-flops yanked him back into the present, and there stood Lauren. One glimpse of honey-gold hair—loose and tumbling over her shoulders—and her smile, bright as a summer day, rendered breathing impossible. A flowing blue floral sundress hugged her in all the right places. Glossy yellow-painted toenails provided a touch of the unexpected, and a pair of delicate gold necklaces highlighted her freckled shoulders and collarbones.

"Hi." She clutched the handle of her huge, colorful purse. Ocean-blue eyes sparkled with excitement but were overlaid with a healthy dose of suspicion. Trepidation, maybe. An *oh, crap, what have I done?* expression.

She looked exactly like he felt.

"Hey." He followed her slight frown to the sprig of cilantro in his hand, which he set back with the rest of its leafy cousins.

"I wanted to thank you." She wrapped a bracelet-covered arm around her midsection. "For, uh . . . having me on the show."

"They just started this thing. My boss was looking for local food talent. I thought it might help you out." He sought her gaze. "I hope it does."

"Okay." She tilted her head, long earrings brushing her neck, and peered at him in that way of hers that simultaneously accepted his surface answer but was waiting for the real one.

"Plus, y'know . . . it's nice. Seeing you again." *Nice* didn't begin to cover it.

"So you bring me on the noon newscast?" She let out a sigh that sounded both amused and exasperated. "What happened to 'let's grab a coffee and catch up'?"

"Would you have said yes to that if I'd asked?"

The question hung between them, heavy as a nimbus cloud. Her mouth opened, but no sound came out. His heart vaulted into his throat. Was she about to say yes? No? What should he even hope for?

The door creaked, and Lauren stepped back. Carter turned to see who'd shattered the moment.

It was Morgan, the producer, her purple-streaked dark hair pulled back in its usual ponytail. She nodded to him and extended a hand to Lauren.

"Lauren Anderson? Hi. Morgan Segars. We spoke on the phone."

"Hi." Lauren returned the handshake. "Thank you so much for having me."

"Everything you asked for is right in here, but if there's anything we missed, let me know. When you're ready, just head through this door and take a left, and we'll get you into makeup." Morgan bustled toward the studio door.

Lauren nodded. "Thanks, Morgan."

The door squeaked open and thumped shut, and Lauren returned her focus to him. Her gaze lingered on his face for a stretched-thin moment. Then she grabbed her voluminous quantity of hair and pulled it behind her head. "Look, let's just do this, all right?"

Tugging a thin elastic band from the pile of bracelets on her wrist, she corralled her hair into a messy updo. Carter swallowed hard. He remembered that hair. How it once seared his fingers with its softness.

Lauren's flip-flops cut through the thick silence as she disappeared behind the backdrop. A second later, the door thudded shut.

Well. That was that. Her nonresponse was all the response he needed. Her presence here was purely professional, and anything beyond that was out of the question.

Fine. That was fine. He was fine.

"Right." In the empty studio, no one could hear the rasp in his voice, but he cleared his throat just the same.

Striding toward the weather center strengthened his resolve. Lauren Anderson or not, this was his job. And he knew how to do his job.

"Yeah." Teeth clenched, he dug through the drawer for his mic pack. "Let's do this."

><

The second those bright set lights clicked on, Lauren understood exactly why the studio had been so frigid. Barely a minute into their cooking segment, sweat already pricked under her arms and at her hairline.

Or maybe that was just from nerves.

Not that she had any reason to be nervous. It was only her first-ever television appearance. And her partner in culinary crime was only her ex-boyfriend. Who, aside from five minutes in the makeup aisle a couple weeks ago, she hadn't interacted with in any way for over a decade. So . . . yeah. No reason for nerves. Nope. None at all.

The situation suddenly seemed so ridiculous that she almost accompanied the scrape of the can opener with a bark of laughter. Surely there was some cheese-tastic rom-com out there with pretty much this exact scenario.

Black beans, shiny under the set lights, gushed into the colander. "So we'll need to drain and rinse these . . ."

"What's that do for us?"

Carter sure didn't look nervous. But why would he? Staring into the TV camera's all-seeing eye came naturally to him. The presence of an audience—regardless of size or location—had always made him come alive.

He'd never lorded that over her, though. Instead, he'd reassured her. Believed in her, even when she didn't believe in herself. Like backstage at *Fiddler* on opening night, when a case of stage fright had held her in a viselike grip.

"You sing like an angel," he'd told her. "Your acting is top notch. Your dancing is way better than mine. And nobody's worked harder than you. You *are* Hodel, my love." With a quick kiss to her cheek, he'd straightened her kerchief and given her that knee-weakening smile. "Now go out there and show them."

Now, all grown up, under the lights of the Channel Five studio, Carter wore that same look of quiet confidence. The slight lift of the chin, the radiant eyes, the barely perceptible quirk of the brow. He believed in her. Just as he had back then. He'd believed she was enough.

Until he didn't.

No. Not now. She could go back to hating him after this was over, but for now she needed the jolt of assurance his confident expression gave her.

"Draining and rinsing removes excess starch and salt." She picked up a bright-red spatula and gave the beans a stir. "It lets the beans' true flavor shine through, and you can season them exactly the way you want."

"Makes sense." Carter turned back toward the array of produce before them on the wooden countertop. "So what's next? The onion? The pepper?"

"Depends. Do onions bother you?" She picked up the onion and sliced down the side to peel it. "I'd hate to make you cry on air."

Carter's dark brows lifted, and a genuine smile cracked through his professional veneer. At the sound of a chortle, Lauren glanced toward the news desk, where Carter's impossibly blonde co-anchor hid her giggles behind a giant mug of coffee.

Tension bled from Lauren's shoulders as she looked back at Carter. His eyes shone, just as they had onstage all those years ago. *See? You're killing it.*

He reached for the other chef's knife. "I'll tackle the pepper, then."

"Good call."

Lauren made quick work of the onion. Its pungent aroma, the neat concentric circles falling into a perfect dice, sliced away her leftover nerves and furthered her sense of being in control.

Control was why she cooked. It had always been about control.

"Wow, that was fast." He sounded impressed, and she grinned.

"It's not my first onion." Tossing the onion skin into the garbage bowl, she turned to Carter, who hadn't even started on the poblano. He held the knife in his right hand, index finger extended over the handle. The hallmark of a novice cook.

"You'll never have any control holding the knife like that. You need to grip it more." She lifted her own knife to show him.

Carter's fingers flexed. "Like this?"

"Not quite. It's more like . . ." Without thinking, she placed her hand on top of his and adjusted his grip. His fingers stirred, then stilled beneath hers, and she froze. Goose bumps rose along her arms despite the heat of the lights.

This hand—and its twin—had felt oh so right once upon a time. They'd caressed her cheeks. Drifted through her hair. Made her feel loved. Adored. Wanted.

But in the cold, sober light of day . . .

Those hands had built her. Broken her.

And now, after thirteen years, their hands had found each other once more.

"So, uh . . ." He cleared his throat. "Now what?"

She jerked her hand away, hoping the thick makeup hid the heat rushing to her cheeks, and retrieved her own knife. "Rock the knife back and forth. And move the food, not the knife." She reached for the cilantro, slid it beneath her blade, and demonstrated.

"Like this?" A more hesitant chopping rhythm mingled with her own.

Carter's technique wasn't perfect yet, but it was much improved, as evidenced by the neat pile of pepper slices on the other side of the knife. His sleeves were rolled to the elbows, and his forearm rippled with the motion of his chop. His skin was a few shades lighter than she remembered—he doubtless didn't spend his summers lifeguarding anymore—but his arm was definitely more muscled.

"Yeah. You're, uh . . . you're doing great." She tore her gaze away and attacked the cilantro. Control. She needed control.

"Okay, chef." Carter's knife settled softly on the counter. "All sliced and diced. What next?"

"Into the skillet." The sizzle in the pan told her he'd followed her instructions, and she added the onion, stirring the uniform bits of deep green and pale white into a delicious mosaic. "Grab the garlic too, would you?"

"Sure thing, Boss." A moment later the garlic she'd minced landed atop the mixture.

"Thanks." She glanced up into his smile. Faint crinkles around his eyes were an attractive new addition to the face she'd known and loved. As were barely visible creases on either side of those full lips . . .

No. *No.* She couldn't look at his lips. Couldn't look at *him.*

They were over. Had been for ages. This was just moldy leftovers of the insecure, clueless teenager she'd once been.

She wasn't that teenager anymore. And there was no room for leftovers. No room for a slip in control.

"Okay." Her voice was as bright as the skillet she reached for. "Thanks to the magic of television, what's supposed to take six to eight minutes is done in less than one. Here's what we're looking for with those sautéed veggies. Soft and translucent."

"Bean time now, right?" To her left, Carter reached for the bowl of drained black beans.

"Yep. Go ahead and dump those on in there."

"Consider it done."

She reached for the little bowl of sea salt to the left of the stove. "And remember how we rinsed those beans?"

"Take off the excess salt and starch, right? So we can season it how we like?"

She glanced up. "Very good."

"Hey, I pay attention when it's important." That same flirtatious note, the one he'd trotted out in the makeup aisle, crept into his voice. Except he hadn't known who she was then.

Now he did.

But he was flirting with her anyway.

And it sparked an irritating sense of joy.

Leftovers. Just leftovers.

"I like to use sea salt when I can." She pinched a fingertip full of sparkling white crystals. "It's full of essential minerals to boost immunity and reduce inflammation. Plus it adds a little brightness to the flavor."

"Pepper too?" Carter reached for the pepper grinder.

"Absolutely. Just give it a few turns."

When the rasp of the grinder quieted, she reached again for the spatula. "Now give it a stir, and it's pretty much done. You can serve it over whatever you like. I have quinoa here, but you could use brown rice, cauliflower rice . . ." Setting the spatula aside, she grabbed a ladle and poured the steaming concoction over the quinoa she'd cooked earlier.

"Wow, that looks fantastic."

Lauren set her ladle in the spoon rest and looked up into warm brown eyes shining with admiration. Pride. *You crushed it, my love.* She could practically hear those long-ago words, words spoken in a dimly lit backstage amid a sweeping curtain and thunderous applause. Soaring with exhilaration and relief, she'd grabbed his face between her hands and poured weeks' worth of emotion into a single impassioned kiss.

"Yeah." She reached for a lime and thwacked it in half with a cleaver. Juice dribbled over whitened knuckles as she choked the life from the innocent fruit. "Just top it off with a squeeze of fresh lime juice. It's a flexible dish, so you can use any sort of topping you want. Scallions, red pepper flakes—"

"Hey, is this some kind of cheese?"

"Cotija, yeah," she said. "And if you're vegan or off dairy, there are plenty of delicious alternatives."

Carter reached for the container of crumbly white cheese and shook a generous amount over the plated beans. "Cheese makes everything better."

Couldn't argue with that. "Throw on a little cilantro for color, as well as vitamins A and K . . ." Lauren scraped up the remaining cilantro leaves, sprinkled them over the cheese-covered beans, and stepped back. "There. Perfect."

"Sure wish all you out there in viewer land could smell this, because it's amazing." Carter reached for a fork, then paused. "We do get to taste it, right?"

She laughed. "Of course. That's the whole point."

"Good." Carter's fork plunged into the dish. A second later his eyes fell closed and he issued a hum of delight that shot straight through to the tips of her toes.

"Lauren." Her name slid from his mouth, sauced in pleasure. "This is incredible."

"I'll, uh . . . I'll take your word for it." Her voice sounded like a croak.

His eyes flew open. "You haven't tried it yet?"

"Well, I make it all the time at home, so—"

"Yeah, okay, whatever. Come on." Carter dug for another bite, and before she could react, he'd slipped a warm forkful of cheese-covered beans into her mouth. Whether it tasted good or not, she had no idea. Because Carter was *right here*. His spicy cologne mingling with the kitchen aromas. His hand hovering just a few inches from her face. Dark glittering eyes locking on hers. Sliding to her lips.

Then he froze in place. His brows inched together, and his mouth opened a fraction. Had the arrows of déjà vu she'd dodged the last few minutes found a new target?

Oh. Oh, *no*. She could deal with leftovers if she was the only one feeling them. But if he felt them too? If they were in this together?

That, she couldn't control.

Carter's throat rippled with a hard swallow. Then he turned back toward the camera and slapped on a smile that looked a bit off around the edges.

"Okay, you guys can see how amazing this is, right? It's great for you, it's delicious, and, hey. If I can make it? You can too."

He kept talking, but his voice sounded a million miles away. Because somehow, after all the pain and heartache, after months of bingeing and purging and forcing herself into a shape she thought he'd want, after therapy and recovery and healing, after all the work she'd put in scrubbing away Carter's memory, the terrifying possibility loomed that it was all for naught.

Because here she was. Thin, Healthy, Confident Lauren.

Feeling things—wanting things—with Carter Freaking Douglas.

CHAPTER SIX

THE END-OF-BROADCAST THEME music had barely faded out when a horde of reporters and production guys converged on the kitchen set, their target the still-steaming dish on the stove. Even Melanie, she of the constant coffee and meal-in-a-bottle shakes, reached for the pile of plasticware someone had brought in from the break room.

Ducking the crowd, Carter headed straight for the weather center, where he stashed his mic pack and stowed his jacket, grateful for the coolness of dimmed lights and removable layers.

"Does it taste as good as it smells?" someone asked from the outer rings of the kitchen throng.

"Better," came the reply around what sounded like a massive mouthful.

Jerking his tie loose, Carter rummaged in the drawer for the package of makeup-remover wipes. The package Lauren had thumped onto his chest in that micro-instant before he knew who she was. Before his past roared into the here and now with all the subtlety of an EF5 tornado.

He scrubbed the makeup from his face, welcoming the bracing chill and artificially fresh fragrance. Man alive, he'd grossly underestimated how being near Lauren would affect him. The simple touch of her hand on his, a jolt of a moment that rocketed him back in time and awakened a desperate ache he'd buried long ago, still had his head spinning. His knees shaking.

He'd expected to notice her beauty, sure. How could he not? But he'd gone far beyond noticing. The grace and ease with which she moved around the kitchen, the surety in her knife strokes and her thorough knowledge of ingredients, the uncertain yet eager glimmer in her blue eyes . . . he'd been mesmerized.

And the way they'd worked together. He'd been counting on no small amount of awkwardness, especially given how things had gone between them before the show. But once the cameras were rolling, they'd settled back into the steps of the dance they'd learned so well onstage that long-ago summer. Playing off each other's micro-expressions. Seeming to read one another's thoughts. Taking what she gave and handing it back one better, then watching her do the same with him.

Now, as then, they'd sparkled. Sizzled. Made magic.

That had been the biggest surprise of all.

He spun at the click of high heels behind him. A smiling Mel held a fragrant, piled-high plate.

"Saved you some," she said.

With a tight smile, he tossed the wipe into the trash. "No thanks. I'm good."

"I'll bet."

"What's that supposed to mean?"

"It means"—Kathleen rounded the corner into the weather center—"that Melanie picked up on the same sizzle I did. And I'm not talking about the stove. Yee-*ow*."

Carter's stomach lurched. Had it been that obvious?

"No joke." Mel's fork scraped against the Styrofoam plate. "You got something going with Bean Girl?"

Bean Girl? "No. Not . . . not with . . . no." Heat blasted his cheeks. Maybe he shouldn't have been so quick to scrub off his makeup.

"Our social pages are blowing up." Kathleen held out her shiny silver phone, where a steady stream of enthusiastic comments popped up on-screen almost faster than Carter could read them.

That dish looks sooooooooo yummy!

Lauren Anderson is a blast! Bring her back ASAP!

Carter Douglas? Cooking? With those rolled up sleeves? I DIE. This followed by a string of fire emojis, along with several heart eyes. The number of likes that comment had already received indicated the agreement of multiple viewers.

Kathleen pulled her phone back and pounced on the latest additions. "Ooh, another vote for the rolled-up sleeves look." Her gaze flitted from the phone to his face. "I think we've got a hit in the making, Carter. As much as the bored housewives already love your weather segments, with a little kitchen action and those sleeves, our noon show's ratings'll be *en fway-go*."

Carter stifled the urge to roll his eyes at his boss's mutilated Spanish. At her fixation on his forearms rather than his forecasting ability.

"That little ad lib there at the end was pretty good too." Mel scooped up another bite.

"'If I can make it, you can too.'" Kathleen gave his shoulder a playful shove. "That was *genius*, Carter. A subtle nod to the station motto and everything."

"Glad you picked up on that." In truth, whatever popped out of his mouth had been totally unplanned, a desperate midcourt heave at the final buzzer. Because that had been mere moments after he'd fed Lauren a bite of her own cooking—why on God's green earth had he not just handed her the fork like a normal person?—and the way she'd looked up at him made his heart skip, trip, and face-plant.

How could something so old, so dead, burn so bright?

And the stunned shimmer in her sapphire eyes told him he might not be the only one asking that question.

"If Carter can make it, you can too!" A grinning Mel elbowed Kathleen.

The news director gasped. "There it is. There's our slogan. It's perfect."

"Perfect. Yeah." Movement out the studio door caught his eye. A flutter of wavy, dark-blonde hair heading for the stairs . . .

"Would you excuse me?" Without waiting for a reply, he made a beeline for the door.

He had no idea what he wanted to say to Lauren. No clue how she'd react. But he jogged downstairs and through the glassed-in lobby anyway. He needed to be near her. Needed to tempt fate or play with fire or at the very least look into those eyes one more time.

To see if he'd imagined what he thought he saw earlier.

He shoved open the door and stepped into the broiling midday sun just as she reached the driver's door of a crimson Jeep. "Lauren."

She turned, keys in hand. A hot gust of southerly wind plastered a wave of hair across her sunglasses. With her free hand, she brushed it aside. "Hey."

"I . . . just wanted you to know how amazing you did in there. My boss says we're blowing up our social media."

She gave a dry chuckle. "That a good thing?"

"To her it is. And since a common theme is how awesome you are, I'd say, yeah. It's a good thing." He'd leave out the part about his shirtsleeves.

Lauren wrinkled her nose. "I'll take your word for it. For me it was just chaos and nerves and awkwardness."

"If you were nervous, it didn't show. You crushed it, Lauren. *Crushed* it."

"Yeah?" Her lashes fluttered behind her sunglasses, and her chin lifted.

His heart squeezed. She always looked so in control, so on top of things, but when she let her inner insecurities shine through, her desperate need for reassurance and encouragement . . . he had no defense against that. None. Never had.

It was looking more and more likely he never would.

"Absolutely. You were confident, knowledgeable . . ." *Beautiful.* "And hey, I know how to hold a knife the right way now, so . . ."

A corner of Lauren's mouth lifted. "Okay. Maybe it wasn't a total fail."

"It wasn't. I promise." He gave a rueful chuckle. "Lot better than my first broadcast, that's for sure. I was a wreck."

Her brows arched. "You? Nervous? Never."

"Scout's honor." He lifted his right hand. "And now look at me. Now they trust me on air with knives."

Lauren laughed. "You did great, Carter."

"I had a great teacher."

"We made a good team." She sounded wistful. Almost like she didn't want to use the past tense.

Neither did he.

"So, hey." His voice came out huskier than he'd like. "You, uh . . . you never answered my question earlier."

She fought another gust of wind for control of her hair. "What question is that?"

"Would you have had coffee with me? If I'd asked?"

Her cautious smile flickered and died. "I'm not so sure that's a good idea."

"It's just coffee. Catching up. Thirteen years is a long time."

"But with you . . . with us . . ."—the word smacked him in the solar plexus—"I don't think it could ever be just coffee."

He rubbed the back of his neck, already warm from the sun's rays. "Look, when I invited you on the show, I never expected, never thought we'd . . . but it was like magic, Lauren. Just like *Fiddler*. After all these years, all that happened between us, we still made magic."

Two lines appeared between her brows. "Carter, just because we made magic in a six-minute TV segment, that doesn't mean . . ." She sighed. "Losing you broke me. And it took a long time—a *long* time—to get put back together again."

She worried her lower lip between her teeth, and the gesture melted him, just like always. It meant she was unsure. Afraid. That the thing she wanted was almost within reach, but she wasn't yet willing to take hold.

He knew all too well what that fear felt like. It was what he'd allowed to shatter them in the first place.

But fear wouldn't call the shots anymore. Not with her. Not with them.

"It broke me too." He caught her gaze and held it. "I was a mess. That whole part of my life . . . I was a stupid, screwed-up kid who didn't know he was about to destroy the best thing that ever happened to him. It took me years to get over that mistake. And right now, standing here, looking at you . . . I'm not sure I ever did."

Her lovely lips curved in a slow, sad smile. "And that's why it can never be just coffee."

The taillights of her Jeep lit with the click of her remote, and panic tore at the tattered remnants of his common sense.

"Okay. So maybe it's not just coffee."

She paused, door halfway open.

"Maybe it's coffee with a side of . . . of angst and longing and regret. Because I screwed up with you. So badly, I screwed up. And not a day goes by I don't wish I could undo the pain I caused you. But somehow, some way, you're here. And I'm here. We're older. Maybe we're wiser. I don't know. I mean . . . I hope we are, because . . . it's *you*, Lauren. It's *us*." His stomach churned. He wanted to flee back to the air-conditioned sanctity of the studio. Even Kathleen's comments about his shirtsleeves would be less excruciating than this.

Nope. Couldn't do that. Deep breath. Finish strong.

"So forget this 'if I'd asked' nonsense. Because it's not an 'if.' It's an actual ask. Would you be willing to have coffee with me?"

A distant siren punctuated the heavy silence. Lauren draped her fingers over the open door of the Jeep. His heart jackhammered as she looked at him. Looked for a long time. A look that said everything. And nothing.

"I don't know." Her gaze fell to the painted white stripe beneath her sandals. "I'll have to think about it, all right?"

"Sure. Yeah." He stepped back. "Take all the time you need, okay? No rush. You, uh . . . you know where to find me."

"Yeah, I guess so." A slight grin melted into another long, searching look. "Thanks, Carter." Then she climbed into the Jeep and shut the door.

Carter turned back toward the studio and palmed the sweat from his forehead, his shaky exhale mingling with the soft rumble of the Jeep's engine, the scratch of tires on gravelly asphalt.

What had just happened? Where had all those words come from? They'd taken total control. Stormed up from his heart in a verbal explosion, and now its rubble was strewn all over the parking lot, the wreckage both horrifying and impressive.

No way to take it back, though. All he could do was wait. And hope.

No, *no*. Not hope. He didn't want to hope. Hope had crushed him in the past. Over and over he'd reeled from its blows.

But hope had swooped in and settled anyway.

Because of all the things Lauren had said to him, the one thing she hadn't said was *no*.

➸➛

How many times had Lauren had this fantasy?

Carter Douglas. In the flesh. Acknowledging how badly he'd screwed up. Practically begging her for another chance.

And always her fantasy had ended the same way: with merry laughter, a cheerful *not in a million years*, and firm instructions for him to get up off his knees and run along. Watching him slink away, dejected.

Hurting him as he'd once hurt her.

But now, here she sat, in a shady spot a couple blocks away from the studio. Hands shaking so badly she almost couldn't drive.

Because in all the times she'd imagined Carter asking for another chance, never had she pictured actually considering his request.

Was it the pleading in his eyes? The depth in his voice? No, she'd dreamed those things. Immunized herself against them.

But the depth of his regret, the glimpse he'd allowed of the raw, wounded soul whose baggage she could only guess at . . .

Oh, come on. Was she crazy? She wasn't some silly teenage girl desperate for a second glance from a boy—*any* boy. She was Thin, Healthy, Confident Lauren. No way should she even be considering this. Had she forgotten that night? That night when he'd said those pretty words and she'd given him something she could never get back?

Ugh. Her hands gripped the steering wheel, and her stomach knotted with regret. She'd let him see her. *See* her. All of her.

She'd thought he loved her. He'd said he did.

But then, after he saw her—all of her—suddenly he didn't want to see her again.

And now he did. Was it because she was thin now? Was that it?

No . . . he'd talked about the magic. The chemistry between them. The way they fell into step with each other as though thirteen years of hurt had never come between them. That was what he'd said, anyway, and the tortured sheen in his eyes, the tightness in his jaw . . .

Her phone jangled in her purse, and she jumped. Maybe it was Carter. Oh crap. What if it *was* Carter?

After all this time, all she'd been through, she was still obsessing over whether Carter Douglas was responsible for her ringing phone? Really?

With a frustrated growl, she grabbed the phone from her purse.

It wasn't Carter.

She lifted the phone to her ear, grateful for the distraction of her future sister-in-law. "Hey, Sloane."

"Hey." Sloane paused. "Did I catch you at a bad time?"

"Nope. All good." She tossed her hair over her shoulder and tried to sound breezy.

"Good. How'd your cooking segment go?"

"Fine. At least . . . I think it was fine." Understatement of the millennium. "I honestly have no idea."

"I'm at work, so I couldn't see it live, but I DVRed it. I'll watch it later and let you know."

Lauren's grip on the phone tightened. "Yeah. Great. That's . . . that'd be great."

"So, hey, changing the subject. I've been looking through some of your grandma's old stuff, trying to figure out who Ephraim is, and I think I may be on to something."

Lauren straightened. "Really?"

"Maybe." A page flipped in the background. "I found your grandma's yearbook from Roosevelt High, class of 1955. Her senior year. And there's an Ephraim James in her class. With the last name added, does it ring any bells?"

Lauren furrowed her brow. "Sorry. That doesn't help. Did he sign the yearbook or anything?"

"Not that I can see. There's one entry that's unsigned, though. It reads 'R plus J Forever.' *R* for Rosie, no doubt, but I don't have a clue who *J* is."

"Maybe a secret admirer, then? Or a clandestine crush?"

"It's entirely possible. Rosie seems to have been quite the popular gal. Cheerleading, Y-Teens . . ."

"Wow. I never knew any of that." Had Grandma been that closed lipped about her high school days? Or had she tried to share her stories, and her grandchildren had been simply too self-absorbed to listen?

"Here's Ephraim's picture again. Looks like he and your grandma were in choir together."

"Really? So this could be the right Ephraim?"

"It's possible. But if it is, if there was any sort of friendship between them, that'd be very intriguing."

"Why do you say that?"

"Okay, this is 1955, remember."

Apprehension hovered in Lauren's chest. "Okay . . ."

"And Ephraim James is black."

CHAPTER SEVEN

September 1954

"SOMEONE'S SURE LOOKING swell this morning!"

Rosie's best friend's voice cut through the locker-door slams and excited chatter. Classmates showing off new flattops and poodle skirts, gossiping about baseball games and the latest flicks at the drive-in. Which couples were still going steady after the long summer break and which ones had called it quits.

Her own pink poodle skirt swished around her legs as she twirled, and there was Vivian Lane hurrying to catch up, flame-red curls bouncing as always.

"Thanks, Viv. You look pretty swell yourself." Rosie flung an arm around her friend. "I haven't seen you all day! How's your morning?"

Vivian wrinkled her nose. "Lots of homework this year, I'm afraid."

Rosie offered a sympathetic glance as they rounded the corner. "Guess they have to get us ready for college and all." Since the middle of sophomore year, she and Viv had planned to attend Kansas State Teacher's College together. To teach at the same grade school someday, to look out on row after row of eager, freshly scrubbed faces and share with them the joy of learning . . . until babies came along, of course. Then it'd be living next door, sharing a coffee after their respective Mr. Rights went off to work. Hanging laundry and chatting over the white picket fence while their children laughed and played in the yard. Walking kids to school, going to church together, and watching their young families grow.

But all that—adulthood, responsibility, maturity—was a long way off. For now, her senior year, Rosie planned to have as much fun as possible.

"Can you believe it, Viv? Our last first day of high school."

"I know." Vivian's curls bounced, her voice an excited squeak. "We've almost made it."

The crowded hallways brought bittersweet excitement, with familiar faces and features Rosie would soon leave behind. Steel-gray lockers. Black-and-white tile floors, shiny from a summer polishing. The ornate clock suspended from the wall just outside the choir room, where she and Vivian would have a class together for the first time all morning.

Looked like they wouldn't be sitting together, though. A peek at Mr. Bishop's seating chart delivered the unwelcome news. With her clear bell-like voice, Viv would be on the far right with the first sopranos, whereas Rosie, a second soprano, found herself next to the tenor section. Right between Peggy Wells and . . . Ephraim James? She'd never seen that name on the roster before.

"See you later." Vivian gave Rosie a quick squeeze.

"I'll save you a seat at lunch." Rosie blew her friend a kiss, slid her music folder from its cubby, and climbed the stairs to the second row of the soprano section. When she found her seat, she flipped open the leather folder—Roosevelt Raider red, naturally—and glanced toward the blackboard to see what they'd be rehearsing first.

But blocking the board was Mr. Bishop, all unruly hair and horn-rimmed glasses, talking to a student.

A black student.

When Daddy's job at Boeing meant a move from the farm to Wichita right before Rosie started junior high, she'd encountered black people up close for the first time. Well, perhaps not up close. The small handful of black students with whom she shared hallways and lunchrooms largely kept to themselves, and the white students tended to ignore them. In fact, she'd never sat next to a black student before. Never even spoken to one.

Looked like she was about to, though, judging from the eyeball Mr. Bishop was casting in her direction. Sure enough, the choir director jutted his chin toward the empty seat to Rosie's left. The new student gave a slight nod and headed up the stairs.

Aha. This must be the mysterious Ephraim James.

Rosie moved her things and slid her knees to the side as he squeezed past, dressed in the standard coat, tie, and crisp white shirt. He was lanky, but not too lanky. Tall, but not overly so. Hair cut high and tight. In every way but one, he looked just like the rest of the boys in choir.

Everyone's got something different about themselves. Auntie Boop had said that years ago when Rosie had asked her favorite aunt about her Sicilian accent. *So you've got two choices. You can try to hide that difference, or you can embrace what the good Lord gave you.* The saucy sparkle in Auntie Boop's golden-brown eyes made it obvious which option she'd chosen. Even during the war, when her homeland was the enemy, her heritage still shone through in her speech.

But Auntie Boop's philosophy didn't apply to everyone. Because Ephraim James couldn't hide his difference even if he wanted to. His skin was deep brown, his hair midnight black, and his eyes a beautiful shade between the two.

Those eyes locked on hers, his expression suspicious, the silence between them awkward. Filling a silence was never a problem for Rosie, but what could she say to Ephraim? What was allowable in this mixed-but-separated world?

Well. She could say hello. Wasn't that what the Bible said? To do for others what you'd want them to do for you?

And when she'd been the new girl, wide-eyed and overwhelmed, that first friendly *hello* meant the world.

She applied her warmest, most welcoming smile. "Hello."

His head tilted slightly, as though he wasn't certain she'd spoken to him.

"I'm Rosie Gibson."

"I know. We had biology together last hour."

"Oh." Her cheeks warmed. She'd been so busy catching up with her friends that she'd not even noticed his presence.

The look in Ephraim's brown eyes softened. "But Mr. Sullivan seems pretty strict. 'Eyes front and center, ladies and gentlemen. Front and center.'" His voice deepened in an imitation of their no-nonsense teacher.

Rosie giggled. "That's him, all right."

Her laughter carved a parenthesis in Ephraim's right cheek. "I'm Ephraim James. Just moved here over the summer."

Her heart went out to him. How difficult must it be to come to a new school—a new city—when everyone was already grouped up and paired off? Especially when there were so many more white students than black ones?

"Well, welcome to Roosevelt High, Ephraim. I think you'll like it here."

With a slight wiggle of dark brows, he flipped open his choir folder. "Guess we'll see."

CHAPTER EIGHT

YES, YOU CAN absolutely use frozen blackberries! Just allow a couple extra minutes of cook time to soften the texture and release the juices.

Lauren scanned the latest reply to a comment on her blog, then pressed Post and sat back with a sigh. Normally, she gave both herself and her laptop a break on Sundays, but her blog subscriptions had nearly doubled in the past three days. Increased traffic brought an increased workload, with many new subscribers leaving comments on multiple posts. Replying to the comments devoured a good deal more time than usual. So on this Sunday, only her cats—Nigella stretched out beside her on the couch and Alton loafing atop the bookshelf—observed a Sabbath rest.

No doubt her TV appearance was behind the uptick in blog traffic. Carter himself had shared the video—a video she still hadn't summoned the courage to watch—on his Facebook page. And this morning before church, after debating the possible ramifications for way too long, she'd sent him a friend request.

Networking. Just networking. That was all it was.

Right.

When his acceptance pinged after lunch, she'd spent an almost embarrassing amount of time combing through his page. His posts consisted mostly of weather information, support for his alma mater's basketball team, and photos of cool lightning strikes and gorgeous sunsets. He'd listed his religious views as Christian, his relationship status as single, and his political views as "Nope," something which drew a quiet chuckle.

Several photos featured him grinning in the cockpit of a small plane, and her heart had given a curious thump. He'd mentioned wanting a pilot's license way back when, but she'd dismissed it as a pipe dream.

She shouldn't have. As usual, he'd spied something he wanted, gone after it, and gotten it. Those pictures made her proud.

And a little uneasy. Because that smile—not the plastic one he wore on TV, but his real smile, the one that lit his whole face—did nothing to squelch the old attraction.

Coffee. With Carter. No good could come from that. But the idea simply wouldn't leave her alone. It perched on her shoulder day and night, a constant squawking companion whose cage she had no way to cover.

And why? Was this some sort of test from God, to see how much she'd truly grown up? Or was he giving her—him . . . *them*—a second chance? These questions had been the subject of many prayers since her cooking segment, but so far God had provided no clear answer.

Setting her laptop aside, she rose and crossed to the small kitchen to make a snack. A smoothie, maybe. Yes. Fresh berries and greens from the farmers' market. Greek yogurt. Raw honey. Good stuff. The ritual of prepping the ingredients, plopping them into the blender, and pulverizing them into thick purple goo took the edge off her chaotic thoughts.

She was pouring the smoothie into a big plastic cup when her phone chirped. Another blog comment? *Ay yi yi.*

But it wasn't a comment this time. It was an email. From Penny LaMont, better known online as the Gluten Free Goddess. Lauren's bookshelves boasted all four of Penny's cookbooks, and rumors swirled that the woman even had a TV show in the works. She was everything Lauren dreamed of being, and beyond.

Kitchen lights glinted off Lauren's silver thumb ring as she clicked on the email. It was probably just Penny's weekly newsletter. Usually those dropped on Mondays, but maybe she had something else this week, or—

Top of the afternoon to you, Lauren!

Wait. What?

Soooooo I saw that cooking segment you did for your local news, and I LOVED it. That recipe is genius!! It's so versatile—I've added chicken and tofu so far, and I'm making it with salmon tonight! I kind of hate that you're the one who came up with it and not me. KIDDING!!!

Lauren's eyes widened. A squeal bubbled in her throat. Penny LaMont. The Gluten Free Goddess. Saw her video. Liked her recipe.

I've been looking through your blog, and I think you'd be a great fit for a guest post on GFG! Interested? We'd love to have you, so LMK and I'll get you on the calendar!

The squeal escaped. The phone slid from her hand, and the smoothie followed a split-second later. Frigid goop jetted from the cup and splorped onto the countertop, but who cared about a little mess when Penny LaMont—*the* Penny LaMont—wanted *Lauren* to do a *guest post*?

"Are you *kidding*, Penny LaMont?" Lauren shrieked at her phone, and both cats lifted wary heads. "I am there. I am *so* there. I am a thousand million percent there."

Hands shaking, she reached for the phone to fumble a reply. But when the screen lit, something caught her eye. A couple sentences at the bottom of Penny's email. Sentences she'd glossed over in all the excitement.

PS—picture me singing "It's a Small World," because it so is. The Gluten Free Husband used to work with your pal Carter at Channel 6 in Springfield. They're still buds on Facebook, and that's honestly the only way I'd have seen your vid. Might wanna buy that dude a cup of coffee!

"Oh, for—" She slammed the phone down and looked skyward. "Are you kidding me?" She'd been praying for guidance. A clear-cut sign. But never had she imagined staring down written instructions to do the exact thing she'd been stewing over for the past three days.

Maybe it could be just coffee with Carter. Maybe it couldn't.

But maybe that didn't matter so much anymore.

Grinning, she reached for her phone. "Very funny, God. Very funny."

❋

"Look who bothered to show up." This was how Carter's oldest sister, Natalie, greeted him when he ducked into his mother's warm, fragrant kitchen that afternoon and rolled shoulders tense from his three-and-a-half-hour drive to his tiny hometown of Joyce Center. Nat's honey-streaked brown hair was pulled back into its usual thick ponytail, and the dark circles beneath her eyes indicated another long day delivering babies.

"Yeah, yeah." He shook out his stiff right leg. "The plane was already spoken for, so I had to get here the old-fashioned way."

His younger sister, Sara, added spices to a vat of what looked suspiciously like her famous onion dip. "Oh, you poor thing," she cooed. Her brown eyes shone warm through chunky cat's-eye glasses, and her hair was cut short, dyed black, and streaked with bright purple. Thanks to her job at a bustling style salon, he never knew quite what to expect her to look like.

Grinning, he exchanged hello kisses with his sisters and tamped down the familiar claustrophobia this little house on Miller Drive always brought. Square footage wasn't the main reason, although growing up sharing a bathroom with three sisters meant brushing his teeth at the kitchen sink more often than not. And it wasn't the addition of boyfriends, husbands, and kids to make an even dozen when everyone was together.

No, what made the walls close in was the mixed bag of memories. Some warmed his heart with nostalgia, but just as many made him down-on-his-knees grateful to live over two hundred miles away.

That distance, as well as his screwball schedule, meant he was excused from most Sunday family dinners, but he still tried to make the trip once a month or so. Any less often meant worried calls from his mom and guilt-trippy texts from his sisters.

Aromatic steam wafted up from the pan of chopped bacon his mother stirred on the stove, and his stomach growled as he wrapped an arm around her soft, comforting shoulders.

"Carter. If it weren't for your forecasts, I'd have forgotten what you looked like." Deep crinkles fanned around Alicia Douglas's eyes as she rested the spoon in the sizzling pot and stretched to kiss his cheek.

"Good to see you too, Mom." He dropped a kiss atop his mother's dark hair.

The back door gave its familiar creak-slam, and Carter's two-year-old nephew, Lucas, barreled toward him. His red hair and Paw Patrol swimsuit were drenched from a romp in the backyard sprinklers, and his smile shot straight to Carter's heart.

"Lucas, my man." Crouching, he held his arms open for an embrace. The toddler lurched into them, and Carter scooped him up with an exaggerated grunt. "You're getting so big."

"Tell me about it." Cassandra chased her son into the kitchen, towel in hand. "Lukey, stop. You're getting Uncle Carter all wet."

"Nah, I don't mind." Pressing a kiss to his nephew's freckled cheek, Carter lowered Lucas to the floor and eyed his sister's rounded belly. A scant sixteen months separated Carter and Cass, and she was the sister he felt closest to. "How you feeling?"

Cassandra met his eyes over the top of her son's head as she toweled him off. "Better. Helps that I'm not throwing up all the time anymore."

Carter grinned. "I'm glad the baby is finally cutting you some slack."

"Me too. Believe me." Cass straightened and extended a hand to her small son. "C'mon, buddy. Let's get you into some dry clothes."

As Lucas's small footsteps thudded down the hall, Carter turned to his mother. "Need any help in here before I go out back and say hi to the guys?" On nice Sundays, the men and kids usually escaped to the backyard for expanded square footage and extended grilling sessions.

Nat's smile turned sly. "Oh, yeah, that's right. You're not completely useless in the kitchen anymore."

Mom peered up at him and gestured to a pile of chives on a wooden cutting board. "Those need chopping, if you're looking for a project." Wiping her hands on a kitchen towel, she glanced at Nat. "Could you take over with this? I need to go see how your father's doing on the steaks."

As the back door shut behind his mother, Carter scanned the offerings in the knife block beside the sink and chose the weapon that looked the most like what Lauren had used on the show. Chef's knife, she'd called it. Well, he was still nowhere close to a chef, but he did know how to hold a knife now. Warmth tinged his cheeks at the memory of Lauren's hand on his own.

"Not sure which had more sizzle on that show." Sara grinned at him, bowl of onion dip in hand. "The stove or the chemistry between you and that blog girl."

Nat fished a potato chip from its plastic sack with one hand while stirring bacon with the other. "You two more than just cooking buddies?"

"Nope." Carter kept his focus on the pile of chives in front of him. *Food to knife, not knife to food.* Lauren had met his family just once, at the final performance of *Fiddler*, and only in passing. As much as his dad's drinking had already destroyed, Carter refused to let it touch the beauty that had blossomed between Lauren and him.

Of course, nothing was safe from the talons of addiction. He'd found that out the hard way.

But that was over now. Dad had been sober for six years. He'd gotten a fresh start.

And because of that, maybe Carter and Lauren could do the same.

"Looked like you could be," Natalie replied around her mouthful of chip.

"Or at least like he wants them to be." Sara nudged his shoulder and dissolved into giggles, which Nat quickly joined.

"All right, all right." Carter set down the knife and gestured toward the neatly chopped pile of chives. "There you go. Chives disassembled. I'm out."

He started for the back door, but a wail from the next room stopped him. A moment later Cassandra appeared, strands of dark brown escaping the haphazard knot atop her head, a screeching Lucas on her hip. "Nobody in here would happen to have seen Petey, would they?"

Petey. Lucas's beloved—and bedraggled—stuffed blue octopus. Why Carter had chosen it as a baby gift for his nephew, he couldn't remember, and why Lucas had grown attached to that toy, of the thousands at his disposal, remained a mystery. Nonetheless, that was how it had happened, and it was rare to see one without the other. And judging from the big tears spilling down Lucas's cheeks, that wasn't going to change anytime soon.

"No, but I'll help you look." Grateful for the escape route, Carter clapped his hands and held them out, offering to relieve Cassandra's squirmy, crying burden. "Come on, little man. Let's go find Petey."

Lucas refused Carter's offer to carry him with an even tighter grip around his mother's neck, but the wailing subsided. A partial success, at any rate.

"Where'd he have it last?" Carter ducked through the large kitchen doorway into the living room, all beige carpet and blue furniture and wall-to-wall photos of him and his sisters through the years.

Cass reached into an enormous gray diaper bag near the front door and withdrew a sippy cup, which she handed to Lucas. Blessedly, sobs were soon replaced with a quiet *slup-slup-slup*.

"I know he didn't have it outside," she said. "The last place I saw it was in here, but he also might've dropped it when I changed him into his suit."

"Want me to look in the bathroom, then, and you look here? Divide and conquer?" He strode in the direction of the small bathroom off the kitchen, but Cassandra stopped him with a hand on his chest.

"I'll take the bathroom." Her lips curved. "I heard Nat and Sara giving you the third degree."

Grinning, Carter kissed his sister's rounded cheek. "You're a peach, Cass."

"And don't you forget it." She and Lucas rounded the corner and disappeared.

"Okay, Petey." Carter cracked his knuckles and glanced around the small room. "Game's up. Show thyself."

But Petey apparently had hidden quite well, because he wasn't on the sill of the big picture window looking out on the street. He wasn't under the sofa either, nor between any of the cushions. And that odd corner behind Mom's favorite chair, the plushy one with the worn armrests, was empty except for a stray emery board and a couple dust bunnies.

"C'mon, Petey. Ain't got all day." Carter knelt in front of his father's armchair, the carpet scratching his knees, and lifted the fabric flap on its front. Could that be it? Way in the back? He stretched an arm beneath the chair, felt around, and brushed a pair of plush, nubby tentacles.

"Jackpot." Scooting toward the back of the chair, he lifted the edge, retrieved Petey, and set the colorful little toy on the end table.

But as he lowered the chair, something wedged between the table and the wall caught his eye. Something cylindrical. Metal.

A Coke can? Here? He reached to retrieve it, and his stomach plummeted.

It wasn't Coke.

It was a beer can.

The cold, thin metal in his fingertips, the yeasty whiff of leftover Coors started a roar in his ears and a spinning, swirling sensation so strong he gripped the end table with whitened knuckles. No. *Please, God, no.* Not again. Dad had been doing so well.

Logic broke into the storm, enough for a shaky breath. Maybe it wasn't Dad's. Maybe there was some other perfectly reasonable explanation. There had to be. Because Dad wouldn't. He *wouldn't.*

But how many beer cans and whiskey bottles had his father squirreled away over the years? Cans and bottles that had led to shouting matches and shattered dishes and sincere-sounding apologies. Always the apologies. The excuses. The empty promises.

The reason Carter had made so many excuses and empty promises himself.

"Petey!"

At Lucas's joyful yelp, Carter stashed the can back in its hiding place. Scrambling to his feet, he slapped on a smile. "Yep. Hid himself pretty good under your grandpa's chair."

The toddler grabbed Petey in a chubby embrace.

"What do we tell Uncle Carter?" Cassandra prompted.

"Thank you." Lucas flung his arms around Carter's legs.

His nephew's exuberance, his sheer innocence, took the edge off the painful shock of a moment before. "You're welcome, little man." Carter patted the small back.

After a moment, the boy trotted off toward the kitchen.

Cassandra blew a stray strand of hair out of her face and gave Carter a tired smile. "You're a lifesaver, little brother." But as her eyes met his, her brow creased. "What's wrong?"

"Nothin'." He scrubbed a hand over his face, raspy with weekend stubble. "It's just . . . how's Dad doing?"

"Seems fine. Why?"

"I, uh . . . I found a beer can. Just now. Behind his chair." A jerk of his chin indicated the spot.

Cass's brows slammed together. "What? But that's impossible."

"Not *impossible*." Carter's jaw clenched. "But I don't wanna think he's . . . not after all this time."

Cass shook her head. "No. No. I'd have noticed. Mom would've said something."

Carter snorted. Principal of Joyce Center Middle School for as long as anyone could remember, his mother was a formidable woman who didn't take any crap from anyone, but she nursed a huge blind spot when it came to her husband.

"Okay, fine, maybe she wouldn't." Cass pursed her lips. "But I honestly think that beer can is Brad's."

Carter's brows lifted. "Brad?" Cass's paramedic husband.

"Dinner last Sunday," she explained. "Brad took a break from the grill and came inside because it was so hot. He had a can of something when he did, and he sat in Dad's chair. He had it in a Koozie though, so I don't know what it was."

Had this explanation come from anyone other than Cass, Carter would've dismissed it outright. But while Mom enabled his father's drinking, Nat tried to cover it up, and Sara pretended it didn't exist, Cass had always been a staunch ally in acknowledging the problem. So if she thought the can was Brad's, then there was at least a reasonable chance that was the truth.

Lips pressed together tightly, Carter squatted and reached blindly for the can. He couldn't look at it. Didn't want to see it. Didn't want to think it could be real. "Wish Brad wouldn't drink around here." *Or at all. Ever.*

No. That wasn't fair. Brad didn't drink often and was always responsible when he did. His enjoying a cold one every now and again wasn't anything to stress about.

"Want me to talk to him?" Cassandra asked. "See if it was his?"

Carter shook his head. "Nah. I'm probably being paranoid."

"You? Paranoid? Never." With a warm smile, Cass laid a hand on Carter's shoulder. "I'll keep an eye on Dad, okay?"

Sliding an arm around his sister's waist, Carter nodded and swallowed hard. He hated to add to her already-full plate, but maybe he could finagle another trip out here in a couple weeks to shoulder his share of the load.

"Yeah. Okay."

Cass motioned toward the can. "Want me to take care of that?"

"Nah, I got it. Thanks, though." With a kiss to her cheek, he rounded the corner to the bathroom.

No sooner had he switched on the light than his phone gave two quick buzzes in the pocket of his shorts. With a quick glance toward the kitchen, he pulled it out. Mom had a strict device-free dinner policy, but dinner wasn't ready yet. Besides, it was probably just work, and he—

Oh.

Not work.

Lauren.

Hey, Carter! Thanks again for having me on the show, and for sharing our video. Blog traffic is through the roof, thanks to you. PLUS—I still can't believe this—the Gluten Free Goddess wants me to do a guest post on her blog!

He had no idea who the Gluten Free Goddess was, but based on the string of surprised-smiley and confetti emojis, this was a good thing.

Anyway, I just wanted to say thank you. And if that coffee offer is still open, I'd like to take you up on it. My treat. Maybe this Friday?

Coffee.

With Lauren.

What changed her mind? What convinced her to take the leap? What—

The snapping of fingers jerked his attention from his phone to Cassandra, whose hazel eyes glimmered and mouth quirked with amusement.

"There you are," she said. "Where'd I lose you?"

He tucked his phone back into his pocket but kept it in a loose grip. "Just the social media rabbit hole."

"Well, you better climb back out, 'cause dinner's ready." She jerked a thumb toward the backyard. "We need help lugging all this stuff out there."

"Okay. Be there in a sec." Carter waited until Cass was safely in the kitchen, then pulled the phone from his pocket and read the message again. And again.

The knot in his chest relaxed its grip at the mere sight of that name, those words, on the screen. Lauren Anderson had always been the one person who'd made it possible to forget who he was, where he came from, and who he believed himself doomed to be. The one person whose love had inspired him to dream of being more.

He glanced at the beer can, still in his left hand. The symbol of all that had gone wrong with his life. With him.

With Lauren.

With a grunt, he tossed it toward the wastebasket next to the toilet. It banked off the wall and clattered in, and Carter switched off the light.

The can was Brad's. It almost had to be.

He wouldn't allow himself to think it could be anyone else's.

CHAPTER NINE

AS MUCH AS Lauren loved her apartment's kitchen, with its exposed brick and clever storage nooks, there was just something about the kitchen in her grandparents' old farmhouse that brought immense joy whenever she cooked there. The big windows behind the sink. The natural light that streamed in, perfect for photography. Knowing she stood in the spot where her mother had learned to cook, and her grandmother, and her great-grandmother, back through the generations for almost as long as the home had existed.

And to think, if not for Sloane and her birth mother, it would've been drowned at the bottom of a ski lake. As it was, the two of them had purchased the house, and Sloane had moved in and begun needed renovations, honoring the past while updating to the best of the present. Riding a wave of immense gratitude, Lauren added an extra swoosh of pomegranate sauce to the chicken she was plating for Sloane.

"Here we go." Dishes balanced on her arms waitress-style, Lauren swept into the dining room, where Garrett and Sloane were setting utensils and glasses of iced herbal tea at each place. Garrett didn't live here—not yet anyway—but he was over so often, it almost seemed like he did.

After Garrett blessed the food, they all dug in, and Lauren watched as her brother froze, wide-eyed, freshly emptied fork halfway back to his plate. "Whoa. Lauren. This is incredible." He shoveled another bite into his already-full mouth. "You really outdid yourself this time."

Sloane flashed a thumbs-up. "I'd say more, but I'm too busy eating."

Lauren beamed beneath their effusive praise. "Thanks, guys. I'm thinking of this recipe for my guest spot on Gluten Free Goddess."

"You got on GFG?" Garrett stopped inhaling his dinner long enough to glance at her across the table. "For real?"

"Yep. A week from Tuesday."

"Wow." Grinning, Garrett extended a closed fist, which Lauren bumped. "Nicely done."

"That's great, Lauren," Sloane mumbled around another large mouthful, brown eyes shining through black plastic glasses. "How'd you land that?"

Lauren loaded her fork with a slice of chicken, a few leaves of kale, and a dab of sauce. The perfect bite. "It was that cooking segment on Channel Five. Penny saw the video on Facebook. I guess her husband used to work with Carter."

"Ol' Carter came through for you, did he?" Garrett returned his attention to his plate and jammed his fork into the chicken thigh. "'Bout time."

A smile touched Lauren's lips, even as painful memories washed over her. Garrett was the only one who knew just how fierce an opponent bulimia had been. The one whose tearful pleas had finally convinced her to seek help. He'd always blamed Carter for her illness, and Lauren had done nothing to persuade him otherwise.

Nothing to convince him—or herself—that Carter wasn't solely responsible for their disaster.

"He really did." She swirled her chicken in a dollop of sauce. "In fact, we're, uh . . . having coffee Friday."

Garrett's head snapped up. "Are you sure that's a good idea?"

"Honestly? No." Thank the Lord Garrett hadn't witnessed their conversation in the K-KAN parking lot, or he'd be even more overprotective. "But I've prayed about it, and I feel like it's something I need to do."

Garrett's blue gaze held hers, long and searching. "Okay." He resumed cutting his chicken. "Just be careful, will you? Please?"

"I will. Promise." Lauren scooped up a forkful of greens. "So totally changing the subject, did you guys see Grandma yesterday?"

Sloane nodded. "She was in pretty good spirits."

"No mention of Ephraim," Garrett added. "And I didn't push it. Seemed best to leave that alone."

Sloane reached for the dish of extra pomegranate sauce. "I think I found him today, though. Or at least where he was back then."

Lauren paused, fork halfway to her mouth. "You did?"

"They just released the 1950 census, so I looked there first. All the Jameses listed there were white." Sloane slathered her chicken with sauce. "But the city directory had a James family living on Lorraine Avenue starting in 1954. City directories don't list race, but that area would've been in the heart of the black neighborhood back then. They were the only James family I found in that part of town, so I'm almost positive that's Ephraim."

"Do we know where he is now?" Lauren asked. "Or if he's even still living?"

Sloane shook her head. "That's all I found so far. And this James family, whether they were Ephraim's or not . . . they don't appear in Wichita after 1957. No idea where they went or why. And your grandma's yearbook is the only record I can find of Ephraim James anywhere."

Lauren drooped with disappointment. "So we still don't know anything about him."

"No. Not yet anyway." Sloane grinned. "But don't worry. I'm just getting warmed up."

>←

October 1954

Squeak. Squeak. Squeak.

Normally, the echoes of student chatter and slamming lockers drowned out any contribution from Rosie's still-new saddle shoes. But now, the school day long over, the hallway was empty enough for those black-and-white leather shoes to take center stage. If anyone else were here, she'd be mortified.

Thank goodness no one was.

Wait. Someone was.

Faint piano music bled from beneath the closed door of the choir room, Rosie's destination after forgetting her gloves at rehearsal. Mr. Bishop listening to one of his records, no doubt.

But if it was, it was unlike any music Rosie had heard before. While it contained the major and minor chords her piano teacher had tried—with mixed success—to show her, several different notes blended in. Notes that sounded at first like the clunkers that always plagued her during her ill-fated three years of lessons. But instead of sounding sour, like they did when she played them, these notes were undeniably sweet.

So was the voice floating on top of it. Agile and rangy, yet smooth as velvet.

Wait. She knew that voice.

She heard it to her left every day during choir.

But she'd never heard Ephraim James's voice do *this*.

She paused, hand on the choir room's cold metal doorknob, and stood on tiptoe to peek through the little glass window. Sure enough, Ephraim sat at the old upright, eyes closed, swaying to the rhythm. His long brown fingers danced up and down the keyboard with all the grace and ease of Fred and Ginger.

Rosie cracked the door and crept inside. She didn't want to disturb him. She definitely didn't want him to stop. But she was so focused on the music—and its source—that she bumped into a chair. It slammed into the riser behind it, and the music came to an abrupt halt.

"Sorry." Ephraim shot to his feet. "I didn't know anyone was here."

"No, no, *I'm* sorry." Rosie's hand fluttered to her chest. "You don't have to stop. And I'm not here. Not really."

One ebony brow arched.

"Okay, fine. I'm here. But not for long. I just . . . I . . ." Oh, why *was* she here? "Gloves. I forgot my gloves."

Ephraim returned to the bench, and his hands feathered onto the keys. "Might want to look under your chair. I think I saw them there earlier."

Sure enough, there they were, neatly folded behind the front leg of her chair. She climbed the stairs and bent to retrieve them, then tucked them into her handbag and descended the steps, her attention pulled, magnet-like, to the piano. Despite hours of practice and Mrs. Mayberry's patient instruction, Rosie had never pulled the kind of music from the keyboard that Ephraim did, seemingly without effort. It flowed from somewhere deep inside him. Straight from his soul.

"Where'd you learn to do that?" The words came out over a river of notes in a scale she'd never heard.

"Listening, mostly." A rapidly descending trio of chords punctuated his answer.

"You never took lessons?"

More chords, immediately followed by a quick arpeggio. "Had a few back in Arkansas."

Arkansas. That explained the slight Southern tinge to his voice.

"Nothing formal," he continued. "Our church organist just showed me some things."

Rosie's eyes widened. "This is church music?"

"At my church it is."

"Not mine." Rosie let out a chuckle at the thought of such music filling the solemn room of stained glass and wooden pews.

Ephraim's smile widened. "Yeah, I heard white church is all stuffy and quiet. Lots of rules for how you're supposed to behave." He shook his head. "That don't sound like church to me."

"No?" Rosie set her books on top of the redwood upright. She'd never thought much about church before. It was just what she did on Sundays. Where she went to learn about Jesus.

But Ephraim had a point—it was no sock hop. The music was . . . well, boring was probably the wrong way to describe it, especially since it was church. But six verses of the same song could get a little monotonous.

And sure, church had times to stand. Times to sit. Times to be quiet. Most of the time, that last one. But she'd never thought of the rhythms of church as restrictive rules, merely the right thing to do. Church was God's house. One ought to treat it with reverence. Listen with respect to the teaching of God's servant.

But maybe, just maybe, that servant could let up—just a little—with the hairy eyeball every time she and Viv so much as glanced each other's way.

"I'm right, aren't I?" Ephraim's voice broke into her thoughts. Brown eyes gleamed with amusement, and his full mouth broke into a grin, then a laugh as musical as the chords beneath his fingertips.

His infectious smile summoned one of her own. "Maybe."

"No maybe about it. White church is just history class with hymns."

"All right." She folded her arms across her chest. "What's your church like?"

"Music." His voice was rich with feeling. "Music like this. No matter what's going on, there's music."

Rosie's brows lifted. "Even during the sermon?"

"It's wild. Energetic. If your church is history class, then mine's . . ." His brow furrowed. "More like a football game."

A *football* game? Reverend Jeffries would flip his lid.

"You ask me, that's what it should be." Ephraim turned to look at her. "We got someone willing to take away all our sin and let us live with him forever in exchange? Seems worth celebrating to me."

Maybe it was the music. Maybe it was Ephraim. Or maybe it was the truth of his words resonating deep in her soul like the strings inside the piano. When he put it like that, when she truly thought about all Christ did for her—for all of them—following rules and maintaining strict silence didn't seem to fit quite as well as it once did.

Rosie propped her elbows atop the piano and rested her chin in her hands, the vibrations of the music traveling throughout her body. "Do you play here a lot, then? After school?"

"Usually. Sometimes I get brave and play the grand in the auditorium." Ephraim's fingers danced through a dizzying series of arpeggios. "Don't have a piano at home, so Mr. Bishop lets me practice here."

"Is that what you want to do after you graduate, then? Play?"

One slim shoulder lifted. "Dunno. Maybe. What about you?"

"I'm going to be a teacher."

Ephraim gave a quiet chuckle. "Surely not like Mr. Sullivan."

"No. Not high school. Grade school, I think. First grade maybe. There's just something about teaching a child how to read that calls to me."

"Kinda like playing does for me, I reckon."

At the next series of chords, curiosity drew Rosie closer. She came around the back of the piano and studied Ephraim's hands, her ponytail whispering across her neck. "How are you *doing* that?"

"Just a basic seventh chord."

Seventh chord. If she'd ever learned such a thing, it had long since been crowded out by chemistry formulas and Shakespearean monologues.

The music stopped, and Ephraim rested his fingers on three white keys. "Like, okay, this here's C major, right?"

The bright sunshine of the C-E-G combination resonated throughout the empty choir room. C major. That, she remembered.

"So then just throw in this note here—" He added a B-flat with his pinky, and the chord shifted from sunny to sultry. "There it is."

"Huh." Rosie rested her own fingers on the keyboard a couple octaves above Ephraim's, mirroring the notes beneath his hand. C. E. G. She sounded the keys one at a time, then cautiously pinged the B-flat on the top. Wow. That black key—the only one in the chord—was all it took to create that beautiful color.

Summoning the scant remnants of her piano knowledge, she created a few more seventh chords in various keys. F. G. D. A.

White keys. Black keys. Ebony and ivory. A piano wouldn't be a piano without both.

So why couldn't people get along like piano keys did?

"There you go." Ephraim nodded his encouragement. "You're getting it now."

She smiled, warm and genuine. "Thanks for teaching me."

All right. So maybe the races as a whole hadn't figured out how to get along yet. But she and Ephraim?

They were getting along just fine.

CHAPTER TEN

MEME.

Humble brag.

Political rant.

Another version of the same meme.

Rolling his eyes, Carter clicked out of Facebook and tucked his phone into his shirt pocket. What an idiot he'd been, to think social media would distract him from his pounding heart and churning stomach.

Cups and silverware clinked, and he glanced across the brick-walled coffee shop to the large clock behind the bar, nearly obscured by a cloud of steam from the hissing espresso machine. Still five minutes before he was due to meet Lauren. Why had arriving early seemed like a good idea? The longer he sat at this little wooden booth, the more his palms dampened and his chest tightened. He hadn't been such a wreck waiting on a woman since . . . since . . .

Since the last time he'd been waiting on Lauren Anderson.

The door creaked open, and there she stood. Radiant in a flowing skirt and bright-blue tank top, half her hair was pulled up in a knot, while the other half tumbled over her shoulders. Her friendly wave dissolved the last of his *she'll actually show up, won't she?* anxiety and replaced it with a wholly different source of stress. One that caused him to fling a silent plea heavenward.

Please don't let me screw this up.

He slid from the booth and stood. "Hey."

"Hi, Carter." Her smile was bright, but the slight roll of her lower lip between her teeth was her tell. She, too, was fighting nerves.

He reached for her waist from pure instinct, but stopped himself. That seemed a little much. But a handshake or fist bump didn't seem right either. He settled for stuffing his hands into his pockets.

Lauren glanced around the interior of Beantown. "This is sure a step up from that cheap place we went to way back when."

Carter slid into line beside her. "Who could forget Tito's?"

"Would you believe that place is still there?"

"It is? How?"

"It's definitely not their coffee." Long tasseled earrings danced with Lauren's slight shrug. "I've had better lattes at gas stations. Y'know, back when I bought food at gas stations. And drank lattes."

She didn't drink lattes anymore? Uh-oh. But his slight panic was alleviated when they reached the front. After perusing the menu and asking a few questions of the barista, she settled on an iced hibiscus tea, while he quickly ordered his usual iced cold brew.

They retrieved their drinks and settled at the cozy booth in the corner, where a vintage-looking pendant light illuminated a polished wooden table and brick walls surrounded them with black-and-white photos of Wichita's past.

"So you must know where to find all the good caffeine, with your shift and all." Lauren's sweet smile clenched his insides. "What time do you get up in the mornings?"

"Usually a little before three."

She gave the wince he'd come to expect when someone learned his schedule. "Ouch. And I thought I got up early."

"It's not too bad once you get used to it. And I've got quiet neighbors. That helps."

Lauren sipped her tea and leaned her elbows on the table. "So how'd someone who wanted to be the next Anderson Cooper end up doing weather?"

The smile that had sprung to his lips so easily suddenly took work to maintain. He kept a polished, surface version of the story in his back pocket at all times. A version he could rattle off without thinking. Without feeling.

But Lauren deserved more than the surface version.

"I did news for a while. Beat reporter a couple different places. Anchored as a fill-in a few times down in Alabama. Had the lead anchor chair right in my sights." He sliced the air with his hand.

"But . . ." She made a *keep going* gesture, the light glinting off a funky silver ring on her middle finger.

"But after the initial excitement wore off, I realized just how depressing most of the news is. Murders, car wrecks, political nonsense . . . Seemed like all I was doing was bringing people down." He shifted in the booth. "But the kicker was a tornado about five years back. They sent me out for a live shot, and I'm standing there talking at the camera while people behind me are sifting through splintered rubble that used to be their home. A mom and two kids died half a mile from where I stood. All I could do was come in afterward and tell everyone else how horrible it was."

Twin lines appeared between delicate brows. "You must've felt so helpless."

"Helpless. Yeah." He stared into the near blackness of his coffee, the rotation in his stomach picking up speed. "It was, um . . . it was a feeling I grew up with."

"What do you mean?"

He forced his head up. Made himself look into those blue eyes. "Remember when I said I had a lot of family stuff going on?"

One brow shot skyward. "The night you broke up with me? Yeah. I remember."

Crap. He shut his eyes against the sharp edge in her voice. This wasn't going well.

Didn't matter, though. Because the truth was long overdue.

Some of it, at least.

He shoved the words from his lips. "My dad's an alcoholic, Lauren. He drank pretty much my whole childhood."

"Oh. Wow."

The sharpness was gone. Thank God.

"It's better now. He's sober." *Probably.* "But growing up, y'know, it was just one disaster after another. And all I could do was stare at the rubble." Carter picked up his glass, cold and slick between his fingers. "So when I felt that same way as an adult—at work—something had to change. I couldn't do anything to prevent the bad stuff, but I could warn people it was coming. Give them the power to protect themselves. And if I could do that, then . . . maybe I wouldn't feel so powerless myself."

She studied him. "Did it work?"

"It did. And I love doing weather. Even more than I thought I would." He replaced his glass and leaned his elbows on the table. "You can't control everything, Lauren. It's stupid to try. But whatever you can control, whatever will keep your life from spiraling into total chaos, then you find that and give it all you've got."

"Yeah. I get that." Her voice was barely above a whisper, her gaze fixed on some distant point in the corner.

Oh. Man. He needed to lighten things up before she decided he was too much of a mess.

"Okay. Phew." Pulling out his TV grin, he pantomimed wiping his forehead. "I don't usually get that heavy on a first date."

Though her focus shifted to him, her eyes never lost that faraway look. "Since when is this a first date?"

Wait. Was she saying this wasn't a date? Or . . .

One corner of her mouth quirked. "If I remember right, our first date was a midnight Taco Bell run in that falling-apart Pontiac of mine."

His grin turned genuine as the grip of tension relaxed. He raised his glass to her in silent toast. "You make an excellent point."

→←

Lauren clinked her glass against Carter's, but only part of her focus was in the here and now. The rest tried to reconcile what he'd said just now with what he'd told her thirteen years ago. Examine those dusty old words in a new day's light.

Lauren, I'm—there's just . . . there's a lot going on right now—with my family mostly—and adding you into it is . . . it's too much, okay? I'm sorry. I'm so sorry. But I can't. It's just too much.

How many hours had those words echoed in her head? How many times had she assumed they were just a flimsy cover for the real reason he didn't want to be with her?

But the hollow look in normally radiant eyes, the twitch in his jaw, the tightness of his lips . . . those words that long-ago night weren't some lame excuse. They were stone-cold truth.

His father. An alcoholic. It made so much sense. Oh, she could only imagine what his childhood had been like.

So why hadn't he loved her enough to tell her then? To let her walk the rock-strewn road with him instead of insisting on walking it alone?

What if she hadn't been too much?

"Okay, Lauren Anderson." Carter's voice gently tugged her attention back into the here and now. "I told you how I got into weather. What about you and health food?"

She gave a dry chuckle. "If you don't want things to get heavy, that's not the right question to ask."

"I did open the door." He reached for his coffee. "Lay it on me."

Lauren fortified herself with a swig of tea, then set the glass down and faced him. "You remember my mom had cancer."

"Yeah . . ." He gave a brief frown, but when his eyes went wide and his lips parted, she knew he'd zipped to the story's predictably tragic end. "Oh. Lauren. No. I'm so sorry."

He thunked his glass onto the table and placed his hand over hers. His fingers were cold and damp from the drink, but their gentle pressure was a comfort. Like finding an old favorite pair of jeans and realizing they still fit.

"When?" he asked.

"It's been seven years now. And she wasn't overweight, didn't smoke, didn't drink—none of the risk factors. If it could happen to her, it can happen to anyone." Her gaze fell from Carter's face to their hands, his smooth beige, hers freckled ivory. "And suddenly there I was, with the twin albatrosses of being overweight and having a family history. So I started researching, and I learned cancer rates were much lower when people ate food the way God intended. Before we started messing with chemicals and pesticides and GMOs. So I stopped eating out, learned to cook, started taking pictures of the stuff I cooked . . ."

"And a blog is born."

"Pretty much." She summoned a smile. It was a good answer. A truthful answer.

But not a complete answer.

She'd left out the lifelong pattern of stress eating that ballooned to disturbing proportions with Mom's diagnosis when Lauren was a freshman. The reflection in the mirror seeming to grow larger by the day.

Summer theater before senior year had been a welcome reprieve. A chance to block out the constant anxiety about her mother and throw herself into her role.

And into Carter's arms.

He was The One. Or so she'd believed, with every fiber of her desperate teenage being. And so, that warm night by the creek when he'd told her he loved her more than he ever could've imagined loving someone, she'd given herself to him. Body, mind, and soul.

Less than a week later, it all came crashing down. And coupled with the pain of loss was the crippling guilt. Her lifelong plan to save herself for her husband had been thrown away for a night of passion, and now she was damaged goods. A chewed piece of gum. A rose with all its petals pulled off. Forgiven, sure . . . but never restored. Never the same girl she would've been if she'd just stayed in control.

Her faithful friends Ben and Jerry had been there for her. As had Pizza Hut, chocolate cake, and store-brand ruffled potato chips.

The first time she threw up was an accident. A natural consequence of eating too much, too fast.

But the second time wasn't.

Neither was the next time. Or the next.

"My blog is like weather is for you." She shut the door on her memories and reached for her tea. Zero calories. Sugar-free. Antioxidant-rich. "Controlling what you can in a world that's uncontrollable."

"Sounds like your blog's doing pretty well, then." Carter moved his hand from hers to his glass of coffee. "Gluten Free Goddess? She sounds like kind of a big deal."

"She is." Lauren swirled the straw in her tea. Ice cubes rattled and clinked against the glass.

"So why don't I detect the same excitement as last week, with all those emojis?"

Carter's gently teasing question drew a chuckle. "Because Penny's strongly encouraging me to do a video. She says guests who do those get a whole lot more hits."

"Okay, and? You just did a video."

"That was different."

"How?"

"Because it was with you." The words were out before she could evaluate their merit. "You were driving that whole thing—"

"What? I barely knew how to hold a chef's knife. Heck, I'd never even heard of a chef's knife."

"But we played off each other, just like we always did. And you did that thing you do, where you're calm and confident and awesome, and—"

"Lauren." Carter tilted his head and sought her gaze. Just like he'd done during *Fiddler*, when she'd been on the verge of freaking out. Those endless brown eyes, that smile that grew tight at the corners, like he was holding back a belly laugh . . . That always helped her relax. Breathe.

"It's an act," he said. "Being comfortable in front of a camera is a learned skill. And as well as you did on our cooking segment? You're gonna rock this video. I know it. You're a natural."

She couldn't suppress a grin. "You're doing it again."

"Doing what?"

"Being awesome. Making me believe in myself."

Laughter slipped out, deep and warm. "What, you want me to apologize?"

"No, it's fine." She slid her lower lip between her teeth and stared at the little stamp on the corner of the table. *Handmade in Wichita.* "I've missed it."

Missed you. Those words didn't make it out of her mouth, but they might as well have, what with the sudden shimmery energy between them. It pulled her attention from the tabletop to that familiar-yet-unfamiliar face. To the parted lips. The slightly furrowed brow.

It was the same look he'd had last week on set. The look that meant whatever she was feeling and re-feeling and grappling with the reality of . . . he was feeling it too.

Could it be their mistakes might not have destroyed their magic?

"Look, what if I gave you some pointers?" He reached for his coffee. "We'll do a dress rehearsal. You make the food, talk your way through it, and I'll be right there to coach you. I'll even run camera if you want me to. Long as whatever you use isn't as complicated as those studio cameras, I should be good."

"Yeah. Okay." Her apartment. Her blog post. Her food. Controlling what she could. "I think . . . maybe I can do this."

"Worth a shot, right?" His lips curved in that confident smile. The one that had buoyed her through countless anxious backstage moments. The same exact smile.

Except not. It was an adult version. *He* was an adult version.

And so was she. They'd grown up. Learned from their mistakes. Been honest with each other. Well, mostly honest. But they'd made progress. They'd moved forward.

"Yeah." Smiling, she swirled her straw in her iced tea. "Definitely worth a shot."

Chapter Eleven

By the time Lauren walked into the lobby of Plaza de Paz the next afternoon, Garrett was already waiting beside the elevator. She resisted the urge to roll her eyes. To her big brother, early was on time, on time was late, and late was . . . Well, she wouldn't know what Garrett called "late." He'd never been late in his life.

Tucked beneath his arm was the faded red Roosevelt High yearbook. Grandma's doctor had suggested a little reminiscence therapy: presenting her with familiar objects from that time in her life, in order to coax these long-term memories to the surface. Help her cope. Help them learn her story.

"Here goes nothing." The Up button lit beneath Lauren's finger. Beside her, Garrett cleared his throat and jangled his keys in his pocket.

What should they even hope for? Pray for? That Grandma would remember Ephraim when she saw his yearbook picture, even though it might upset her? Or that the yearbook would receive the same blank look so much else did these days? If she didn't remember it, she'd escape any potential pain . . . but that would mean these stories, these memories, were lost forever.

The elevator dinged its arrival, and they stepped inside.

"So." Garrett pushed the button for the fourth floor, and the metal doors slid shut. "What's new? You and Carter have that coffee yet?"

"Yeah. Yesterday."

"How'd it go? Not too awkward, I hope."

"No, it was . . . a little weird at first, but after that it was fine. We've both grown up. A lot." She tossed an errant wave over her shoulder. "Especially him."

Garrett chuckled as the elevator shuddered to a stop. "There was room."

"He offered to help with my recipe video for Gluten Free Goddess." The doors slid open, and Lauren stepped into the lobby of the Memory Care Unit. She felt like a teenager, running a new relationship through the litmus test of her parents' approval. Except with Mom gone and Dad having eloped to Florida with his internet girlfriend, Garrett's was the only approval Lauren sought.

Not that she'd give him the satisfaction of knowing that, though. Ugh. The gloating would never end.

"He did?" Garrett pushed the call button. His lips twitched, like he planned to say something else, but the click of the Memory Care Unit's double doors cut off whatever words might've escaped.

"Yeah." She kept her voice light. "He says comfort on camera is a learned skill. He's giving me some pointers."

They rounded the green-carpeted corner and stopped in front of the white-columned artificial front porch that marked the entrance to Grandma's suite. Lauren's gaze slid toward Garrett. "You still don't trust him, do you?"

"It's not that exactly." Garrett paused, his hand on the silver door handle. "I just don't want to see you get hurt again, all right?"

"I don't want to *be* hurt again. That's why we're going slow."

"Fair enough." Garrett kissed the top of her head. "I'm just looking out for you."

"I know." Her heart full of the mixture of affection and irritation that so often accompanied interactions with her brother, she rapped the back of the door. "Hello?"

"Nobody home," came Grandma's cheerful reply.

That was always a good sign.

Inside the overly warm suite, Grandma sat in her usual favorite blue armchair, a Texas-sized smile on her face. "Well, hi, sug."

The old endearment brought a bittersweet pang. Lauren's resemblance to her mother meant Grandma had called her Barbara on occasion, though she'd always quickly corrected herself.

A couple years ago, though, the corrections stopped.

Grandma didn't even call her Barbara anymore. Now, she was just *sug*.

Lauren settled into Grandpa's recliner, while Garrett pulled up a chair from the small kitchen table and sat across from them. After some small talk confirmed Grandma was indeed in a good place, Garrett retrieved the yearbook from the end table where he'd laid it.

"So, Grandma, we found this yearbook at your old house." He placed the embossed red-and-black book in their grandmother's age-spotted hand.

"Oh, mercy." Through her glasses, Grandma's gaze caressed the cover. Her fingertips followed. "I haven't seen this thing in ages."

Okay. She remembered the yearbook, and the feelings it brought about seemed pleasant enough. This was good.

"We wanted to show you a picture of someone." Leaning over, Lauren flipped musty pages to where Garrett had bookmarked the senior class portraits. And there, peering up in black-and-white from the center of the page—dark skin, close-cropped hair, and a smile that could light up Times Square—was Ephraim James.

"You were talking a few days ago about someone named Ephraim, and we found an Ephraim James in your senior class." Tapping the photo, Lauren glanced toward her grandmother, but the wrinkled face betrayed no emotion. "Is this the same person? Is this the one who was supposed to meet you?"

Grandma took in a sharp breath. Pale fingertips, the nails neatly filed and polished shiny pink, rested beneath the young man's photo. Silence stretched to the point of discomfort.

"Grandma, do you—"

"O, Romeo, Romeo, wherefore art thou Romeo?"

Lauren drew back at her grandmother's unexpected response.

"Deny thy father, and refuse thy n-name." Grandma's fingers curled into a fist. Her voice was strong yet shaky.

Lauren met Garrett's eyes over the snowy curls and saw her own bewilderment staring back at her. Since when did Grandma quote Shakespeare?

One question, however, seemed to have been answered by the wobble on the last word. The sheen of tears in pale-blue eyes, the fond smile curving crepey cheeks.

At least on some level, in some part of her disease-riddled brain, Grandma remembered Ephraim James.

"Or, if thou wilt not, be but sworn my love." Grandma caressed the photo again, her smile growing wider. "And I'll no longer be a Capulet."

❧

November 1954

Please don't let her call on me. Please don't let her call on me. Please, please, please don't let her call on me.

Rosie slid into her desk, chanting her silent prayer. It wasn't that Miss Greer was mean. Far from it. And it wasn't that Rosie was shy, because she wasn't, or because she wasn't good at reading out loud, because she was. One of the best in class, in fact. Couldn't be much of a teacher if she didn't hone those skills.

But all that skill and confidence evaporated in the face of Shakespeare's plays.

Plays were meant not merely to be read but to be performed, Miss Greer insisted. So they always read them aloud in English class, with their pretty brunette teacher making sure everyone had a turn in the spotlight. And most of the words were recognizable enough. But all the *doths* and *forsooths* tangled Rosie's tongue and brain alike. So focused was she on preventing mistakes when reading that she frequently had no idea what Shakespeare was talking about. No clue why someone with such a simple nickname—the Bard—would use such complex, flowery language to make his point.

Being a grade school teacher was looking more and more appealing.

Vivian slipped in at the bell, sliding into her usual seat at Rosie's left with a sheepish smile. Flushed cheeks broadcast the likely reason for her near tardiness. Doubtless Bobby Duvall was afflicted with the same reddish tinge and mad dash to class. Rosie hid a giggle behind her fingers, and Viv's hazel eyes widened.

"Shh," she hissed, finger to her lips.

On the other side of Vivian sat Ephraim, who caught Rosie's gaze over the top of Viv's head. His dark eyes reflected her own amusement, and she had to fight to keep from giggling outright. Her blossoming friendship with her black classmate, fed and watered by clandestine after-school meetings in the choir room, was still a secret. But when the sunshine of his smile warmed her from head to toe, even here in English class, how much longer could it stay that way?

Rising from her desk, Miss Greer clapped her hands, and the chatter quieted. "Good morning, ladies and gentlemen. We will resume where we left off. Act one, scene five."

Textbooks thumped open, and the rustle of pages filled the rows of desks. Miss Greer consulted her notes. "Mr. Tubbs, you'll read First Servant. Miss Winslow, Second Servant. Mr. McIntyre, you'll make a fine Lord Capulet."

A smile shone on the face of the clean-cut strawberry-blond quarterback to Rosie's right, a smile he aimed in her direction. She gave a brief one in reply, then turned her attention to her textbook. She liked Gordon McIntyre well enough. Outgoing and charismatic, he made for an entertaining friend. But his cockiness, bordering on arrogance, meant her interest in him ended there.

She couldn't say the same for his interest in her.

"Mr. Waters, you'll be our Second Capulet." Miss Greer peered over the rims of her glasses. "Mr. James, if you'll read Romeo, please. Mr. Huffman, Tybalt—"

Gordon gave a derisive snort. "A colored Romeo? Yeah, right."

Behind them, a couple students snickered, while Miss Greer's smile froze in place and fastened on Gordon. "I'm sorry, Mr. McIntyre. Did you have something you'd like to share with the class?"

Rosie tensed as Gordon leaned back in his chair, a smirk on his lips, and looked Miss Greer dead in the eye. "I said, ma'am, that I don't think a colored boy should play Romeo. Given that it's in Italy and all. Figured you'd want to be as historically accurate as possible."

Rosie stared straight ahead, mortified for Ephraim. She didn't dare look his way.

"It's interesting you mention historical accuracy, Mr. McIntyre." Miss Greer's blue-green eyes twinkled with dangerous glee. "Because if we're being strictly accurate, we'd remember that all the actors in Shakespeare's day were men. This means it would be well within my rights—in the interest of accuracy, of course—to cast *you* as fair Juliet."

A hushed giggle rippled through the class. Rosie stifled hers as best she could, but a titter slipped out. She hazarded a glance at Ephraim. He, too, fought back a chuckle.

Miss Greer peered at Gordon over the rims of her glasses. "Now, the balcony scene is coming up. Shall I choose those parts with historical accuracy in mind?"

A bright flush climbed Gordon's pale neck, and a muscle in his jaw twitched. "No, ma'am."

"Very well. I'm glad we've reached an understanding." Miss Greer turned back toward the blackboard, but not before Rosie glimpsed the catlike smile on her crimson lips. The teacher assigned the rest of the parts without incident, and Rosie nearly melted with relief that none of them went to her.

But her relief gave way to apprehension for Ephraim, who followed the lines in the play with a fingertip. How would he do? She'd never heard him read aloud before. And to be given such an important role while one member of the class waited to pounce on even the slightest mistake . . .

Lord, help him. Her fingers tightened to fists beneath her desk as Romeo's first line approached.

"O, she doth teach the torches to burn bright!" Ephraim's voice rang out loud and clear, and Rosie sat dumbfounded. "It seems she hangs upon the cheek of night like a rich jewel in an Ethiope's ear."

Rosie fought the urge that tugged her gaze two desks to the left. This was beyond reading. It was like the words had leaped from the page, taken root in her friend's heart, and now sprang forth with new life in his Southern-tinged voice.

"The measure done, I'll watch her place of stand. And, touching hers, make blessed my rude hand."

Miss Greer's shining eyes mirrored the joy in Rosie's soul. Ephraim spoke with such emotion he was either a top-notch actor . . . or he was imagining a real-life girl in place of the fictional Juliet. He'd never mentioned anyone, but how else could these words have the depth of feeling he gave them?

"Did my heart love till now? Forswear it, sight!" Then Ephraim's gaze left the page and slid directly, inescapably, toward her.

Rosie stopped breathing. Her heart jumped into her throat.

"For I ne'er saw true beauty till this night."

Rosie's mouth turned dry, her palms damp. There was no doubt now. Ephraim *did* have someone in mind. He wasn't conjuring up some Juliet in his head.

He was looking right at her.

Somehow she managed to close her mouth. Arrange it into a wobbly smile. And the one he gave in return, sweet and shy, turned her heart to mush and her legs to Jell-O.

Was this as obvious to everyone else as it seemed to her? Oh, what would Miss Greer say? And what on earth would her friends say? What would Viv say? What would Gordon say?

Thoughts fizzed to the surface but popped like bubbles under the gentle force of that gorgeous smile. The room faded to nothing. Sound stopped. Time stood still. Everything disappeared except their beautiful secret.

"Thank you, Mr. James. Wonderful job." Miss Greer's voice, soft though it was, broke the spell, and Ephraim's gaze darted away, as though remembering somewhere else it needed to be. If he was blushing, his brown skin hid it, and Rosie envied him. No doubt her cheeks flushed a deep shade of Roosevelt High red.

Vivian glanced her way, and Rosie froze. But all her best friend said was a whispered, "Wow, he's good," with a jerk of her head toward Ephraim.

Nodding her agreement, Rosie returned her attention to her textbook. Must not be as obvious as she'd feared, if even Viv didn't notice. And despite sharing nearly every second of the last six years with her dearest friend, Rosie was relieved. This strange new thing that had happened— *was* happening, shouldn't, *couldn't* happen—was like a snowflake floating down to land on a woolen glove. Too precious, too fragile, too magical to share with anyone.

Thank heavens Miss Greer had given shy, studious Helen Prescott the part of Juliet. As terrified as Rosie had been before, she'd be doubly so now. But as Ephraim and Helen flawlessly read the flirtatious back-and-forth of the young lovers' first meeting, Rosie found the words imprinting on her mind. Her heart. Words that had once seemed arcane, foreign, impossible to understand, now sprang to resonant life.

Though four centuries and the thick curtain of reality separated her from Juliet, Rosie's heart squeezed with sudden kinship.

Because a young girl, sweet on the absolute last person she should be sweet on?

Rosie now knew exactly what that felt like.

CHAPTER TWELVE

WALKING DOWN THE hallway of Lauren's apartment building the following Wednesday afternoon filled Carter with serious déjà vu. All the way to the end, last door on the left. The same directions for finding her dorm room during Sunflower Summer Theater. Similar wrought iron light fixtures on the walls, the same type of nondescript carpeting forming a sound-muffling aisle on hardwood floors.

Only in these halls, there was no need to deaden the sound. Doors stood tightly shut, with only the barest hint of conversations and TV shows bleeding from beneath them. Not at all like Sunflower, where doors were constantly flung open, the halls a hub of shouting and singing and the raucous, exuberant laughter of teenagers convinced they were living their best life now.

And just like with the hallway, the Lauren who peeked through a chain-latched door, then opened it wide was familiar enough to be comfortable, but different enough for him to notice. Deep-blue eyes still knocked the wind out of him. Her smile still carved dimples into freckle-kissed skin.

But the smile now ended with that uncertain, lip-between-the-teeth gesture. Her eyes now glinted with caution. Uncertainty.

"Hey, you made it." Even her voice was a shadow of its usual confident self.

"Last door on the left, just like always." His own nerves humming, Carter stepped inside and glanced around the apartment. Instead of the Kelly Clarkson and Taylor Swift posters that had covered her walls back then, now her place featured funky pottery on the shelves and a framed print of Van Gogh's *Sunflowers* on the far wall. She'd echoed the theme with a vase or two filled with fresh versions of the cheery yellow flower that had always been her favorite.

Instead of the *Wicked*-obsessed red-haired roommate she'd had that summer, Lauren now shared her space with a cat. No, make that two. The white one on the couch had been easy enough to spot, but the orange tabby on the bookshelf who eyed him with undisguised suspicion had escaped first glance.

"I see you met Alton and Nigella." Lauren indicated each cat in turn with a sweep of her wrist, then made her way into the kitchen. Granite countertops had been swept clean of all but a knife block, a mason jar with a few spoons, and a handful of ingredients. Meanwhile, the kitchen table practically groaned under the weight of spice jars, cooking utensils, bottles of oil, and who knew what else. That was more like it. The familiar clutter drew a grin.

He sank onto a counter stool at the bar across from her. "What are you making?"

"Pomegranate-glazed chicken with farro and spiced kale. Pretty simple, but it should be a winner."

Carter chuckled. "The only part of that I understood was 'chicken,' so if that's simple, I don't want to know what you'd call complicated."

She laughed, but it was a high-pitched, hollow laugh. The sides of her neck were taut, her shoulders hunched as she moved around the kitchen.

His brow creased. She was just nervous about the video, right? Or . . . was it about him? She'd seemed okay with him helping out when he ran it by her last week, but now that he was in her apartment, now that they were actually about to do this, maybe she was having second thoughts. Had he pushed too hard? Was it too soon in their—well, probably better not call it a relationship yet—for him to insert himself into her life to this degree?

"Can I get you a drink before we start?" Her clipped tone did nothing to answer his questions, but that three-o'clock wake-up call also wasn't helping.

"Don't suppose you've got any coffee, do you?"

"Iced hibiscus tea's the best I can do."

"Caffeinated?" He tried to rub the beginnings of a headache from his temples.

She offered a tight smile. "Nope."

"Okay, but no promises I won't fall asleep."

"I'll try not to be too boring, then." Lauren gave a small laugh as she reached into the cabinet for a glass.

"Hey, if our cooking segment is anything to go by, boring is the last thing you'll be." He shifted on the stool, and it creaked again. "How'd you feel about that thing, anyway?"

"Great." Ice clinked into the glass from the dispenser in her freezer door. "The dish turned out well, and your Facebook page blew up with all the comments."

Suspicion niggled within. He was no detective, but that response had seemed a little too quick. A lot too bright.

"How'd you feel when you watched it, though?" he pressed. "You wanted me to come coach you. What'd you see that you'd like to improve?"

Tea sloshed into the glass, and her shoulders hunched further.

Uh-huh. "You haven't watched it yet, have you?"

Defeat whooshed out in a sigh. "No."

"Come on. You did a great job. Confident, enthusiastic, knowledgeable . . . it was all there. Just a couple tweaks and you'll be ready for prime time."

She whirled, glass in hand. "You watched it?"

"Of course I did. A time or two." Or ten. "Can't be much help if I don't see the finished product."

"Ugh." She slid the glass toward him.

He studied the clear red-tinged liquid, then took a cautious sip. Not too bad. A little plant-y tasting, but . . . not bad.

"I *hate* watching videos of myself." Lauren's fists clenched on the counter. "I sound like a twelve-year-old, and I look like a cheap hippie Giada de Laurentiis."

Having not a clue who that was, Carter wasn't going there. But relief tugged his lips into a grin. Maybe her apartment was unfamiliar, maybe this new, adult version of Lauren wasn't someone he knew well yet.

But the in-need-of-a-confidence-boost Lauren? Her, he knew like the back of his hand.

"Lauren, no one likes watching themselves on video, okay? No one."

She leaned against the counter. "Not even you?"

"Oh, heck no." He waved a hand. "I always think my neck's too skinny, my nose is too big, and my mouth looks weird when I talk. But we're all our own worst critic. No one else focuses on our flaws quite like we do."

"Yeah?" That single, soft syllable, her wide-eyed look, struck him with almost physical force. He was a sucker for that look. He'd kick down doors, scale a wall, climb Mount Everest for that look.

No matter how badly he'd screwed up in the past, he'd always somehow known what to say, what to do, to bring her out of whatever wormhole her thoughts dragged her into. Though she'd never admitted it and probably never would, she needed him.

Just like he needed her. He couldn't fix his dad. Couldn't prevent tornadoes or flash floods or hailstorms.

But here was a sliver of hope. A small corner of the world where he could make a difference.

So he'd give that corner everything he had.

Taking her silence as assent, Carter fished his phone from his pocket. "Come on, Lauren." He patted the stool beside him. "Time to rip off the Band-Aid."

⇥⇤

Lauren winced at the tiny version of herself scraping onions into a sizzling pan. Good *night*. She looked like someone had injected her eyelids and cheeks with Botox to freeze them in that wide-eyed smiling position.

"Ugh," she groaned. "I look ridiculous."

"No, you don't." Carter's automatic reply did nothing for her confidence.

"Yes, I do." Unable to stomach any more, she turned away. "I don't think I can do this, Carter."

"What?" He pressed the screen with his thumb, freezing their images in laughable expressions. "Come on. You brought the house down as Hodel. What's so different about this?"

Because she didn't have to watch the video. Because she didn't have to try to convince herself that "the camera adds a few pounds."

Because she could lose herself in someone she wasn't and forget about being the person she was.

She sketched an absent pattern in the puddle of condensation at the base of her glass. "Being Hodel—performing for real people—was fun. But this isn't a performance. I'm not playing a character. And there aren't any real people here. There's just this big evil eye. Staring at me. Judging me. Waiting for me to screw up."

Carter drew back, blinking. "Never thought about it that way." A grin cracked the surface. "Not sure how I feel about tomorrow's show now."

"Stop it." She shoved his shoulder.

"No, I get it." His warm brown gaze fastened on hers. "But on the other side of that camera *are* real people. People who want to learn from you. Who care what you have to say. That camera you're so scared of? That's just a portal to reach them."

She sipped her tea, considering his words.

"Besides, if they see what I see . . ." His gaze locked on the fridge, lips pressed together, seemingly trying to decide whether he wanted to release whatever words had built up behind them. "Lauren, when I watch you on camera, I see someone who's passionate about what she does. Someone who wants people to be healthy and feel good. I see someone who's charismatic and engaging and . . . and freakin' gorgeous, all right?"

His hand rested on hers, cool and smooth. "I always thought you were beautiful. Always. But now that you're all grown up . . . now you're so gorgeous, it almost hurts to look at you."

Beautiful. Gorgeous. Words that always watered the desert places in her heart. Words he'd said before, words she'd accused him of uttering solely so he could get what he wanted from her.

But there was no pretense in his eyes. Instead, they radiated genuine wonder. Awe. Amazement that the sparkle between them, the magic . . . thirteen years had done nothing to erase it.

And his lips, had they drawn closer? Or was it she who'd moved?

Her heartbeat skittered; her mouth tingled with anticipation. She knew exactly what this felt like. She knew how intoxicating those lips had been, how they'd—

A flash of movement behind him and then a startled yelp from Carter. Was that—

It *was.* Alton had leaped down from his bookshelf perch to rest on

Carter's back. She dissolved into laughter as the orange tabby climbed up and over his shoulder, then plopped onto the counter before him, drawing his fluffy tail beneath Carter's nose.

"Guess I passed muster?" Carter gave the cat a scratch behind the ears and was rewarded with wild purring.

"Guess so." Oh, Alton. She could've kissed him. Because she'd almost kissed *Carter*. She'd almost lost control. One coffee date and ten minutes of a video coaching session, and she'd been *this close* to falling into the trap that had claimed her thirteen years ago.

They were taking it slow. Testing the waters.

And kissing him would have blown all those noble intentions to smithereens.

"Okay. Come on." She rose and slapped the countertop. "Let's do this. Before I lose my nerve."

He looked surprised. Maybe a touch relieved too. "You sure you're ready?"

"Guess we'll find out." She fetched the video camera from the cluttered kitchen table and plopped it into his palm. His sleeve brushed her bare arm. *No. Focus.*

"You're gonna be great, Lauren."

He was still looking at her, lining up his shot, but it was through the lens of the camera. And that small black circle, the one that had caused so much stress ten minutes ago, now was a shot of cool relief. Compared to Carter's soulful, all-seeing brown eyes, that camera was a piece of cake.

"Okay, you ready?"

Lauren wiped her hands on her skirt. *It's not the camera. It's the people. They're not judging me. They want to learn.*

She pulled in a breath and shaped her lips into a warm smile. "Ready."

⊰⊱

Sneakers squeaked a slow rhythm on the weather office floor the following Monday, and Carter smiled at the sound. Days like today, when the computer models all predicted bumpy weather, meant overtime for him and an early arrival for Jim Ford, K-KAN's venerable chief meteorologist. For

Carter, the forecast late-day squall lines signaled both a respite from the heat and the chance to hang out with one of his favorite people.

"How's the radar looking?" Jim set down his trademark green canvas bag, which doubtless contained the sack dinner his wife always packed for him when he'd likely be stuck in the studio during his usual break.

Carter glanced at the nearby monitor, where a long line of green and yellow blobs had taken up residence over the viewing area's westernmost counties. "Storms are popping up right on schedule." Though he'd long since learned to ignore the cracks about meteorologists missing their forecasts, it always felt great to nail one.

He talked shop with Jim for a few minutes, energy zinging through him as it always did when brainstorming with the wizened chief. He'd first met Jim at Cassandra's wedding—the older man was a longtime friend of her in-laws—two months after the tornado in Alabama made him rethink his career. Since that fortuitous meeting, Jim had taken Carter under his wing. Answered countless questions. Helped him study for exams. And when the time came, the chief went to bat for him with the Channel Five brass. Convinced them to hire a rookie in a market where unpredictable, occasionally dangerous weather sometimes meant lives were on the line.

Their deep friendship extended past the weather office to church on Sundays, where Carter sat with the Fords at weekly services. Though he'd always liked the idea of faith, and welcomed the grace he knew he desperately needed, his father's model of Mass on Sundays and Mick's Tavern the rest of the week sure had taken the shine off religion. For years Carter had been a submarine Catholic, surfacing only for family occasions, Easter, and the requisite midnight Mass on Christmas Eve.

But Jim was different. His quiet, steadfast faith, a faith that permeated every aspect of his life, a faith that looked the same Monday through Saturday as it did on Sunday . . . *that* was the faith Carter wanted. A faith that, after countless deep conversations and sometimes-uncomfortable questions, Carter had made his own.

He'd never been overly blessed in the dad department. But what God had withheld biologically, he'd given in spades through Jim Ford.

"So, hey." The rolling chair creaked as Carter turned away from the computer. "You're taking Ethel up this weekend, right?" The flying club to which Carter and Jim belonged had purchased a gently used Cessna 172 Skyhawk, nicknamed Ethel, and members shared maintenance costs and flying privileges.

The keyboard clicked beneath Jim's derisive grunt. "Well, I *was*, but Peggy made other plans. Some friend's niece's college roommate's wedding that we apparently RSVP'd to three months ago."

Carter couldn't resist a chuckle. Only two things could turn Jim Ford into a curmudgeon: the Oklahoma Sooners losing a football game, and being deprived of quality time with Ethel.

Carter reached for a pen. "Mind if I take her up, then?"

"Reckon she'll get pouty if she doesn't get her usual attention."

Inspiration simmered in Carter's chest, as it had since last week's video shoot with Lauren. He'd asked her to dinner, and she'd hesitantly accepted, but they'd yet to agree on a restaurant. And just yesterday, a former colleague—one who shared Lauren's passion for health food—had raved on Facebook about a new restaurant just outside Dallas, a convenient few miles away from the Mesquite Airport.

"Where are you taking her?"

It took Carter a moment to realize Jim was asking about the airplane, not his date. "Thinking about Lake Randeau, Texas."

"What's in Lake Randeau?"

"A restaurant. Organic, farm to table, all that. Supposed to be really good."

"And whatever girlfriend has you into all that nonsense, she in Lake Randeau too?"

Carter grinned. He never could put one past Jim Ford. "No. She's here."

"Mmm." Jim clicked at the computer. "Must be a special one."

"Yeah." Carter's heart squeezed. "She is."

"Then Ethel's all yours." Jim eyed Carter over the wire rims of his glasses. "Just don't screw it up, Douglas."

Carter frowned. "The plane?"

"No. The girl."

Chapter Thirteen

"Come on, Grandma. Right this way."

Grandma. Grand-ma. Grand. Ma.

I recognize the syllables. The word is one I've heard countless times. But for the life of me I can't remember what it means.

That handsome man is here. Sandy hair, blue eyes, and a dimple in his chin. He looks so familiar, and the way he acts toward me, I must mean something to him.

But who *is* he? *Think, Rosie, think.* My tongue wants to form a word that simply won't come, no matter how hard I try.

He takes my arm to guide me through the door of what smells like— oh, fiddle. Can't remember that word either. That place, you know, where people go to eat when they don't want to cook.

I can't name any of the smells, but they're delicious. Familiar. My heart soars and sinks at the same time. Like I'm home and yet not, in this place I can't recall and don't know if I've ever visited.

"Party of four?" A perky woman in a blue dress, her hand full of shiny cardboard rectangles, smiles at my handsome companion. He nods, and she leads the way past tables and chairs, all edged in chrome. She moves fast, but I cannot. Handsome stays back with me, hand on my arm, while the two women with us keep up with Blue Dress.

I study the floor to steady myself. Black square. White square. Left foot. Right foot. The ordered pattern provides a cool drop of calm. Helps me keep my rhythm.

"Here we are, Grandma." Handsome pulls out a chair and helps me sit. Across from me is the woman who looks like Handsome. The dark-haired woman is here too, the one I call Auntie Boop. She always answers to the name, but her polite smile tells me she's only playing along.

I don't know who they are, these people. Not anymore.

But I still know I love them.

"Rosie? What looks good?"

Auntie Boop is holding up one of those shiny cardboards, brows arched over her glasses. It takes me a minute to realize I'm supposed to look at it and pick something to eat.

There *is* something I want. Can't remember the name, of course, but I can taste it. Red. Fruity. Bubbly. Like a shot of pure joy. And with it a thin piece of meat between two bread circles, and those delicious hot sticks. Crispy on the outside, tender on the inside, with just the right amount of salt. Dipped in . . . in . . . something from that red bottle, right there in the center of the table, next to a chrome box filled with napkins.

Napkin. *Napkins!* I remembered.

But no one notices, of course. Handsome is leaning in, pointing to things on the cardboard. "I've heard their hamburgers are the best in town. Would you like one of those? Maybe some fries?"

"Or, ooh, how about a cheeseburger?" Auntie Boop sets the cardboard down, a smile on her face. "That's what I'm having."

Girl Handsome flips her cardboard over and frowns at the back. "Do they have any salads?"

"Not gonna find any tempeh or tofu at Clyde's Diner, Lauren," Handsome jokes. "This isn't that kind of place."

Girl-Called-Lauren sticks her tongue out at Handsome but doesn't look up. "The chicken tortilla soup doesn't seem *too* bad." She worries her lower lip between her teeth. "As long as I make sure the tortillas are corn and get them to leave off the sour cream . . ."

"Are we ready to order?" Another perky woman approaches, this one with hair so blonde it looks almost white. Like Marilyn Monroe.

Another name! I feel like I've just stepped to the plate and hit a lead-off double.

The women order first—Girl-Called-Lauren asks that poor waitress an awful lot of questions—and then Handsome orders for me. The Number Fifteen Special.

Marilyn scribbles on her notepad. "And to drink? We have Coke products, house-made root beer, cherry phosphate, Green Rivers—"

"Cherry phosphate." The words leap from my mouth, like they've been waiting all day for just the right moment. They don't mean anything to me. No picture comes to mind, no taste to my mouth, to fit those words. They're just words.

But somewhere, deep down, I must have remembered.

"Great choice." Marilyn clicks her pen and sticks it into the pocket of her dress. That dress—white with red polka dots—looks like one of mine. One I wore to a sock hop last year. Kenneth Maynes was my date, and Viv went with Bobby . . . but they were just Viv and Bobby at the time, not *VivandBobby*. And Gordon was still going steady with Imogene Harris, right before the big game against East . . .

We're gonna win, won't lose or tie! Roosevelt, Roosevelt, Roosevelt High!

Wait. Am I late for cheer practice? I *am*. It's got to be past four by now. Heart racing, I start to get up.

"Grandma? Everything all right?" Handsome looks worried, and I feel silly. My stiff, aching joints remind me I'm not in high school anymore. But it *feels* like I am. Like if I thought about it for a minute, I could remember the rest of the cheer. The red-and-white pom-poms. The high kicks. The wobbly exhilaration of standing at the top of the pyramid.

Blue Dress swishes by, leading a group past our table. A woman with long hair—red, almost as red as Viv's—carries a baby dressed all in pink. She's got a bow in her hair too—dark curly hair without a hint of red. And her face, her arms, her chubby thighs, all are a light milky brown. Not ivory like her mother.

A little boy is next. Older. Three, maybe four. Same light-brown skin, same curly black hair. He trots along in fits and starts, fascination gleaming in his dark eyes. When he crouches for a closer look at something on the floor, I catch a glimpse of his T-shirt. White script across a vivid blue background. I'd know that script anywhere.

Royals.

A kindred spirit!

"Harrison." A tall man with dark-brown skin, long ebony braids, and a pleasant face puts his hand on the boy's small back. "Come on, son."

Son. They're a family, this group.

A family.

"Here you are," Blue Dress says, and the tall man slides into the booth and smiles up at her.

"Thank you much." He takes a shiny cardboard from her outstretched hand.

My heart aches. My eyes sting. And I can't for the life of me think why.

Marilyn returns, balancing a tray. "Got your drinks."

I sit up straighter. That brilliant red drink with the straw sticking out, that's mine. That's what I'm craving. The little bubbles rising and popping. I can almost taste the fizz on my tongue.

But as Marilyn starts to hand it to me, the cup slips from her grasp. It smacks onto the floor and rolls, crimson liquid and chunks of ice gushing out.

"Oh. Oh my goodness. I'm so sorry." Flustered, she sets the tray on an empty table behind her, grabs a handful of napkins—napkins! The word I remembered!—and mops up the mess.

"Here." Handsome yanks out a whole handful of napkins from our dispenser, while Auntie Boop and Girl-Called-Lauren leap up to help.

But they'll have to do more than this. Soda has already soaked through all the available napkins. Bright red bleeds through crisp white in the middle of that black square of tile.

Wait . . .

My heart quickens. My breath catches.

There's a memory. Shy. Uncertain. Hovering just out of sight. If I don't move, don't blink, don't breathe, maybe I won't frighten it.

Maybe, just this once . . . maybe the memory will stay.

→←

November 1954

Eddie Fisher's resonant voice streamed from the jukebox as Rosie took her first drink of cherry phosphate. *Ahhh.* Perfect. Exactly what she needed after a long day of classes and exams and cramming her brain full of information she'd probably never need.

Of course, there was every possibility that her brain felt so full because of all the space Ephraim was taking up.

Beside her, Viv leaned across the table to sip from the root beer float she and Bobby were sharing. Instinctively, Rosie scooted her drink closer. She wasn't sharing. Not her cherry phosphate.

And definitely not with Gordon McIntyre.

She'd raced to the choir room as soon as the bell rang, but Ephraim hadn't been there. He wasn't in the auditorium either. The door had burst open, and she'd turned, heart skipping, but it wasn't Ephraim.

It was Viv.

"Did you forget your gloves again?" she'd asked, half chiding. "I've been looking all over for you. Everyone's heading to Clyde's."

Rosie had drawn a shaky breath and tried to swallow her disappointment. If Ephraim wasn't here by now, he probably wasn't coming. Besides, her presence with the gang at Clyde's was practically required. Her questions—Did he really mean it, looking at her while he'd read the part of Romeo? And what on earth would she do if he did?—would have to find their answers another day.

If she'd even be bold enough to ask.

It was only after her arrival at Clyde's that she discovered *everyone* included Gordon, who'd plopped down in their booth with a wink and a grin. Rosie hadn't particularly wanted his company, but with Viv and Bobby practically fusing into a single, starry-eyed entity, she felt very much like a third wheel. At least this way the table was evenly matched.

She didn't want Gordon getting any ideas, though. Not after how rude he'd been to Ephraim in English.

That was why she'd bought her own soda.

Gordon liked to talk, and Rosie was content to let him so her thoughts could drift to where they really wanted to be. Ephraim. Reading Romeo's lines. Looking right at her. Making her feel . . . Oh, it was so wrong, the way she felt toward him. It was barely permissible for black and white to be friends. More than that? A cardinal sin.

Although if he counted the minutes until the bell rang like she did, if the sweetest moments of his day were spent in the choir room after school, talking and laughing and making music together, if the same soul dwelt in two bodies whose only difference was their color . . . why was it so wrong?

A familiar lanky figure out the window caught her gaze, waiting to cross Main Street, and her heart jumped into her throat. Ephraim. Had her very thoughts summoned him?

The light changed, and he crossed the street. He was heading right toward Clyde's. Oh, what she wouldn't give to be able to kick Gordon out of the booth and gaze into those brown eyes across the table over a shared root beer float. But Ephraim couldn't even come inside Clyde's. Black people had to order at a window and wait for their food to be brought out in a paper bag.

Well. Maybe he couldn't come inside.

But nothing could keep her from going out.

Taking advantage of everyone else's distraction, Rosie knocked over her soda. Brilliant red liquid streamed across the table and gushed over the side in a waterfall. Her yelp was genuine as the frigid drink splashed onto her legs. Her shoes. Her socks. Her skirt.

Everyone at the table leaped up at once.

"Rosie, my gosh!" Viv yanked a handful of napkins from the dispenser. "Are you okay?"

"Fine. Just clumsy is all." Rosie dabbed at the crimson stain spreading on her gray felt poodle skirt. Would it come out? She hadn't considered that.

"Oh, honey. You better get some cold water." Viv handed her another batch of napkins.

Rosie hid her smile. Her plan was working. "You're right, I should."

"Need me to help you?" Viv started toward the ladies' room, but Rosie waved her off.

"No, no, I got it."

While Bobby flung napkins at the mess and Gordon flagged down the waitress, Rosie streaked through the diner, down the hall toward the ladies' room, and out the back door into the crisp, cloudy afternoon. A heavyset cook with a streaked apron and stained white hat leaned against the diner's brick exterior, snuffing out the nub of a cigarette with the toe of his shoe. He lifted a brow but didn't say a word as she hurried from the alley and rounded the corner onto Main.

Her timing was so impeccable she almost collided with Ephraim.

"Ephraim." A broad smile leaped to her face, and the chilly air faded from notice. "There you are. I've been looking all over for you."

But he didn't return her smile. Dark eyes darting this way and that, he hurried her into the same alley she'd just come out of. She glanced back toward Clyde's, but the cook had gone inside, leaving the two of them alone.

"What are you doing?" Ephraim asked in a fierce whisper, looking behind him once more. "We'll get in big trouble if we're seen together."

Her cheeks flamed. What a stupid idea. Stupid, stupid, stupid.

"I know, I just . . . you weren't in the choir room after school. Or the auditorium."

His shoulders lowered a fraction. "It's Wednesday, remember? I never stay late on church night."

"Oh, of course." Heat rushed to her cheeks. Had he scrambled her brain so much she'd forgotten what day it was?

A gust of late-autumn wind chilled the sticky soda on her bare legs, and she shivered.

"You all right?" He started to shed his jacket, but she stepped back, and he paused. "I'm fine." She clasped her hands in front of her skirt, suddenly mortified at the mess she'd made. "Spilled my drink just now. I'm, uh . . . heading home to get cleaned up."

"Oh. Okay." He shrugged back into the jacket. "Well, don't let me keep you. It's chilly."

He started to stride off, but she reached out. Plucked his sleeve.

He stopped. Turned. His face looked drawn. Tired. Older than his eighteen years.

"What do you want, Rosie?"

She blinked at his bluntness. "Nothin'. I just . . . you did a good job today. Reading."

"Thank you."

"How'd you do that?" The words rushed forth, like the phosphate from her glass.

"You're surprised I read well?"

"No. No. It's not that. It's just . . . you put so much feeling into it." She summoned all her courage and stared straight into his dark-brown eyes. Maybe he'd read her questions there. Questions she was too afraid to ask.

"*Romeo and Juliet* is my mother's favorite play," he replied. "She even has it on a record. I've heard it a lot."

"Oh." Her gaze fell to the bricks between her soda-stained saddle shoes. So he hadn't meant anything by it. He just knew the play well. Had heard it performed by professional actors, and with his ear for music, he'd doubtless absorbed all the emotion and nuance as well.

And the fact that he'd looked at her? Smiled?

Mere coincidence. Had to be.

It was good, then, that she'd imagined the whole thing. Right? It was good. Because she was a senior. On her way to teacher's college in the fall. She didn't need any crazy complications. Didn't need—

"But . . ."

The tremor in his voice drew her attention to his uncertain smile. His shining eyes.

"It was easier than I thought it'd be to put myself in Romeo's shoes. Knowing what it is to be looking right at the prettiest girl you've ever seen."

Her eyes widened. Her mouth fell open. "Oh."

Words, Rosie. Come on. Words. You can do this. You're good at words.

But they deserted her.

His smile faded, his gaze left hers, and he turned to leave. "I'd, uh . . . I'd best get home."

"No. Ephraim. Wait."

He stopped. Turned back.

"I'm not very good at Shakespeare," she blurted. "I don't understand most of it. But in that scene, I kinda think Juliet thought Romeo was pretty swell too."

What was she doing? What had she done?

Nothing but tell the truth. Surely there was no sin in that.

Ephraim tilted his head. "Did she?"

"That's what I got out of it."

"Well." A smile broke through, sunshine this cold, dreary day had no hope of hiding. "All right, then."

"All right." She clasped her hands behind her back and swayed to and fro.

He chuckled. "You better go get yourself cleaned up, Rosie girl."

Rosie girl. *Rosie girl.* She felt dizzy. Lightheaded. She'd never heard her name spoken with such affection, such poetry before.

"Yes. I should." But she didn't move.

"And I gotta get home." He didn't move either. He still stood there, a few feet away, eyes dancing.

"Me too."

"I know you do."

Finally, he broke the spell. Strolled toward the street, his shoes scraping against the bricks, then looked back over his shoulder. "I'll, uh . . . I'll definitely be in the choir room after school tomorrow, if you'd care to join me."

It wasn't a root beer float at Clyde's. It wasn't a movie at the Orpheum. But it was a date nonetheless. The best kind she could imagine.

She beamed. "I'll be there."

Chapter Fourteen

For Lauren, the summer of *Fiddler* had been peppered with quick jaunts with Carter for tacos and donuts and lattes. Late-night movies, moonlit strolls along the river, and one particularly memorable evening exploring the abandoned Joyland amusement park.

She'd always been the driver. Carter had left his car back home, so Lauren had facilitated their dates in her rickety red Pontiac Sunfire. Taylor Swift was always their soundtrack, volume cranked to compete with the roar of a barely functional air conditioner.

On this Saturday night, though, Carter was more than making up for it. Not in a car, either. A plane. One he shared with his flying club. Instead of fighting construction traffic on Kellogg, now that congested highway was a thin ribbon beneath them, the cars barely visible specks. A crystal-blue cloudless horizon stretched before them.

The headsets they wore for noise protection and communication distorted Carter's voice and gave a curious sense of distance, but their physical proximity more than compensated. They were practically glued together from shoulder to knee, a sensation that sent shivers down Lauren's whole left side. The constant vibration in her seat coupled with the rumbly whine left her insides unsettled. But Carter's grip on the yoke, the confidence in his voice as he rattled off a string of Alphas and Charlies and niners to the control tower, underpinned that unsettledness with a warm sense of peace.

She soared nearly a mile above the earth's surface with the man who'd once made her crash and burn. And that didn't frighten her nearly as much as it should.

Carter flipped a switch, then laced his fingers together, stretched his forearms, and leaned back in the pilot's seat with a sigh so deep and contented Lauren felt it in her toes.

"This is it." He indicated the vast horizon with a sweep of his hand. "This view. Can't get enough."

"It's incredible." Lauren pressed her fingertips against the smooth glass window, gawking at the beauty beneath them. The sky, such a brilliant liquid blue it almost hurt to look at it. The ground, a patchwork quilt of bright greens and earthy browns, the carefully ordered grid of farms and roads teased by meandering silvery trickles of rivers and creeks. The simple grandeur stole her breath and squeezed her heart.

"At first I figured no way would all those flying lessons be worth it." Carter's voice cut in through the headset. "All the studying and checklists and money. But the first time I got up here and felt this freedom . . ."

She glanced into brown eyes crinkled at the corners through a pair of aviator sunglasses. "Worth it?"

"Oh yeah." Grinning, he shifted in the small seat. The sleeve of his navy polo shirt pressed against her shoulder. "All my problems, all the stress . . . my job, my family, my dad, my—" He broke off and shook his head. "No matter how huge a situation seems on the ground, being up here makes it feel tiny. Insignificant. Flying helps me get my head on straight."

What had he stopped himself from saying? No, she wouldn't press. Not when his skin glowed with such joy, when his smile shone so bright.

"I don't want to sound like that five-year-old kid who thinks God literally lives in the sky," he continued. "But I can't deny that being up here makes me feel closer to him."

She turned her head so fast the headset nearly fell off. "Really?"

He chuckled, deep and warm. "I was pretty disillusioned with church back then. With everything, really."

"Yeah, I remember." The night they'd poked around the tumbledown remnants of Joyland's Whacky Shack, he'd cracked open his locked-tight soul. Let some questions sneak out. About whether sitting in church every Sunday made any kind of difference. About whether following Jesus could really change someone. Was any of it real, he'd asked, or had he just been sold a bill of goods?

As for answers, she'd been fresh out. She was the girl who'd lived and breathed youth group. Who'd gone to revivals and church camps and helped with vacation Bible school. Who'd grown up under the umbrella of faith, who'd been in church nearly every time the doors were open, and who consequently had never heard anyone voice the questions Carter had.

But had all those church services and youth camps, all the praise choruses and altar calls, really changed her?

Apparently not, if her life could be derailed so dramatically. So fast.

"You were different, though." The crackle of Carter's voice broke into her thoughts.

She fought the cynical urge to laugh. "Yeah? How?"

"You walked the walk. Faith was a real thing to you."

Her eyes widened. "But I had no answers for you, Carter, because I'd never been where you were. I'd never wondered any of it."

"I didn't need answers, Lauren. You—the way you were—that was answer enough. You tried to do the right thing no matter what day of the week it was. You loved God, and that shone through loud and clear."

Until it didn't. Until she'd lost control and tossed her standards out the window. Until he'd left and Mom got worse and Lauren started throwing up.

Until the girl who'd never questioned anything started asking the same questions Carter did.

"My friend Jim's like that too." Carter tapped the screen of a tablet. "And I finally decided that the kind of faith he has, the kind *you* have, that's what I wanted. I've still got a long way to go to be who I want to be, but I know it's all real. Everything's true. And you're one of the people I have to thank for that."

Lauren turned his words over, the way she'd examine a piece of fruit at the farmers' market. The time in her life when she thought she knew everything, when the overconfident youth-group girl was about to realize just how close she stood to the cliff edge, that was the time—and she was the one—God chose to use.

Despite everything, Carter had seen something. Something God used to draw him a step or two closer.

They weren't the same kids they'd once been. Carter wasn't a floundering, check-the-box Christian anymore, and she wasn't the know-it-all youth-group girl either. Her maturity hadn't come cheap, and she bore the battle scars to prove it. But her struggles had birthed a deeper, more refined faith. A faith that could survive the tough questions.

It sounded like the same was true for Carter too.

His voice broke into the headset then, more Alphas and Charlies and niners, and she had to grin. Perhaps flying her to Texas for dinner was a little over the top, but he wasn't doing it to show off. He was doing it to let her in. To show her who he'd grown up to be. To welcome her into his sacred space, his sanctuary in the skies. To introduce her to what brought him closer to God. To the thing that made him feel most alive.

He wasn't trying to impress her. Not really. But he was doing it all the same. Because yes, she was flying a mile above the earth with Carter, but it wasn't the same Carter. And she wasn't the same Lauren. God had changed them both.

And maybe, despite all the ways in which they'd failed, he was giving them a precious second chance.

>←

After a dinner every bit as delicious as advertised—even if it was healthy—Carter's bare feet sank into the soft sand at the shores of Lake Randeau, leaving a trail of short-lived footprints behind him. Cold lake water lapped at his ankles, and his shoes, dangling in his left hand, brushed against his knees.

He was as earthbound as they came. But with Lauren Anderson next to him, he was soaring.

When had she slipped her hand into his? Or was it he who'd taken hers? Or had their hands simply found each other, drawn together like magnets by history and habit?

Did it even matter?

Probably not. What mattered was that he and Lauren had fallen back in step, their fingers interlaced. The thirteen years that separated them seemed to have been quietly erased, like their footprints in the lake's gentle waves.

A lilting hum drew his gaze to the right, and the power of breathing deserted him. Gentle winds from the west whispered through Lauren's long, loose hair and pinned her skirt to her legs, highlighting their gorgeous shape. Eyes closed, she tilted her face toward the setting sun, and her sweet soprano shot an electric current straight to his heart.

It had been years since he heard that voice.

Her eyes opened, and her cheeks turned as pink as the sky. "Sorry."

"No, don't let me stop you. It's nice. Hearing your voice again."

"Thanks. I've always got a song stuck in my head, seems like, but . . ." Her eyes met his, and her smile cut him off at the knees. "I only hum when I'm happy."

He gave her hand a gentle squeeze and answered her smile with a cheek-aching one of his own. "That's the best thing I've heard all day."

Lauren returned his squeeze, and he fell into step with her once more, taking in the perfection spread out before them. The lake rippled deep silver in the fading light. Bright-white contrails streaked a crimson sky. Miles away to the southeast, a lone thunderstorm had popped up in the humid evening air. Flickers of blue-white pierced billows of gray, and a veil of rain melted from the cloud's leaden bottom. It wouldn't interfere with their flight home, but it did make for some killer special effects.

Carter couldn't have ordered up a more perfect evening if he'd tried.

Lauren must've thought so too, because she started humming again. Her happy little tune bounced over the rustle of wind through nearby cottonwoods, the irritated quacking of a couple mallards, and—

"What *is* that song?" Lauren stopped walking, brow furrowed. "Oh man. That's gonna drive me nuts."

Carter turned toward her. "Hit me with a few bars. Maybe I know it."

She hummed again. The tune was jaunty. Energetic. And familiar. After the first stanza, the melody welled up in his chest. Burst from his throat. Which meant . . .

"Wait." Lauren stopped. Her hand flew to her forehead. "That's . . ."

"*Fiddler.*" Nostalgia tugged at his lips. "Our dance. By the river."

She gave a quiet laugh. "Must be why I couldn't remember the words, then. There weren't any."

"Ah, but do you remember the dance?" Tossing his shoes to the side, he summoned the spirit of Perchik. Passionate. Intelligent. More than a little self-assured. He squared his shoulders, lifted his chin, struck a pose, and grinned at Lauren.

Those twin lines appeared between her brows. "You're insane."

Perchik might be a little of that too. Or maybe the insanity was all Carter. But for her sweet smile, the slight shake of her head, the hint of lavender wafting from her hair to tease his senses, insane was a title he'd carry with pride.

"C'mon." He held out his hands. "Let's see if we can still do this."

The breeze blew a gust of blonde hair across Lauren's face, and she brushed it back. "I think the question isn't if we can still do this"—her mouth quirked, and her eyes flashed a warning of mischief—"but if *you* could ever do it at all." She punctuated her teasing declaration by grabbing his hands in hers.

Laughter burst forth as he launched into the backward hops that started the dance. "Hey, them's fightin' words." But not untrue, given how quickly she'd discovered his Achilles' heel. For whatever reason, the control he had over gangly limbs on the basketball court totally deserted him onstage. Ironic, given that Perchik's role in the scene was to teach Hodel the new dances he'd learned in Kiev. In reality, it was Lauren leading him through the choreography. Patiently working with him, hour after hour, until he moved with almost as much grace as she did.

But their practice paid off, because even now the opening steps were locked deep in his muscle memory. There was a big difference, though, between character shoes on a stage floor and bare feet in lake-lapped sand, a fact he discovered when he nearly lost his balance. His big toe grazed Lauren's through the grit, and he didn't miss the triumphant gleam in her eyes.

"Aha. Stepping on my toes. Of course."

"Hey," he said amid laughter. "Sand doesn't exactly give the best footing."

"Sure, that's your excuse now. What about then?"

"Oh, now you're asking for it." Grinning, he tugged her into the rest of the dance. The hops. The running steps. The twists. The turns.

And Lauren. Deep-blue eyes sparkling as they spun arm in arm. Head thrown back in joyous laughter. Strong fingers digging into his shoulder. The ripple of muscles in her lower back beneath the thin fabric of her dress.

He felt whole with her in his arms. Alive. Thirteen years he'd been walking around with a piece of his heart missing, and now that piece had fluttered back from its wandering and settled into place. As snug and complete as if it had never left. The dull ache of its absence disappeared without a trace.

Home. He'd come home.

He'd also completely lost his place in the choreography. He expected Lauren to talk trash, but she didn't. In fact, the teasing was gone from her eyes, and her smile had melded from sheer triumph to something softer. More intimate.

"Sorry." He stopped. "Just realized I have no idea what comes next."

She blinked up at him, lips curved. "Next is when Hodel and Perchik stop, look into each other's eyes . . . and realize the crazy chemistry they have together."

He swallowed hard. "Right."

He braced himself for her to pull away, but to his pleasant surprise she drew nearer. Her left hand slid behind his neck, while her right wandered up his arm toward his shoulder. He slipped his arms around her waist and pulled her as close as he dared, his heart thundering so loudly she could probably hear it.

Her fingertips trailed along his cheek then, and he shut his eyes against the rush of feelings her feathered caress brought. He was all about control in the chaos, but there was no control. Not here. He couldn't control his surging emotions any more than he could alter the path of an oncoming tornado.

When her fingers found his nape, he forced his eyes open. Allowed one hand to explore the silky tousled waves of her hair. Her gaze, a deep navy in the fading light, lowered to his mouth, and her full lower lip slipped between her teeth. He couldn't stop looking at that lip. At its twin, not quite as full, but with an adorable bow at the top. His own mouth tingled. The genesis of lightning, the invisible current, the sizzle before the bolt . . .

"Carter." She was looking at him, lips parted, eyes wide with want but overlaid with caution.

He pulled back. "Yeah."

Her shaky exhale teased his lips. "If we're gonna do this—if we're gonna try again—we have to get out of the past. The past is painful. Messy. We have to do it different this time."

Lauren's trust, her vulnerability, terrified him. Made him want to hop back into the Cessna's welcoming cockpit and fly far, far away. The gift she offered was too precious. He'd just screw it up. Like he did before. Like he did with everything else.

Disaster was in his DNA.

"But I think maybe we can. Because I'm not the girl I was. And you're not the guy you were either." Her slight smile, her belief in him, the trail of her fingers through his hair, took the edge off his terror. "You're who you are now. And I *like* who you are now. So if this is going to work . . . we can't go back, Carter. We have to go forward."

Forward. Forward. He could do forward. He could—

And then her lips were on his, and he couldn't do anything but feel. Strong, soft hands cupped the back of his neck, and he wove his fingers through her mass of soft, beautiful hair. So soft his knees buckled. Lavender filled his senses, sweet and heady, and the rapid beat of his heart was the rhythm of her name. *Lauren. Lauren. Lauren.*

If he'd thought he was soaring before, now he'd been flung into the stratosphere.

CHAPTER FIFTEEN

December 1954

ROSIE'S FEET BARELY skimmed the tile floor of the hallway leading to the music wing. When the final bell rang, she'd gathered her books and shot out of her seat, begging off the usual trip to Clyde's with Viv and Bobby and the gang, this time with a phony excuse about needing Mr. Bishop's help with a passage of music for their Christmas concert next week. It was a tricky balance, coming up with believable reasons to skip while putting in enough appearances that no one got suspicious. The knot of guilt grew ever tighter when she lied to Viv, even though those lies slipped off her tongue more and more easily.

But she couldn't tell anyone where she was going.

Who she was really going to see.

Above the pounding of her heart in her ears and the skittering of her footsteps came the faint waves of glorious music for which she'd hoped, seeping from beneath the doors of the auditorium, where choir rehearsals were taking place in the days leading up to next week's concert. She cracked open the door, and a wave of sound engulfed her. Chromatic harmonies and soulful rhythms filled the cavernous space and echoed off the wooden walls. And there sat Ephraim. Center stage, exactly where he belonged. Eyes closed, long slender fingers pulling sweet music from the big black grand.

The door gave a quiet click as it shut behind her, and she made her way down the center aisle. Like . . . like a bride almost. Walking toward her groom. Toward her destiny.

"There you are." A cascading series of chromatic chords punctuated his words. "Been wondering."

"Sorry." She deposited her books on the edge of the stage and made her way up the creaky stairs. "Got caught up. But I'm here."

"And my day just got a whole lot better, now that it's just us."

"Mine too." With a happy sigh, she sat on the bench beside him. Sights, smells, and sounds once foreign had now become familiar. The tight coils in close-cropped hair. Tiny bumps on his deep-brown neck. His fresh, clean scent. The arpeggios rippling up and down the keyboard like the creek on her grandparents' farm. This had become her safe spot. Her haven.

Just us.

The first few meetings after school had been fraught with fear. She was alone. With a fella. A black fella. The amount of trouble she'd get in if anyone found out was unimaginable. But with each successful encounter, every hour that passed undiscovered, her fears faded like morning mist. If Mr. Bishop knew their secret, he never breathed a word. And that stately old grand, as well as it sang under Ephraim's expert touch, wasn't about to talk. Nor were the heavy black curtains, the white spotlights, or the sea of red velvet chairs.

"Have I told you I love watching you play?" she asked over another ripple of chords.

"Once or twice." He grinned. "And like I said before, I'm just makin' stuff up."

"That's what I like about it." She sighed and scooted an inch closer. "You make it look so easy."

"You play?" *Deedle-dee-deedle-dee-daht.*

Rosie laughed. "I did for a while. Mother was desperate to hide any hint of our country roots, and for some reason piano lessons were a part of that." She looked down at her fingers, short and stubby and not at all graceful like Ephraim's. "I suffered through it for three years, and finally Mrs. Mayberry told Mother the lessons were a waste of both time and money."

Ephraim laughed, warm and rich. "Guess you must've been pretty bad."

"Oh, I was." Somehow the admission wasn't as embarrassing here, in the world of just them. "But I do still love the sound of the piano. I love to watch people play."

"Works out well, then. 'Cause I love to play."

There it was. That word. From his lips. It sounded better, deeper, warmer, more musical, coming from him. More so than she'd ever heard before.

She gazed at her hands in her lap. "Guess so."

The unfamiliar melody, the syncopated rhythms, melded seamlessly into another tune. Ephraim's fingers danced over the keys. Caressing them. She could watch his hands forever and never get tired of it.

"They sing this one at your church?" he asked.

She shook her head. "Unless you've fancied it up so much I wouldn't recognize it."

He chuckled. "Well, here's one I bet you'll know. Fancied up and all."

Rosie tilted her head. Listened. Amid the bluesy notes and complicated harmonies arose a melody she'd known since practically infancy. She smiled. Looked up at him. "Amazing Grace."

Ephraim acknowledged her correct answer with the subtlest of nods, then closed his eyes, opened his mouth, and sang.

Amazing grace, how sweet the sound
That saved a wretch like me

Rosie sat, spellbound. If her life depended on it, she couldn't have moved a muscle. She knew these words, knew this hymn. It was knitted into the very deepest part of her, but she'd never heard it this way before. In Ephraim's capable hands, with his melodious tenor voice, it came alive. Each word held more meaning than ever before.

I once was lost, but now am found
Was blind but now I see

Ephraim went off on one of his musical bunny trails, but Rosie stayed stuck on that last line. Turning it over and over in her head, like the crank on the ice crusher Daddy had bought Mother for Christmas.

Blind. She'd been blind to any world but her own. Any way of doing things but the way she'd always done them.

But now she saw. The world was more vibrant, more colorful than she'd ever dreamed.

And Ephraim James was the reason why.

"Bet you never heard it like that before." Ephraim's voice broke into her thoughts, and she glanced over at him.

"No." She smiled. "This way is so much better."

Ephraim lifted a slim shoulder. "Not better. Not worse. Just different."

Different. That was precisely it. That was what they were. His skin was brown; hers was white. His hair was black; hers was blonde. His church was like a football game; hers was history class. His music contained flats and bluesy notes and rippling arpeggios, and hers was a choir singing from a hymnal.

But were they really that different? They both loved Jesus. They both loved music. They had the same sense of humor. And they liked each other, in a way that both thrilled and terrified.

The piano keys danced beneath Ephraim's capable hands. The tinkly chords and deep bass notes resonated with a sudden shift in key, one that raised the pitch of the familiar tune. White keys and black keys worked together in perfect harmony, and a thought struck her with such force it jumped instantly from her brain to her mouth, with no thought of whether it was gay, charming, or smart.

"I think we're like the piano, Ephraim."

Ephraim opened his eyes and glanced at her. "What do you mean by that?"

"Look at the keys. Black. White. They're all different, but none of them are better or worse than the other. None of them are more important. They all work together to make beautiful music." Her breath caught when she looked into his eyes, so deep and dark she could drown in them. Oh, she was being forward. Too forward. Mother would faint if she knew.

Then again, Mother would faint at everything that was happening here. And when a thousand different rules lay shattered on the stage floor, what was breaking one more?

Ephraim played a series of chords up the keyboard. "Your people don't want that."

"No. They don't."

"And mine aren't too sure either." The key changed again. His improvisation picked up speed and passion. "They want us to be treated equal, sure. But they don't want too much mixing going on."

Rosie paused. She knew her world was against them. It hadn't occurred to her that his world would be as well.

"But . . ." He took a deep breath, and hers hung suspended, awaiting what he'd say next. "Right here, right now . . ."

"It's just us."

The music faded and fell silent. Rosie tried not to furrow her brow too much as she studied him. His hands, hands that were so steady and certain on the keyboard, now shook slightly. He slipped his fingertips beneath the sleeve of his crisp white shirt, a shirt that was a touch too long for him. The silence was loud. Far louder than the music had been.

"And since it's just us . . ." Eyes shining, he slipped something from his wrist and cradled it in the palm of his hand.

Rosie's world stopped at the sight of the slender silver links. The circular metal plate engraved with his initials.

His ID bracelet.

"I wondered if maybe you might want to wear this for a while."

Her mouth fell open. She'd dreamed of the moment a young man offered her his bracelet. Told her she was pretty and asked her to be his girl. To go steady with him. To belong to him. To be his.

But in her dreams, the gesture was always held up by the framework of propriety. By him shaking her father's hand and promising to have her back by nine thirty. By sharing a Coke after school or taking in a movie at the Orpheum. Dragging Douglas. Going to sock hops. Being his date to the prom.

Accepting Ephraim's bracelet—being his girl—would mean giving up those things. She wouldn't even be able to wear his bracelet in public. There would be no proper handshakes or dates to the movies. She wouldn't watch his face light up at the sight of her in her prom dress. She couldn't shout from the rooftops that the most wonderful man she'd ever met had asked her to be his.

But a secret relationship with Ephraim was miles ahead of a public relationship with anyone else.

"I . . . I can't wear it." She sought his eyes. "Not . . . not like I could if—"

"If I weren't black."

"Or if I weren't white."

He wrapped the bracelet in a gentle fist. "I'm sorry. I shouldn't have—"

"No." She stopped him, her fingers on his. "I didn't mean . . . I *want* to wear it, Ephraim. I do."

His eyes met hers. Widened slightly when he caught her meaning.

"I could wear it in here," she suggested. "When it's just us."

A smile bloomed, slow and sweet. "You could."

Her grip on his hand tightened. "I will."

The smile widened, and she thought she might die of joy at the sight. Slowly he unwrapped his fingers, and her gaze fell from his smile to the bracelet in his palm. A palm not much darker in color than her own.

Her heart going a mile a minute, her mouth desert dry, she held out her wrist. Ephraim draped the cold metal over her skin. With trembling fingers, he fastened the clasp, and it was done. She wore the bracelet.

She was Ephraim's girl.

"It looks good on you." The smile in his voice was like warm sunshine.

"It does." She couldn't stop looking at it. At the little glimmer of silver around her ivory wrist, just beneath her cardigan's red sleeve. At the delicate, dancing black shadow it cast on her skirt.

The world—hers, his, the world at large—would try to convince them it was wrong. But it was right, and all that came of it would be right.

And she didn't have to convince anyone right now.

Because right here, right now, on an empty stage, it was just them.

She wished it could stay like that forever.

CHAPTER SIXTEEN

"Now, tomorrow night, this frontal system slides on through, but without much moisture to work with, our rain chances stay pretty low. Good news for everyone out here at the fairgrounds."

On this warm mid-September afternoon, Lauren hung back in the shade of a cottonwood a few yards behind the K-KAN cameraman as Carter finished a live weathercast from the Kansas State Fair. As usual, she couldn't take her eyes off him. Something about his well-fitting navy polo and aviator sunglasses turned her into a giddy seventeen-year-old all over again.

But unlike her seventeen-year-old self, she now saw beneath the attractive surface. She understood the source of his passion for weather. The heart-wrenching story behind the easy, relaxed manner. And she knew how deeply he cared for the people he reached through the camera.

It was that care she'd tried to channel in her video for Gluten Free Goddess. Far beyond likes and clicks, she prayed her audience would win their own battles with food and discover the joy of healthful eating. With that as her mission and Carter smiling his encouragement from behind the lens, she'd forgotten all about her fears of how she looked on camera. It was some of the most fun she'd ever had cooking. An entirely new way to think about her blog. And Carter Douglas had helped her get there.

When the newscast wrapped, Carter thanked the camera crew and headed for Lauren with an eager grin.

"All right, my lady." He laced his fingers with hers. "Next three hours, I'm all yours. Where to first? Fried Snickers bar on a stick? Amelia Earhart sculpted entirely out of butter? A pumpkin the size of my high school?"

Lauren giggled and squeezed his hand. "Those pumpkins can't be *that* big."

"You never saw my high school." Carter stroked the back of her hand with the pad of his thumb, a gesture that brought a pleasant shiver despite temperatures still nudging ninety.

"I definitely don't want to miss that pumpkin, but . . ." She stopped in front of a large brick building. DOMESTIC ARTS, white letters over the entrance declared. "I actually want to start with the cakes and pies, if you don't mind."

"Baked goods? You?"

"Grandma won lots of prizes for her tomatoes." Lauren's throat thickened at the memory of all those county and state fair ribbons—mostly blue, with some red and white thrown in—once prominently displayed in a spare bedroom of the farmhouse that now belonged to Sloane. "But one year we got a whole bunch of rain, and her blackberry bushes went crazy. I talked her into entering a pie, and she said she'd only do it if I helped her come up with the recipe."

Carter wrapped an arm around her, and she leaned into his firm embrace, blinking against the sting of memories that brick building brought. "Not only did it win a blue ribbon at county, it won here too. She insisted I keep that ribbon, because the whole thing was my idea." Lauren pressed her lips together. "I still have it."

"So your grandma taught you how to bake, then?"

"My mom never cooked, Carter. Like, ever. She was so good at so many things—decorating, painting, anything artistic—but her idea of a gourmet meal was Hamburger Helper. So everything I know about cooking, about food, came from Grandma, and I miss her." A hot tear sneaked from Lauren's right eye, and she swiped it away. "Which sounds silly, because she's still here, she's still alive, but yet she's not. The grandma I remember is gone, and the one who's here now is lost in memories of a guy I've never heard of."

"I'm so sorry, love."

The old endearment whispered across her hair as he pulled her close and kissed the top of her head. She'd obsess later over whether he'd meant something by it or merely slipped into an old habit. For now she'd simply relax into his warmth. His strength. His being here.

"But she's still my grandma. And we were always so close. I guess I just want to connect with her any way I can. So maybe it's nuts, but I want to find Ephraim James. Or at least learn their story. And maybe that way . . ." She sighed. "Oh, I don't know. It's a long shot at best, and even then . . ."

"You love her, Lauren. That's not nuts at all."

"Thanks, Carter." Her cheeks warmed. "I'm sorry. I didn't mean to turn this whole thing into a sobfest. It's the state fair. Giant pumpkins and butter sculptures and deep-fried cholesterol on a stick."

"Yeah, but to a lot of people, it's a lot more than that." Dark eyes shone with the same compassion he showed on camera. The same knowledge of his audience and what they most needed to hear. Once again, he just *got* her. Like no one before or since.

With a cleansing breath, she slipped from his arms, took his hand, and stepped into the coolness of the Domestic Arts building. They strolled in contented silence down an aisle flanked with tables of glittering jelly jars, the preserves within shining like a rainbow of jewels.

"So while we're on the subject of your grandma and Ephraim . . ." Carter cleared his throat. "I had an idea this morning. Something I'm ninety-five percent sure the station would go for, but I wanted to run it by you first."

Lauren glanced up from her perusal of a beautiful jar of peach jam. "What kind of idea?"

"What if we did a human-interest feature on your grandma and Ephraim? Show some pictures of her from high school, maybe Ephraim's picture from the yearbook, talk about what we know of their story and see if we get any leads that way?" Carter's brown eyes gleamed. "With social media, this thing's got the potential to spread all over the country. So whoever's left from her high school, whoever would remember her or Ephraim, wherever they are, this story could reach them."

A feature story. About Grandma. Ephraim. To be shared on social media.

Carter was right. When done well, social media was unmatched in bringing people together. And while the class of '55 probably didn't spend hours scrolling through their newsfeeds, their kids and grandkids, scattered all across the country? They might.

Carter's idea, his excitement, was as enticing as a clear blue swimming pool, but caution held her back from jumping in. "I'm not sure how good an interview Grandma would be, Carter. Or how she'd react to strangers with cameras. If we catch her on a good day, she'd probably be her usual charming self. But if it's a bad day, there's no telling."

"I thought of that." Carter's voice was soft but confident. "And the guy who I'd pitch this to, Gary Grattenberger—"

"The guy who does the *People of Kansas* stories?"

"Exactly. He's been doing these for thirty years. He's got a God-given gift for knowing how to put people at ease, no matter their situation. Plus, his own mom had Alzheimer's. So I can't think of a single person who'd be better to talk with your grandma."

Relief loosened Lauren's shoulders. "Yeah. Okay."

"And given the circumstances, your grandma would probably just be on there for a couple sound bites." Carter squeezed her hand. "It'd be a group effort. I figure we'd get Sloane for the historical part, if she's willing, and for the personal touch . . . you. And Garrett, of course, but you too." He peered deep into her eyes. "If you're okay with being on camera."

"Are you kidding?" She nudged his shoulder. "I've had private coaching from one of the top broadcast professionals in the state. I'll be fine."

His proud smile shot straight to her toes. "That's my girl."

They strolled down the aisle, his thumb resuming its gentle caress to the back of her pale freckled hand. It looked right, their laced-together hands. Felt right. Like she could conquer anything with this man by her side.

"You'll be there? When we do the interview?" Insecurity slipped out, and Carter stopped and turned to face her.

"Of course I'll be there, love. I'll always be there."

That word again. That promise. She scanned his face, unblinking. Was he just talking about the interview with Grandma? Or was that huskiness in his voice, the sheen in his eyes, the answer to a much deeper question?

Did she even dare hope, after last time?

Could she trust the promise fluttering between them after it had fallen flat on its face before?

❧

Just helping out a friend. That was how Carter had spun it when he pitched the Rosie Spencer interview idea to Gary and Kathleen. Predictably, Kathleen had spent the next several minutes talking in circles, trying to figure out how to get Carter on camera too. Gary, for his part, hadn't said a word, but that slightly raised silver eyebrow had told Carter in no uncertain terms that his cover was blown. Three decades of journalism would give someone a pretty good crap detector, Carter decided. Either that or his feelings for Lauren were just that obvious.

Thankfully, Gary hadn't said a word, and Kathleen had rather huffily signed off on the story despite Carter's insistence on staying off camera. Now here he was, arranging spotlights in the cozy yet ornate library of Plaza de Paz, much to the delight of Mitch the cameraman, who seemed gleeful at the opportunity to boss around on-air talent.

His tasks finished and the interview about to begin, Carter settled into a plush pink recliner while Sloane and Lauren perched on the edge of a stiff-looking velvet sofa, Rosie's high school yearbook between them. Whether it was Carter's coaching or the typical Gary Grattenberger magic, Carter couldn't be sure. But Lauren finally looked relaxed. At ease. Comfortable on camera. And she knew it too, judging from the dazzling smile she shot him over Gary's head. Carter's heart swelled. All those *Fiddler* shows, yet he'd never been more proud of her than now.

When the women's interview was over, Lauren's brother, Garrett, arrived with Rosie clinging to his elbow, gawking at the lights and the cameras. Lauren sprang from the sofa and rushed to her grandmother's side, explaining for probably not the first time why they were all gathered in the library and what all those reporters and cameras were doing there.

Gary strode toward the older woman, extending a hand and a warm smile. "Mrs. Spencer, hello. Gary Grattenberger from K-KAN. I've heard so much about you."

Rosie's wrinkled face creased into the grin of someone much younger. "Well, don't believe everything you hear, Mr. Grattenberger." She and Gary shared a hearty laugh, then Rosie turned toward Lauren.

"Are you with the station too, dear?" she asked.

Carter's breath caught, and Lauren's smile froze.

"Grandma . . . it's me. Lauren."

No recognition in those pale-blue eyes. None at all.

"Lauren Anderson. Barbara's daughter."

"Barbara." Her snowy brow furrowed. "I knew a Barbara once . . ."

Lauren's pain-filled eyes cracked Carter's heart in sympathy. He knew the anguish of looking into the face of a loved one so far gone they weren't even sure where they were. He'd seen his dad in that state too many times to count.

But in those times, the condition was temporary. Self-inflicted. Rosie Spencer's was neither. She wouldn't sleep it off or snap out of it with black coffee and a cold shower. She couldn't go through twelve steps or stop cold turkey. This was permanent. It would never get better. In fact, it would only get worse.

That had to sting like crazy.

Lauren helped her grandmother settle onto the couch, gentle and patient as ever despite the hurt etched on her face. The sight was so beautiful, so heart wrenching, that Carter could barely stand to watch. But he couldn't look away. Not here, not now, because he was so in love with Lauren.

He was in love with Lauren.

He'd always been in love with her, hadn't he? And he wanted nothing more than to spend the rest of his life being in love with her. Caring for her as tenderly as she cared for her grandmother. Encouraging her. Supporting her. Folding her into his arms and kissing her pain away, if only for a moment.

The force of this new yet old, fresh yet long-standing knowledge pressed him deeper into his chair. He stared, helpless against it, as Rosie and Lauren bent their heads together over the yearbook, as Lauren's lips curved and Rosie's mirth fizzed forth at a joke Gary must've told. No doubt this lighthearted moment would show up in the finished interview. It had to. Carter had never seen anything more beautiful.

As predicted, Gary spent only a few moments with Rosie, after which Lauren helped her up from the couch while Garrett retrieved her walker.

"It's very nice to meet you," Rosie said to Gary, then smiled at Lauren and gave her upper arm a squeeze. "And you too, dear, although I'm sorry I can't remember your name."

That same heartbroken smile, along with a gentle pat to the fragile hand. "Lauren."

"Lauren. Right." Once more, no recognition flickered on the older woman's face. "Well, it was lovely to meet you. Good luck with your story."

Sloane sidled up next to Rosie, yearbook tucked under one arm. "Ready to go back to your room?"

Rosie grinned. "Sure thing, Auntie Boop."

Sloane guided Rosie toward the elevator, Garrett close behind, while Gary and the crew packed up. Carter rose to offer what assistance he could, but Lauren's approach drove all else from his mind.

"Hey." He leaned in and kissed her cheek. "You did great."

"Thanks." Her shoulders slumped with relief.

"So who's Auntie Boop?"

Lauren offered a lopsided grin. "That would be Grandma's great-aunt Domenica, who's actually an ancestor of Sloane's. The two are practically identical. I've seen pictures. It's almost creepy."

But Lauren's attempt at lightness didn't hide her grief, and Carter pulled her close. "I'm sorry she didn't remember you." He walked her from the warm, stuffy library around the corner to a quiet hallway, far from all-seeing journalists and nosy camera crews. "That must be difficult."

Her brave smile broke his heart. "It's okay."

"No, Lauren. It's not."

Lauren took his hands in hers. "You're right. It's not. But you're here. And that helps more than you can possibly imagine."

A precious ache seized him. This was what he was meant for. This. Right here. Making Lauren smile. Being here for her. Easing her burdens. Lightening her cares. Bringing joy to the face and the heart of the woman he loved.

"Hey." He slid his fingers beneath her chin. "I promised I would be."

"I know. And it means the world."

She slid her arms around his neck, and his heart thumped. The caution was gone from her eyes, her guard fully down. She was trusting him. Holding out her heart—a heart that bore scars from wounds he'd inflicted—and giving him another chance.

Letting him love her.

Cotton-mouthed fear seized him as he slipped his hands around her waist and feathered a kiss to her cheek. As much devastation as his mistakes had caused before, if he made them again, if he hadn't changed . . .

Oh, God, help me. Help me. Please. Help me.

Help me not screw this up.

Help me not hurt her again.

Chapter Seventeen

March 1955

Rosie hadn't lied to her parents. Not really.

She'd spent the last two hours at the library, as she'd promised, and was now heading to a friend's house for dinner, like she'd said.

She'd just never told them which friend's house. And mercifully, they'd never asked.

A cool early-spring wind kissing her cheeks, she moved closer to Ephraim, who'd met her at the library moments before and guided her first steps into his neighborhood. His world.

Grid-like streets boasted grocers, barber shops, churches, even a movie theater. Faint music mingled with lazy wisps of smoke from a nearby chimney. A woman in the backyard of a boxy little house took down the wash, while a man in the next house sat in a cozily lit window reading the evening paper and a pair of laughing children sprinted off toward home at a mother's singsong call. At first glance, it wasn't that different from her own neighborhood.

But here, every last person was black. And even though none of them seemed to have noticed that Rosie wasn't—her scarf covered her blonde hair, and fading evening light shadowed her pale complexion—self-consciousness crawled through her frame. For the first time in her life, the color of her skin marked her as different. *Other.*

Was this conspicuousness, this unwelcome spotlight's shine, what Ephraim faced every time he walked down the hall at school? Every time he left this little enclave at Ninth and Cleveland? Compassion taking the edge off her discomfort, she slipped her hand into the crook of his elbow and gave a quick squeeze.

He leaned closer. "You all right, Rosie girl?"

"Fine. Just wishing I had darker hair. Darker skin."

Ephraim stopped. Turned her to face him. "I don't."

"Why not? I might blend in better."

"But I don't want you to blend in. I want you to be *you*. You're my Rosie girl. Blonde hair, blue eyes, white as a bottle of milk. You wouldn't be you if you blended in around here."

He stepped closer and caressed a lock of blonde hair tucked beneath her scarf. And there, in a neighborhood full of people who looked nothing like her, on a street her father always drove out of his way to avoid, Ephraim's quiet care made Rosie feel more like herself than ever before.

"Okay?" he asked.

Adoration tugged her lips. "Okay."

"Okay, then." Shoulders square, Ephraim interlaced his fingers with hers and led her down the street once more.

But the farther they progressed down this tree-lined avenue, the louder her pulse thumped and the damper her palms grew within her gloves. Ephraim had told his parents about her two weeks ago, and although his report indicated they weren't thrilled to know their son was seeing a white girl, they'd still asked her to dinner so they could meet her.

Meet her.

She'd never met a fella's parents before, at least not in that way. Not unless you counted Wayne Farnesworth's parents, which she didn't, because she knew them from church. Besides, Wayne Farnesworth only lasted a couple of dates.

Not like Ephraim.

That was why excitement zinged amid jangled nerves. No longer were they locked in their after-school world of just them. Gone were the whispers and secrecy. Now they walked down the street, hand in hand, like any normal couple. So what if their outsides didn't match? Their insides did. And in a few short minutes, with any luck at all, someone besides the two of them would see that.

Near the end of the block, Ephraim stopped before a cozy-looking white house. Curtains graced the windows, and a pair of rocking chairs greeted visitors from the porch. A blue jay called a greeting from the top of a large tree dotted with tiny green buds.

"This is me." Ephraim squeezed her hand. "You ready?"

Rosie summoned her bravest smile. "Ready."

"That's my girl." Escorting her up the steps to the front door, he pushed it open. "Mama? Daddy? We're here."

A man sitting in a corner chair lowered a copy of the *Beacon*. Rosie's breath caught as he laid the paper aside and rose. He was tall—taller than Ephraim, even. Broader too. Silver touched tight black coils at his temples, and an uncertain smile hovered beneath his mustache, as though he wasn't sure whether this was a dream or whether there really was a white girl standing in his living room.

A slender woman strode around the corner, wiping light-brown hands on a clean white apron. Black hair shone smooth in a style not unlike Rosie's own. Ephraim's mother peered at Rosie in a thorough evaluation, one Rosie recognized in an instant. Ephraim looked mostly like his daddy, but those eyes came straight from his mother.

"Mama, Daddy, I'd like you to meet Rosie Gibson." Pride tinged Ephraim's voice.

"How do you do, Mr. and Mrs. James?" For the first time, Rosie was grateful for all her mother's *don't let them know we used to be country bumpkins* etiquette lessons. She made eye contact and extended a hand to Ephraim's father.

His dark eyes widened behind black-rimmed glasses, but after a brief pause, he returned the gesture.

"Glad to meet you, Rosie," he said.

Rosie extended a hand in turn to Mrs. James. "It's a pleasure to make your acquaintance, ma'am."

"Likewise." Ephraim's mother returned the handshake loosely, giving Rosie another thorough once-over. Rosie's muscles tensed, and she resisted the urge to squirm or look away from the penetrating stare. Had she thought the spotlight shone brightly on the street? It was doubly bright—and warm—in here. Gratitude washed through her as Ephraim slid her stylish red coat off and cool air rushed in.

"Would anyone care for something to drink? Iced tea, perhaps? Lemonade?" Mrs. James's face was a smooth, unreadable mask.

"Oh, I'd love some lemonade, ma'am. Mrs. James." Was it always this uncomfortable, meeting a fella's parents?

"Lemonade sounds wonderful, Mama." Ephraim's rich tenor, his calming presence, steadied her nerves.

Ephraim's father handed his wife an empty coffee mug, regarding her with a warmth that had been absent until now. "Top me off?"

"Of course." Mrs. James responded with a cool curve of crimson lips. "Rosie, dear, would you mind giving me a hand in the kitchen?"

Out of the frying pan, into the fire. "N-no, ma'am. Not at all." With a quick glance at Ephraim, she followed his mother into a small yet neat kitchen. Empty mixing bowls stood beside the sink, and Rosie's mouth watered at the sight of a pie cooling on the windowsill. Pots and pans on the stove boiled and simmered, releasing unfamiliar yet delicious aromas.

"It smells wonderful in here, Mrs. James."

"Thank you." Her voice was butter smooth. "I'm certain my son had the same to say about your mother's cooking, when you invited him to dinner."

Rosie stopped. Her mouth dropped open.

"He *has* met your folks, now, hasn't he?" Lemonade sloshed into a glass. "Surely, as long as you've been seeing each other, he's come to the front door, at least, to shake your daddy's hand."

Rosie licked her lips, the wax of her lipstick bitter against a tongue as dry as sand. "Well, ma'am, you see, it's . . ."

"Mm-hm." The pitcher thunked against the counter, and Mrs. James whirled around, her mouth a thin line. "What are you doing?"

Rosie blinked. "Helping with the drinks, ma'am."

"No, not now. I meant with my son. Dozens of girls his own color would give their eyeteeth to be with him, but he wants *you*." She spat the word like it tasted bad. "A pretty little white girl. Do you have any idea how hard this makes things for him? For us?"

Rosie blinked at the barrage of questions. Which should she answer first? How could she even begin?

"What's so special about you, Rosie Gibson? Why does my son think you hung the moon? Why's he willing to turn his back on his own people for the likes of you? And why—*why* on God's green earth—are you messing with him? With *us*? What's in it for you?"

Rosie focused on the ordered pattern of shiny black-and-white tiles between her shoes and shot up a quick prayer for bravery. How could she prove to Ephraim's mother that she meant no harm? That she stood in this kitchen not because she wanted to create further hardship for Ephraim or his family, or because she was the sort of girl who toyed with a young man's affections, but because, for her, Ephraim . . . hung the moon?

"Mrs. James. Ma'am." She laced her fingers behind her back, the fabric of her woolen skirt rough against her knuckles. "I know you just met me. And I know you don't trust me. But the reason I'm standing here right now, is because your son is . . . he's—"

"Go on." An ebony brow arched, and Rosie would've given anything for a swallow from that cool glass of lemonade at the woman's elbow.

She took a quick breath. "I'm in love with him, ma'am."

Mrs. James's eyes grew as large as the serving platter on the counter.

Rosie gripped the back of a chair to steady herself. Love? She'd never said the word. Not out loud. Barely even to herself.

But it was true, wasn't it? That beautiful *something* she and Ephraim shared, the something that gave her the bravery to wear his bracelet on her wrist, to resist the urge to burst out the kitchen door, run through the alley, and never look back, the something that could never be contained in the world of just them. Their beautiful something had a name.

Love.

A strange urge to giggle rose within, but thank the Lord she managed to swallow it. "I've never felt this way before, ma'am. Not about anyone. And my folks would hit the roof if they knew. Everyone thinks it's wrong for black and white to be together—"

Mrs. James gave a dry chuckle. "You can say that again."

"But if it's so wrong, then why does it feel so *right*? Why do butterflies zoom around my stomach whenever Ephraim's near? Why is he my last thought at night and my first thought in the morning? Why does the best part of every single day happen after school, when I get to sit beside him on that creaky bench and listen to him pull the most beautiful music I've ever heard out of that old, out-of-tune piano?"

Rosie expected an argument, but none came, and she pressed her advantage. Her feelings wouldn't be denied.

"We sing together, Mrs. James. We worship the Lord together. And when we do that, we're not black and white. We're just . . . Ephraim and Rosie."

Heart hammering, she sought the older woman's eyes—eyes so like Ephraim's. "I know you don't trust me. But I hope and pray you will someday. Because I . . . I'm in love with your son. With all my heart, I love him. And I don't expect that to change anytime soon."

"You really mean all that?"

She turned at the familiar voice. Ephraim. Framed by the kitchen doorway, one hand braced on its wooden edge. A smile spread across his face, a flame to which she fluttered. Resting her hands on his shoulders, she drank in that beautiful face. He even had tears in his eyes, bless him, and his image blurred with the sting of her own.

"Yes." She'd never meant anything more in her life.

"Well, shoot, Rosie girl. I love you too." Warm hands slid around her waist, and his quiet chuckle vibrated beneath her palms. "Wow. I never said that to anyone but my mama and daddy before."

Joy bubbled up in a breathy laugh, and she bounced on the balls of her feet. "Me neither."

When he bent his head, she hesitated only a moment, then cupped the back of his neck and pressed her lips to his.

Maybe there was a stifled gasp behind her. Maybe the clatter of a dropped coffee cup. Or maybe she'd imagined those things. It didn't matter. Ephraim was kissing her. *Ephraim.* Was kissing *her.*

It wasn't their first kiss. But it was the first time they'd kissed outside the world of just them.

Was it just them, though? Had it ever been at all? Could a love like theirs have a prayer of being contained?

Ephraim withdrew, slid his arm around Rosie's shoulders, and faced his mother. "Do you believe her now, Mama?"

"Oh, I believe her, all right." Mrs. James's brown skin seemed to have paled a shade or two. She stared at the two of them, back and forth, back and forth, while the pots on the stove steamed and a splash of spilled coffee crept silently across the counter.

The pressure of Ephraim's arm around Rosie's shoulders increased, and she snuggled into his protective warmth.

"And?" he asked.

His mother turned, grabbed a dishrag from beside the sink, and attacked the puddled coffee with vigor. "Lord have mercy, child, now I just feel sorry for the both of you."

CHAPTER EIGHTEEN

"ARE YOU SURE you gave it back to me, Garrett? I thought you said Sloane wanted it for something." Lauren directed her question to the phone on the coffee table the following Saturday while flipping through the stack of cookbooks on her living room bookshelf. Alton, snoozing in a patch of late-afternoon sun, opened one green eye at the commotion. She hated to disturb him, but she needed this cookbook. Those turnip greens she'd planned for her blog wouldn't cook themselves, and she couldn't for the life of her remember how Grandma had seasoned them. The answer lay within the age-softened pages of the Jamesville First Christian Church cookbook. Which Lauren couldn't find.

"She did. She wanted the coffee cake recipe." Garrett's reply squawked through the phone. "But she brought it back weeks ago."

"Well, I can't find it."

"You can't find one cookbook out of the thousands you've stuffed in every nook and cranny of that apartment? I'm shocked, Lauren. Truly."

"Shut up." Lauren glared at the phone. "I keep all my older cookbooks on this exact shelf, and it's not here."

"Then obviously it's somewhere else."

"Literally the only other place I'd keep it is the cabinet above the fridge, and I've looked through that half a dozen times." With a huff, she shoved the stack of cookbooks to the side and started in on the next shelf. "I promise you this cookbook isn't in my apartment—"

Wait. What was that? The tiny spiral-bound book pinned between back issues of *Victory Through Veganism* and *3-2-1 Paleo*?

"Anywhere." The slim pale-blue volume seemed to wink at her as she slid it from the shelf.

"You found it, didn't you?" Garrett was practically chortling in glee.

"Again, shut up." Let that brother of hers gloat. Whatever. She'd found the cookbook. That was what mattered.

"So you no longer need me. Which, come to think of it, you never did in the first place."

Garrett kept talking, but the words floated through her skull unheard. Because slipped into the middle of the cookbook, amid pages of recipes for potato salads and Jell-O dishes that would do any church potluck proud, rested a little folded piece of paper, yellowed with age. It was stuck in there so well she had to peel it from the typewritten pages. Faint, clinging ink marks from Eunice Schwartzkopf's Seven by Seven salad recipe testified to the decades the paper had spent pressed inside these pages.

Roosevelt High School Junior-Senior Prom Royalty 1955, the paper read. Beneath it was a list of finalists for prom king and queen, one of which was Rosie Gibson.

Lauren's breath caught. Grandma's name was circled in faint pencil, along with a line of scribbled handwriting.

Forever my queen.

If she wasn't mistaken, that handwriting was the same as the *R + J Forever* inscription in Grandma's yearbook. Could it be?

"Garrett." Her voice trembled. "Garrett, did you know Grandma was up for prom queen her senior year?"

"No. Why?"

"Because I just found this." Adrenaline surging, she described the aged paper fluttering in her hand.

"Whoa," was Garrett's reaction.

Lauren set the cookbook down next to the phone. "I feel awful. She probably told us this story a hundred times, but we were too busy or self-absorbed to listen, and now—"

"Maybe she didn't, Lo." Garrett's reassurance came calm and quiet. "Grandpa was always the yarn spinner. Not Grandma. And if she and Ephraim really were romantically involved, then there could be dozens of reasons not to talk about it. A mixed-race couple back then would've had to keep that secret under lock and key."

"But it's no big deal now," Lauren protested. "Surely she'd know we wouldn't judge."

"Or maybe it had nothing to do with that. Could be the relationship was either too precious or too painful for her to revisit. You don't go telling everyone *your* darkest secrets, after all."

Conviction knifed her gut. "True." Garrett was the only soul alive who knew about her struggle with bulimia. She hadn't written a word about it on her blog. Hadn't breathed a word to Carter. The truth was too painful. Too embarrassing.

Had Grandma thought her relationship with Ephraim was embarrassing? Painful? Or did she, even now, fear her family wouldn't understand? Did she not trust them enough to reveal the truth?

Did Lauren trust anyone with her secrets?

Even Carter?

To an extent, of course she did. She trusted him with her present.

But she didn't trust him—didn't trust anyone—with her past.

Otherwise, she'd have already talked about it.

"That *People of Kansas* feature hasn't aired yet, has it?" Garrett's tinny voice broke in from the coffee table.

"No. Last Carter heard it was still in editing."

"Maybe send him a photo of this note, then. Couldn't hurt."

"Of course. You're right."

"Always am."

She could practically hear the grin in his voice as they ended the call. Still feeling unwound, unraveled, Lauren carried the note to the other side of the room, where the light was best, and grabbed her camera from the drawer where she kept it.

Decades, this little scrap of evidence had nested in the depths of a small town church cookbook, waiting to be discovered. A silent secret, a symbol of something too precious or painful to reveal.

Pain was indeed a powerful motivator for keeping secrets. Lauren knew that all too well.

But maybe uncovering her grandmother's secrets would give her the courage to reveal her own.

><

April 1955

"Fancy running into you here, Miss Rosie."

Rosie jumped at the sound of Gordon's greeting from the other side of her locker door, but covered it with a smile and a slight roll of her eyes. "Stop clowning around, Gordon. You know perfectly well this is my locker."

"Did you hear the news?" Gordon dangled a slip of paper between two fingers. "You're up for prom queen."

"I am?" She took the paper and scanned the list of names. Sure enough, hers appeared, along with Vivian's just below. She thrilled at the sight. Truth be told, she'd be just as happy to see Viv wear that tiara as she would be to have it on top of her own head. "That's swell, Gord. Thanks for telling me." It really was swell. These popularity contests meant less and less as she inched toward graduation, toward adulthood, but it was still nice to know she was well-liked. Well-thought-of.

"You saw whose name's right across from yours, didn't you?" He pointed to another name on the opposite side of the page.

Gordon McIntyre.

Of course.

"That's neat, Gordon. Congratulations." Smiling, she stuffed the paper into her pocket, then shut her locker.

"Wouldn't that be something, Rosie? You and me? King and queen? Sounds like destiny."

"Right. Destiny." They'd known each other since junior high, so in a sense it would be something. But it was becoming more and more clear that their destinies pointed in opposite directions.

"Look." Gordon leaned against the bank of lockers, the *R* on his letterman's jacket a resplendent red in the light. "Since we both have to be there, and we're both on the ballot . . . it'd only make sense for us to go together, wouldn't it?"

Rosie's heart seemed to stop beating.

Prom.

With Gordon.

Ever since she even knew what prom was, since she saw the full, flouncy dresses and heard tales of romance and magic from older students, she'd longed to experience it herself. To be a fairy-tale princess, if only for a night.

But what was a princess without her prince?

She couldn't, of course. *They* couldn't. No one knew their secret, save Ephraim's parents. And she couldn't spill it now. Life was already difficult enough for him. For his family. She wouldn't be the cause of further hardship.

But she knew Gordon well enough to know he wouldn't buzz off easily. Not without a really good reason.

Clutching her books to her chest, she applied her winningest smile. "Gosh, Gordon, that's sweet of you, but I . . . I'm seeing someone." *Quick, Rosie. Quick. Make someone up. Anyone.*

Gordon's cocky grin faded. His eyes narrowed.

"Who? I haven't seen you with anyone."

"He, uh, he . . . he doesn't go here. He's . . . older. In college. At KU." *Oh, God, forgive me for lying.* "He's studying to be a doctor."

"A college boy, huh?" Gordon's red-blond eyebrows furrowed. "How'd you keep that a secret?"

The web of lies unfurled as fast as she could spin it. "We met at church. Christmas Eve. His parents just started attending, and my mother found out about his career aspirations and immediately introduced us." Rosie waved her hand with an airy laugh. "You know her."

But Gordon didn't share her amusement, instead folding his arms across his broad chest. "What's his name, then?"

"Jimmy. Jimmy Edwards." The right initials, even if reversed. And Jimmy was a nickname for James. Should she feel proud of herself for weaving so many kernels of truth into her lies? Or should she fall to her knees and repent on the spot? *God, please don't let Gordon dig too deep. Please. I don't know how much more lying I can do.*

But rather than press further, Gordon merely grinned. "Well, now. Since this Jimmy Edwards is so far away—and no doubt piled high with homework, if he's studying medicine and all—it sure looks unlikely he'd be able to slip away for a dinky little high school prom, now, doesn't it?"

Oh. Oh. No. She'd spun the web, but it was she who found herself stuck fast and struggling in its stickiness. "I suppose not."

"So maybe he wouldn't mind if you went with your old pal Gordon." Pale-blue eyes penetrated deep. "If he loves you, he wouldn't want you to miss your senior prom, would he? 'Specially if you get crowned queen."

Oh, this was a disaster. "Just as *friends*, Gordon." After a split-second debate, she extended her wrist. The one bearing Ephraim's ID bracelet. Silvered links clinked together as she wiggled her wrist, fast enough Gordon couldn't read the initials. "Jimmy's the jealous type."

Gordon raised both hands in surrender. "Far be it from me to violate the trust of a doctor. Who knows? I may need his help someday."

Rosie replied to his chuckle with a weak smile. "I suppose you're right. But I will need to talk with Jimmy first. Make sure he's all right with this."

"Of course." Gordon gave a gallant dip of his head, then looked up with a grin. "But if he is? Then may I escort you to our inevitable coronation? As a friend?"

Rosie hesitated. It was expected of her, this senior prom. She might be crowned queen. But the moment she'd dreamed of her whole high school career, now that it was in her grasp, so close she could almost taste it, the honor thudded dull and empty. How had she been so satisfied with the superficial? How could popularity have been the only thing she cared about?

But it was this very popularity now that made her real dreams impossible. Sure, she could skip prom, but everyone would notice. Everyone would wonder why she wasn't there. And if she sought to protect Ephraim, protect the love that bloomed in her heart, then she needed to lie. She needed to follow through with what was expected of her.

She squared her shoulders. "If Jimmy's all right with it, then yes. As friends."

"Good." Gordon's grin widened, and he pushed himself off the lockers. "Then I'll be looking forward to it . . . my queen."

><

"Rosie girl!"

As usual, Ephraim didn't turn around when she entered the choir room. He simply greeted her over the rippling, bluesy arpeggios. Normally the sound soothed her, but today it merely worsened the churning in her gut. Two hours removed from her conversation with Gordon, and she still didn't know how to tell Ephraim. What if he didn't understand? What if he thought—heaven forbid—she liked Gordon?

The music fell silent as she sank onto the bench beside him, and the warmth of his gaze caressed the side of her face.

"Oh, come on, now. What's wrong?"

Her eyes stung at the compassion in his voice. "Gordon McIntyre just asked me to prom."

"I see." Ephraim rolled his lips together. "Do you want to go with him?"

"No, no, of course not. I don't want to go to prom with anyone except you."

He reached for her hand. "Aw, Rosie girl. You know we can't."

"I know." Her free hand balled into a fist in the lap of her red poodle skirt. "I know, and I hate it. I hate it. I hate it. I *hate* it."

"Easy now." Ephraim wrapped her in his warm, secure embrace. She laid her head on the shoulder of his crisp white shirt, inhaling the fresh scent of his shaving soap.

"But I'm up for prom queen."

"I saw." The smile shone through in his voice. "I voted for you."

She lifted her head. "You did?"

"Course I did." Mischief gleamed in his dark eyes as he slipped a folded piece of paper from his shirt pocket. "Your steady girl's up for prom queen, you darn well circle her name."

He handed her the paper. Sure enough, her name was circled, with a penciled note next to it. *Forever my queen.*

"Ephraim." Her eyes stung again, but for an entirely different reason. She pressed the paper to her overflowing heart. "That's just the sweetest."

"Keep it," he said. "I snagged an extra. Didn't put any editorializing on the one I slipped in the ballot box, though."

Laughing, she squeezed his hand, then returned her head to its nest on his shoulder. The spot where it fit so well, as though God himself had designed it to lay there.

The lightness of the moment faded, and she sighed, studying the ballot he'd given her. The ballot with her name circled.

"I have to go to prom," she said. "It would be too suspicious if I didn't."

"I know."

"And Gordon cornered me. Asked me to be his date before I even knew what was happening. I told him I had a boyfriend, but—"

"You did?"

She grinned. "I had to think fast. So if anyone asks, your name is Jimmy Edwards, and you're at KU studying to be a doctor."

"A doctor, huh?" His brows lifted. "Mama'd be proud."

"So I told Gordon I'd go with him as a friend only, if Jimmy approved." *Oh, please let him understand.* "And I wish I didn't have to. I wish I could go with you, Ephraim. I wish we could let everyone know how much we love each other."

"I know." He pressed a kiss to her hair. "But your man Jimmy, he's okay with it. Because he just had an idea."

Rosie's eyes widened. "What kind of idea?"

"You mentioned church, and that made me think of this friend I got there. Ruby's her name. And she really does have a fella far away. He's in the army, and I'm guessing they don't view senior prom as a reason to skip out of boot camp."

Rosie chuckled. "I suppose not."

His eyes shone. "So if I take Ruby, and you go with Gordon . . ."

"We'd both be at prom." Cautious joy bubbled within.

"Not together exactly, but who's to say we couldn't sneak off to the choir room for a dance?" His fingertips whispered along her cheek, and she shivered. "Set a time, watch the clock, make up some excuse for our dates, and then come on in here."

"Just us."

"Just us. I'll put on a record, and we'll have ourselves a dance."

Her eyes slid closed as his lips followed the path his fingertips had taken. "I won't want just one dance."

"Me neither, Rosie girl." His husky whisper tickled her earlobe. "But even if it is just one, I'd rather have that one dance with you than a million with anyone else."

Her heart bursting with joy, Rosie looked into the eyes of the man she loved so much. "Ephraim James, are you asking me to be your date to the senior prom?"

He touched the brim of an imaginary cap. "Why, yes, ma'am. I do believe I am."

Her smile was so big, her face didn't even have room for it. "Then I gladly accept."

Chapter Nineteen

"C'mon, old girl. Up and at 'em."

Pale golden light peeked over the hangar as Lauren watched Carter tug on the tow rope to lead the small airplane from its metal cave. The Cessna slowly emerged, the first blush of a late-September dawn kissing shiny white wings.

"If even Ethel is complaining, maybe it is a weensy bit on the early side." Lauren sipped a smoothie spiked with extra ginseng. At this time of day, she needed all the alertness she could get.

"What, you too now?" Carter let go of the rope. "Normally I'm having lunch at sunrise, not breakfast."

"A fair point." Lauren brushed back a lock of hair, an escapee from her messy updo. On this rare Saturday without a wedding to photograph, she and Carter were headed for southwestern Oklahoma to hike a trail he couldn't stop raving about. Mountains, he'd promised her. Waterfalls too. Whether Oklahoma truly held such wonders, Lauren couldn't be sure. But she was thrilled just to be with him. Even if it was barely sunup.

"Oh, quit whining," Carter said to the plane, tossing the rope back into the hangar. "I'll get your wake-up juice in a minute." Glancing Lauren's way, he retrieved his keys from the pocket of his shorts. "Wanna pull the car in?"

"Sure." She reached up just in time to receive the gently arcing key ring. It landed in her palm with a soft jingle and only the barest of stings.

Carter's smile appeared, bright against a dark thatch of Saturday stubble. "Nice catch."

"Nice throw." Lauren headed around the corner of the hangar to where Carter had parked his gunmetal-gray Dodge Charger. Opening the door, she slid behind the driver's seat, and *ouch*. There was that pinch again at the waistband of her shorts. The same pinch she'd felt earlier when he'd come by to pick her up.

Anxiety clawed at her chest. She hadn't weighed herself in years, not since her therapist recommended tossing the scale completely and focusing instead on how her body felt and her clothing fit. She hadn't worn these shorts in a while. And it was the time of the month when she tended to bloat slightly.

But hormones didn't explain the snugness of her tank top or the effort it had taken to tug it on. Nor the filling out of the hollows beneath her cheekbones.

She turned the key in the ignition, trying to breathe away her worries over the Charger's rumbling engine. So what if all these dinners and lunches with Carter had caused her to put on a few pounds? She was happy. She still felt good. She hadn't lost a step in her workouts. Those things were what mattered, weren't they?

With a sigh, Lauren pulled the car into the hangar and grabbed their gear from the floor of the back seat. Maybe she could convince Carter to add a couple miles to their hike.

When she emerged, he was frowning at his phone. Only a few puffy clouds hovered overhead, but perhaps storms brewed elsewhere. Occupational hazards of dating a meteorologist, she'd quickly learned.

She set her backpack down in the shade of Ethel's wing. "Tell me that's not the station."

Carter glanced up, blinking from beneath a worn Broncos ball cap as though he'd forgotten she was there. "Oh. No." He slid his thumb across the screen. "Just my sister."

"Which one?"

"Nat." He stuffed his phone back into his pocket and crossed toward the fuel pump.

"She normally call this early?"

"Sometimes." Carter jerked the thick black fuel hose in Ethel's direction with a quiet grunt. "She's an OB-GYN, so her hours are as screwy as mine.

Half the time neither one of us knows what day it is." With a slight grin he set the hose down and returned to the pump, wallet in hand. "Probably just one of her ... gentle reminders, let's call it, that I haven't been out to see them for a while. Usually start getting those calls after six weeks or so."

"Has it really been that long?"

"Longer. Last time I went to see them was in July." He scanned his credit card at the pump, the morning breeze ruffling his faded cobalt T-shirt.

Quick mental calculations proved the estimate correct. Not even three months, then, since their surprise reunion in the grocery store's makeup aisle.

"That escalated quickly." Lauren grinned at Carter as he bent to pick up the hose.

"Time flies." He climbed the ladder leaning against Ethel's smooth side and stuck the nozzle into a hole on the wing. A whiff of pungent fuel permeated the fresh morning air. "Hey, how's our interview with your grandma doing? Any leads?"

Gary Grattenberger's *People of Kansas* feature had aired the previous Wednesday. The story had come together beautifully and had touched hundreds, if all the comments were anything to go by.

"Still getting a lot of traffic," she replied. "And we've heard back from a couple Roosevelt alums. I've heard some good stories and seen one super-cute picture of Grandma in her cheerleader uniform. But nobody seems to remember much about Ephraim."

Carter pulled his phone from his pocket and gave it another glance. "He wasn't there very long though, right? Just the one year?"

"Right. And the white students—which are the only ones we've heard from—probably wouldn't have interacted with him much."

"Sad, but true." He replaced the phone.

"Speaking of sad, Sloane found out yesterday that Grandma's friend Vivian died in 2007."

"Oh no." Tugging the hose free, Carter peered over his shoulder. "I'm sorry to hear that. And I'm sorry you don't have any solid leads yet."

"Thanks. It's not surprising, though. So much of the class is already gone, and their memories along with them. For all we know, Ephraim himself is gone too. We'll probably never know the whole story."

Carter's biceps flexed as he backed down the ladder, hose in hand. "So that's it? You're giving up?"

"Not yet. Because there's a chance he's still alive. And maybe he's been happily married for sixty years with eight kids and twenty-two grandkids—"

"That's awfully specific."

She laughed. "Shut up. I'm having a moment here."

Eyes crinkled at the corners, Carter made a lips-zipped gesture and dragged the hose toward the pump.

"Anyway. Maybe he's completely content with his life and has no desire to reconnect with Grandma. Maybe he doesn't even remember her. But there's also a chance he does. And maybe all these years later, he's still thinking about her. Wondering where she is and what she's doing." Her heart melted as Carter strode toward her. "I know I would be if it were you and me."

He slid his hands around her waist, and she looped her arms over his shoulders. "Sounds pretty crazy, huh?" she asked.

"Nope. I don't think it's crazy at all." He pulled her close. "I think it's generous. Sweet. One of the many reasons I love you."

Her mouth fell open. "It is? You do?"

His smile was doubtless as broad and goofy as hers. "Yeah. Without a doubt."

"Carter." Joy welled deep inside, traveling from her heart to tug at her lips.

A long buzz sounded from his pocket. His phone again. But he reached in and silenced it. "Whatever that is"—his fingertips skimmed along her jaw—"can wait. Because right now, the way you're looking at me, the way the light's hitting you, it's one of the most gorgeous things I've ever seen, and I just want to stop and enjoy it. Enjoy *you*."

He claimed her lips, and Lauren's overfull heart burst. So much of her life, she'd chased perfection. The perfect figure, the perfect photo, the perfect meal. She'd tried so hard. But God had gift wrapped perfection on this fresh September morning in the form of Carter Douglas. *Carter Douglas.*

It would've taken a miracle for something like that.

And a miracle was exactly what this was.

⤞⤝

That *I love you* had slipped out a bit before Carter intended.

Oh, telling her had always been part of his plan. He'd just meant to wait until their hike. The scenic resting spot by the waterfall.

But at the sight of Lauren's freckled skin glowing in the sunrise, blue eyes bright with hope, his brilliant plans went out the window. His heart was so full of love he had to let some of it out. Like a cloud so heavy and swollen the rain had no choice but to fall. And fall it did.

And fall *he* did. He was falling still. Deeper with every movement of his mouth against hers, every molecule of smooth skin beneath his fingers, every whisper of her hair across his knuckles. He was falling and falling and nothing could catch him. Nothing could save him. He was—

His phone buzzed twice in his pocket. Another text. Probably Nat again. He deepened the kiss. Whatever was going on back home could wait. He and Lauren couldn't.

But it was barely past seven. And even when his mom and sisters were at their guilt-trippiest, calls and texts never came in a cluster like this.

Carter pulled back from Lauren and cupped her beautiful face in his hands. Sparkling eyes, flushed cheeks, those *lips*—

No. *No.* Something was wrong. Something bad.

"Lauren." He struggled for breath. "I'm so sorry. But my phone's blowing up. And as much as I'd like to toss it into that field over there and never look at it again, it's my family."

Kiss-swollen lips curved in a rueful smile. She stepped back, and the cool damp of morning rushed in, tormenting skin heated by her touch.

"It's okay, Carter."

He gritted his teeth. No. It wasn't. It *wasn't* okay.

His phone buzzed again, and his gut churned.

It wasn't okay.

Otherwise he wouldn't be getting so many calls.

THE SONGS THAT COULD HAVE BEEN

Heart thumping in his throat, he fished out the phone.

Cass. *The baby.* Little man wasn't due for a couple months yet, but what if . . .

"I'll make it as quick as I can." With a kiss to Lauren's cheek, he strode into the shade of the hangar, slid his thumb across the screen, and lifted the phone to his ear. "Cass?"

"Oh, Carter, thank God." Her voice broke, and his heart along with it.

"Is . . . is the baby . . . is he—"

"No, no, the baby's fine."

"Then wha—"

"There's been an accident."

His stomach plummeted to the pavement. "What kind of accident? Is anyone hurt? Who . . ."

"It's Dad, Carter. And it doesn't look good."

CHAPTER TWENTY

CARTER'S TENSE FINGERS splayed against the roof of his car. An accident. *Dad.*

"What happened? How bad?"

"I don't know the details." The words tumbled from Cass's mouth, tremulous and tear filled. "Just that he rolled his pickup on the highway. Broken ribs, head trauma, something about his spleen, I think. They were talking about airlifting him to Wichita, but I don't know if they've decided anything yet."

Cass kept talking, but her words streamed through his ears unabsorbed. His relationship with his father had never been the best. The responsibility for so much heartache and humiliation lay squarely on that man's shoulders.

But still . . .

"There's something else." His sister's lowered voice cut through decades of resurfaced pain. "You were right."

Blood drained from Carter's face. A silent prayer welled in his gut at the inevitable, the ominous rotation of a low-hanging wall cloud. *No. No. No, no, no, please, God, no. Please.*

"The police ordered a blood test."

He squeezed his eyes shut. Clenched his fist on the Charger's hood. Tried to fling as many solid surfaces between himself and the storm as he could. "They get the results back yet?"

"No. At least not that I've heard."

In the darkness, he could picture Cass as clearly as if she were standing there, twirling a chunk of long dark hair around her index finger, the way she did when she was stressed.

"So that doesn't necessarily prove anything, them asking for a blood test, then, right? I mean, maybe the cop's just checking boxes. Maybe it's standard operating—"

"They could *smell* it, Carter." The words cut in on a sob. "Brad said when Shane and the crew got there, it was obvious. The cops didn't order the blood test to see if Dad was drinking. They ordered it to see how much."

The tornado he'd been trying to escape burst through with roaring fury, sucking him from his flimsy shelter and tossing him around in the vortex. Debris socked him in the gut. Knocked the wind out of him.

Dad had succumbed to his demons yet again.

Shoulders slumped, Carter lifted the ball cap from his head and tossed it onto the roof of his car. "What can I do?"

"I don't know. Brad's on call until six tonight, and his mom has Lucas. Our mom's a wreck, Nat won't stop grilling the doctors, and I can't get hold of Sara. She went camping with some friends this weekend, so she's off the grid."

Carter's heart squeezed. The glue that held the family together, that was Cassandra. And from the sound of it, someone needed to hold *her* together.

"I'll be right there." His mind raced with the hasty alteration of plans. "I have the plane now. I can be there in about an hour."

"You *can*?" His sister's relief melted into the phone.

"Yeah." He swallowed hard. "Hang in there, okay? I'll see you soon."

"Thank you, Carter. Thank you."

He ended the call a moment later and stepped from the shaded hangar. Ethel shone in the sunrise, the ladder still leaning against her side. And there was Lauren, crouched beneath the wing, her camera raised toward the propeller and clicking madly. Her sneakers scraped across the pavement with her graceful movements, and a smile played at her lips.

He stood there in the doorway with a bittersweet pang. Five minutes ago, it was dawn, pale blues and pinks and golds swirling in the sky and highlighting a handful of cirrus clouds. But now the sun had crested over the eastern horizon, bathing everything in glorious light. The golden hour, Lauren called it. Every photographer's dream. No wonder she wanted to take advantage.

Five minutes ago, his day held nothing but hiking and waterfalls and perfection. Five minutes ago, he was mesmerized by the softness of Lauren in his arms, by the play of predawn light over her smooth, freckled skin.

Five minutes ago, he'd told her he loved her.

Because five minutes ago, his father was six years sober, and the demons that had stalked three generations of Douglas men were still in hiding.

Longing shot up from his heart, so strong he almost shouted with the force of it.

What he wouldn't give for it to still be five minutes ago.

><

Lauren shuffled a couple awkward, squatted steps, her hamstrings protesting the movement. The shot would be worth it, though. Brilliant, liquid sunlight, framed by the sharp, solid angles of the plane's propeller. Not her usual subject matter, granted. But what a beautiful photo, if she could just . . . *There*. Perfect.

"Make sure you get Ethel's good side. She's kind of a diva." Carter's voice cut in over the clicking shutter and brought a smile.

"The pretty ones always are." Lauren stood and shook out stiff legs, glancing at the LCD panel on the back of the camera. *Yes*. Got it. The perfect shot. "Most of my photos are brides, babies, or stuff for the blog, but look at . . ." The words faded, her enthusiasm waned, when she saw Carter. His hair was disheveled, the Broncos cap nowhere to be found. His skin had paled a shade or two, and his familiar grin seemed hastily applied and not at all secure.

He looked like he'd aged five years in the last five minutes.

"What happened?" she asked.

"It's my dad. There's been an accident."

"Oh my word." She set the camera down on her backpack and hurried to his side. "What kind of accident? Will he be all right?"

"We don't know yet. That's what all the calls were about." He raked a hand through his hair. Sweat sheened his forehead. "I guess he rolled the truck? He's hurt. They don't know how bad. Broken ribs, I think? Something about his spleen . . ."

Lauren pulled him into her arms. "Oh, Carter. I'm so sorry."

His hands found her waist, but not with the passionate purpose of before. "I can't go hiking. Not today. I have to go out there. I'm sorry."

"It's okay," she murmured close to his ear. "I don't care about hiking. I care about being with you."

His shoulders stiffened. "I'm not sure how long I'll have to be gone. Might be a few days, or they might airlift him here and I'll have to turn right around and come back. I can't ask you to come along when it's so up in the air."

"You're not asking me. I'm volunteering."

"I'm sorry." He stepped back. Pulled out his keys and wiggled the Charger's fob off the ring. "Look, take my car, okay? Park it at your place until I get back. I don't want this to be a hassle."

"It's not a hassle." She clasped his hand in both of hers, stilling its frantic movements. "I love you, all right? And I want to be there for you. *With* you. It's not a hassle at all."

She expected a hint of joy in his eyes. A trace of the magic from a few minutes ago. Relief, if nothing else. But instead he looked pained, as though her words had lanced a wound and made it bleed.

"Lauren . . . not like this." He pressed the key into her hand, his cheeks flushed, his breathing fast. "It's not that I don't—it's just . . . I can't. Not right now. Not with my—it's too much."

His words stole her breath. Her senses.

Too much.

Those words were what unraveled them—unraveled *her*—on the phone that awful night years ago. Then, as now, the weight of family issues nearly crushed him. Then, as now, she'd wanted to help.

And then, as now, he'd told her it was too much.

She was too much.

The clank of the ladder brought her back. "I'll make it up to you when I get back. Promise," he called from where he was stashing the ladder. "I'll get Ethel, we'll get a good flying day, and we'll take that hike."

It's not about the hike. But the words wouldn't come.

Ladder stowed, he came back to her. Wrapped her in his arms once more. "Because believe me. There's nothing I want more right now than to sit with you beside that waterfall and watch the world melt away."

He caressed her cheek with his thumb, and her fist tightened around his key. Maybe this would recapture the magic. Maybe now he'd hear her.

"But right now I have to go."

Or maybe not.

She swallowed around the lump in her throat. "Okay."

Carter cupped the back of her neck and pressed a fierce kiss to her forehead. She tilted her face up, looking to answer with one of her own, but he'd already drawn back. Pain darkening his eyes, he turned and climbed into the cockpit of the small Cessna. A moment later, the propeller rumbled to life, and Carter taxied down the runway without a backward glance.

Without her.

Eyes stinging, she slipped the car key into the pocket of her ill-fitting shorts, then bent to gather her camera. Moments ago it had captured a slice of perfection. The perfect shot on a perfect day. Now it lay on a dark-green backpack, hastily discarded at Carter's haggard appearance. Where once it had rested beneath the shade of the airplane's wing, now it sat in full sun. And the plane that had shaded it now hurtled toward the western sky, the vibrations of its engine feathering the soles of her feet.

What a fleeting thing, perfection.

Blinking back her tears, she clapped the lens cap back on the camera and stuffed it into the backpack, all desire to capture any part of this day gone. Frantic emotions and snatches of prayers tumbled through her chest. For Carter. For his father. For herself. For them. For his two-syllable sucker punch from the past to be coincidence rather than the head of a familiar, pain-strewn trail.

For some sign, some hope, *something*, to reassure her that it really would be different this time.

Slinging her backpack over her shoulder, she reached into the side pocket for the bag of trail mix she'd packed for their hike. Shook a pile of colorful fruits and nuts into her palm and tossed them into her mouth. Maybe she could crunch her anxiety into oblivion like she did this delicious, sweet-salty mixture of dried cherries and apricots and pumpkin seeds and almonds.

It was different this time. He was different. They were different.

If only she fully believed that was true.

CHAPTER TWENTY-ONE

May 1955

FLUFFING HER VOLUMINOUS tulle skirts, Rosie stepped before the mirror to survey her reflection. A squeal rose in her throat. She'd fallen for this frothy white confection ornamented with black flowers the moment she'd spied it at the Innes Department Store. And despite her mother's attempts to sway her, she'd held her ground.

"Try this one on, Rosemary, dear." Mother had swept into the fitting room, her eyes barely visible above an armload of chiffon the same shade as bubble gum. "It's your favorite color, after all. Or what about this one?" The same dress in pale blue, peeking from beneath the pink. "It matches your eyes, and heaven knows you could use some color."

Color. Yes. That was the whole point. The reason this dress had spoken to her. Black and white could mingle on a prom gown and no one would bat an eye.

A subtle way to convey the message she couldn't speak out loud.

Mother's reflection in the bedroom mirror plucked white evening gloves from Rosie's bed and approached, blue eyes shining.

"Here you are, darling." Mother slipped her fingers into the opening of the glove, and Rosie held out her hand. "I must say, you do look stunning."

"Thank you, Mother." The glove slid up to Rosie's elbow, cool and silky smooth. "I feel like Cinderella."

"The blue dress would've made you look more like her." Mother's smile was warm, but there was a coolness to her words as she slid the remaining glove onto Rosie's right hand.

The doorbell rang, and Rosie's heart slammed into her throat.

"Oh good." Mother clapped her hands together, looking and sounding closer to Rosie's age than her own. "Gordon's here."

Rosie forced enthusiasm into her voice. "Time to go, I guess." Bracing herself, she gathered her skirts, but Mother stopped her with a hand on her gloved forearm.

"Now, don't go down yet." Mother's crimson smile was coy. Teasing. "Make him wait a minute or two. Anticipation is the best part."

That, Rosie could agree with. The anticipation of seeing Ephraim, of stealing a dance with him in the choir room, of those precious, fleeting moments where everything would disappear except the two of them . . . the thought raised goose bumps on her upper arms. Would he wear a suit? A white dinner jacket? Either one would positively melt her. As would his arm around her waist. His hand on the small of her back. His other hand laced with hers. That adoring gaze, the one he saved only for her . . .

"Ah, *there* it is." Mother reached up to pat Rosie's cheek. "The bloom of a young girl in love. Finally you've seen Gordon for the catch he is."

Cheeks flaming, Rosie retrieved her clutch from the bureau. Maybe it was best, Mother thinking she loved Gordon. "Well, he's—"

"Rosemary." Her father's voice floated up the stairs. "There's a handsome young man here to see you. Can't imagine what for."

Would that teasing lilt be present if Ephraim waited in the foyer instead of Gordon?

"That's your cue, darling." Mother gave her a gentle nudge, and Rosie glanced in the mirror one last time, slipping into the role she'd be playing for the better part of the evening. The popular blonde cheerleader on the arm of the star quarterback, whose concerns began and ended with dresses, hairstyles, and the announcement of prom queen.

A few months ago, it wasn't an act. But then a dashing black man with the voice of an angel turned her world upside down and made the role fit as poorly as clothing two years outgrown.

Just as a body could be forced into too-small clothing with the help of a girdle, though, Rosie could force the charade for an evening. Applying a bright smile, she gathered her skirts and glided down the stairs.

Gordon was at the bottom, muscled shoulders swathed in a well-fitting white dinner jacket, a red rose corsage in his hands. His charming smile broadened, his eyes opened wider, at the sight of her.

"Rosie. My gosh. You look simply gorgeous."

The words and smile were polite, but the path his eyes took as they traveled from top to toe and back again was anything but.

"Doesn't she though?" Mother sidled up beside her, cool hands on Rosie's bare shoulders. "This dress wasn't my first choice, but I admit she wears it well."

"Gotta admire a girl who knows what she wants." Gordon stepped forward, and Rosie extended a hand to receive the corsage he slipped over her wrist.

"That's our Rosemary." Mother bent forward and air-kissed Rosie's cheek, though Rosie wasn't certain whether it was to keep from disturbing her makeup or Mother's own.

"Now, look here, son." Daddy stepped between Rosie and Gordon, arms folded and expression stern. "I don't think I have to remind you that I'm entrusting you with my little girl."

Gordon nodded. "Of course, Mr. Gibson, sir. I understand."

"And I'll need you to remember—aw, shoot, who am I kidding?" Daddy's scowl melted into a grin. "I thought I could make it through that with a straight face. I know you'll take good care of her."

"Phew. You had me worried there for a minute, sir." Gordon pantomimed wiping his brow. "But you have my solemn assurance that I'll take the best possible care of Miss Rosemary. In fact, I won't have her back a minute past ten thirty."

"Make it eleven," Daddy replied. "Senior prom only comes around once."

"Oh, yes, sir. Thank you, sir." Gordon pumped Daddy's hand, then turned to Rosie with a shining smile. "Shall we?"

She stood rooted to the spot. At one time, going to prom with Gordon McIntyre would've been the most natural thing in the world. Maybe she'd have made her mother's dreams come true for real and actually fallen for Gordon. A few scant months ago, this wouldn't have been a performance, but reality.

But that was before Ephraim. Before she knew what it was to truly love another person for who he was deep inside. To feel that same love in return. To have someone look beyond the pretty cheerleader and see her for more.

And now the charade sickened her. Part of her wanted to run upstairs, lock herself in her room, and be done with it all.

But she wouldn't. She couldn't. Because the charade, this prom everyone else thought she should have, was the only route to the prom she actually wanted.

"Of course I am." Smiling at the thought of what awaited her on the other side of a couple hours playacting, she rested her fingers lightly in the crook of Gordon's elbow.

"You kids have fun now," Mother cooed.

Fun. Yes. Not a doubt in her mind she'd have fun.

She just had to make it through the rest first.

→←

Roosevelt High's familiar gymnasium had been transformed into an island paradise. Large paper palm trees stood proud in every corner, and flowers of all colors and sizes danced from their branches. Soft white lights twinkled from the rafters, while yellow construction-paper stars completed the picture of a tropical night sky.

"Place looks all right," Gordon remarked to her left. "I didn't think the juniors had it in them."

"They did a swell job." Rosie switched her focus from the decorations to the people, searching for familiar faces amid the dinner jackets and bow ties, the frothy foam of formal gowns.

Oh, there was Viv. Closer to the makeshift stage where the band played, looking stunning in the pale-green dress Rosie had helped her select. She lifted a hand to wave at her friend, but Viv's eyes were for Bobby and Bobby only.

Not that Rosie blamed her. She was looking for a particular someone too. That spotlight of a smile. Those deep, dark eyes.

He wasn't here yet. She'd know in a heartbeat if he was. The butterflies in her stomach flapped even faster. What if he didn't show? Oh, that'd just spoil the whole night. Her senior prom would be a disaster. No. Worse than a disaster. It'd be—

"Rosie?" To her left, Gordon let out a quiet chuckle. "Where'd I lose you?"

"Oh. Nowhere." She fluffed her skirt and firmed up the edges of her smile. "I was just getting a big tickle out of how pretty they made this smelly old gym. I'm sorry. What were you saying?"

"I was asking if you'd like to get some punch." Gordon indicated the refreshments table with a sweep of his hand. "Shall we?"

Rosie nodded her acceptance and headed toward the gaily decorated table, still scanning the crowd, Gordon's hand resting lightly at the small of her back. Classmates, choir friends, and cheerleaders alike all squealed their greetings. Rosie played along, but only with her body. Her face. Her mind and heart still searched for Ephraim.

A cup of punch appeared in her hand, courtesy of Gordon, and she took an automatic sip. The punch was cold, and probably delicious, but her cotton-dry mouth couldn't taste a drop. She waved to another classmate as an excuse to scan the crowd once more while Gordon stood off to one side, chortling with a few members of his offensive line.

"You in that dress, Rosie girl, it's gonna be awful hard to pay the kind of attention to my date I'm supposed to."

Her breath caught. Ephraim. He was here. He was *here*.

Joy bubbled in her chest, fighting to slip out in a squeak. She bit smiling lips in an effort to stifle it and resisted the urge to whirl around. Mother was right about one thing. Anticipation really was the best part. And she wanted to savor every second.

Slowly, she turned, and . . . oh my.

A few paces away, a glass of punch in each hand, Ephraim hadn't gone all out like Gordon. His simple dark suit was slightly too long in the sleeves and too big in the shoulders. Instead of the elaborate boutonniere Mother had insisted on for Gordon, a single red carnation peeked from the buttonhole.

Yet with his wide, shining eyes and knee-weakening smile, Ephraim could've shown up in a cardboard box and he'd still be the best-looking fella here.

His mouth gaped a fraction as he took in her hairdo. Her dress. Not the way Gordon had, like she was meant for consumption. Ephraim's gaze was full of reverent admiration. Like he was studying a masterpiece.

"I knew you'd be beautiful tonight." His voice was low. "But I had no idea how beautiful."

The compliment warmed her to the tips of her satin-covered toes. "You like it?" She resisted the urge to spin in a circle. To hold up her fluffy skirts for his admiration. There'd be time later.

He started to step forward, then stopped, seeming to remember where he was. "I never saw true beauty till this night."

Her heart turned to Jell-O at the reference to *Romeo and Juliet*. "Thank you."

"So." She had to strain to hear him as he glanced toward the large clock on the gymnasium wall. "Same time?"

She nodded. Yesterday in the choir room, after school, they'd agreed on eight thirty as the time when the world would go away and their few precious minutes—their prom—would take place.

"Till then, Rosie girl." And then he was gone, weaving back through the crowd.

Feeling flushed, Rosie took another sip of punch. It really was delicious. Fruity. Definitely some orange juice in there somewhere, and something to make it fizz. Her tongue came alive at the taste. The room burst into brilliant color. The music pulsed through her. Her heart sang along with the band.

Ephraim was here. She'd seen him. They'd spoken.

And now prom could really begin.

"Sorry about that." Gordon was at her elbow. "I told the fellas they only got me for a couple minutes, and then I'm yours the rest of the night."

This was supposed to thrill her, no doubt. She applied a smile. But before she could respond, Gordon gave a derisive snort. She followed his gaze to the edge of the gym, where Ephraim stood with his date, a pretty black girl in a fluffy lavender dress.

"Didn't realize their kind would be here too."

Rosie clenched her jaw and ordered her smile to stay in place. "Why not? They're seniors, same as us."

"They may be seniors, Rosie, but they're not the same as us."

You're absolutely right. Because Ephraim James is ten—no, a hundred, no a thousand—times the man you'll ever be.

Rosie bit back the retort and forced calm into her chest. "Come on, Gordon. Forget about them." She held out a hand. "Let's dance."

Her plan worked. Gordon's attention snapped back to Rosie, and he took her hand. "Well, now. I can't think of anything I'd like better."

Rosie could.

And it was only one hour and eight minutes away.

CHAPTER TWENTY-TWO

THE SUN CARTER had watched crest over the hangars in Wichita now hovered well above the strip of tarmac and scattered storage buildings that made up the Joyce County Regional Airport. The air was long devoid of morning crispness, but also free from the oppressive humidity the eastern part of the state sometimes featured. Climbing from Ethel's cockpit beneath a brilliant blue sky, he headed across the tarmac, where Cassandra's red SUV waited for him.

His sister wriggled out of the car as he approached, and his heart wrenched at the sight of her. The dark circles under her eyes, circles that had arrived about the same time Lucas had, were more pronounced, and her mouth was tight with worry. "Thank you for coming." Cass melted into his arms as he pulled her into a warm embrace made slightly awkward by her ever-growing belly.

"Anything for my favorite sister." He kissed her forehead. "What's the latest? Any news?"

"They took him back to surgery about half an hour ago." Cass pulled her phone from the back pocket of her jeans and gave it a glance. "The doctors said not to expect any updates for an hour or two. Nat was pestering them, but she got called up to L and D for one of her own patients."

"Much to the delight of Dad's doctors, no doubt."

With a wry grin, Cass tucked her phone away. "Yeah, I don't imagine any of them are complaining."

Carter hopped into the Tahoe's sun-drenched passenger seat. Its keys were still in the ignition, a quiet *ding* serving as a reminder. "So are they still talking about airlifting Dad to Wichita?" The click of the seat belt punctuated his question.

Cass slid behind the wheel with a grunt and reached for her own seat belt. "I don't know if that's entirely off the table, but they had to get in there and remove his spleen right away before he bled out. They'll assess once he's stable."

Bled out. Assess. Stable. The words landed like punches as Cass pulled onto the main road into town.

They rode in silence for a few minutes, the familiar sequence of landmarks whizzing past the window. The dilapidated drive-in, closed down for nearly a decade, where Dad had taken him—just him, without his sisters—to see movies ranging from *Chicken Run* to *Revenge of the Sith*. The little ice-cream place with scattered benches where they always went afterward. The grid of gravel roads stretching to the horizon, the roads where he'd taught Carter to drive.

Bitter, booze-drenched memories were what Carter expected to be front and center. Instead, these bittersweet snapshots surfaced, bringing a lump to his throat and a quiet desperation to his heart.

He studied his sister's profile, stark against the morning sun. "What happened, Cass? Do they know?"

Cass's blinker clicked with her change of lanes. "Mom said he went to play poker with some friends in Ulysses. He was coming in on 260 and took the curve too fast. Rolled a few times and landed on the roof. Brad said a farmer called it in a little after five. It looked like Dad had been there awhile. Lost a lot of blood."

"So no one else was involved?"

"No, thank God."

Relieved gratitude swept through Carter in a silent prayer. That was a silver lining, at least. Dad could've easily hurt someone. Killed someone.

Another tragedy Carter would've been powerless to prevent.

Cass hung a left onto Main Street. "Even so, if what Brad's guys said was accurate, we're still looking at a DUI."

Carter's gut tightened. "Not his first one either." He knew the consequences that could result. Fines. A suspended license. Jail time.

A litany the cop had delivered with cool detachment when Carter got his own DUI.

It was the night after his return from Sunflower Summer Theater. From ten weeks of magic with Lauren, ten weeks away from Dad and home and everything that went along with it. But the minute he dropped his bags on the bedroom floor, the clouds of his old life—his real life—rolled in. The guys threw a party to welcome him back, celebrating in their usual way: beer and Jell-O shots, courtesy of Mulligan's older brother.

And Carter partook, as he always did. The cold refreshment of the beer. The burning sweetness of the shots. The euphoria. The release. The escape.

In the past, he'd always slept it off on Mulligan's couch. But not that night. He had to get home to FaceTime with Lauren. After two and a half months of near-constant togetherness, her absence was so profound it had become, in itself, a presence. A tangible thing even alcohol couldn't erase.

The rest of the evening was a blur. The snakelike pattern of Maple Street's center line. The glittering red and blue lights in his rearview mirror. The pit in his stomach as he pulled over. The disapproval on the face of the heavyset cop. Officer Morris. The father of one of his cross-country teammates.

"Well, well, well. Carter Douglas." Morris had eyed his license, then shaken his head. "Looks like the apple doesn't fall far from the tree, does it?"

Those words were the wake-up call Carter had needed. What he'd long considered normal partying was, in reality, the same demon that stalked his dad. And his granddad. And who knew how many Douglases before that.

He hadn't talked with Lauren that night. Or the next. Or the next. Finally, on the fourth day, he'd placed the call that broke both their hearts.

He hadn't told her the truth. How could he? The holding cell. The suspended license. The interlock device that would be on his car for the next year. It was so humiliating, so sickening, he couldn't form the words. Instead, he'd spun excuses about family problems and not having the resources to devote to a serious relationship. Nothing he'd said was a lie, but he'd also left out the lion's share of the truth.

She deserved more. That had never been a question. But letting Lauren Anderson, the love of his life, see who and what he really was? To carry on with her knowing the kind of life she'd be sentenced to if she stuck with him? That would've torn him apart.

Booze hadn't touched his lips since that night. He'd sobered up, performed his required hours of community service, and done his best to ensure his misstep didn't define the rest of his life. For the most part, it didn't. It hadn't.

But the quiet fear remained, a constant worry simmering in the back of his mind, that no matter how many times he politely turned down a casually offered drink, no matter how many times he steered clear of the beer fridge at the grocery store, no matter how much he tried to convince himself he'd changed, that he wasn't truly free. That the monster would always live inside him.

Sure, the monster was dormant now. But could he truly promise himself—promise anyone else—that it wouldn't wake up to wreak havoc someday?

He'd thought he could. But with Dad having tumbled off the proverbial wagon after six rock-solid years, now he wasn't so sure.

⊰⊱

Like every other hospital waiting room Carter had visited, the one at Beckham Memorial was filled with fake leather chairs and smelled of stale coffee. Nat was nowhere to be found, but her husband, Jeremy, sat in a corner chair scrolling on his phone. A few spots over, eyes closed in prayer, hands clasped around her rosary, sat Alicia Douglas.

Greeting his brother-in-law with a nod, Carter sank into a chair next to his mother.

Her eyes flew open. "You're here already? That was fast."

"All those flying lessons come in handy every now and then." He pulled her in for a quick embrace.

Cass waddled across the room and poked Jeremy's shoe with the toe of her own. "Any news?"

Jeremy glanced up from his phone and shook his head.

"Okay." Cass rummaged in her purse. "Little man is leaching out all my life force, and there's a bag of M&M's in that vending machine calling my name. Can I get anyone else anything?"

"Pretty sure I spied some beef jerky in there." Jeremy stood and stretched his lanky frame, seemingly relieved to have something to do besides sit and wait.

When his sister and brother-in-law had rounded the corner, Carter sought his mother's gaze. "How are you holding up, Mom?"

"Oh. I'm getting by." A smile tugged at her lips, then fell flat, as though the effort was simply too much. The lines around her red-rimmed eyes seemed to have deepened since he'd seen her last. She'd colored her hair for years, but he'd never seen so much gray at her roots before. Never seen her normally squared shoulders quite so slumped.

In all her years of raising kids and running herd on middle schoolers and building her take-no-prisoners reputation, he'd never seen his mother look so spent. So beaten down by life.

How long, Mom? How long has he been drinking again? How long have you known? How long have you been covering for him?

And how long will you keep on doing it?

To his horror, his mind suddenly morphed his mother's golden-brown eyes to a deep sapphire. Dark-brown hair lightened to shimmering gold. And suddenly it wasn't his mother sitting there at the end of her rope.

It was Lauren.

"Look what the cat dragged in." Snacks in hand, Cass waddled back into the waiting room flanked by Jeremy and a scrub-clad Natalie. Relieved at the distraction, Carter rose and embraced his oldest sister.

"Any word?" he asked.

"Not much." The reply was shaded with Nat's usual annoyance at the world's stubborn refusal to fall in line and do her bidding. "Travis won't answer my texts, so they must still be in surgery. At this point, I'd say no news is good news."

Carter glanced toward his mother's seat. She nodded, gave another weak smile, and returned to her rosary beads.

"And your patient?" he asked Nat.

"Mom and baby girl are both doing fine. Seven pounds, four ounces, nineteen inches long. Good healthy lungs too." Nat gave a wincing grin and tugged at her right ear.

Carter chuckled. "Congrats."

Natalie's smile faded as she glanced across the room at their mother. With a few quick jerks of her head, she called an impromptu Douglas Sibling Huddle.

"I did call in a favor with the lab and got Dad's test results back." Nat's dark eyes were intense behind her glasses.

Carter's abs tightened. "How bad?"

"Point one one."

The blow stole his breath despite his preparation. Point one one. Well above the legal limit. And that was after his arrival at the hospital. God alone knew what his number was when he left Ulysses.

Cass made the sign of the cross. "Thank *God* he didn't hurt anyone else."

This had to be a nightmare. Any minute now, Carter would wake up in his own bed, drenched in sweat and down on his knees in gratitude that it wasn't real. Dad didn't drink anymore. He was sober. Had been for six years.

But this wasn't a nightmare. It was living, breathing, wide-awake horrible life. And the hope he'd clung to? The hope that maybe he and his dad could both beat the family curse?

Maybe that was a vapor too.

"That's the thing about stuff like this." Jeremy had joined the huddle, his arm around Nat, his mouth a tight line amid his full blond beard. "Sometimes no matter how far you run, it's always got you on its leash, ready to yank you back and sink its claws right into you. There's no escaping something like this. Not really."

Carter turned away. Clenched his fist. Bit his lips until he tasted blood.

His brother-in-law had just given voice—given *life*—to his deepest, darkest fear.

CHAPTER TWENTY-THREE

NORMALLY, LAUREN ENJOYED the time she spent in social media groups, connecting with the Dollop of Delicious community and fostering relationships among like-minded foodies. The task absorbed all her brain power, boosted her confidence, and reminded her of her mission. Her ministry.

But today concentration was impossible, thanks to the presence of her phone on the sofa, snuggled up to her left thigh. Since Carter's sudden departure early this morning, she'd lived and died by his occasional brief texts.

Dad in surgery. Will update when I hear more.

Surgery went well, but doc says next 24 hours are critical.

No change. Will keep you posted.

She responded to each text with a flood of encouragement, reminding him of her love and promising her prayers. And while she didn't expect a Shakespearean sonnet in reply, a *Love you too*, or even a heart emoji, might have been nice. Instead, all she got was the ever-inscrutable *Thx*.

The phone had been still for the last hour or so, but she picked it up and glanced at the screen anyway, just to make sure. Nope. Nothing new. She tossed it back to the sofa, irritated with herself more than anyone. She'd been in Carter's shoes. During Mom's cancer battle, it was all she could do to keep her head above water. Texting updates to well-meaning friends and family, fielding the same questions, explaining the same complicated treatments, had been exhausting. And who knew how many others Carter had to keep informed about his father's condition.

So this wasn't like last time. He wasn't pulling away just because things weren't perfect at home. Once the situation was resolved and Carter was back in Wichita, he'd be fine. *They'd* be fine.

Wouldn't they?

She reached for another kale chip from the bowl on the coffee table, but came up only with fingertips full of salt and a few deep-green crumbs. She hadn't eaten them all already, had she?

Wow. So she had.

Clearly it was time to make more.

She rose from the sofa, bowl in hand, and crossed to the kitchen. Rummaged in the crisper drawer for another bunch of kale. She'd just pulled a knife from the block when her phone jangled from the sofa.

Her bare feet skimmed the floor as she ran to answer. Of course the phone would ring the moment she stopped waiting for it. See? There was nothing to worry about. Carter had just been waiting for a quiet moment, a moment when he could duck outside and talk away from prying eyes, when he—

But it wasn't Carter. The call was from a Massachusetts number she didn't recognize.

Brow furrowed, she lifted the phone to her ear and answered.

"Hello there," came an elderly woman's voice. "Is this the Lauren Anderson who appeared on K-KAN with her grandmother in that human-interest story?"

Lauren perked up, all thoughts of Carter momentarily shoved aside. "Yes, this is that Lauren."

"Oh good." The woman chuckled. "I was worried for a second the station thought I was a crackpot and gave me a fake number just to get rid of me. Frances Beatty's my name. I live in Lexington now, but I'm a Wichita native and graduate of Roosevelt High in fifty-six. We've still got some family down there, and my granddaughter—she's surgically attached to her phone, always on some social media this or that—saw the interview."

"Wow, that's amazing." Lauren paced the floor in front of her bookshelf, hope percolating in her heart. "So did you know my grandma?"

"Not well." Frances gave a dry chortle. "Rosie Gibson was quite a few rungs above me on the high school social ladder. But she was always smiling, always friendly."

"Sounds like Grandma." Lauren smiled into the phone. "And what about Ephraim James? Might you have known him?"

"No, I didn't even know his name. But I sure did recognize him from that yearbook photo your grandma shared. Brought back a lot of memories I thought you might want to hear."

"Always." Lauren retrieved her laptop, ready to write down all she could capture. Memories—especially where Grandma was concerned—were like jewels. Precious and rare.

"It was prom night, fifty-five. I was a junior that year, so I attended only as a yearbook photographer." Frances's voice grew warm and burnished, like a cup of hot cider. "Your grandma arrived on the arm of Gordon McIntyre, Mr. Senior Class himself. As for Ephraim, he brought a girl I knew from the newspaper. Ruby . . . Johnson, I think her last name was. Or maybe Jackson . . ."

Lauren's mind whirled. Grandma and Ephraim arriving with other dates sure put a kink in her theory. Back then, though, a mixed couple would've had to keep things on the down low. No way could they attend prom together.

Unless they came with other dates as cover.

Lauren's breath left in a whoosh. If that was how it happened, then what a dangerous game Grandma had played. But how brilliant. How gutsy.

How madly in love she must've been.

"Anyway." The word spiraled from Frances's lips with great leisure. "I was there to capture as much of prom as I could. Point and click, keep it going, sort through the photos later. That sort of thing."

Lauren grinned. "Yup. I'm a photographer too, so I get it."

"A kindred spirit." Frances's smile came through loud and clear. "So you know, then, that sometimes a shot just leaps out at you, saying *this one. This one is the one.*"

"Oh, absolutely."

"Well, I had that photo. I knew it'd cause some controversy, given the times, but I submitted it anyway. As I expected, they shot it down so fast it'd make your head spin. But I kept the print and the negative. Of all the photos I took for the yearbook, that one is a favorite for sure."

"Is it something you'd be willing to share?" It had to be, or Frances wouldn't have called. But Lauren's heart thumped, her body humming with silent pleas, just the same.

Frances replied with a throaty laugh. "Of course it is. But I'm going to have to get my granddaughter to help me, because all this new-fangled technology ties my fingers in knots. Hang on one second, Lauren, if you would. Payton?" she called, her voice softer.

Muffled conversation ensued, with references to "this confounded thing" from Frances and "just push this button" from another voice, presumably Payton.

Then Frances came back on the line. "Okay. You should be getting a text."

Lauren's phone buzzed. "Got it. I'll put you on speaker, okay?" She pressed the icon, opened the text, and ... *oh.*

Grandma stood by the refreshments table, young and gorgeous in a fluffy white tulle skirt adorned with black flowers. Buttery blonde hair perfectly coiffed, slender arms covered in satin gloves and an ornate corsage. And a few paces away, holding two glasses of punch and wearing a suit that looked a tad too big, was Ephraim James. He gazed at Grandma like she made the sun rise and set. And Grandma's smile. Even an aged black-and-white photo couldn't hide her flushed cheeks. Her glowing skin.

Lauren had photographed hundreds of couples. She knew the look of love.

And there it was, staring up at her from almost six decades ago.

"Wow." Her eyes burned. The photo blurred.

"You can see why the yearbook refused to publish it." Frances's voice was stiff with disapproval.

"No joke. But I'm so glad you kept it. That you shared it. It means the world." Lauren zoomed in on Grandma's lovestruck expression. "Do you know anything more about that night?"

"Nothing definitive, but boy, did I hear rumors." Frances hesitated. "I didn't tell anyone, because Rosie seemed like a good girl. I didn't want anyone to think ill of her. Not that she did anything wrong, necessarily, but back then . . ." She paused. When she spoke again, her voice was clear and crisp. "Anyway. That night I was changing out my roll of film, getting ready for the royalty announcement. I happened to glance up and see Rosie leaving the gym without Gordon. I thought she was just headed for the powder room, but a few minutes later, Ephraim went the same way, and Ruby was nowhere to be seen."

Lauren's breath caught. "Do you think they were meeting somewhere?"

"Hard to say," Frances replied. "There were some pretty wild rumors after prom, and to this day I don't know whether there's a lick of truth to any of them. But one thing I remember for sure—your grandma didn't come back in until a split second before the coronation."

><

May 1955

Rosie's skirts swished as she orbited the choir room. The rhythmic tick of the clock on the wall moved much slower than her frenzied footsteps.

It was past eight thirty. Four minutes past. Sure, Ephraim was known to run late, but they only had these precious few moments together, and now he wasn't even *here* yet, and she had half a mind to—

The door opened. "Hey there, Rosie girl." Ephraim sounded breathless.

"Where *were* you?" She crossed the room, gesturing toward the clock. "We said eight thirty."

"I know. I'm sorry." He rubbed her bare shoulder, flooding her skin with warmth. "I was just fixing to leave when a song came on. Reminded Ruby of her fella overseas. I couldn't very well leave her right then, could I?"

Rosie's irritation zoomed out of her like air from a deflating balloon. "Well now, if that isn't the sweetest excuse I've ever heard."

Smiling, he strolled across the room and placed the needle on the phonograph. Music filled the space, the same sort of bluesy seventh chords like the one he'd taught her. But this song added drums, bass, and a few saxophones along with the tinkly piano. The effect was intoxicating.

As a deep, growly voice began to sing, Ephraim turned toward her and opened his arms. "Would you do me the supreme honor of this dance, Miss Gibson?"

Oh. She melted. Melted to the spot. "I'd be delighted, Mr. James."

He met her beside the piano, grasping her right hand in his and settling his other at the small of her back. His cheek pressed against hers, cool and smooth. He wasn't so much guiding her in the dance as keeping her from floating up into the rafters.

"Did I mention you look gorgeous tonight?" The words tickled her ear. "I mean, you always do, but tonight you look like a princess. No. Not a princess. A queen."

She snuggled closer, breathing the fresh scent of his shaving soap. "Do you like the colors on my dress?"

"I do indeed."

"I chose them on purpose. Black and white. Maybe we can't dance together out there, maybe we just get this one dance in here, but I'm still your girl. This dress is to say so."

He smiled against her temple and pulled her close. "One dance with you won't ever be enough, Rosie girl."

She snuggled against him, her chin resting on his broad shoulder, her lungs filled with his scent. Oh, that she could freeze time. Right here. That the relentless march of seconds would cease and she wouldn't have to think about coronation. About tomorrow. About finals or graduation or college or any of it. That she and Ephraim could spend the rest of forever right here in the choir room, arm in arm, heart to heart.

"Seem pretty deep in thought for just a dance," he ventured.

"You know we graduate in two weeks."

A corner of his mouth quirked. "I know. No more homework."

"No more exams."

A deep chuckle rumbled in his chest. "No more of Miss Greer's ridiculous essay questions."

"But no more choir room. No more auditorium." She stopped and peered up into the face she loved so well. "What then? What happens to this? To us?"

His grip on her waist tightened. "I don't know. But I don't want us to end."

"Me neither." The love in her heart fizzed over the sides, like a bottle of shaken-up soda. "I want this—us—to last forever."

The music swelled, but his steps slowed. "That's a mighty heavy word, Rosie girl. Forever."

Panic pierced the fizz. "Is that not what you want?"

"Never said that." His voice was low and husky. "I just don't see how we can make it happen, things being the way they are."

"Then maybe we can change things."

He arched a brow. "Does your mama know why you wanted that particular dress? Why you chose those colors?"

Her optimism thudded to the ground as quickly as it had taken flight. "No."

"What about your friend Vivian? You tell her about us yet?"

"I chose this dress," Rosie protested. "With these colors. That's a step."

"Forever's gonna take a lot more than a dress, Rosie girl. 'Specially if no one but us knows what it means."

Rosie's frustration escaped in a sigh. "I know. I just . . . I'm not . . . Let's not argue, all right? Not during our one dance."

"I'm not arguing with you." He pressed his lips together. "Just making sure you know there's a difference between wanting forever and doing what it'll take to make it happen."

He had a point. He'd told his parents. He'd invited her to his home. His neighborhood. She'd stepped into his world.

But her world?

No one in her world knew he existed.

Her stomach knotted. As uncomfortable as meeting his parents had been, bringing him to meet Mother and Daddy would be three times worse. Not for her. She'd take whatever punishment her parents cared to dish out. But she could only imagine the kinds of things Daddy might say to Ephraim, and she wouldn't have it. Not for a second.

Ephraim wasn't a secret from her world because he embarrassed her or because she was afraid for herself.

He was a secret because she feared how badly they'd treat him.

When the song ended, Ephraim pulled back, leaving her skin cold and bereft where it no longer touched him.

She put on a mock pout. "That was short."

"We could dance to that whole album and it'd still feel short." He lifted her gloved hand to his lips and pressed a kiss to the back of it. "But you've gotta go."

Her brow creased. Why? Why did she have to leave this beautiful world of just them, where all was as it should be and other people's opinions didn't matter?

Why did there have to be anywhere else but right here?

His quiet laughter penetrated her confusion. "Don't tell me you forgot you're up for prom queen."

"Oh, two hours from now it won't even matter."

"Yeah, but it will two minutes from now, when your head's not there for them to put a crown on."

She waved a hand. "Viv'll probably win."

"Even so."

"Okay. I'll go." She stepped back. It was no use pretending. The outside world was there, it was real, and she had to leave here to go rejoin it. The thought was nearly unbearable. "As long as we can have a few more minutes. Later."

Ephraim's brows shot up. "Later? Ruby's daddy wants her home by ten."

"So come back after." Inspiration ran wild and free. "Your neighborhood's only a few minutes' walk. Take her home and come back. If you walk fast, you might even be back by the last dance."

A lazy smile lit his face. "I might. 'Specially if I take her home a little before ten. Y'know, just to make doubly sure I get her home on time."

Rosie's thoughts zoomed. "If I'm queen, I'll pretend all the excitement's too much. And if I'm not, I'll pretend like I can't stand to see some other girl wearing that crown. Either way I've got an easy escape."

"You realize the risk we're taking." Ephraim's voice was quiet.

"I don't care." She resisted a sudden, childish urge to stamp her foot. "You say we have to do what it takes to have forever, then this is a risk I'll take."

"We shouldn't. There are too many people here. It's too dangerous." He took her hands loosely in his and swung them gently back and forth. That smile pierced the dim room. "But I can't say no to you, Rosie girl."

"Then I'll see you back here. Right before the last dance." She eyed him with mock severity. "Better not make me wait this time."

"I won't." He pressed a soft kiss to her lips. "I promise. I'll never make you wait on me again."

CHAPTER TWENTY-FOUR

DOC SAYS DAD's doing as well as can be expected. Recovery looks like it'll be slow but complete. Not sure about release yet but probably toward the end of the week.

Carter scanned the outgoing text to make sure autocorrect hadn't obliterated his meaning, then pressed the Send button. As expected, the phone vibrated with Lauren's response a few seconds later.

So glad to hear that!!! Praise God!! Will keep praying!

He let himself linger on her response and the accompanying string of heart, kissy-face, and praying-hands emojis. A sliver of time when the world disappeared, when he could imagine himself resting in her arms and basking in her sunshine. Maybe, if he closed his eyes, he could conjure up that mountainside waterfall. Feel her fingers interlaced with his. Hear the melody of her voice. Smell the clean air mingling with her warm floral scent.

No. The stale, sterile hospital smell was too strong. The beeps of the monitors attached to his father were too loud.

Pretending was useless.

Carter tucked the phone into the pocket of the shorts he'd worn for two days straight and leaned not into the reassuring softness of Lauren's arms but the stiff, squeaky embrace of the uncomfortable plastic recliner that served as both chair and bed to whoever was stationed at Dad's side. At the moment, that duty belonged to him. Nat and Cass had finally convinced Mom to come with them for a bite to eat, but she agreed only so long as someone stayed with Dad. So Carter volunteered.

Dad was quiet now. Sleeping. A far cry from the big, barrel-chested man who'd raged at Mom and thrown dishes and backhanded Carter across the mouth for smarting off. The man who'd sulked in a chair, glued to a baseball game, while Carter stood beside him, glove in hand, begging him to come out and play catch before it got too dark. The man who'd shown up so sloppy and embarrassing at graduation that Carter had sneaked out the back door of the high school gym. Here in this hospital room, hooked up to all those monitors, his father looked almost helpless.

And yet Carter had never been more furious with him.

Dad had done so well. For six years he'd resisted the siren song of alcohol.

Unless he hadn't. Maybe he'd pulled one over on everyone who cared about him. Hidden it so well that even those closest to him didn't suspect.

Carter drained another sip of lukewarm coffee from its cardboard cup and flitted through the last few years. Holidays. Barbecues. Weddings. Funerals. Nothing was out of place. He'd spied none of the telltale signs. Dad had even started working out again a couple years back. Lost some weight. Looked healthier—and happier—than he had in years.

So either the man had plunged off the proverbial wagon, or he'd become a master of disguise.

Carter turned the coffee cup in his hands, studying the bland pastel pattern on the side. If Dad had pretended sobriety for the last half decade, then it was still possible to believe that addiction was beatable if he'd actually try for once. But if he'd truly given his all and succumbed anyway, then that meant even his best efforts, his hardest work, everything he had in him, still wasn't enough.

And if *that* was the case, then . . .

No. The coffee cup crumpled in his hand. He wouldn't go there. Not today.

A stirring from the bed drew his gaze, and Dad's dark eyes opened. Blinked a few times.

"Carter."

"Hey, Dad." Carter stood and tossed the cup into the wastebasket beside the bed. "How you feeling?"

"I think I'll live." His father's sturdy hand, covered with IV lines and hospital bracelets, groped around the bedcovers. "Be nice if I could sit up."

"Here." Carter handed his father the remote. Nodding his thanks, Dad pushed a button, and the bed hummed and rose into a sitting position.

Carter took the remote from his father and set it on the bed. "Can I get you anything?"

"I could use a drink."

"'Fraid all they got here is water."

"That's what I meant."

Carter gripped the plastic pitcher of water on the tray beside the bed. "You'll forgive me for not being sure."

"Should've known you only came here to judge me."

"Nope." Carter bit off the retort as ice and water tumbled into the large plastic hospital-logo cup. "Not judging. Just stating a fact. You're an alcoholic. You've always been an alcoholic. You'll always *be* an alcoholic. Might as well give in, right? Sobriety's just too dang hard."

"It was one slip." Dad accepted the cup from Carter's outstretched hand.

"One?" Carter replaced the pitcher with a thunk. "Then what about that beer can I found behind your chair last time I was here?"

His father's silence, the guilty expression over the rim of the cup, was answer enough.

"How long have you been playing us?" He hadn't meant to ask the question, not now, not like this, but it was out there. Now all he could do was wait for the answer he probably needed but definitely wasn't sure he wanted.

Dad sighed and replaced the cup on the tray beside the bed. "Since last fall."

"Last fall?" Carter dragged a hand through his hair. Why was he surprised? Nothing his father did should surprise him anymore.

"They passed me over for supervisor at the plant again. That's the third time." His father plucked at the covers. "They won't tell me it's because they know I'm getting close to retirement—they're smarter than that—but that's why."

Or maybe it's because they want someone they can depend on. No. That wasn't fair. His father had always been a great employee. He was, for the most part, a highly functional alcoholic.

But an alcoholic nonetheless.

"So that's it, then?" Carter's vision tinged red. "You decided to prove they're right not to promote you?"

But Dad didn't take the bait. He simply studied Carter, the wrinkled skin beneath his brown eyes bunching in a slight squint.

Carter squirmed beneath the penetrating gaze. "What?"

"You really think you're so much better than me."

"I don't think I'm better than you."

"Yes, you do." Heavy, graying brows lowered. "I can see it in your eyes. Your mouth. You're disgusted with me. You of all people can't fathom how hard it is to stay sober."

Something inside Carter snapped. "Okay. You're right. You got me. I have no idea what's wrong with you that you can't just *stop*. Do you have any idea how worried Mom is? She hasn't eaten since you got here. Hasn't slept."

Dad opened his mouth to reply, but Carter silenced him with a look. "You drove drunk, Dad. Your BAC was—well, the test said point one one, but that was hours later. How many drinks did you have? How drunk were you when you got behind the wheel? You could've hurt someone. Killed someone. You risk your own neck, that's one thing, but you put every other soul on the road in danger because you can't stay sober."

"And you can."

Carter set his jaw. "Haven't had a drop in thirteen years."

"Then you're a better man than I am. That what you want to hear?"

"No, Dad. Because I'm not a better man than you. I'm just like you. But I quit drinking. So, no. I don't understand why you can't."

Dark eyes flashed. "I *have* quit, Carter. Plenty of times. But what you haven't realized is that it's always got its claws in me. I can fight it. I can ignore it. I can work the steps, score a few points against it. I even pull ahead for a while. But that need to drink will always be inside me. And mark my words." One thick finger jabbed the air. "There'll come a day, an hour, a moment, when you're weak too. You're beaten down. You've got nothing left. And if you're anything like me, that monster will be more than you can handle. It'll sneak in and it'll beat you. Just because it hasn't happened to you yet doesn't mean it won't."

Carter's hands balled into fists so tight his knuckles ached. He wanted to punch the words from the air, or, failing that, to flee as he'd done in childhood. To lock himself in the hall bathroom, turn on the tub full blast, and cover his ears so he wouldn't hear the screaming. The shouting. The broken dishes and those awful, awful words. Words that pummeled him like body blows. Words to which he had no response.

Because he knew, deep in his bones, that they were true. The proof lay before him, helpless in a hospital bed.

Someone bumped him from behind, and he started. There was his mother, a beatific smile on her face.

"Hey, Mom." He moved to embrace her. "Feeling better now that you had something to eat?"

"Some." She rested her head on his shoulder for a brief moment, then pulled the plastic chair closer to the bed and sank into it. Murmuring endearments, she kissed her husband's stubbled cheek. Her delicate fingers swept salt-and-pepper locks from his forehead. Her eyes radiated nothing but adoration and forgiveness. A willingness to be caught in the trap yet again.

Carter closed his eyes against the heartwarming, horrible scene. In a flash, he conjured a future version of himself, lying in a hospital bed just like this one, Lauren at his side. Haggard and exhausted from whatever he'd done to her, but still all in for whatever else he cared to dish out. He saw her stationed on the opposite side of the kitchen, face flushed, eyes streaming angry, heartbroken tears at the chasm between them, the chasm caused by the demon he couldn't defeat. And there, crouching in the hallway, a little boy. His little boy. Hands over his ears, eyes wide with terror—

"Carter? Are you okay?"

Cass. Only she sounded like she was in a tunnel a hundred miles away.

"Yeah. Fine." He tried to arrange his face into something resembling a smile. "Just . . . need some air."

Before she could reply or argue or insist on coming with him, he bolted. Banged the door open and barreled for the nearest exit.

Outside was an oven, but he welcomed it anyway. Leaning against the sunbaked bricks of the hospital's exterior, he tried to pray, but all he could muster was a frantic snatch here and there. Not even words. Just rage and desperation and agony.

His fist slammed against the rough bricks. It wouldn't work. Not here. He needed to be off the ground. High in the air, above all this. Maybe then he'd have a shred of clarity.

Maybe then he could breathe.

He pulled out his phone but stopped just before his shaking thumb landed on Cass's number. He couldn't call her because she'd talk him out of leaving. Not with words. She'd urge him to go. But her tired eyes would sing a different tune.

And he'd stay. For her, he would stay.

But he'd break if he did, and the pieces might never get put back together again.

Before he could save anyone else, he had to save himself. He could be a good brother, a good son, later. But he had to put on his own oxygen mask before he could help anyone else with theirs.

So he did what his father should have done Friday night and called for a cab.

Chapter Twenty-Five

May 1955

For the second time that evening, Ephraim was late. So for the second time that evening, Rosie paced skirt-swishing laps before the risers in the choir room, one eye on the clock.

He'd promised she'd never wait on him again. But it was barely ten after ten. If she knew her Ephraim, he was safely showing Ruby Johnson to the door and bidding her a friendly good night. If anything, Rosie was early. But the opportunity to slip out had presented itself, and she'd taken it.

Gordon and Vivian had been crowned king and queen, an answer to Rosie's fervent, wobbly-kneed prayers as she waited with the other candidates for the announcement. Because tradition decreed that the king and queen share the last dance.

Which meant that swirling around the dance floor, cheek to cheek, would be the two people who would most likely notice her departure.

So she really could slip out. Share the last dance with Ephraim.

It was destiny.

And if anyone did notice, it would be all too easy to pretend jealousy of Viv. Her best friend wearing the crown and dancing with *Rosie's* man? A practiced pout and a couple flouncy foot stomps, and no one would question it.

But no one ever asked. No one even glanced her way as she hurried out of the gym, tossing popularity aside like a rejected dress and slipping down the dark corridor to the safe oasis of the choir room. The one place in the entire school where she could love whoever she wanted to love, not who her parents expected or society dictated.

The click of the door brought a smile to her lips and a song to her heart. She clasped her hands and whirled around—

But the face staring back at her from the doorway was pale and freckled, not deep brown. The hair was strawberry blond, not midnight black.

Rosie gasped. "Gordon."

Blue eyes narrowed. "You were expecting someone else."

It wasn't a question, but Rosie smoothed her skirts, pretending it was all the same. "No, I was just . . . I—I was upset, you know. That I didn't win prom queen." The story resurfaced in the nick of time, and she flung herself into the role and stamped a high-heeled foot. "I couldn't stand watching Viv prance around with that tiara on her head, not when she knew how long I'd been dreaming of—"

The slap came out of nowhere. It rattled her teeth. Stung her mouth.

"Good thing you're not in drama class, doll, because you're a terrible actress." Gordon's lips curled in a sneer, and she blinked back the tears both his slap and his betrayal had brought forth. To think she'd once called him a friend. Her lips were numb now. Tingling. She put her gloved hand to them—the satin came away stained crimson. Was it just lipstick, or was there blood in the mix?

"Gordon—"

"Save it. I know why you're here."

Rosie's heart leaped into her throat. Her stomach lurched. He couldn't know. Could he? *Could* he? Terror hummed in her ears, a high-pitched whine.

"I saw you at the punch table with that—" Gordon snarled a name so foul it made Rosie flinch.

"We're in choir together, Gordon. I stand next to him. We were just saying hello." That morsel, at least, was true.

"Oh, sure, *that* time." Frosty blue eyes thawed for a fraction of an instant. Just enough for her to see the hurt he tried to conceal. "But I saw how you looked at him. How he looked at you."

Her stinging lips parted. Gordon was sweet on her. That bravado, the way he constantly, jokingly pursued her . . . it wasn't a joke, was it? He had feelings for her. Probably had for a while now and used humor as a cover.

Gordon McIntyre, Mr. Roosevelt High himself, was as shy and vulnerable as anyone else.

But the further hardening of his eyes, the set of his jaw, quickly snuffed out what little sympathy had surfaced.

Gordon stepped closer. "I know you sneaked in here with him too."

"Wha—*how?*"

Laughter escaped in a bitter bark, and Gordon flung a hand skyward. "You won't even deny it." He paced a couple steps away from her, then whirled. "You disappeared on me. That nerdy photographer said you'd gone to the little girls' room, but you were gone so long I started to worry. I came down this way just to make sure, and I heard music. *Music.* Coming from in here." He leaned closer. "Only music that's supposed to be going on tonight is out there. Not in here."

His blue-flamed glare revealed the rest, and the blood drained from Rosie's face. Horror clawed at her throat at the thought of him witnessing such a precious, private moment.

"I thought I was seeing things." Gordon laughed again. "Thought maybe I'd been a little too deep in the stuff Mayhew brought to add to the punch."

Rosie's brows shot up. "Have you been drinking?"

"Don't change the subject." He grabbed her by the shoulders, his hands warm and clammy on her bare skin, the scent of booze wafting from his breath. "Have you *been* with that . . . that—"

"No." Rosie jerked free from his grasp. "I haven't been wi . . . with anyone. Not that it's any business of yours. We're here only as friends." The word was as false as any she'd ever uttered, but maybe her desperation move would knock some sense into him.

"Friends. Right. Like you and I are *friends*." He stepped closer, his footfalls on the tile echoing like gunshots. "And as your *friend*, Rosie Gibson . . . I need to teach you a little lesson about the way things are."

He loomed over her, and her heart hammered double time. "Gordon, please." She tried to back up, but her shoulders met the cold brick wall.

"White women belong with white men." Gordon's meaty hand mauled her from cheek to neck to shoulder in a way that made her stomach roil. His class ring was cold on her upper arm. "And maybe the whole reason you're so hung up on *that* is 'cause you don't know what it's like to be with the kind of man you're supposed to be with."

Rosie put her hands on Gordon's chest and shoved, anger giving her an extra burst of strength. "I know perfectly well what kind of man I'm supposed to be with. I'm supposed to be with a *good* man. A *kind* man. One who's smart and funny and treats me with love. With respect. With—"

The words turned into a scream as Gordon's mouth crashed down onto hers. The force of his lips bruised tender flesh, especially on the right half of her mouth where he'd slapped her. She tried with all her might to fight him off, but he pinned her in place with relative ease. His hands roved over her, touching places no one had touched—no one other than her husband *should* touch—and his body became a truck roaring onto her, crushing her to the wall.

He wouldn't stop even long enough for her to draw breath, let alone scream for help. Stars dancing before her vision, all she could do was pray. Cry out in silent desperation to the God who was her only hope.

"Hey. *Hey.* Get off her!"

Ephraim. She'd never heard such anger in his voice. Such authority.

Thank you, God.

Her knees went weak with relief as the weight of Gordon's body released, and a fist flew across his face. A dark-brown fist.

Ephraim's fist.

Blood spattered her dress. Bright crimson marred black and white. She stared at the brilliant drops, then up at the boys, who'd frozen in place. Gordon lifted a hand to his nose, the source of the flow. Thick fingertips smeared shiny red.

And Ephraim—even Ephraim stared, like he couldn't quite believe what he had done.

Gordon growled an obscenity, and all hell broke loose. Scraping chairs and angry shouts and the thud of fists against flesh and more cursing and screaming—the last of those came from her, almost inhuman in its terror and rage. Because Ephraim was strong—surprisingly so for one so skinny—but Gordon was both enormous and furious. His eyes were nearly neon in their anger, and Rosie had never seen such vile hatred in someone's expression before. How long could Ephraim truly last against such violence? Such pure evil?

The doors banged open, and in burst two chaperones, three teachers, and the principal, Mr. Thompson. With angry shouts of their own, they separated the boys and flung them to opposite corners of the room. Blood poured from both faces, and Rosie's heart broke for Ephraim, whose cheek was swollen and whose chest heaved for breath. His eyes met hers, dark with sorrow and regret. But what did he have to regret? What on earth could he possibly have to be sorry for?

"What's going on in here?" Mr. Thompson demanded.

"This *animal* was trying to take advantage of Miss Gibson, sir." Gordon's feigned innocence sickened her stomach. "I came upon the scene just in time to prevent the compromise of her honor."

Rosie's hand flew to her mouth. Horror escaped in a squeak.

Mr. Thompson's black-framed glasses turned in her direction. "Is this true, Miss Gibson?"

No. No. It's not true. It's the opposite. But the alternative was to spill the truth about their relationship—their precious secret—to the administration. The faculty. To everyone in the whole wide world, and she just needed a minute to think how to do it, to—

"Come on." Mr. Thompson must've taken her silence as assent, because he grabbed Ephraim by the elbow and jerked him toward the door.

"No, no, no, that's not what happened. *No*, that's not . . . *he* didn't . . . It wasn't Ephraim who did those things to me. It was *Gordon*."

But the words she'd found at last fell on deaf ears. Ephraim cast one sorrowful glance over his shoulder, and then the beloved face disappeared behind the closing door.

"It wasn't Ephraim." The protest tumbled from her lips over and over, like a prayer. "It wasn't Ephraim."

"There, there. It'll be all right." Gordon tried to put his arm around her, but she screamed and shoved him away.

"No, it *won't*." She gathered stained skirts in two fists. "It won't because I *love* him. And you . . . you—" Her throat closed with rage and grief and the bleeding remnants of her fear. Tears pooled in her eyes. Coursed down her cheeks. There wasn't a word vile enough for what Gordon McIntyre was.

A murmur arose from the chaperones, pinging off the edges of her awareness. *She's obviously had quite a fright, poor dear. We've got to call her parents. Get her home.*

No. Not her parents. She wanted to tell them—was going to tell them—but not . . . not like this. No, please, please, not like this.

But Rosie couldn't speak. All she could do was sob from the depths of her shattered heart as they led her away.

Chapter Twenty-Six

LAUREN THUDDED THE door of her Jeep shut and turned to face the rear entrance of the K-KAN studios. It was just past the end of the noon newscast on a day that finally felt like fall, and Carter's car was still parked beneath the sun-dappled shade of a cottonwood a couple spaces away.

That car had been parked at her apartment since she'd driven it home from the airport Saturday morning. She'd intended to give him a ride when he returned, but he'd taken an Uber home instead, hitched a ride with a colleague that morning, and retrieved his Charger under cover of darkness. He'd texted to let her know, promising dinner that night, but when a hole popped up in her schedule right around his quitting time, she'd seen no reason to postpone their reunion.

The heavy steel door creaked open, and Carter emerged. One hand tugged a dark-blue tie loose, while the other held his phone, thumb dancing across the screen.

"Excuse me." Smiling, she leaned against his car. "Aren't you Carter Douglas, that super-hot weather guy?"

Carter glanced up and blinked, and Lauren reveled in the micro-moment before recognition, the anticipation of his dazzling ear-to-ear smile.

But the true smile never materialized. Just a weary flex of his mouth as he tucked his phone into his pocket.

"You're a sight for sore eyes." He wrapped his arms around her waist, and his lips found hers, but the kiss was short. A "hi, honey, how was your day" sort of kiss, the kind she'd expect of a long-married couple who'd settled into the comfortable and routine. Not the fiery kind she and Carter were known for.

"A photo shoot got rescheduled, so I had some unexpected free time. And"—she reached through the open window of her Jeep and withdrew a basket covered with a colorful towel—"I come bearing treats. Chocolate chip zucchini muffins. With real chocolate and everything."

"That's sweet, Lauren. Really."

She flipped back the towel. "Try one."

Carter held up a hand. "I wish I'd known or I wouldn't have pigged out quite so much after the kitchen segment."

"Oh. Right. Federico Mottola." She lowered the basket. "I recorded it but haven't watched yet. How'd it go?"

"Great." Carter stripped the tie from around his neck and unbuttoned the top couple buttons of his shirt. "We made some kinda . . . shoot, I can't remember what he called them. Little potato dumplings or something."

"Gnocchi."

"Yeah. That's it. Anyway, it was . . ." He kissed his fingertips. "Couldn't eat another bite if I wanted to."

"Right. Sure." Who was she to think a lame-o batch of homemade zucchini muffins could compete with gnocchi from the head chef of Wichita's favorite Italian restaurant? "Take them home, then. They'll keep."

"Yeah, absolutely. Thanks." He took the basket and set it on the curb. "And now that I have my hands free . . ."

He opened his arms to her, and she stepped into them once more. Tilted her face up to his for a kiss. A real one this time. None of that old-married-couple nonsense.

He obliged. His lips moved against hers with appropriate pressure and passion. But his neck was tense. His shoulders stiff as twin loaves of stale bread.

He ended the kiss with a groan. "You have no idea how glad I am to be home."

Was he really? She searched his eyes but found them only dark and unreadable.

"How's your dad?" she asked.

"Doing better." Carter raked a hand through his hair. "They're think-ing he'll get to go home Friday."

"That's great." Lauren cupped the back of his neck, trying to relieve some of the tension. "So, hey. Let's get outta here. Go look at the mums at Botanica or walk around the zoo or something. I hear from a reliable source it's supposed to stay seventy-two and perfect all afternoon."

On any other day, her quip would've brought a chuckle or a witty come-back, but on this day it drew only a weak upturn of his lips.

"Nice as that sounds, Lauren, I'm just beat. My schedule's all screwed up, and right now the only thing in the world that sounds good is a nap."

She let her hands fall to her sides, swallowing selfish disappointment. Of course he was exhausted. Who wouldn't be?

"Absolutely. Yes. Go home. Take a nap. And we'll go out to dinner tonight after you wake up. Or, hey, if you don't feel like going out, we can stay in. I've got this whole passel of produce from the farmers' market I need to do something with, and—"

"Lauren." He laid a heavy hand on her shoulder. "I'm so sorry, but I just . . . I can't, okay? Not today."

Irritation sparked before she could tamp it down. "What is it about going back home that makes you suddenly not able to handle us?"

Whoa. Simmer down. You're blowing this way out of proportion. He's just—

But her inner scolding quieted at the quick jerk of his head. The slight twitch of skin beneath his left eye. The pale line around his lips.

Had she hit on something? Stumbled across some truth?

Was he really having second thoughts?

"This isn't about you, okay? My dad's just . . ." He sighed, as though the mere effort of speaking was more than he could bear. "This weekend has been a lot, and it's too much for me to handle right now. Not without a nap, anyway."

He flashed a lame, half-hearted grin, but it barely registered. Those two fateful words bounced around her head. Her heart. Her stomach. *Too much. Too much. It's too much.*

It was just like thirteen years ago. The same deadpan inflection. The same words clawing through the fabric of time to puncture her heart once more.

"I'll call you later, okay?" He brushed a kiss to her forehead, then climbed into his car, started the engine, and pulled from the parking lot without a backward glance.

And without the muffins.

Lauren blinked back tears as she bent to retrieve the basket. Fought the rising panic. Okay, maybe his choice of words could've been better, but it had to be a coincidence. His father had been in a car accident. Could've died. Was still hospitalized. Who wouldn't be a little overwhelmed?

And Carter's sleep schedule. She couldn't fathom keeping the hours he did week after week. The human body wasn't designed to violate circadian rhythms the way his shift required.

So this was different. *He* was different.

Wasn't he?

With a sigh, she picked up the top muffin from the pile, peeled back the wrapper, and took a bite. Wow. Tender, moist, just the right amount of sweetness. She polished off the rest in a single bite and grabbed the next before she'd even finished chewing.

They really were very good muffins.

⋊⋉

Lauren rolled over in bed, her mouth dry and foul tasting. Wha . . . what time was it? How long had she slept?

Needles of sunlight stabbing gritty eyes were at least a partial answer. Head throbbing, stomach roiling, she sat up to get her bearings. Was she hung over? No. She didn't drink. Didn't like the taste. Booze was about the only thing she'd never binged on, though, and . . .

Oh.

The basket of zucchini muffins she'd polished off before she'd even left the studio parking lot. The mad dash through the grocery store, grabbing whatever would fit in her cart. The pastries. The pretzels. The deep-dish pepperoni pizza from the little place down the street.

She fell back into bed with a groan. No wonder she felt like she'd eaten a bowling ball. Several bowling balls. And now they were rolling around inside her, lurching with every movement.

Gingerly she reached for the phone on her nightstand to check the time, but the screen was black. Dead. Had she forgotten to plug it in last night? Wait. No. She'd switched it off herself when the clock had ticked well past Carter's usual workday bedtime and she'd realized that not only had he not called, he wasn't going to.

That was when she'd ordered the pizza. Nausea surged at the memory.

You can take advantage of that, y'know.

The whining voice popped up from nowhere.

You're probably about to throw up on your own anyway, what with all those calories and carbs and trans fats and God alone knows what else you crammed down your gullet last night. Do it yourself. You're in control.

Her eyes flew wide. Her pulse pounded. No. She hadn't heard that voice in years. She'd thought its whining had forever ceased. But here it was. Taunting her.

No. She couldn't go down that road.

Oh, don't make it sound so dramatic. This won't become a habit, just like eating a whole entire pizza won't become a habit. You had a weak moment. It happens. Just get rid of what you can, work off what you can't, and get back on the wagon. No harm, no foul.

As if in agreement, her stomach pulsed, and another wave of nausea clutched at her guts. She probably would lose it all on her own pretty soon. And once that happened, she'd feel so much better.

What was the harm in speeding it along?

Hating herself with every step, she rose from the bed and padded to the bathroom. Knelt in front of the toilet. Bile rose. Her stomach churned. Sweat beaded on her forehead as she assumed the familiar posture. Lifted a trembling hand to her mouth. Extended her index finger and aimed it for her throat . . .

"Lauren?"

Her brother's voice, the rattle of keys at her apartment door, froze her every muscle. The door creaked open, then thudded shut. One of the cats meowed a greeting, and Garrett's keys clanked onto the counter.

"You okay, Lo?" The vibrations of his footsteps on the floor beneath her bare knees made her cringe. He was in the living room now, doubtless taking in the empty Oreo package. The Cheetos bags. The pizza box . . .

"I tried to call—a whole bunch of times, actually—but your phone was off, and since I was—"

He rounded the corner into the bedroom, and she realized, too late, that she hadn't shut the door behind her. And there Garrett stood, in all his judgy big-brother glory.

But he wasn't judging. His mouth opened slightly, his face paled, and his eyes radiated not superiority, but sorrow.

Maybe that was worse.

"Oh, Lauren."

It was the sadness in his voice that broke her. Tears flooded her eyes, and she shoved away from the porcelain throne, disgusted with herself. With what she'd done last night. What she'd nearly done this morning. What she'd done years ago, over and over for months. How easily she'd almost fallen back into it.

Garrett sank onto the floor of the tiny bathroom, and she fell sobbing against his chest. He gathered her into his arms and smoothed her hair, as Mom had always done. Was the gesture intentional or merely a subconscious product of habit and heredity?

Either way, it worked.

When her sobs subsided and she'd used half the roll of toilet paper to blow her nose, Garrett sought her watery gaze. "What's going on, Lo?"

"It's Carter. Although you probably already guessed that." She tossed a crumpled wad of tissue toward the trash can. "Things were going great. *Really* great. But then his dad had a car accident, and Carter went home to be with his family, and now he's back, but he's shutting me out, just like before. He says he needs to process, or whatever. That I'm too much to deal with."

Garrett's sandy brows inched upward, but he said nothing.

"I thought he'd changed. And maybe he has. Maybe I'm just overreacting because I'm not totally over when he hurt me before. Maybe this is just me making a big deal out of nothing." She paused, studying the white tile between electric-purple toenails. "But maybe it's not. Maybe he hasn't changed. Maybe he's still the same Carter."

"Whether he is or isn't, you're not the same Lauren. This"—he swept a hand around the bathroom—"isn't who you are anymore. God's changed you in ways you probably don't even realize. You're healthy now. You're strong. You're capable and compassionate and beautiful and . . . and one of the most amazing women I've ever known, bar none. Whether Carter Douglas sees that or not, I do."

Lauren squeezed her brother's hand, warmth seeping into her soul. "Thanks, Garrett."

"You're welcome." He shifted on the floor. "So . . . we're done here?"

She shut the toilet lid, shuddering at how close she'd come. "Yeah. We're done."

"Good." Garrett hoisted himself off the floor with a grunt, then held out his hand to help her up. "You wouldn't happen to have any pizza left over, would you? I haven't had lunch, and I'm due back at the office in a few."

Lauren blanched. "If there is, it's all yours." Ugh. She would never eat pizza again as long as she lived.

"And maybe we should get you some ginger ale or Pepto or something." Garrett slung his arm around her shoulders.

She grinned. As usual, her big brother was right. About the Pepto, sure . . . but about the rest of it too.

Normally, his being right all the time annoyed her.

Not this time.

This time, it was a relief.

CHAPTER TWENTY-SEVEN

May 1955

As usual for a Saturday morning, Rosie's plate was piled high with eggs, bacon, and toast. Twin cups of coffee steamed at her parents' places, and the *Wichita Eagle* lay neatly before her father, as it always did.

But coffee, newspaper, breakfast, all remained untouched. The stretched-thin silence was broken only by the timid twitter of birds out the open window.

Across the table, Daddy stared at the headlines. His mouth was tight, and that vein in his forehead bulged. Any minute now he'd blow his stack and let fly with a few cross words. But as quick as Edward Gibson was to get frosted, it blew over just as quick. So she wasn't really worried about Daddy.

But Mother. Usually coiffed to perfection, Mother's bottle-blonde hair flew in all directions. She wore no makeup—had Rosie ever seen her that way before?—and her eyes over the untouched coffee cup were rimmed red and shadowed with bluish circles. She looked like she hadn't slept at all.

That made two of them.

Principal Thompson had driven Rosie home last night in an Oldsmobile that reeked of cigar smoke. Explained to her parents in his usual monotone that an altercation involving her had taken place between two boys—Gordon McIntyre and a Negro student—

"His name is Ephraim James," Rosie had spat. "And I love him." There was no point in hiding it. Not anymore. Ephraim was God alone knew where, facing God alone knew what consequences. The least she could do was be honest. To say the words she should've said weeks ago.

To tell the world who held her heart.

Heavy silence had descended then, with Mother gasping, then fleeing upstairs, Daddy going deathly pale and following her, and Mr. Thompson awkwardly showing himself out.

No one had tried to remove the bloodstains from her dress. No one had soothed her split lip or the bruises she was sure would crop up by morning. No one had asked if she was all right.

No one had said a word.

No one had said anything this morning, either. The tick of the old grandfather clock in the foyer and the quiet rustlings of Daddy's newspaper and Mother's cooking were the only sounds at breakfast.

Finally, her father looked up from his paper, set it down slowly, and cleared his throat. Fixed her with a granite gaze. Here it came . . .

"What were you *thinking*, Rosemary?"

"A Negro boy?" Her mother's hand fluttered to her chest.

Their objections tumbled out, one over the other, like bowling pins.

"It's appalling."

"It's not proper."

"It's inconceivable."

"It just isn't done."

"I've never been more disappointed in you."

"What on earth was wrong with Gordon McIntyre?"

Rosie's brows shot up at her mother's latest volley. "Oh, I don't know, Mother. Maybe *this* for a start?" She pointed to her swollen lower lip.

Daddy averted his gaze. "Perhaps you wouldn't have that if you weren't mixed up in something so vile."

"*What?*" The words knocked the wind from her. This was the man who'd let her dance on his socked feet while Benny Goodman played on the radio. The man who'd promised no boy would ever hurt her and get away with it. The man who'd always been there to protect her. Defend her. And now, not only was he not defending her, he . . . he was *blaming* her.

"All this sneaking around you've been doing. The dishonesty. The lying for—oh, I don't even want to know how long you've been looking us in the eye and lying to us. To your teachers. Your friends." Daddy shook his head, his lips a thin line. "Trust takes much work to gain, Rosemary, and you've lost mine."

The chastisement cut swift and deep. *God, forgive me.* She had been dishonest. She'd woven so many stories she could scarcely keep them straight.

At least now she wouldn't have to.

"To say nothing of the sort of company you were sneaking around with." Her father's voice shook. "There are only two types of women willing to be seen with a colored boy, Rosemary. An insane woman and a woman of ill repute."

"Or a woman in love."

Had she really feared saying those words? Now they flew from her lips like they'd always been part of her.

Daddy flung up his hands and looked toward Mother. *I've done all I can with her,* his expression seemed to read. *It's your turn now.*

Mother folded her hands on the table and flicked a weak smile. "Rosemary. Darling." She spoke slowly, as though to a dim child. "I've nothing against this boy as a person—"

"His name is *Ephraim.*"

"Ephraim." Mother's nose wrinkled, like she'd just smelled something unpleasant in the Frigidaire. "Yes. I've nothing against him or his kind as people, per se. I'm certain many of them are lovely. But mixing the races . . . it's unbiblical."

"The good Lord separated mankind at the tower of Babel for a reason," Daddy said in reply to Rosie's open-mouthed stare. "Confused their language. Scattered them over the whole earth so they wouldn't be so prideful. Even the apostle Paul said it wasn't a good idea. We're not to be unequally yoked. Reverend Jeffries said so in his sermon just this past Sunday."

"Did you hear the *rest* of his sermon?" Rosie's words burst out over the chiming clock. How could the people who'd taught her God's Word twist it so deftly? Mangle it to suit their own preconceived notions? "Paul was talking about believers and unbelievers, not black and white. Ephraim and his family may worship differently than we do, but they worship the same God. The same Jesus. It doesn't matter one bit to him that our outsides don't match, because on the inside, Ephraim and I are the same."

Mother and Daddy exchanged a cryptic look, and Mother straightened her already ramrod posture. "Even if that were true, where would the two of you live? A neighborhood like ours certainly wouldn't accept you. And his neighborhood . . ."

Rosie's eyes narrowed. "What's wrong with his neighborhood?"

"I'm sure it's fine, but it's no place for a girl like you."

"That's funny." Rosie lifted her chin. "I got along just fine when I visited."

Mother gasped. "You've been there? Did anyone *see* you?"

"Relax, Mother." Rosie's injured mouth twisted into a parody of a smile. "None of your fancy white friends saw me, so there's no need to worry."

"That's enough, Rosemary." Her father's voice sliced like a knife.

Mother closed her eyes and rolled her lips together. "All right. Suppose you do find a place to live. What about the children that would come from such a union? Not white. Not black. They wouldn't be accepted anywhere."

"Then maybe they'd be brown." Rosie met her mother's worried gaze. "And they could be accepted here, if you so chose."

Daddy paled. "Are you . . . *with child*, Rosemary?"

"Daddy!" Her face heated. "No. Ephraim and I haven't—we've done things the right way."

"There is no right way. Not with this." Daddy slipped off his glasses and set them on his paper. For the first time, she noticed red rimming his eyes too. "I'm afraid you leave me no choice."

Mother jerked toward him. "Edward, no."

"What would you have me do, then?" His hands splayed wide. "It's clear things can't go on like they are. And our daughter is still blind to how sinful her actions are."

"What's sinful is your refusal to accept a brother in Christ—the man I love—simply because of the color of his skin." The words were out before she could evaluate their merit, and her father's wide-eyed stare mirrored her own astonishment. Never had she talked back to her parents to this degree. Never had she rebelled so irrevocably. There was no telling what they'd say. What they'd do.

But she'd never known, to the very deepest part of her, that she was right. And they were horribly, inexcusably wrong.

Daddy's surprise hardened to cold steel, so much so that it made her shiver. He was looking at her like he didn't even know her.

Maybe he didn't.

"You will go upstairs this minute, Rosemary." His voice was deathly calm. "You will pack your things, get in the car, and I will drive you to your grandparents' house."

Rosie's brows flew to her hairline. "The farm?"

"I spoke with them this morning and shared only that a situation has arisen that makes your living here no longer feasible. Unless you want to send them to their graves, you'll say nothing further."

"But they're almost an hour away. How will I get to school?"

"That is no longer your concern," her father snapped.

"But, *Daddy*. Graduation is in two weeks."

"And you will not participate."

"Edward." Mother turned pleading eyes on Daddy. "Missing her own graduation? What will everyone say when she's not there?"

"We can't take any chances, Helen. As long as Rosemary is in the throes of this ridiculous adolescent infatuation, we can't so much as let her lay eyes on the boy. A little distance from him, and perhaps she'll come to her senses."

"It's not infatuation, Daddy." Tears stung. "I love him."

"All the more reason for you to get away from him, then," her father retorted. "I'll speak with Mr. Thompson. Arrange for you to receive your diploma from a distance. Certainly he'll understand our reluctance to expose you to additional risk from this boy."

"You mean from Gordon McIntyre." That, at least, would be a silver lining to life on the farm.

Mother's simpering gaze turned her way. "Gordon comes from a good family."

"Too bad it didn't rub off."

"Rosemary!" Her father smacked the table, and the dishes jumped. "Upstairs. Now."

Rosie tossed her napkin on her untouched plate and stormed toward the stairs. If this was the way it'd be around here, then fine. Send her to that creaky, dusty old farmhouse out in the middle of nowhere. Miles away from Ephraim. From everyone.

She paused on the landing, her right hand resting on the polished banister. Miles away. From her parents. From school. From that awful Gordon McIntyre. From everyone who said she and Ephraim shouldn't be together.

Perhaps the fresh country air, the freedom it represented, was just the ticket.

The only thing she needed was to get a message to Ephraim.

CHAPTER TWENTY-EIGHT

BLINDING SUNSHINE STUNG Carter's eyes as he stepped from the chilled confines of the studio into brilliant autumn sunshine the next afternoon. Forecast sunshine, though. At least it had that in its favor.

He pulled his buzzing phone from his pocket, shielding the screen from the sun with a cupped hand. Updates from Cass usually landed right after his shift, and sure enough, here was today's. Dad was being released as soon as the paperwork was in order.

Carter replaced the phone with a sigh. It was good, of course, Dad being released. But what would he be released *to*? He still faced a lengthy recovery, not to mention pending legal issues from a second DUI. And even if he made it through those minefields, what then? Would his first excursion from the house be to the liquor store around the corner? Or would his addiction switch from alcohol to painkillers? He'd be on them for quite a while, and knowing Dad, one addiction could well replace, or even join, another. Would he—

"Hello, Carter."

For the second time in as many days, a member of the Anderson family awaited him in the shady oasis where he'd parked his car. But this time it was Lauren's brother, Garrett. Carter had only met the guy once, but the resemblance between brother and sister had not dimmed with the passage of time.

He greeted the taller man with a cautious smile. "Garrett. Been a while. What can I do for you?"

"You can stop jerking my sister around, for starters."

Carter blinked. "Come again?"

Garrett folded his arms across his chest. "I'll be honest—I've never been your biggest fan. But I've been willing to give you the benefit of the doubt, because I remember how much Lauren loved you."

The brutal beginning to this unexpected conversation was like that substate basketball game against Ulysses his senior year, when his team started slow and quickly found themselves in a double-digit hole.

"She gets this special smile when you're around. One I haven't seen since the two of you were together before." The hard edges of Garrett's gaze softened slightly. "And when you started flying her off to parts unknown just to take her to eat at a place you knew she'd like, when you jumped in with both feet to help us try to find Ephraim James, I thought, hey, y'know what? Maybe the guy's changed. And even more importantly, Lauren thought you'd changed. But now you're doing the same thing you did way back when. You love her one minute, but you won't even text her back the next—"

"Look, pal." Carter stepped forward, a dull throbbing in his temples. "Not that it's any of your business, but I'm going through a lot of stuff right now, and—"

"You ever stop to think, *pal*, that maybe she is too?" Garrett's eyes narrowed. "You know she binged yesterday for the first time in over a decade?"

"Binged?"

"When Lauren's upset, she eats." Garrett flung his arms wide. "She eats, and she eats, and she eats, and then she throws it all up."

The words were an elbow to the gut, a stolen ball, a blow so sharp and sudden it doubled him over, the swish-and-score at the other end of the court just a blur.

"The first time she did that was right after you dumped her all those years ago." Garrett's words were softer, but their impact hadn't lessened. "She had bulimia for ten months after that, Carter. *Ten months*. None of us had any idea how bad it was. I'm not even sure I know now. But she finally got help. Got through it."

I didn't know, his heart shrieked. *I didn't know how fragile she was. I didn't know what she'd been through.*

"Now, maybe Lauren was close to the edge of the cliff anyway. Maybe she'd have started purging whether you were in the picture or not. But you were. And don't think for a minute either one of us has forgotten how she came home from theater camp all moony-eyed and giddy, and four days later you broke her heart."

A blue jay streaked from one tree to the other, its shrill cry underlining Garrett's words.

"I was willing to let bygones be bygones. Until last night, when she binged again." Garrett shook his head, his lips a thin line. "My sister is nowhere near as okay as she pretends to be, and I won't stand by and watch you wreck her all over again. So if you're not all in with her, if you can't guarantee you'll do whatever it takes to make sure it works this time, then if you care about her at all, just leave her alone. She's got enough problems. She doesn't need you adding to the mix."

Garrett climbed into his car and pulled away, leaving Carter standing hands-on-knees at center court, blinking up at the final score and reeling from an offensive onslaught he never saw coming.

Bulimia. Lauren had bulimia.

Bulimia brought on by his actions. His words.

Him.

Garrett was right. He was no good for her. No good for anyone.

No matter how much time had passed, no matter how much work he'd put in, he was the same guy he'd always been. The tornado signature, the angry red hook on the radar, an unrelenting march of devastation toward some unsuspecting town.

And just like in his job, he couldn't do anything about the impending doom.

All he could do was warn the poor souls in its path.

><

Lauren's bare feet thudded across her apartment floor in her hurry to answer the doorbell. She hadn't been expecting any visitors, but here one stood in her hallway. The one she'd been trying to reach since about this time yesterday.

"Carter." She blinked at his appearance. His eyes had darkened to near ebony and glistened with unshed tears. A tawny patch of makeup he must've missed clung to a darkly stubbled jaw. Pale skin outlined pressed-together lips.

"Come in. Come in." She hurried him inside. "What's wrong? Is it your dad?"

"No, it's not—not really. He's getting released today, but . . ." Carter shook his head, still studying her with a mixture of sadness and horror. "Bulimia, Lauren?"

Her stomach plummeted. "*What?*" She couldn't have heard him right. He hadn't said what she thought he said. He couldn't. He didn't know. She hadn't told him.

"You make yourself throw up?" His brow creased.

"No. I . . . I don't do that. Not anymore." Never mind how close she'd come just a couple hours ago. "Who told you?"

Carter flinched, as though her words were confirmation he'd been praying not to receive. "Garrett. He came to see me just now. After work."

Lauren looked skyward. "Great. That's just . . . that's *great.*"

"Why didn't you tell me?" Carter's voice nudged the edge of composure.

"Because it's over." She flung her arms wide. "I got treatment. I went through boatloads of therapy. I'm not that person anymore."

"So that binge you went on last night was what, exactly?"

Her face stung like she'd been slapped. She'd never felt so humiliated. So betrayed.

"I don't know, Carter. But when you told me I was too much, I just—"

"What?" Dark brows creased. "I never said *you* were too much. I said *this* was too much."

"How is that different?"

"Because it's got nothing to do with you." He emphasized his point with a slashing gesture. "All right? It's not about what you look like, or . . . or what you weigh. I love you no matter what size you wear. It's not about any of that."

"Then what *is* it about?" The question that had haunted her for thirteen years hovered between them. She probed his gaze for answers.

Carter dragged a hand through his hair. "No one else has ever made me feel even half as alive as you do. No other woman has ever worked her way so deep into my heart." His eyes met hers, tortured and pleading. "I've never loved anyone the way I love you, Lauren. Never."

Stepping closer, she took his hand in hers. "Then why do you keep sabotaging it?"

He looked down at their clasped hands, and the muscle in his jaw worked. "Because my dad's drinking again." Barely audible words, but they bathed everything in a new hue. "I suspected as much last time I went home, but I didn't have proof until now. That car crash . . . he was drunk."

Murmuring his name, Lauren slid her arms around his waist and tucked her head beneath his chin. His arms came around her, and his chest rumbled with the depth of his sigh.

"There's nothing like growing up in a small town with a dad who's a drunk. 'Cause everyone knows. That bruise your mom tries to hide with makeup? Everyone knows she didn't walk into a doorframe. Your sister's perfect GPA, her medical degree, everyone's proud of her, sure. But no one forgets who her dad is." His heartbeat sped beneath her cheek, and his grip on her shoulders tightened. "And when you get pulled over for a DUI when you're seventeen? No one's surprised. Because you're a chip off the old block. You're Rick Douglas's son."

Lauren drew back. "Wh . . . what are you saying?"

The pain in his eyes shattered her. "I'm saying I'm just like him." He slipped from her embrace and paced the floor, the wood creaking beneath his dress shoes. "It started in high school. Parties. Some kid hands you a beer, you chug it without even thinking. One turns into two, then three, and then drinking only at parties turns into drinking at home after school. A shot or two before the big game, just to calm your nerves."

Precious memories flickered in a new, horrifying light. "Were you drinking at Sunflower? When we were together?"

"Not after we met." He stopped and palmed the back of his neck. "Being with you made me realize who I wanted to be. But coming home, falling back into the old trap, getting a DUI, all that reminded me who I really was."

There it was. The long-sought why. After all the years of guessing, of assumptions, of thinking it had something to do with what they'd done together, or what he thought of her body, the truth was far more heart-breaking than she ever could've imagined. The weight on his shoulders far heavier than anyone could guess.

The question hovered on her lips, then burst forth. "Are you still—"

"*No*. After my DUI, after we broke up, I quit. Cold turkey. Haven't had a drop since."

She stepped toward him and threaded her fingers through the close-cropped hair at his temple. "Carter, that's been years. Surely after all this time you know you can beat it."

"But it's in me, Lauren." He pulled back, eyes dark and desperate. "It's part of my DNA. I can make all kinds of promises, tell you anything you want to hear, but in my heart of hearts, do I know for absolute certain I'll always have the strength to say no? Do I know beyond all doubt that it'll never come back? That I'll never treat you the way my dad treated my mom, treat our kids the way he treated us?" His hand balled into a white-knuckled fist. "Doing to you what he did to her—it would destroy me. But how can I know we won't end up just like them?"

"Because people can change, Carter." Tears clogged her throat. "Temptation might come, but that doesn't mean you have to give in."

He plucked an empty Cheetos bag off the coffee table. "You sure about that?"

Her stunned silence lasted a beat too long, and Carter's gaze fell to the floor. The bag fluttered down after it.

"We're too broken, Lauren." What began as a bitter laugh ended in a choked sob. "Both of us. We're too messed up. Drunk, sober, bingeing, not . . . as long as we've both got this kind of damage, I don't see how this works."

She exhaled with the gut-punch of his statement. He was right, though. As long as he remained unconvinced they could change, what chance did they have? No matter how good it was between them, what guaranteed their old demons wouldn't resurface to burn everything to the ground?

She loved him. So much it made her chest ache.

But all the baggage that came with him?

He'd been right all along.

It really was too much.

Lauren swallowed hard and looked up at him through stinging eyes. "I don't see how it works either."

Carter reached for her. Tucked a lock of hair behind her ear, the touch of his fingertips making her shiver. He attempted a smile, but it faded as the reality of what they'd just said, what they'd just done, what it meant, settled over them like a thick blanket.

Then he bent his head, and she met his lips without hesitation. His kiss held a lifetime of regret, of apology, of a yearning, heartrending ache for a way—any way at all—for things to be other than what they were. And Lauren poured it back in equal measure. Gripping his face between her hands, she memorized the feel of him, the taste, the way every movement of his lips careened through her body, setting her nerves alight and filling her heart to the point of pain. No matter who she found in the future, no matter whose lips claimed hers, she'd never come close to the way she felt when she kissed Carter Douglas.

Then the kiss changed. Regrets had passed, emotion spent. The golden hour was over, the sun had slipped away, and now . . . now it was goodbye.

Carter pulled back and gazed into her eyes, his rapid breaths tickling lips that cried out for more. More. Always more.

But with *more* came *too much*. And neither one of them could bear it.

She blinked, and loss dove down her cheek in a single scalding drop. Carter brushed it away with his thumb, his eyes so dark and depthless she could drown in them. Tears pooled in their inner corners, and one sneaked out to trickle down the side of his nose and finish the shattering of her heart. He pulled her in for a quick, fierce kiss, then slipped from her apartment without a word.

Lauren followed slowly, breathing deep the remnants of his cologne, and locked the door behind him. Leaned her forehead against its cool wooden surface. Gripped the knob, as though somehow able to absorb the remaining molecules of his presence. Maybe that, somehow, would be enough to last the rest of her life.

The pain had been inevitable. From the moment she'd spotted him in that makeup aisle, she knew she'd someday be watching him walk away.

At least this time she understood why.

Chapter Twenty-Nine

May 1955

ROSIE'S THIN BLOUSE was no match for the rough cottonwood bark pressing into her back, but she leaned against the big old tree anyway, toying with a fallen green leaf, listening to the burble of the creek. Shadows danced in warm late-afternoon sunshine, and red-winged blackbirds trilled in the reeds poking up from the creek's muddy banks.

Mother and Daddy had meant this return to the farm as a punishment. And for the first day or two, that was exactly what it had felt like. No phone. No friends. No Roosevelt High.

But no pretending either. No struggling to fit in to the increasingly ill-fitting molds of Rosie the Society Girl for her mother, Rosie the Carefree Cheerleader her school friends expected her to be, or Rosie the Rebel, as society's ridiculous disdain of mixed-race couples had forced her to become.

Here on the farm, she was just . . . Rosie. The girl who loved who she loved, regardless of what others thought. Who sat quietly in this little clearing by the creek, sunshine warming her right arm, the big white farmhouse a stately, reassuring presence to her left. It had always been her favorite place in the world, this farm. She always felt better here. Always at peace.

Always home.

It had been her home, once upon a time. When Daddy had gone off to fight the Germans, Mother had grudgingly moved back in with her folks, and some of Rosie's earliest memories included trotting alongside Grandpa Thomas as he cared for the horses or helping Grandma Louisa gather the eggs. There were endless spaces to roam. To pretend she was a fairy, flitting from flower to flower. To run and climb trees and explore the farmhouse's nooks and crannies. To her little-girl heart, there was no better place in the world to grow up. Nowhere she'd rather be.

But when the war ended and Daddy came home, Mother insisted they move back to the city. Back to civilization and culture. Back to a place where Rosie could learn to be a proper lady. And so the endless backyard shrank to a fenced-in patch of grass, the big white farmhouse to a brick two-story on Second Street. And the farm went from home to a place they visited only on holidays. A place where everything melted away and the outside world ceased to exist.

It sure had that effect now. Less than a week, but she might as well have flown to the moon with how little she'd heard from anyone in town. None of her friends, not even Viv. Not Gordon, thank the Lord. But not a word from Ephraim either. Not surprising, since he was probably in as much hot water as she was. How had his folks reacted? Had he been back to school yet? Was he—

"Hey there, Rosie girl."

Rosie gasped and whirled around. This had to be a dream. Or maybe she missed him so much her imagination had conjured that velvet voice. His brilliant smile lighting up the whole woods.

The smile stretched wider. "You look like you've seen a ghost."

"I can't believe you're . . . you're here, right?" She jumped up. "Is that really you?"

Ephraim opened his arms. "Come here and find out."

Rosie covered the distance between them in about two steps, and then she was squeezing him tight. Breathing him in. Spinning in dizzying circles, her feet nowhere near the ground. The past five days faded in a single heartbeat. Had she thought this place felt like home before? Now it was doubly so.

Ephraim was here, and her world was complete.

"How'd you get here?" Her imagination tripped over the possibilities. "Did Mother and Daddy see the light? Did they bring you here?"

"My pop drove me." Ephraim took her hand and led her back to where she'd been sitting. "He wasn't thrilled about it, but I had to see you. Had to tell you in person."

The joyful flutters in her stomach took on an apprehensive edge. "Tell me what?"

Ephraim sank onto a log in the clearing. "Word on the street is Gordon's family is threatening to press charges."

She stared at the fading bruise on his right cheek. "Wha—*Gordon's* family wants to press charges?"

He nodded. "For assault. I think it's just a scare tactic, but Mama says—"

"But he assaulted me! *He's* the one who—"

"I know."

"And you were just defending me!" Rosie's fists clenched at her sides. "He has no right to even . . ." Her words trailed off as frustration closed her throat and burned her eyes.

"Well, I did get the better of him, I think," Ephraim replied. "He's big and all, but I'm pretty quick."

Laughing through her tears, Rosie dropped onto the log beside him. How could he be so calm? So steady in the midst of such a storm? He was right, of course. He was pretty quick. Smart as a whip too.

Optimism took the edge off her anger. "Surely a judge will see that, if it gets that far," she said. "The truth will come out."

Ephraim plucked a blade of tall prairie grass. "I'm not so sure about that, Rosie girl."

"But you're in the right."

"And I'm up against a white boy whose folks have money and connections." He turned, dappled shadows dancing across deep-brown skin. "Most times that doesn't work out in our favor."

"I'll testify, then. I'll do whatever it takes, *say* whatever it takes, to make them see the truth." Rosie gripped his shoulder. "I'll fight for you, Ephraim. The way you did for me."

She expected a quick response. A dazzling grin. But he simply stared at the blade of grass, twirling it round and round. "Much obliged, Rosie girl. But there's no need for you to go through that."

Why did his voice sound so strange? Why did it feel like clouds had blotted out the sun?

"I'm going away for a while."

His words thudded into her midsection. "What? Going away? Where?"

"Philadelphia."

"Phila . . ." Her lips couldn't form the word. She bent forward, probing his gaze. "Why?"

"My cousin moved there a couple years back. Got a job doing dishes at a hotel. He says there's lots of turnover, so they can probably take me on as soon as I get up there."

"Dishes?" Rosie gaped. The blade of grass whirled faster between Ephraim's lean, limber fingers. Those fingers, those hands—they could play anything on a piano. Trip up and down the keyboard, arpeggios rippling like the creek in front of them. Those hands were the vehicle through which his music flowed, the surest way to a glimpse of his beautiful soul. To think of them wrinkled in hot suds for hours on end, skin cracked and bleeding from harsh detergent—

"No." Her vehemence shattered the wrenching image. "Your hands—you can't. What about your music?"

"Hotels have pianos." A smile sprang to his lips, but the skin beneath his eyes didn't crease as it usually did. "I'll still make music. I can't *not* make music. And the hotel gig won't be forever. Just until I can find something better."

Rosie leaped to her feet. "How can you let Gordon McIntyre do this to you? To *us*? He's done enough."

"It's not just about Gordon." Round and round, the blade of grass twirled. "Truth be told, Mama's been talking about Philly for months. Her sister—my auntie—moved there four years ago, and she says it's better there. She wants us all to come. We came here because Daddy could make more at the airplane plant. Save enough to get us there faster."

Ephraim. Leaving. He'd never planned to stay.

"And you're telling me this *now*?"

"There's not enough money for all of us to go yet. And I thought in the time it'd take to save up that much, I could talk her out of it. Let me stay here, where I'm happy." He tossed the grass aside. "But now, with all this, she won't hear a word of it." Pain-filled eyes met hers. "They already bought my ticket."

Ephraim. Leaving. Ephraim . . . no. Her world was spiraling out of control, and she grabbed for the only thing she could reach. Clutched it tight. "I'm coming with you."

Dark brows shot up. "What?"

"If you're so dead set on going to Philadelphia, Ephraim James, then . . . then I'm coming with you." Her heart hammered at the base of her throat. A dizzying whirl started in the pit of her stomach.

He stood, wide-eyed. "Rosie girl, no. That's . . . I can't ask you to do that."

She clasped his hands in hers. Precious hands. Beautiful hands. Hands that would steady her.

"You're not asking me." Her voice quavered. "I'm telling you how it's going to be. I'm coming to Philadelphia with you. We'll get married, and we'll make beautiful brown babies, and we'll have a life together, just like we want."

He looked down at their hands. "I don't know if Philly'll be any friendlier to a couple like us than Wichita is."

"Even if it isn't, I don't care." She did care. It was terrifying. But the idea of never seeing him again was worse.

She squared her shoulders. "I don't know what the future looks like, but I don't want one without you in it. So I'm coming with you. Deal?"

Ephraim blew out a breath . . . and then that smile. The smile she'd do anything for.

"Deal."

He bent his head, and their lips met. Oh, she loved him. The feeling of his mouth on hers, the strength of his arms around her, the clean scent of his soap, and the warm smoothness of his skin beneath her hand. She clung to him. His love was the only thing in her world that made sense. So that would be enough to carry them through whatever their future held.

Wouldn't it?

His kisses traveled up her cheekbone toward her temple. "Best pack your bags," came the husky whisper against her skin. "The train leaves Friday night."

Her mouth fell open, and she pulled back. "What? Friday? *This* Friday?"

"This Friday." Was it her imagination, or was there a trace of fear in his eyes?

She swallowed the anxious lump in her throat and forced a brave smile. "Okay, then. The future starts Friday."

Friday.

This Friday.

Philadelphia.

What in the world had she done?

CHAPTER THIRTY

LAUREN'S SHARP KNOCKS to the apartment door that evening were soon met by the click of the lock and Garrett's puzzled-looking face through the crack in the doorway.

"Lauren." He slid the chain latch and opened the door. "How are you? Are you feeling better?"

Avoiding eye contact, she brushed past him on her way to the kitchen, the basket of food she'd brought weighing heavy on her forearm. "If you're asking if I've stayed away from the potato chips, yep. I'm right as rain." She plopped the basket onto Garrett's minuscule kitchen counter, the thud mingling with the play-by-play of some baseball game on TV. "Sloane's not here, is she?"

"No. She's working late, setting up the new exhibit." Garrett's frown came through in his voice. "Did I . . . miss something? Had we planned for you to come over?"

Lauren unloaded a freshly purchased package of salmon fillets and stuffed it into Garrett's refrigerator. "Nope. Just thought dinner might be a nice surprise."

"Far be it from me to turn down a free meal." The baseball chatter silenced, and one of Garrett's counter stools creaked. "What are we having?"

She continued unloading ingredients, setting each on the counter with a satisfying smack. "A mixed green salad for starters, topped with sliced almonds, dried cranberries, and my homemade honey-mustard vinaigrette. For the main course, seared salmon in a mustard glaze, served alongside mustard-spiced roasted potatoes, covered in extra mustard sauce. With more mustard for dipping."

"You, uh . . . you know I hate mustard, right?"

"Mm-hm." With a perversely bright smile, Lauren removed the brand-new jar of gourmet European mustard she'd purchased on the way over.

"Ah. So you're mad."

"Brilliant deduction, Sherlock." Resisting the urge to fling the jar at her brother, she set it down and grabbed the head of romaine. "I cannot *believe* you told Carter about my bulimia."

She yanked a knife from the block on the counter, and Garrett raised his hands in self-defense. "He needed to know, Lauren. He needed to know what this hot-and-cold nonsense was doing to you."

"But he needed to hear it from me, especially since I'm the only one who knows the whole reason why I binged. I can take care of myself, *Garrett*." She vented her anger on the defenseless green leaves.

"Pizza and Oreos and God alone knows what else last night. I'm not so sure."

Her chopping intensified, and the lettuce disintegrated beneath her vigorous knife strokes.

"Well, Carter and I broke up a couple hours ago. That should make you happy." She scraped the lettuce from the cutting board into a wooden salad bowl and slammed the knife to the counter.

"I'm sorry to hear that."

"No you're not." She unwrapped a head of Belgian endive from its nest of paper towels. "You got exactly what you wanted."

"You're hurting. That's not what I wanted. It never is. But I can't watch you go down that road again. Seeing you by that toilet, seeing how broken you were, I just . . . snapped, I guess."

She picked up the knife and slid it through the endive, albeit with somewhat less aggression. "I didn't mean to scare you. I thought I was past this."

"What *is* it about Carter?" Blue eyes peered deep. "I've watched you, y'know, since you broke up the first time. And once you got well, you never relapsed. Even when Mom died, you held it together. I don't think you binged once."

Lauren shook her head. He was right. She'd kept it in check.

"Same thing when Dad moved to Florida. And when Grandma got sick, and Grandpa died, and you came down here . . ." Garrett shook his head in amazement. "I thought it was stress, but you've been through so much, yet you've stayed on the right side of the line."

Careful intake. Healthy ingredients. Reading labels. Perhaps it was the right side of the line. Or maybe the wrong side of a different line. Who knew anymore?

"And boyfriends. There've been a couple others since Carter, but you never relapsed with them, either."

"That's probably because Carter's the only one I . . ." She trailed off, cheeks warm, at the memory of that long-ago night. Fervent, whispered words of promise that turned out to be nothing but fantasy. Words, kisses, that caused her to shed her standards as fast as she'd cast aside her clothing.

Lauren sliced through the rest of the endive, along with her memories. "It doesn't matter. I thought that was the reason, but it wasn't."

"You thought what was the reason?"

"Carter and I . . . went further that summer than we should have. Did things we shouldn't have done." Slice, slice, slice. "So when he broke up with me as soon as we got home, I thought it was because he'd seen me— *all* of me—and didn't like what he saw."

She expected judgment from Garrett, but instead received only a slow nod and the pursed-lip look that meant the wheels were turning in his ever-active, always-logical mind. "Did he say something to that effect?"

"No, and it was all in my head. I know that now." Her knife scraped, and the endive tumbled into the bowl. "He really did have some pretty heavy issues going on—issues that have cropped up again, and that I'll keep in confidence, because that's what you're *supposed* to do with people's secrets."

Garrett gave a sheepish grin. "Yeah, I deserved that."

"Anyway, bottom line, he thinks we're both screwed up beyond repair. And after last night, I'm not so sure he's wrong. His issues, my issues, when you put them together, it's . . ."

"Kablooie?"

"Pretty much." She sawed into a head of brilliant purple radicchio. "Serves us right, I suppose."

"What's that supposed to mean?"

Heat crept into her cheeks. "I gotta spell it out for you, Mr. I'm-

Planning-a-Wedding? Carter and I had sex. Just the one time, way back when. But still, I gave him something I'll never get back. Something I'd promised God I'd save for the man I married."

"That's nothing God can't forgive, Lo," Garrett said quietly.

"Oh, sure, he forgives." Tears blurred the radicchio on the cutting board. "But now I'm just a treasure chest missing half its gold. A rose with its petals pulled off. Insert your favorite damaged-goods metaphor here."

"Yeah, I was there for all those youth-group guilt trips too." Garrett grabbed the salt shaker and turned it over in his hands. "Never really bought it, though. I mean, if Jesus's death truly covers all our sins, if he could wipe the slate clean for people like Peter who denied knowing him, or Paul, who straight-up murdered Christians, and use those two guys to build his church, then I think it seems pretty inconsistent for him to give up on someone who loves him and wants nothing more than to follow him, all because of a momentary loss of control."

Control.

Her whole world had spun out of control that summer. Life had become a whirlwind of Mom's chemo sessions and oncologist visits and *if* and *maybe* and *wait and see*. Things she'd always counted on—having her mother at her college graduation, at her wedding, beaming down at her grandbabies—suddenly were anything but certain.

And Lauren had lost control with Carter that night. One kiss, one look, and she was gone.

Food was the one area where she could jerk back the reins. Resume control over her body. Her life.

Wait a minute.

God wasn't the one punishing her for her mistake with Carter.

She was.

"So—not that you asked—I don't think anyone's ever truly screwed up beyond repair."

Garrett's gentle voice broke into her thoughts, and she slowly resumed her disassembly of the radicchio. "No one?"

"No one who's willing to change, anyway. Willing to surrender to someone who can make everything new again." A grin tugged the corners of his mouth. "It's kinda like the farmhouse, y'know? I thought that thing was a lost cause. Too many issues, too many repairs to be practical."

"I remember." Months of back-and-forth with her profit-and-loss, black-and-white big brother had nearly doomed the family's century-old farmhouse to a date with the wrecking ball.

"But then someone came along who loved it enough to redeem it, fix it up, and make it something new, all while honoring the builder's original intention." Garrett's eyes shone. "I think God does something like that with us. We've all got our own version of peeling paint and rickety porches, but God fixes those up and weaves them into his perfect plan. The only way we're screwed up beyond repair is if we don't trust him to do that."

Something shifted inside Lauren at his words. She might not be binge-ing and purging anymore, but had she truly trusted God to heal her? Or had she merely exchanged one method of grasping at control for another? She loved feeling healthy and taking care of her body. But she needed to move food off the throne and let Jesus resume his rightful place.

Jesus, the one who forgave. Who'd restored Peter. Who'd turned Paul's life completely around. Who'd used them, and countless more just like them, to spread his message of love and redemption.

He loved and forgave Lauren every bit as much.

He'd just been waiting for her to realize it.

Garrett leaned his elbows on the counter. "Hey, do with this information what you will, but your old therapist?"

Lauren blinked stinging eyes. "Lisette?"

"Unless there's another therapist named Lisette St. Pierre-Pakpreo, it looks like she's moved her practice to Wichita. Not too far from my office, in fact."

Smiling, Lauren scraped her knife on the side of the bowl and set it down. Lisette's combination of tender loving care and no-holds-barred honesty had seen Lauren through the worst of her bulimia. Going for a few sessions now would feel like curling up on a comfy couch with an old friend. "Guess I probably better give her a call."

"Couldn't hurt."

Lauren dried her hands on a nearby dish towel. "I hate that you're always right."

"I'm not always right, believe me." Garrett stood and made his way into the kitchen. "I overstepped with Carter. I had no right to tell him about your eating disorder. You clearly wanted to keep it private, and I should have respected that."

Lauren slid an arm around her brother's waist. "Thank you. I should've told him earlier, though. For me, if nothing else."

He pulled her close. "Are you okay?"

"Not yet. But I will be."

"Yes, you will." He stepped back to lean against the counter. "And for what it's worth, all that stuff I said about people not being beyond repair? That applies to Carter too. Whatever his damage."

She rolled her lower lip between her teeth and turned away, the mention of his name pricking her heart with fresh pain. "Too bad I couldn't convince him of that."

"Maybe you can't. But I bet I know someone who can." Garrett's gaze flicked skyward.

Blinking rapidly, Lauren launched a heartfelt, wordless missive heavenward. That someone, someday, would speak truth into Carter's life the way Garrett had for her. It was too late for them, that much was clear. But it wasn't too late for *him*. As long as he lived and breathed, it was never too late.

Feeling as though a massive weight had lifted from her shoulders, Lauren glanced around the kitchen at the scattered ingredients and fought the urge to giggle at the jar of gourmet mustard she'd planned to force-feed her brother.

"Y'know?" She glanced up. "I'm suddenly not in a mustardy, salmon-y kind of mood."

Grinning, Garrett pantomimed wiping his brow. "*Thank* you."

She gave him a playful shove and reached for the salad bowl. "How about I stick all this in the fridge and we'll go grab some tacos instead?"

"Tacos sound amazing." Garrett grabbed his keys from the bowl on the counter. "You sure they're on your Approved Food List?"

Lauren slid the basket into her brother's fridge. "I have a feeling there might be a few more foods on that list from now on."

He gripped her shoulder, warm and fierce. "That's the best thing I've heard all day."

Was he just talking about the tacos? Or did the richness of his tone indicate a deeper meaning?

Didn't matter.

Both were a marked improvement over her original plan.

CHAPTER THIRTY-ONE

THE SOUND SYSTEM warbled with one of those interchangeable female country-slash-pop singers, a curious soundtrack to the late-season baseball game flickering on a muted TV behind the bar. Carter glanced up long enough to watch a Red Sox player launch a homer off a hapless Royals reliever, then turned his attention back to the glass in front of him.

Jack Daniels. Neat and tidy.

He hadn't had any yet.

Yet being the operative word.

He'd been here awhile. An hour at least. Just sitting. Staring at the crystal Collins glass filled with amber liquid. Looked like a little more than the usual pour, though maybe the bartender was in a generous mood. Or maybe she just felt sorry for him. Given the sympathetic tilt of her head when he'd slid onto the stool, the quirk of her penciled brow when he'd mumbled his order, it was probably the latter.

Carter picked up the glass and inhaled the pungent aroma. His eyes snapped shut. Just one whiff and a lifetime of memories tumbled through him. His father's shouts. His mother's tears. The stinging smack of a hand across his mouth. Frustration. Humiliation. Disappointment. Most of his life, this simple liquid had made him feel a thousand kinds of bad.

But beneath all that lingered the agonizing truth. This simple liquid had made him feel a thousand kinds of good too.

Throw back two or three of these and he'd burn his heartbreak into oblivion. A couple more and he'd forget he ever even knew a girl named Lauren Anderson. For a blissful hour or two, he could escape the searing pain of her absence. The gaping hole through which his life's blood seeped, the hole he'd never managed to fill with anyone or anything else.

Right now, he wanted that escape. So badly his teeth ached.

But the very fact that he wanted it meant he'd been right to break it off with her. She deserved someone who wouldn't hurt her every time he turned around. Someone who didn't have a monster lurking inside him. Someone from a functional family with a healthy outlook on life.

Someone who wasn't a disaster waiting to happen.

He picked up the glass and swirled it. Blew out a breath.

Time to get on with it.

"To-go order for Ford."

Carter jumped at the words, and a few drops of the still-untouched drink sloshed out onto his thumb. He knew that voice. How could he not? That steady, soothing baritone delivered the weather forecast every weeknight at five, six, and ten. And it was 7:12. The heart of Jim Ford's dinner break.

Sure enough, there he stood. The venerable chief—Carter's coworker, his mentor, his friend—stood at the corner of the bar, the baseball game reflecting off his glasses. The bartender glanced at her computer screen, then bustled toward the kitchen, and Jim turned his attention to his phone.

Carter averted his gaze. Where were the restrooms? Maybe he could sneak off to the men's room and hide there until Jim left. Couldn't be too long, right?

No dice. Jim stood directly below the thrumming neon arrow pointing toward that particular means of escape.

Okay. No worries. He could fling some money on the bar and try to slip out unnoticed. Well, probably not unnoticed, but possibly unrecognized. He'd have to walk past Jim to do that too, though. Did Pete's Bar and Grill have a back exit? Funny, he'd never needed to know before.

But he'd also never been in a situation like this, where the person he admired most, the person whose respect he valued above pretty much everything else, was about to come face-to-face with the version of himself Carter tried hardest to keep hidden.

Then Jim tucked his phone into his pocket and sat down two stools away. Carter's heart sank. No hope for escape now. Seemed like his best option was to shrink in on himself. Maybe if he avoided eye contact, kept his shoulders hunched, maybe, just maybe, Jim wouldn't—

"Can't remember seeing you here before."

Crap.

Carter sighed and offered a sheepish smile. "I could say the same about you."

"It's not one of my usual go-tos. But they do have a mighty tasty Philly cheesesteak." One broad shoulder lifted. "For some reason tonight I had a hankering."

"Gotcha." Carter turned his attention back to the glass in front of him. Maybe if he acted casual enough, Jim wouldn't question it. After all, lots of people drank and didn't have a problem.

Might help if he actually took a sip.

Jim cleared his throat. When Carter glanced up, the older man nodded toward the very glass Carter had prayed he wouldn't notice.

"I'm gonna go out on a limb and guess this has something to do with a girl."

Carter chuckled. "You're not Wichita's most accurate forecaster for nothing."

"I've learned a thing or two reading the skies. Sometimes it carries over."

At that, something broke inside Carter, and words tumbled out. So many words. Words detailing his childhood. His dad. Lauren thirteen years ago. Lauren now.

"So your father's an alcoholic, and you're a mess, and you're sabotaging things with the girl you love because of it." Jim's kind brown eyes slid to the drink on the bar before him. "And maybe I'm wrong here, but given where you are, and what's in that glass, it's not just your dad who struggles. Am I close?"

Carter gave a quiet chuckle—barely even a sound, just a quick puff of breath—then stared into the glass. What he wouldn't give to shrink down, hop into that glass, and disappear.

"Nailed it, my friend," he said.

"How long?"

"Started drinking in high school. Stopped after I got a DUI."

"Meetings?"

"Nah. Just plain cold turkey."

"Impressive."

Carter picked up the drink. "Don't know if I'd call it that. Because I've been sober for thirteen years. I know what drinking this will do to me. I know what it'll make me become. But right now I'd like nothing more than to toss it back and order a couple more."

"Mmm." Jim shifted on the stool. When Carter finally dared to glance up, his mentor was staring at the silent television. The Sox had added two more runs. Looked like the Royals were digging themselves a hole they couldn't climb out of.

He could relate.

The silence between them stretched. Not unusual for Jim Ford—the man was known for economizing in everything, speech included. Finally, over the hum of conversation and the guitar riff of a song Carter remembered from high school but couldn't identify, Jim cleared his throat.

"Seems to me if you really wanted to drink that, you would've done it by now."

"Huh." Carter pursed his lips and set the glass down. "You're probably right."

"I usually am."

"So let's say I win this round. I get up right now and walk away. There'll always be another round. Another fight." Carter shook his head. "How do I know I'll always be strong enough to win?"

"You won't."

The reply was quick. Firm. Two syllables that thudded into Carter's gut and confirmed everything he'd ever believed.

He wasn't strong enough. He couldn't beat it.

He'd been right to set Lauren free.

"So thank God you don't have to fight it alone."

Carter shook his head. "I don't know if meetings are my thing, Jim."

"Meetings aren't a bad idea, but I'm not talking about those." Jim's words were quiet, but strong as steel. "I'm talking about Jesus. Second Corinthians says that if anyone is in Christ, he's a new creation."

A new creation. Carter had seen that verse before. And it was Scripture, so it had to be true.

So why did Carter feel like the same old creation he'd always been?

"That's not to say temptation doesn't happen." Jim tapped lightly on the bar. "It does. Or that you won't struggle. You might. But for children of God, addiction doesn't call the shots anymore. When you're tempted, he promises to always give you a way out. Sometimes it's hard to see. But it's there."

A way out.

Carter had been seconds away from downing this drink when Jim walked in. To a place he rarely visited, to order a sandwich he craved only occasionally.

Maybe that cheesesteak, then, was more than just a quick dinner.

Jim's gaze seemed to bore holes straight to Carter's soul. "You're not your dad, Carter. You're not your damage or his mistakes—or *your* mistakes. You're a redeemed son of a loving Father. He has a plan for you, one you're not powerful enough to screw up. But you're not powerful enough to fight booze on your own either. Good news is, God's fighting alongside you. Addiction's a formidable foe, I'll grant you. But God is even more formidable."

Those words were the most he'd ever heard Jim string together off air. And together, they sparked hope. Not the tentative, sinking-sand hope he'd manufactured every time his father had sworn this time was different, this time he'd keep it together, this time he was quitting for real. This hope was different. Grounded in granite.

Built on a completely different source.

"Here you go." The raven-haired bartender slid a white plastic bag in front of Jim, who nodded his thanks.

"And don't be so quick to dismiss the idea of meetings." Jim scrawled his signature across the credit card slip and clicked the pen closed. "Wouldn't be where I am today without them."

Carter turned. Blinked. Stared. *What?*

"Got my thirty-year sobriety chip this past July. Wasn't easy, of course. Couldn't have done it without that group and God's grace." Eyes twinkling, Jim stood and gave Carter a friendly pat on the shoulder. "If I can do it, you can too. Seems like I heard that on TV somewhere."

With a wink, Jim grabbed his dinner and sauntered toward the door, whistling a lighthearted tune.

Jim Ford. His mentor. His friend. The person he admired most. He'd fought the same demons. Grappled with the same monster. And he'd overcome it. Thirty years' sobriety. He'd licked it, with God's help.

So maybe . . . you'd help me, too?

"Can I get you anything else?" The bartender paused before him, polishing a beer glass with a white towel.

Carter had almost forgotten about the glass of Jack in front of him. Strangely enough, he didn't want it anymore. Didn't crave the burn, the blitz, the blissful oblivion.

But it didn't bring about that gut-level visceral revulsion either.

For the first time ever, that liquid in a glass was just that. Liquid.

Liquid that no longer held the power over him it once had.

"Y'know what?" He rose from the stool and fished out his wallet. "I think I'm good." He placed a twenty on the bar, told the bartender to keep the change, and headed out into the crisp autumn night, his heart light, his mind clear.

Dad wasn't entirely wrong. Those moments would likely come. Moments of weakness. Being beaten down. Having nothing left. Wanting a drink worse than anything.

Carter had just had one of those moments, but God had come through. He'd provided a friendly face. A sympathetic ear.

An escape route.

One Carter prayed he'd always have eyes to see and courage to run toward.

CHAPTER THIRTY-TWO

May 1955

OF ALL THE seasons and months on the farm, Rosie loved May best.

It was the cottonwoods that did it. The big trees by the creek erupted into full, shimmering leaf, and fluffy white seed pods danced on warm breezes to create a springtime snow. Her bedroom window held the perfect view—trees parted just enough to provide a glimpse of the creek's glimmering gray-brown waters.

She paused, the freshly folded poodle skirt halfway into her suitcase. She was really going to miss this view.

A knock came to her door, and she turned. Grandma, probably. She stuffed the skirt into the suitcase, slid it under the bed, and turned. "Come in." Hopefully, Grandma's slight hearing loss meant the waver in Rosie's voice would go undetected.

But instead of a wrinkled face and a head of cottony fluff, the face peering back at her was young, framed with vibrant red locks.

"Vivian!" On wobbly legs, Rosie crossed the room and swallowed her best friend in a fierce hug. "How did you get here? What are you doing here?" Last time she'd seen Viv, a tiara had sparkled on her friend's head, and she'd swept across the dance floor, while Rosie had scurried off to the choir room, where . . .

"Daddy drove me." Viv slipped off her gloves. "Uncle Ern lives up this way, and Daddy said he was due for a visit."

Rosie blinked, still trying to absorb the utter shock of her best friend from the city standing in the bedroom of her country childhood. "How did you know I was here?"

"My mother ran into yours at Allen's."

Was it Rosie's imagination, or did Viv stiffen a little?

Rosie ran a finger over the lace curtain framing the window. "Did she tell you what happened?"

"No, just that there was—how did she put it?—a situation from which it was best for Rosemary to be removed."

Viv's rounded tones, the exaggerated elimination of rural twang, was a perfect impression of Rosie's mother, and Rosie giggled.

"Anyhow, they handed out yearbooks at school today, and your mother said I could bring you yours." Vivian ducked out of the room for a moment and retrieved a red hardcover book from the small table in the hall. *Roosevelt High School, 1954–1955*, black letters on the front declared.

Rosie cracked open the book, a fresh-ink smell wafting from pristine white pages. Her final year of high school, encapsulated in a sea of photographs. She paused on one of herself on top of the pyramid at a football game, pom-poms high, lipsticked mouth stretched in a permanent dimpled grin.

She remembered that night. The crisp breeze, the last-second touchdown that sent the crowd into a frenzy. Basking in the bliss of that moment, she'd thought that was as good as life got.

But that girl didn't know who she was. What she wanted. She didn't know the exhilarating, yet terrifying strain of pushing against the constraints imposed on her by an image-obsessed mother.

And that girl didn't know what it was to truly love. To be loved. And to have that love challenged, scorned, and fought against from every direction.

The perky blonde atop the pyramid . . . Rosie didn't even know her anymore.

She flipped through the rest of the book with a sense of curious detachment, pausing when she reached the autograph pages in the back. Viv must've collected signatures for her, because the formerly blank white pages were covered with the loopy scrawls of fellow cheerleaders, choir members, classmates, and—

R + J Forever

Rosie's breath caught. There was no signature. No name. But she didn't need one. She'd know that handwriting anywhere. She still had it, scribbled across the homecoming royalty ballot she'd snatched from her bedroom that horrible night.

R stood for Rosie, of course. But why *J*? Had he used his last name and not his first to avoid suspicion? Or—

Oh.

R wasn't her. It was *him*. Romeo.

And J. Juliet.

Hot tears blurred the image at the memory of that day in English, when Shakespeare's timeless words of adoration had come to life in a sweet tenor, when shining brown eyes had made the world stop spinning, when—

"So it's true."

Rosie glanced up. "What's true?" A tear threatened. She blinked it away.

"You're in love with that colored boy." Her friend's expression held an odd mix of judgment, confusion, and sympathy.

She snapped the yearbook closed. "His name is Ephraim."

"Rumors were flying." Viv plopped onto the quilted bedspread. "Everyone's asking me questions about you and him, you and Gordon—"

"Whatever you've heard about Gordon and me is a lie." The words spilled out with far more anger than she intended, and Viv blinked at her with a wounded expression.

"Then maybe you could tell me the truth."

Rosie stopped. She hadn't told the truth. Not about Gordon. The administration, her parents . . . nobody would believe her. And even if they did, they'd probably take Gordon's side.

But if anyone would believe her, if anyone would understand, it'd be Viv.

So Rosie sank onto the bed beside her friend, and for the first time since October, she told the truth. Ephraim. Gordon. All of it. And Vivian's eyes widened. Her jaw dropped. Silent tears spilled. She called Gordon McIntyre something foul and vowed never to speak to him again, "not ever, Rosie. Never *ever*."

The last of the words ran out, leaving Rosie both emptied and filled. And Viv's face was a parade of expressions, one after the other.

"I knew you'd been keeping something from me." Viv picked at a loose cuticle. "You've been off in outer space lately. And then Ephraim came up to me in English today and asked me for your yearbook."

Even after all this, just the mention of his name made her heart leap.

"He only had it for a second, and he tried to hide what he wrote, but I saw it anyway." Vivian blinked up, hurt in her eyes. "I didn't want to believe it, but when I saw your face just now, I—why wouldn't you tell me?"

Rosie's hands knotted in her lap. "Because I didn't think you'd understand."

"You're right. I don't."

"You're telling me if Bobby Duvall were exactly the same person, but his skin was brown, you wouldn't have looked twice?"

"Probably not."

"Then you'd be the poorer for it."

Viv flung a hand in the air. "Rosie, it's not that simple. As much as I love Bobby, if he cost me my family, my future—I mean, what about college? What about becoming a teacher? What about your future?"

"I already have a future, Viv." In response to her friend's questioning look, she squared her shoulders. "Ephraim and I, we're going to Philadelphia."

"Philadelphia? Like for a trip? Or—" Vivian gasped and jumped up. "Oh. No. No, Rosie. No. You can't."

Rosie stood and faced her friend. "His folks want him out of town. Away from Gordon—and me. His cousin already lives up there and says he can get him a job."

Viv's eyes narrowed. "What kind of job?"

"Washing dishes at a hotel."

"Washing *dishes*?" Viv's hand flew to her cheek. "You're giving up everything to run away with Ephraim, and he's going to support you by washing dishes?"

"He says it'll just be temporary."

"And what about you? What will you do? What kind of neighborhood will you live in? What kind of church will you go to? And . . . and . . . what if you have kids?"

Rosie rolled her eyes. "You sound like my mother."

"I'm just—what about our dream, Rosie? What about *your* dream?

Kansas State Teacher's College, remember? We teach for a few years, then marry handsome fellas and move in next door to each other. Don't you remember?"

Of course she did. Standing at the front of the classroom. Living next door to Viv. The kids playing in the yard. The white picket fence. It was a beautiful dream. An easy one. A peaceful one.

But that dream was dead. She'd unknowingly signed its death warrant the moment she'd looked into Ephraim's eyes.

Its loss lodged inexplicably in her throat. "I have a different dream now, Viv."

"But you can't just—Rosie, the minute I met you, you told me you wanted to be a teacher."

"Then I'll teach in Philadelphia. I'm sure children there need to learn to read just as much as the ones here do."

"You'd still have to go to college for that." Viv's voice was quiet, but the words still hit their mark. "And I highly doubt your parents will pay for your schooling if you run away with Ephraim."

Rosie pressed her lips together. No. Of course not. Her parents would likely never speak to her again. Not that she wanted them to, with their horrible attitudes and their twisted Scripture and their—

"Can Ephraim put you through school, Rosie? Can he pay for college washing dishes?"

All right. So she'd have to give up college. And teaching. But she probably only would've been in the classroom for a year or two anyway before she started having babies, so would it truly be that big of a sacrifice?

Probably not.

So why did it feel like one?

Rosie lifted her chin. "I don't know," she said with a bravery she didn't feel. "But we're in love. We'll find a way."

"But . . . but this is your home. How can you just *leave*?"

Hot tears blurred the delicate lace curtains. The view of the creek. After tomorrow, it would all be but a memory.

"And how could I say goodbye to someone who holds half my heart?" She wiped away the tear with shaking fingertips. "Ephraim came to see me yesterday to tell me he was leaving, and I couldn't—I can't—let that be the last time I ever see his face. I can't—what if it were Bobby, Viv? What if Bobby were moving a thousand miles away? What if he came to say good-bye to you?"

"I don't know." Vivian crossed to the window, her pale, freckled hand pushing back the delicate curtain, and stared in silence.

Only a few feet separated them, but it may as well be the Grand Canyon, with Vivian standing on the side of the girl Rosie had been, and Ephraim standing on the side of the woman she'd become. They'd been best friends since eighth grade, she and Viv, but now that closeness stretched to the breaking point. Things would never be the same between them.

Between her and anyone.

Rosie hadn't even left yet, and already her decision was building a wall, brick by brick, between herself and the life she'd known. Yes to Ephraim meant a heavy, resounding, final *no* to everything she'd ever known.

Even her best friend.

"When do you leave?" Vivian's voice sounded thick.

"Tomorrow."

"Are you taking the train?"

"Yes."

"How will you get to the station?"

Rosie swallowed hard. "I don't know yet."

"Then we'll drive you." Vivian turned from the window, lips set in a straight line. "Bobby has a car, and his parents won't blink if we're gone all evening. Mine won't either, for that matter."

Fresh tears flooded Rosie's eyes. "You'd do that? For me?"

"I don't understand what you're doing, Rosie. I think it's a horrible mistake. But you're my best friend. And if you're really doing this, if you're really running away with Ephraim, if this is really what you want your future to be . . ." Vivian's words wobbled. "Then I can't let today be the last time I ever see your face."

How, *how* could one person's heart contain so many feelings? They boiled up and spilled over, like a pot left on the stove too long. Rosie collapsed under their weight, folding in on herself, all the *I'm sorry* and *I'll miss you* and *I love him* and *but I don't want to leave home* spilling out in silent sobs.

In a heartbeat, Viv was there, folding her in an embrace, and Rosie cried all those feelings out onto her best friend's shoulder.

Staying here, saying goodbye to Ephraim, would rip her heart in two.

But she hadn't banked on how much saying goodbye to Viv, to *home*, would do the same.

CHAPTER THIRTY-THREE

FIVE-DAY-OLD LIAM SQUINTED up at Carter from his nest of blankets that cloudy late-October day, tiny nose wrinkled, deep-blue eyes filled with questions.

"Hey, little guy." Carter adjusted his grip on his newborn nephew and bent to kiss the unimaginably small forehead. "I'm your uncle Carter."

Little Liam pursed his lips, and his eyes drifted closed.

Carter ran a hand over the still-squashed-looking head covered with wisps of reddish-brown fluff. The baby's coloring was Brad's, but even at less than a week, the tiny dude was clearly a Douglas.

With a twinge in his heart, he gave Liam another kiss, then gently handed him back to Cass. What would his and Lauren's kids have looked like? Would they have his tawny skin, but Lauren's cleft chin and delicate nose? Or would the baby have had her fair, freckled complexion, but his features? He'd have preferred the former—no reason to saddle an innocent kid with his mug—but at this moment, he'd give anything for a future with Lauren to be a possibility.

But it wasn't. Though he'd attended a few meetings with Jim, started through his steps, and had every reason to believe God would grant him victory over the bottle, he'd broken Lauren's heart twice now. Even if she were willing to go another round, he wasn't. He couldn't risk hurting her. Not again.

Cass walked toward the kitchen, cooing softly to Liam, and Dad shuffled in, heading for his favorite chair. The one in the corner where he'd hidden the beer can Carter had found over the summer. Nothing back there now—Carter had checked when he got here—but his father had only been out of the hospital for a month.

Carter squelched his bitterness and offered a smile. "How you feelin', Dad?"

"Better every day." Rick Douglas sank heavily into the chair.

"Can I get you anything? Water? A snack?"

"Nothing right now. Thank you."

Carter sat on the sofa and stared blankly at the Broncos game on TV. Mutual distrust clouded the atmosphere. His father doubtless expected judgment. Why wouldn't he?

And Carter expected to be let down again.

God, grant me the serenity to accept the things I cannot change, the courage to change the things I can, and the wisdom to know the difference.

He couldn't change his father. Time to accept that.

But he could change how he'd always responded.

And that could start with an apology.

"Dad." He reached for the remote and lowered the volume on the TV. "I need to apologize for last time. The things I said, the way I said them. I was angry, and I was scared to death I'd lose you. But that doesn't excuse it."

His father waved a hand, gaze still locked on the game. "Don't worry about it, son. It's no big deal."

"It is a big deal, Dad. You're my father. You deserve more respect than I gave you."

At that, his father turned and gave a slight nod. "Thank you, Carter."

Carter cleared his throat. "Y'know, Dad, you were right before. That moment you talked about, that moment of weakness, of being tired and beaten down . . . it happened to me."

"Sorry to hear that." An apology, sure, but it was impossible to miss that hint of *I told you so.*

"I ordered a drink, and I sat there for an hour and almost downed it. But I didn't. God gave me a way out, and he gave me the grace to see it."

His father made a rumbling noise deep in his throat. "Good for you. What's this make, then? Thirteen years sober? Thirteen years better than—"

"*No*, Dad." Carter balled his fist. "I need you to hear what I'm saying, not what you think I'm saying or what I've said before. I'm not beating alcohol because I'm strong, or because I have willpower, or anything that has anything to do with me. It's because of Jesus, Dad. It's all him."

His father's brows arched, and Carter didn't blame him. He couldn't recall ever talking with his dad about faith, other than *when is Mass* and *do we really have to go?*

Carter straightened. "It says in the book of Philippians that we can do all things through Christ who gives us strength. Anything God calls us to, he gives us the ability and the resources to do. Because of him, there's a power living in us that's stronger than anything we'll face."

Dad pursed his lips. "That's quite the sermon. Sure you didn't miss your calling to the priesthood?"

Carter gave a wry grin. "No sermon, Dad. Just a story. My story. But God can help you write yours."

"I won't make any promises, Carter."

Carter bit his lip against the all-too-familiar sinking sensation in his gut. Dad had disappointed him again. And how, when he'd been disappointed a billion times before, was he even still capable of disappointment? Surely his heart would be numb by now.

"I won't make promises"—his father swiveled in the creaky recliner to face him—"because I've promised you the moon countless times, and I've always fallen short. So I'll think about what you've said. But I won't promise anything."

"I will." Carter leaned forward to rest his hand on his father's knee. "I'll promise to be here for you. Whatever you need. Anything. All that's between us, I'm working to forgive. Choosing to forgive. All I want is for you to be the man I know you can be, Dad." His eyes stung. "Because I'm just like you. I'm a Douglas. And look how far God's brought me."

Dad didn't say anything. But for the first time, in the older man's eyes, Carter saw a glimmer of hope.

"Hey, you guys got the score?" Brad poked his head in from the kitchen.

Carter reached for the remote and handed it to his brother-in-law. "Broncs are up, ten to six."

"Cool." Brad lumbered into the room, plopped down in the easy chair next to Dad, and pointed the remote at the big screen. Tony Romo's commentary grew louder, and Carter breathed a sigh of relief. That was enough heavy conversation for one afternoon.

His phone buzzed in the pocket of his jeans, and he wedged it out to peer at the screen.

Philadelphia, PA.

Like he knew anyone in Philadelphia. Probably just a scam call. He started to replace the phone, but a strong inward pull made him reconsider. Frowning, he pressed the Phone icon and lifted the device to his ear.

A deep male voice came through the line. "Is this Carter Douglas from Channel Five in Wichita?"

"Speaking." Carter's guard went up. This started like the usual crackpot call. But those callers were usually female. The calls came to the station, not his cell.

And the area code was nearly always the familiar 316 or 620. Not one from Philadelphia.

"Apologies if I've caught you off guard, Mr. Douglas. I tried the station first, but when I told them who I was and what I wanted, the reporter I talked to was most eager to pass along your number."

Okay, if this was a crackpot call, it was officially the strangest one he'd ever received.

The caller cleared his throat. "My name is Ephraim James. I understand you all have been looking for me."

✦

Lauren reached into the cabinet in the farmhouse kitchen for a stack of square white plates. Presentation still mattered, after all, even if dinner was takeout burritos.

She set the plates on the marble countertop and reached into the funky, retro-style pale-blue fridge for a handful of cilantro to serve as a garnish. Her sister-in-law-to-be had done some amazing work on the farmhouse, mixing modern innovations with vintage touches. In fact, with its black-and-white checkered flooring and chrome fixtures, this kitchen might very well take Grandma right back to her high school days.

If any of those memories still remained.

Plates in hand, Lauren carried them into the living room, where Sloane and Garrett sat on the sofa, one of those black-and-white movies Sloane liked so much flickering on the TV above the fireplace.

"I'm still impressed you brought takeout." Garrett accepted his plate with one hand and held out a twenty in the other. "You're coming along nicely."

Lauren gave a slight curtsy and pocketed the cash. "It's still mostly veggies in mine, but they put in real cheese, and I have no idea how many calories or fat grams or anything this burrito has."

Garrett reached for the remote and paused the movie. "I'm proud of you, Lo."

"Thank you." Plates distributed, Lauren took her own—that burrito smelled divine—and settled into a comfy new recliner. Still blue, a nod to the favorite chairs of Grandma's that had moved with her to Plaza de Paz, but minus the worn springs and faded armrests. The cup holders were a nice touch too. Perfect for her tall, icy horchata.

"You two are doing that Wonder Twin thing again." Sloane's dark eyes darted from Garrett to Lauren and back. "What'd I miss?"

Garrett glanced toward Lauren, uncertainty hovering in his expression. Oh, wow. He really had honored his pledge to keep her struggles private. Even his fiancée didn't know. The realization warmed Lauren's heart.

"There's something about me you don't know yet, Sloane." Apprehension clutching at her chest, Lauren unwrapped the burrito. "I'm a recovering bulimic."

Sloane's brows arched over black-framed glasses. "I see."

"It was pretty bad a few years ago, and I'm a whole lot better, but I recently figured out that I'm still dealing with some control issues about food." An understatement, if ever there was one. "My therapist is helping me work through those."

"Good for you." Sloane's smile was warm and genuine. "I'm glad you're being proactive about healing. How can we best support you?"

Relief washed through Lauren, like the spicy steam piping from the burrito. Sloane never came across as judgmental particularly, but still, condemnation, revulsion, rejection . . . those terrified her. Especially after how things had ended with Carter.

"Thank you," she said. "I think mostly just prayer at the moment."

"Then let's do that right now." And Sloane did. After thanking God for the food, she specifically requested that it be a source of strength for Lauren, rather than a stumbling block.

As the petitions and the love within them washed over her, Lauren added a few of her own, along with a good deal of gratitude that God had brought such a fantastic woman into her big brother's life.

When the prayer finished, Lauren dug in. Had anything ever tasted so delicious as this burrito? Spicy roasted poblanos played against pungent onions, crisp bell peppers, and the creaminess of *queso asadero*. For the first time in a long time, she savored the food without obsessing over its nutritional value or shoving it down to deal with unpleasant feelings. Appreciated both the natural ingredients and the skills of those who'd combined those ingredients into such a delicious whole. If heaven indeed had a banquet table, she sincerely hoped this burrito would be on it.

"So I take it things are going well with Lisette?" Garrett's voice cut into her food-induced reverie.

"They are." Lauren swallowed her bite and reached for the horchata. "She says healing comes in layers, and it's perfectly normal to need a touch-up every now and again. It doesn't mean I'm back where I was before, just that I've still got some work to do." Lauren paused and hazarded a glance at Garrett. "She thinks it might be good for me to post my story on my blog."

"Going public?" Garrett's brows arched. "Wow. That'd be a big step."

Lauren sipped her horchata and slid it back into the cup holder, relishing the sweet creamy coolness on her tongue. "I've been afraid to lose authority in people's eyes. Like, what does someone who used to binge on Oreos and then make herself throw up know about health?"

Sloane reached for a tortilla chip. "If anything, I'd say it makes you even more credible. People who might be struggling with the same issues wouldn't feel quite so alone if they knew you'd come through it and survived."

"Could be a real ministry," Garrett piped up around a mouthful.

"Lisette said the same thing." Lauren retrieved a fallen poblano and popped it into her mouth. "I'm working on a script for a video about it. I'm not ready to do it yet, and might not be for a while, but just writing it out has been pretty cathartic." Another understatement. Because the story of her bulimia was the story of her and Carter, and writing them both had helped her sort out where one ended and the other began. He hadn't caused her disordered eating, but his behavior had been a trigger. And learning how to identify and neutralize that trigger had been a key part of her therapy sessions.

"You might get sick of hearing me say I'm proud of you," Garrett said, "but I'm going on the record right now as saying I don't care. Because I am, and I'm going to tell you pretty often."

Lauren grinned. "Not sick of it yet, big brother."

After a pleasant lull in the conversation, Sloane cleared her throat. "So, not to change the subject, but your brother and I were talking earlier, and I think we might be running out of options with Ephraim James."

The leaden disappointment Lauren swallowed along with her burrito wasn't unexpected, but it still hurt. It had been weeks since the interview aired, and though they'd received a flood of responses and had connected with many of Grandma's high school classmates, ultimately those connections had led nowhere. Now the flood had slowed to a trickle, and the combination of six decades, fading memories, and the fact that nobody really knew much about Grandma and Ephraim's relationship to begin with meant concrete facts were nonexistent.

Memories of the interview, and a bittersweet pang, surfaced. Sitting beside Grandma, grinning beyond the cameras to Carter, who waited quietly in the shadows. Supporting her with his unshakable confidence. His calming presence. His reassuring *you got this, Lauren* smile.

She didn't need the confidence boost anymore. Going on camera didn't terrify her as much as it once did.

But my word, did she miss that smile.

"I think the possibility we have to consider is that Ephraim isn't alive anymore," Garrett said quietly.

Leave it to him to bring up the uncomfortable topic no one wanted to address. But just like with selling the house, someone had to. It was time to face the facts.

"It's possible," Sloane replied, "but I haven't found a death certificate for him. In fact, I haven't found much at all. Ephraim James seems to have vanished into thin air. I hunted up obituaries for his parents—his mother died in 1969, his father five years later—and they both mention him as a survivor, but neither obit indicates where he was living at the time."

Lauren slurped up the last drops of her horchata. "Y'know, maybe it is time to let this go. If Grandma still remembers him, and we tell her we can't find him and have no clue what happened to him, would that break her heart all over again? And it's entirely possible she doesn't even remember him now. Maybe those memories bubbled to the surface, burst, and now they're gone, and talking about him would just confuse her."

Garrett reached for his drink, his expression grave. "Hate to say it, Sloane, because I know how you are with unsolved mysteries, but I think Lauren's right. We need to let it go."

"Okay." Sloane reached for Garrett's hand. "If that's what you want, then I'll stop looking."

Garrett's expression mirrored Lauren's relief as he pulled Sloane close. "Yeah. I think it's time."

"Okay." Sloane rested her head on Garrett's shoulder. "I'm sorry it didn't work out."

"Me too." Lauren wadded up her empty burrito wrapper and tossed it onto the plate. Would it have been nice to give Grandma and Ephraim a reunion? Some closure? Maybe even a second chance? Sure.

But sometimes the past needed to stay in the past. Because sometimes second chances were even more painful than the first.

CHAPTER THIRTY-FOUR

"EPHRAIM." CARTER PUSHED the front door open and stepped out onto his parents' front porch. Ephraim James. The man Lauren's whole family had been searching for. This man was on the phone. Right now. With him. "How . . . how did you . . ."

"My great-granddaughter saw the interview your station did with Rosie and her family. Not sure where—probably one of those social network whatsits she's always on her phone about—and it didn't take her too long to put two and two together. Me, on the other hand . . . it took me a while to get up the gumption to make this phone call, if I'm honest. It's a time in my life I don't talk much about."

"Sure." An idea formed and started a slow rotation, like the bottom of a wall cloud. Lauren. Lauren. He needed to tell Lauren.

"I'm not even sure I ever told my wife."

"Your wife?" Uh-oh. Looked like Lauren's happily-ever-after pipe dream was dead in the water.

"The good Lord blessed me with fifty-six wonderful years of marriage to a singer named Beverly. We lost her in 2014, but we had four beautiful children together. Nine grands, fifteen great-grands, with another on the way next month."

Carter sank onto the porch step. "Congratulations, sir. It sounds like you've had a wonderful life."

"Oh, I have. I have." Ephraim's voice was rich with feeling. "But I've never forgotten my Rosie girl. Seeing her on that interview . . . my, my, she's as beautiful as she ever was, and every bit as sweet."

The old man's tender inflection sent truth searing through the phone line. Ephraim had been in love with Rosie. Still thought about her, even all these years later. Even after moving on. Marrying and having a family with someone else.

A cool gust of autumn wind sent dried-up leaves skittering over the sidewalk. Was this what his own forecast looked like? He'd never entertained the idea of marriage, not with any seriousness, but now that he was free from his dad's addiction—his own addiction—maybe he could.

Eventually. After his heart healed.

Oh, who was he kidding? It had always been Lauren. And if the last thirteen years were anything to go by, it'd always be Lauren. No one else could make his heart soar a mile above earth with a single glance of sky-blue eyes.

"I wish I could meet her family," Ephraim continued. "See that grandson and granddaughter of hers. Thank them for learning our story. And to see Rosie again, even for just a moment, that'd be . . ."

The tremor in the older man's voice brought a sting to Carter's eyes. "I'm sure we could arrange that."

"Oh, twenty years ago, maybe. But at my age, flying cross-country gets tough. The wheelchairs, the layovers, the terminals, security. Airlines help as much as they can, of course, but it's still an effort worthy of Hercules on my own."

The rotating idea gathered speed. "So it's not a health issue, then?"

"No, just accessibility. Last time I flew anywhere, my daughter Elaine came with me, but she's taking care of her mother-in-law, so it wouldn't be right to ask her to leave just now."

The idea rotation touched down and kicked up debris. The future—his future, Lauren's future, his father—all that was beyond his control. And for the first time, that thought didn't make him want to weep with help-lessness, because God held it all. And his plans were good.

Serenity. That was what this was. Accepting—even embracing—the things he couldn't change.

And having the courage to change what he could.

Like channeling his helplessness at that long-ago twister into a career in meteorology. Like shattering the belief that he was doomed to be just like dear old Dad.

And Ephraim. Bringing him home. Giving him, and Lauren, and her family—and maybe even himself—some necessary closure.

He gripped the porch railing, a grin tugging at his lips. "Mr. James, I have a proposition for you."

※

There was really no escape, was there?

It had been a beautiful crisp morning, perfect for a trip to the farmers' market for a haul of apples, pecans, and decorative gourds. Recipes simmered in Lauren's imagination, inspired by the ingredients resting in the back seat. It was a perfect morning. *Perfect.*

Until that billboard half a block from her apartment. The one workers in cherry pickers were just putting the finishing touches on.

The one with Carter's face, his toothpaste-commercial smile beaming at her from fourteen feet up.

He didn't beam alone either. Beside him on the kitchen set stood Paulina Ayala, head chef at the hot new taqueria in town—breathtakingly gorgeous and a recurring guest on Carter's increasingly popular noon show cooking segments. Fruits, vegetables, and gleaming copper cookware surrounded them, and the segment's slogan was scrawled across the bottom in a white almost as bright as their twin TV smiles. *If Carter can cook it, you can too!*

Jealousy ripped the scab from the wound of Carter's departure. Doubtless he and Paulina melted the camera with their on-set chemistry. With his charm and charisma, he could cook up chemistry with anyone.

Lauren retrieved her groceries, slammed the car door, and stormed up the stairs to her apartment. All fine and dandy for him. But what about her? Would she ever find that spice, that heat, with anyone else?

Sloane had offered to introduce her to their church's new worship pastor. "He's kinda artsy like you" was her ringing endorsement. Lauren would've preferred *not prone to self-sabotage* or *won't trigger your insecurities and control issues.* But *kinda artsy* was at least a somewhat hopeful beginning.

A beginning she should probably save for a time when seeing Carter's face on a billboard wouldn't ruin her entire morning. When a commercial for his weathercast wouldn't make her run for the remote and nearly sprain her thumb in her eagerness to change the channel. When a gray Dodge Charger could pull up in traffic and she didn't immediately jerk her gaze toward the driver, just to make sure it wasn't him.

There was even a gray Charger in the parking lot, just below her kitchen window.

It was empty, though. She'd made sure to check.

After slipping out of her new red coat and tossing it over the back of the couch, Lauren tumbled the apples into the sink and gave them a quick rinse. She wasn't over Carter yet, not even close. And she needed to get over him. Needed to move on. Needed to—

Knock knock knock.

Answer the door.

"Coming." She shut off the water, crossed the kitchen, flung open the door, and stared.

Carter. In the flesh.

The billboard featured the spit-and-polished suit-clad Carter, whereas the one standing in her hallway was all weekend-stubbly and rolled-up-sleeves delicious. That was the one she'd give anything to get over.

The one Mr. Kinda-Artsy could never hope to compare to.

"I'm guessing by the look on your face you'd prefer I'd called." His mouth tipped up.

She folded her arms as protection from that heart-melting smile. "Well, since we're broken up now, yeah. Probably."

"Crap." He palmed the back of his neck. "If it helps, I'm not here about that."

It didn't help.

"I actually have someone here with me," he said. "Someone you might want to meet, and someone who'd definitely like to meet you."

Lauren recoiled. If he'd brought Paulina Ayala with him, she'd be sorely tempted to put his head through the wall.

But from the shadows stepped a tall, elderly black man. Wire-rimmed glasses accentuated deep creases around his eyes, and a dusty fedora perched atop snow-white hair. He leaned on a cane, but his posture was still straight, and he carried himself with quiet dignity.

And then he smiled.

She'd know that smile anywhere.

"Lauren." Carter's voice sounded miles away. "This is—"

"Ephraim," she breathed. "Ephraim James. You're alive. I knew it. I *knew* you were still alive."

Ephraim extended a slender dark-brown hand, but Lauren pulled him into a hug instead. The tweed of his coat was scratchy against her cheek, and he smelled of coffee and Old Spice and family. *Family.* Though he belonged to a different era and a different race, and though she was just now meeting him, through the searching and discovering and rooting deep into her grandmother's past, he'd become family.

"Well, now," he said as they pulled apart, bracing his hands on her elbows. "That's a mighty warm welcome."

"I just feel like I know you. I mean, we've learned some of your story, but there's so much more—*so* much more—I don't know, and I want to learn, and . . . wow. Ephraim James. You're here."

Twinkling brown eyes swept over her face. "When you get excited, young lady, you get a dimple in your cheek. A shine in your eyes. Just like your grandmother. So I suppose it's safe to say I feel as though I know you too."

"Then what are we doing standing out in the hallway? Come in. Come in." Lauren flung the door wide and took Ephraim's elbow to guide him inside. As he leaned his cane against the wall and doffed his hat, she looked back at Carter, who stood in the doorway, fiddling with his watch.

"How did you find him?" she asked. "We've been searching for months."

Carter lifted a shoulder. "That interview finally found its mark."

The interview. Carter's idea. He'd set up the whole thing. And look where it led. Her heart warmed.

"And you even drove him here?"

"Flew me." Ephraim piped up, hanging his coat on the rack. "All the way from Philadelphia. Your young man is quite the pilot."

The urge to correct him surfaced, but she stuffed it down and stared at Carter. "You *flew* him? All this way? For Grandma? For . . . me?"

Carter nodded, his lips tight. "I just . . . I wanted someone to get their happily-ever-after, y'know?"

Oh, Carter. It took everything in her not to reach for him and wrap him in her arms. To press her cheek against his and whisper her gratitude into his ear. Her whole body cried out for contact, but she resisted the urge. It wouldn't solve anything. Wouldn't change anything.

It'd just make that ripped-open wound even harder to heal.

She wrapped her arms around her midsection instead and swallowed hard. "Thank you, Carter. It means more than you'll ever know."

Avoiding eye contact, he nodded, then ducked through the open door and into the hallway.

"You're welcome to stay, if you like." The idea springboarded from her lips before she could evaluate its merit.

But what was there to evaluate? Regardless of the risk to her heart, to her sanity, she owed him this. The opportunity to stay. To see the fruit of all his labor.

He paused and turned but didn't progress toward her door.

"I got some coffee today at the farmers' market. You, uh . . . look like you could use some." She braced her arm against the doorframe.

His brows lifted. "Coffee? You?"

"I'm expanding my horizons." She grinned, despite a valiant struggle not to. "Garrett and Sloane discovered they had an extra French press between them, so they gave it to me. I'm still getting the hang of it, but I think I can make a decent cup without too many grounds."

A smile flickered, then faded, as he studied her. "Are you sure?"

"Give me a little credit, Carter. Coffee's not that hard."

Color rose beneath his cheekbones. "No, it's not that, I just . . ."

Watching him twist in the wind wasn't quite as much fun as she'd hoped. She stepped into the hall.

"I'm serious. Come in. None of this would've happened without you. You helped us tell Grandma's story. And you need to be here to see how it ends."

"Yeah. Okay. Thanks." Hands in his pockets, he walked back toward her door, then paused when he reached her. "So this is real coffee, right? Not some weird soy-tempe-beet root concoction that—*hey*."

He broke off when she gave him a hefty shove in the shoulder, one that knocked him off balance and brought forth a laugh she felt all the way to her toes. A laugh that took her back to the very beginning of that long-ago summer, before anything got messy or complicated. When they were simply and purely friends.

Maybe, someday, they could return to that. Friends.

He held the door for her, and she walked back into her apartment. Would friendship with Carter Douglas be wise? Could she handle that?

That was a decision for another day. Another time. Because Ephraim James was in her apartment. Sitting on her sofa, polishing his glasses on his shirttail. Doubtless he'd welcome a cup of coffee too.

Excitement bubbled at the sight. Garrett. She had to call Garrett. And Sloane. They needed to get over here. Right now.

Because Grandma's Ephraim, at last, had come home.

CHAPTER THIRTY-FIVE

May 1955

"THIS IS YOUR second call, ladies and gentlemen. Track six to Kansas City, with service to Chicago, Boston, and Philadelphia, all aboard."

Panic swooshing through her, Rosie stood and scanned the crowded station. Searched every brown face, every dark head of hair, for that familiar lanky figure, that smile that lit up her whole world.

Surely he was coming. He'd said he'd be here. Surely he was—

There.

"Ephraim!"

She must've been quite the sight, running through the station as fast as her high heels and heavy suitcase would let her, running toward a black man, but she didn't care what anyone thought. Not anymore. Her time for that was over.

He turned toward her. "Rosie girl. You're here."

She stopped and paused a moment to catch her breath, then smiled into those dark eyes. "Hi."

"I didn't think you'd actually . . ." Trailing off, he reached for her, and she melted into his arms. Into her future. The first step into an irrevocable decision that would dictate the course of the entire rest of her life.

He pulled back to look at her, blinking as though he still didn't believe it. "You're really doing this."

He didn't smile like she thought he would.

"I really am." Oh, was it normal for her stomach to feel knotted tighter than a pretzel? It was normal. Of course it was. She was turning her back on everything she knew. Everyone she loved.

Everyone except Ephraim.

"I'm really doing this." Her grip on the ticket tightened. "I'm really running away. To start a new life. With you."

"With me." His voice wavered.

"With you." So did hers.

The corners of his smile pushed up, but not in the broad, natural way she'd come to expect. "Then let's go."

"Let's do it. Let's get on the train."

But her feet stayed rooted to the black-and-white tiles.

So did his.

"Track six, all aboard!"

She still didn't move.

Neither did he. Neat brown shoes, the same pair he'd worn to prom, formed a vee on the black-and-white squares.

"Rosie girl."

The sudden heaviness in his voice was the same feeling in her heart. His eyes radiated sorrow, not the joy and excitement of new beginnings.

He didn't have to say another word. He would, of course. But whatever came next would confirm what his voice, his eyes, had already told her.

She wasn't the only one having second thoughts.

Slim shoulders rose and fell with a shaky breath. "I can't believe I'm about to say this. And believe me, I don't want to, but . . ."

"You're not sure about this either."

He leaned in and lowered his voice. "Look around you. See how everyone's looking at us."

"I don't care about that. Maybe I did once, but I don't now."

"I know you don't. That's one of the reasons I love you." He caressed her with his gaze. "But prom—Gordon—showed me just how much hate the world has for a couple like us. When it was just us, we could ignore it, but we couldn't stay there forever."

Her eyes stung. She could almost hear her world crumbling around her.

Ephraim clasped her hands between his. "I know in my heart there'll come a time when it won't matter if a couple matches on the outside. When a black man and a white woman and their little brown babies will be accepted instead of despised." His face fell, and he traced the swollen spot on her lip, still tender from Gordon McIntyre's assault. "But I didn't know until now just how far off that day really is. I . . . I don't know if we'll live to see it."

His image blurred. She bit her lip to stop its trembling. "I don't know if we will either."

"You've already been through so much pain because of me. And asking you to endure a whole lifetime of it . . . that's not what love does. Love doesn't insist on its own way."

Rosie caressed the backs of Ephraim's fingers with the pad of her thumb. These fingers should be dancing across a keyboard, giving voice to the music of his soul, not plunged into scalding dishwater for hours on end just to put a roof over their heads. Asking him to delay his dreams—or even cancel them—to provide for her? That would be insisting on its own way.

That, above anything else, was why she still couldn't move toward that train.

That was why she had to let him go.

"Ephraim." She swallowed hard. "There's nothing in the world I want more than to get on that train with you. But doing that means it'd be even longer for you to be able to make music. And if we have babies—which I want, more than anything—then you might never—"

"I know."

His voice broke, and she choked back a sob. She felt like Abraham, standing on the mountain, knife held high, seconds from sacrificing what he loved most. How could she bear this pain?

"The world is hard enough for you on your own," she said. "You don't need me making it harder."

"When you love someone like I love you, you want the best possible life for that someone." He stepped closer. "And the way this world is right now, a life together, that's not the best possible life for you."

Had heartbreak ever been so tender? So loving? The gentle touch of his thumb on her skin, the near whisper of his words, shouldn't have been enough to shatter her heart. And yet they did.

The truth did.

"It's not the best possible life for you either." Her tears spilled over, scorching trails down her cheeks. "I love you, Ephraim. I love you so much."

"I love you too, Rosie girl." A tear traced a shiny line down his right cheek. "And if love were enough, I'd be yanking you onto that train to Philly."

"But it's not enough."

He gave a slow, sad shake of his head. "And you've got no idea how much I wish it was."

"Final boarding call, track six to Kansas City, with service to Chicago, Boston, and Philadelphia."

Panic seared her at the sound. This was it. This really was goodbye. Another minute, maybe two, and Ephraim would be on that train, heading for a new life. One that didn't—couldn't—involve her. How could she possibly say all she wanted to say?

How could she cram a lifetime of love into their few remaining moments?

As if feeling the same panic, he folded her into his arms and pressed her cheek to his chest. She squeezed her eyes shut, committing his strength, his warmth, his scent, to memory.

These scant few seconds would have to last the rest of her life.

"Find someone, Rosie girl," he said in a choked whisper. "Find a good man who'll love you and take care of you and give you a beautiful life."

She couldn't suppress her sobs any longer. Would anyone ever love her again the way Ephraim James did? Would she ever love anyone else?

"You do the same. Find someone who loves you like you deserve to be loved." Oh, it tore her apart to think of her Ephraim with anyone else. "And . . . and don't ever stop making music, okay? No matter what. Never stop playing the piano."

"I won't." He pulled back to look at her. "I'll think of you every time I do."

Rosie wiped the tears from her cheeks and managed a smile. "And I'll think of you every time I hear a piano."

He stepped back, and cold air rushed in where her skin had lost contact with his. His lips tipped up in a watery version of that famous Ephraim smile. "You remember that seventh chord, now."

"I'll never forget it." She would never forget it. Never forget him.

As long as her heart still beat, as long as she still had breath, she would never forget Ephraim James.

Rosie covered her mouth with her hand, muffling her sobs as she watched the man she loved hand his ticket to the porter and board the train. He ducked through the doorway, gave her one last lingering look, and then disappeared.

Ephraim was gone.

Her heart screamed at her to run after him. She still had her ticket—somewhere she did, she was sure of it. She could still get on the train. It hadn't pulled away yet. She could still run away with him. Still start her new life. Still spend forever with the man she loved.

But she wouldn't.

She loved him too much.

With a hiss and a whistle, the train pulled away, taking her heart with it. She watched until it was merely a dot in the distance, then she floated back to earth. Back to reality. Back to the black-and-white tile floor. Back to the suddenly empty terminal. Back to the haze of smoke and the click of footsteps.

Back to the ticket she'd clutched in her hand for the last half hour, the ticket that now lay discarded at her feet, lost somewhere in the melee of farewell.

Back to the hastily packed suitcase she wouldn't be needing after all.

They'd made the right choice. The mature choice. The loving choice.

But that didn't mean it wouldn't shatter her heart.

CHAPTER THIRTY-SIX

"YOU AND GRANDMA almost ran away together?" Lauren gaped first at Ephraim, then at Garrett, whose stunned blinking quietly reflected her own astonishment.

Ephraim leaned on his cane. "Indeed we did."

For nearly the last hour, they'd all clustered around in Lauren's small living room, listening to Ephraim James tell the tale of his relationship with Grandma. He sat at the head of the metaphorical table, in the worn green armchair by the window that served as Nigella's afternoon nap spot. She hadn't seemed to care though, as she'd curled up in Ephraim's lap. His deep-brown hand stroked the cat's cottony fur as he talked.

Sloane and Garrett sat smushed together, all lovey-dovey and engaged, on Lauren's sofa, while Lauren perched beside Carter on her countertop stools. She'd thought about cramming herself onto the sofa. But making a point not to sit beside Carter would make her discomfort obvious, and she didn't want her discomfort to be obvious. Least of all to Carter.

So she sat beside him. Caught the occasional whiff of his cologne. Tried not to admire the curve of his cheekbone or the shadow of stubble on his jaw or the perfect shape of his forearms.

Her discomfort was probably obvious anyway.

Sloane peered at Ephraim through funky vintage-framed glasses. "Do you ever wish you'd done things differently?"

"For a while. Those first weeks, it took everything I had in me not to try and hitch a ride back to Kansas. To find Rosie and grovel and beg her to take me back. To try and carve out some kind of life with her here. But if I'd done that, I'd have never found Beverly. I wouldn't have my kids. My grandkids."

Ephraim half raised out of his seat and withdrew a cell phone from his pocket, which he regarded with a mixture of amusement and disdain. "I don't have much use for this contraption, but I've found the younger members of the family worry about me less if I carry it around. Plus it's a whole lot easier on the ol' back pocket than a wallet full of photos." A slender finger tapped the screen, and then he held the phone out to Lauren. "This is all of us at a reunion the summer before Beverly passed."

Lauren took the phone from his outstretched hand. "What a beautiful family."

Ephraim sat in the center with a woman whose face shone with joy even from the tiny screen of the phone. A passel of middle-aged black people clustered around them, and radiating out from them were younger people, ranging from a toddler with her hair in puffy ebony pigtails to a teenager with long dreadlocks. And off to the right, a handsome black man about Lauren's age—one of Ephraim's grandchildren, no doubt, judging from the identical smile—had his arm around a white woman with long dirty-blonde hair. On her hip perched a baby boy, his arms and legs chubby, his skin a pale brown.

Heart full of joy, Lauren passed the phone to Carter. She tried not to notice when his warm fingertips brushed hers, but the slight contact brought a shiver anyway.

"I think the good Lord gave us wisdom beyond our years." Ephraim rubbed the sleeping Nigella under the chin. "Because Rosie was right. If I'd had her to support, I'd never have been able to take the leap into music. I never would've even found the band, let alone play with them for so many years. Never would've founded RJ Rose—"

Garrett sat up straight. "You founded RJ Rose Records?"

"Son, I am RJ Rose."

Garrett's mouth hung open. "You're ... he's ... RJ Rose ... you're—that was the name on those gospel records Grandma liked to listen to. Your version of 'Precious Lord, Take My Hand' is just sensational."

"Appreciate the love, son."

Lauren met Garrett's astonished gaze. "Do you think Grandma knew?"

"Can't imagine she didn't." She could almost see the wheels turning in his brain, the memories of years gone by suddenly clicking into place. "She had a lot of records by a lot of different artists, but those, she said, were her favorite."

Sloane's brow furrowed. "So that's why all those online searches for Ephraim James came up empty."

Deep creases fanned beside Ephraim's eyes. "Our manager back in the early days told me Ephraim James didn't roll off the tongue. And since I pictured my Rosie girl sitting beside me every time I played, the name just came to me. RJ for Romeo and Juliet. Rose for my inspiration. My muse. The woman who made all this possible."

Garrett turned his open-mouthed stare on his fiancée. "He's RJ Rose. Grandma's boyfriend is RJ Rose."

Lauren stifled a giggle at her discombobulated big brother. Fanboy Garrett wasn't something she'd ever imagined seeing.

"My whole life, I prayed she'd be happy too." Ephraim leaned forward in his chair, urgency in his eyes. "So tell me. Was she?"

Garrett placed a hand on the older man's. "Yes. She was."

"Did she ever teach? I know she dreamed of doing that."

"She did. She and Grandpa were married in . . . fifty-nine, I think?" Lauren glanced toward Garrett, who nodded his confirmation. "And she taught school in Jamesville until Mom was born in 1964. After that she taught Sunday school for a long time."

Ephraim's eyes misted. "Then we did the right thing. And what about her husband? Your grandfather?"

"Orrin Spencer," Garrett replied. "As the story goes, he worked in the campus post office while Grandma was at college."

"They were married almost sixty years." Lauren's eyes stung at the memory of her grandfather. A man she'd have never known if Grandma and Ephraim had made a different decision that night so long ago. "I know she loved him like crazy. They moved into the farmhouse not long after they got married, and—"

Ephraim's eyes lit. "She still lived in the farmhouse?"

"Grandpa was a rural-route mail carrier most of his career," Lauren replied. "But he always said he'd wanted to try his hand at farming."

"During my research last year, I discovered that Orrin and Rosie purchased the farm from Rosie's grandmother after her grandpa passed away in 1960." Sloane's grip on Garrett's hand tightened. "Orrin died a couple years ago, and we moved her to assisted living not long afterward."

A warm smile curved Ephraim's lips. "She always did love that place. I know she was upset when her parents exiled her there, but I think it was only there that she realized what she'd be giving up to be with me." Sharp brown eyes studied Garrett and Sloane. "What happened to the farm? Do you know?"

"Sloane lives there now." Garrett slid an arm around his fiancée and squeezed her tight. "She learned last year that she and her birth mother are direct descendants of the couple who built the place, so when we had to sell it, they bought it together. We've been fixing it up, and I'll move in once we're married."

"I'm so relieved she had a good life." A weight seemed to lift from Ephraim's shoulders. "I knew a few other couples like us through the years. Some were able to withstand the storm of public opinion. Some weren't. I can't be sure where we'd have landed, but I like to think we'd have made it."

"I think you would have." Amusement curved Lauren's lips. "Grandma's pretty stubborn."

Ephraim chuckled. "The good Lord had a different plan, though not a day went by that I didn't pray he'd blessed her as much as he blessed me. I dearly loved my Beverly—still do—but a part of my heart will always belong to your grandmother."

Carter shifted beside her, head bowed, hands loosely clasped between denim-clad legs. Lauren pressed her lips together. Was this her future, too? Would she be in her eighties someday, reflecting on the good life she'd built with someone else—maybe even Mr. Kinda-Artsy—but knowing that a part of her heart would always belong to the first man she'd ever loved?

A deep chuckle rumbled from Ephraim, and a smile creased his weathered cheeks. "Never in my wildest dreams did I think I'd ever get the chance to see her again. Just might be that after all the twists and turns, God's not done writing our story yet."

Lauren could feel Carter looking at her even before she glanced up to receive confirmation. Those deep-brown eyes glimmered with pain and hope and emotions she couldn't even name. They shimmered with the question that had suddenly hooked in her heart.

Could it be God wasn't finished writing their story yet either?

Carter believed they were doomed. He carried a life sentence of alcoholism, while she was forever chained to her food issues.

But . . . she wasn't. Not anymore. Not since she put God back on the throne and learned to trust him. Not since she truly embraced the forgiveness he freely offered and stopped punishing herself for that long-ago mistake with the man who sat beside her. Not since she learned how thoroughly God repaired damage and redeemed brokenness.

Had Carter discovered the same thing? Had he found the same hope she had?

If he hadn't, could her experience point him in that direction?

Ephraim slid his hands beneath Nigella's snowy body and gently lifted her off his lap and set her on a nearby cushion. "And speaking of that story, I'd like to write the next chapter. Provided her doctors say it's all right, of course."

"It should be fine." Garrett paused. "It's just . . ."

Lauren bailed her brother out. "She remembered you a few weeks ago— she knew your picture, remembered your name, quoted parts of *Romeo and Juliet*—but it's been long enough, and her disease is bad enough . . ."

"She might not remember who you are," Garrett finished.

Ephraim's expression melted into a warm smile. "But I remember who she is."

Lauren's throat thickened. Carter's eyes held a sheen too.

"Then what are we waiting for?" Lauren stood and looked away. Those eyes were her Kryptonite. "Besides, this is usually a pretty good time of day for her."

Following her lead, Garrett and Sloane helped Ephraim to his feet, while Lauren fetched his jacket. When she handed it to him, the older man's dark eyes gleamed with youthful mischief.

"Do you know if this place where she lives has a piano?"

><

"Come on, Grandma. There's someone here to see you."

Handsome and Auntie Boop are on one side of me. Girl-Called-... oh, shoot, I can't remember her name. But she's the girl who looks like Handsome. And she's on the other side.

They all seem so excited. Scurrying around like ants. Girl Handsome seems like she's about to burst, like she's got so much energy she wants to run circles around me.

I wonder what the rush is. I'm not quite dead yet.

We round the corner, and there's music.

Music.

I stop for a moment and lean on my walker to listen. It's beautiful, that music. And it makes me feel ... *something.* I can't conjure up a name for it, of course, but it's strong.

And I know I've felt it before.

Handsome leans closer. "Are you all right, Grandma?"

"Yes. Fine. I just need ... I need ..." *I need you to shut your yap so I can listen to that beautiful music.*

"Want to get a little closer?" Even Auntie Boop's eyes gleam with excitement. She puts a hand on my arm, but I shake it off and push my walker toward the direction of the sound. I don't need help. Not now. It's like the music itself is making my legs move. Infusing me with strength I thought I'd lost long ago.

We round the corner, and Girl Handsome can't contain herself any longer. "Grandma. Look. At the piano."

"Chill, Lauren," Handsome says.

Lauren. That's Girl Handsome's name.

And *piano.* That must be the large rose-brown something near the center of the room, the source of that beautiful sound. A man sits there, a black man with silver hair, whose lean fingers fly up and down the keyboard as though that was what they were made to do.

And the music those fingers are making . . . that feeling inside me just gets stronger and stronger. So strong it fills me. Makes it so I almost can't breathe.

There's a memory tied in all this. There has to be, the way I feel. The memory is there, hovering just out of sight. But it won't ever come into view.

They used to frustrate me, these golden knobs to doors that will forever remain locked. I used to fight them. But now I've learned to accept them. Welcome them, even. Because while I may not be able to see my memories anymore, their hushed presence tells me to look for their shadows.

I smile up at Handsome. "This is lovely music."

"Yes. Yes it is." Girl-Called-Lauren answers for him, nodding and grinning like a fool.

A chair scrapes the floor. A dark-haired man I've never seen before—or if I have, I don't remember him—is pulling it up next to the piano. *Right* next to it.

Girl-Called-Lauren motions to it, that smile still plastered on her face. "Come on, Grandma. Sit here so you can see."

I start to wave a hand. I don't want to bother the man who's playing. But the ones who brought me here seem so intent on me sitting there that I don't feel I can refuse. Handsome must've picked up on my surrender, because he takes my elbow, guides me to the chair, and helps me plop down with a bit more grace than I might have otherwise.

The man doesn't look up from the keyboard. Doesn't stop playing. But he does smile.

"Hello," he says. There's a tenderness to his voice. A husky burnished strength. One that brings another sharp stab of that . . . that *feeling*.

It only grows as I watch his hands. Lean, brown hands, wrinkled like mine, but they dance over the keys with the ease and grace of someone who lives and breathes music, pulling every drop of melody and harmony from the black and white.

I close my eyes. Lean into the melody. And then . . .

A swish of skirts around my legs. Full, fluffy skirts.

A whiff of flowers.

The warmth of arms around me. Dancing. Swaying. Holding me like he never wants to let me go.

But . . . *who*? I can't see his face. Can't remember his name.

But I do remember joy. *Joy*. That's the name of the feeling. One of the feelings, anyway. There are a lot of them inside me, all jumbled up in a heap. But there's one stronger than the rest. One that bursts from the bottom of the pile, growing and growing and taking on a life of its own.

It's so strong it frightens me, but I don't want it to go away. Because it feels like coming home, to a place I've never been.

The man ends the music with a ripple of notes, and the people scattered around us clap. But I'm just mesmerized by those black and white strips. Up and down the piano. Back and forth. Black and white. Their ordered pattern is soothing. So pleasing, so right, I want to touch them. Ground myself in them somehow.

So I do.

My feeble old hands find three notes.

C.

E.

G.

Why? How . . . how do I remember the names of those notes? Or even that they're called notes?

But I do. I remember.

They don't sound quite right, though. Not like I want them to. Oh shoot. Maybe I didn't remember right after all. Or maybe there's something missing, maybe another—

"Here."

The man's voice is low and close. His palm brushes my knuckles as he crosses his hand over mine and pings a note at the top of the chord.

"B-flat," he says. "That's the note you're looking for."

Yes. *Yes.* How did he know? How did he know that the three white keys I'm playing needed that one black note to sound right?

I replace his finger with mine, and he moves his hand. Light glints off a red gem in a ring he's wearing.

Black.

White.

Red.

Ephraim.

The name wells from somewhere deep inside and bursts from my lips. It doesn't sound familiar to me. Doesn't bring to mind any time or place or face. But the tears in my eyes and the fullness in my heart tell me it must've once been very important.

The man's deep-brown eyes are crinkled with joy. His smile shows teeth in the midst of a beard that's almost as white.

"Ephraim," I say again. "I . . . I think I knew someone by that name once."

His broadening smile plucks a string deep in my heart. "Call me RJ," he says.

I can't look away. Looking at this RJ, being around him, hearing his music, brings . . . not memories, of course. But shadows. So soothing and warm and happy I want to stay in them forever.

"You look like . . ." I pause, wanting to make sure I get the right words. "You look like someone I'd like to know."

He tilts his head to the side, and the sunshine of his smile warms my face. "I'd like to know you too. Very much."

Then he turns back to the piano. Back to all those black and white keys and the beautiful music he can coax out of them.

I could listen to this music forever. It's my favorite kind.

It's the kind that sounds like love.

CHAPTER THIRTY-SEVEN

SITTING IN THE Fireside Room of Plaza de Paz, watching Rosie and Ephraim reconnect after all these decades, thickened Carter's throat and brought a sting to his eyes. Exhaustion, no doubt. But he'd be kidding himself if he truly believed that was all it was.

Joy ringed his heart at those two crazy eighty-five-year-old kids. Their brilliant smiles, the tender way they gazed at each other, spoke of both old memories and new beginnings. Even after all this time, these two were meant to be.

What he wouldn't give for that kind of clarity, that kind of fresh start, with Lauren. For crystal clear confirmation that it was God's plan for them to be together. Or not.

Carter knew his own heart, of course. Knew it to the very depths of him, without a second thought.

But what God wanted mattered more. Carter would do anything to be with her, but more than that, he'd do anything for her to be at peace. In the center of God's plan for her life. And if that meant never seeing her again, never hearing her sweet voice, living the rest of his days without the sunshine of her presence, then so be it. Just like Ephraim and Rosie had decided the most loving choice was to let each other go, he'd sacrifice his own happiness in a second if it meant Lauren would have hers.

Well. One thing was clear. The aged lovebirds didn't need him hanging around, intruding on such an intimate moment, spoiling its purity with his own mental thunderstorm.

Rising from the chair, he slipped quietly from the room and headed for the double glass doors at the end of the hallway. If God would just give him some kind of sign. Some indication of—

"Carter?"

Lauren's voice echoed off the white-painted walls. Stopped him with his right heel on the ground and his heart burning.

He turned, and breath whooshed out of him. All the times he'd seen Lauren, all the days he'd spent with her and the nights she'd visited his dreams, she'd never been more beautiful. Paused there, her blue skirt swishing around slender legs, her hair glimmering gold in the hallway lights. The dimple in her cheek sunk halfway, suspended by a hesitant yet hopeful smile.

His heart vaulted into his throat. "Hey."

"I wanted to thank you." Her dimple deepened, and her long-lashed gaze dropped to the carpet. "I mean, I probably said it before, but what you did, flying Ephraim in to see Grandma again, to meet us, I just . . . Thanks, Carter." She glanced up again, her eyes a mix of emotions he couldn't hope to guess at.

He swallowed hard. "I'd do it again in a second."

"I know."

She wrapped an arm around her midsection, and panic surged through him. This must've been how Rosie and Ephraim had felt all those years ago, standing in that train station, spending their final few moments together. It was like being on air that first stormy spring day as a tornado bore down on the metro, with thousands of lives depending on his next few words. How could he appropriately convey the gravity of the moment? What could he say to encapsulate all he felt for Lauren, all she meant to him, in the last few seconds of her presence?

"So, uh." He palmed his neck and looked at the ground. "How are you?"

Wow. That was lame.

But at least it was something.

"I'm okay." She twisted that funky ring around her middle finger. "I'm, uh . . . I'm doing really well, actually."

"Good." It was good. And he should be happy for her. If he was a better man, he would be.

But he wasn't a better man, and his heart was breaking. He'd wanted confirmation, and here it was.

Lauren was better off without him.

Her bracelets clinked as she brushed back a lock of hair. "How are you?"

Terrible. I haven't slept in days. And every time I do fall asleep, you're hovering there, just out of reach.

"Good," he replied.

"How's your dad?"

Carter focused once more on the dark-gray swirls beneath his shoes, unable to bear the compassion in her eyes.

"Better. He checked into a rehab facility in Liberal last weekend."

Lauren's eyes brightened. "Oh. Yay. I mean . . . that's good, right?"

"It's very good. Dad's always tried to deal with this on his own, never asking for any kind of help. But you can't really kick this kind of thing all by yourself."

"Yeah, I get that." Her lips curved. "Anyway, I'm glad he's getting help. I've been praying for him. And you."

Her words made his eyes burn. "Thanks. That means a lot."

"Carter." She stepped toward him, rolling her lower lip between her teeth. "There's something I want to make sure you know."

She must sense the looming goodbye as well.

He swallowed hard. "Okay."

"I don't want you to blame yourself for my bulimia, okay? That's my issue and mine alone." She shook her head. "So much was spiraling out of control during that part of my life, and food was the one thing I felt I could grab on to. But that spiraled too."

Carter nodded. "Makes sense."

"God never let go of me, though. I felt like everything was a mess, but he was always in control. Forgiving me. Redeeming and restoring all the messes I made." Her eyes shone with a new intensity. "He's doing the same for you too, Carter. There's nothing God can't restore."

He had to get out of here. Had to get away from her before he grabbed her and kissed her and ruined everything.

He gripped the keys in his pocket. "Listen, Lauren, I want nothing but joy for you, all right? Nothing but the best God has to offer."

"Wait." Her brow furrowed. "Are you saying goodbye?"

His teeth clenched against the emotion that threatened to spill forth. "Isn't that what this is?"

She blinked. "Well, I . . ." A slight chuckle escaped. "Oh man, this is gonna sound stupid." She raised her eyes to his and brushed her hair back. "I thought maybe we could be friends."

Oh, she was killing him. In all the worst-case scenarios that had danced through his head, this one—her moving on, meeting someone, flashing a huge diamond on her left hand, walking down the aisle to pledge herself to some other guy, all while he sat courtside smiling like an idiot and trying to pretend his heart wasn't shattering into a million pieces—had never occurred to him.

It sounded like a horrible way to spend his life.

Even worse than spending it without her in it at all.

"I have enough friends, Lauren." His voice sounded rougher than he wanted, and hurt flashed in her eyes.

"I see," she said, so quietly he almost couldn't hear her.

Shoving caution aside, he reached for her hand. Her eyes widened slightly as he caressed the peaks and valleys of her knuckles with the pad of his thumb. "What I meant was that it's darn near impossible to be friends with someone you're still crazy in love with. Someone who's the first thing you think about in the morning and the last thing on your mind at night. Someone who can make your whole day with a single smile. Someone you know in your heart you'll never, ever, not be in love with."

"Oh." Her mouth stayed that way, in the little O shape, and it was so adorable he almost kissed it.

Almost.

"But sometimes, no matter how much you love someone, love isn't enough."

She pressed her lips together. "You're right, Carter. Sometimes it isn't."

His heart sank to the floor and shattered.

"But God *is* enough. He takes our broken, hopelessly flawed selves, covers it all with his grace, and makes something beautiful with it. And that grace is enough, Carter." She smiled. "God is enough."

Wasn't that what Jim had said? Wasn't that what God had proven over and over the last few weeks?

Tears turned Lauren's eyes a brilliant ocean blue, and she covered his hand with both of hers. "And Grandma and Ephraim showed me that it's never too late for God. Nothing's too far gone for him to redeem it."

Hope surged.

Lauren tightened her grip on his hand. "In *Fiddler on the Roof,* Hodel knew exactly what she was getting into with Perchik. And I know exactly what I'm signing up for with you. I know your family situation, I know your damage, and none of it scares me. Because God's got this, Carter. He's got us. He got me through bulimia. He brought Grandma and Ephraim back together after almost sixty years. He's helped you stay sober for over a decade. He brought us to the same grocery store, the same makeup aisle . . . Is there anything in the world he can't do?"

Had he needed a sign? Well, here was one. Screaming and flashing and blinding in its brightness. Just as God had freed him from alcohol's grip, just as he'd brought Rosie and Ephraim back together, he'd been guiding things with Lauren too.

As much as Carter loved her, that love alone wouldn't be enough. But God and his grace would stand in the gap, make broken things whole, and strengthen him to be exactly who Lauren needed him to be.

"No, Lauren." He freed his hand from hers and ran it through her hair. His eyes filled again, but these were tears of joy. Of love. Of freedom.

He slipped his hands behind her neck and feasted his gaze on her. Her blue eyes. Her adorable freckles. Her full lips. "There's nothing he can't do."

Then he bent his head and claimed her lips, and his heart was home at last.

><

This kiss was just as emotion filled as their last had been. Now, as then, tears stung Lauren's eyes. Her throat held a sizable lump. Her heart felt close to cracking open.

And Carter poured just as much passion into this kiss as he had their last one. His lips on hers were every bit as fervent, his embrace every bit as firm.

But that last kiss had been goodbye.

This one was hello. Welcome home. Forever.

When they finally broke apart, she trailed her fingertips over his temple. His cheekbone. His lips. His eyes fell closed and the muscle in his cheek twitched, as though the storm of emotions inside was too much for him.

"Lauren." His voice was raspy. Still breathless. "I love you. I've loved you since that rehearsal at Sunflower where you first admitted how scared you were. That first moment you let it slip that you needed help, and I was the one who could help you." He captured her hand and kissed her fingertips one by one. "I love you no matter what you look like, no matter what the scale says. And if you ever doubt that, then I'll reassure you." Still clutching her hand, he moved his kisses to her cheek. "Again." Her other cheek. "And again." The delicate lobe of her ear. "And again." The hollow of her throat.

She'd melt to the floor in a boneless heap if Carter weren't holding her so tightly.

"And I've loved you . . ." She looked deep into those rich brown eyes. Trailed her fingers through close-cropped dark hair. "Since the first time we practiced Hodel and Perchik's dance. Remember? You tripped over your own feet, and I realized Mr. Basketball Star was a closet klutz."

His laugh thrilled her to her toes. "Hey. I've gotten better."

"You have." She wiggled her eyebrows. "You've gotten better at a lot of things." To prove it, she kissed him again. And yes, he was a good kisser before. There'd been no doubt. But now . . . now it was like kissing her was what he was born to do.

"And I love you," she whispered against his lips. "No matter who your dad is. No matter what your past is. No matter what wounds and scars and damage you carry around with you. And if you ever doubt that, if you ever start thinking you're doomed to repeat your dad's mistakes, then I'll reassure you." She kissed the curve of his jaw. "And I'll do it again." The corner of his mouth this time. "And again." The other corner. "And again." Her lips came home to his, and he melted into her with a happy groan.

The next time he pulled away, he captured her hand. Kissed the backs of her fingers. "I can't guarantee I won't hurt you, Lauren. I can't guarantee I won't do something stupid. But what I can guarantee is that I will never, ever quit on you. On us. Ever. And I will never stop loving you."

"I'll never stop loving you, Carter Douglas." Oh, how wonderful to have that fact sound hopeful, rather than hopeless. To know that loving him forever wasn't her doom.

It was her destiny.

"Come on." She patted his chest. "You look like you could use some caffeine. Let's get some cold brew in you."

"I'll never say no to that."

"And I have a hankering for a latte."

He turned, brows arched. "A latte? You?"

"Oat milk. No whipped cream." She grinned. "I haven't lost it completely. But I am expanding my horizons."

"Y'know . . ." Mischief gleamed in his eyes. "I know this great coffee place. Not too far on the map. No clouds in the sky, and I'm pretty sure Ethel doesn't have any other plans."

"Then what are we waiting for, Carter?" She took him by the hand and started toward the exit doors. "Let's fly."

AUTHOR'S NOTE

IT IS WITH a great deal of fear and trembling that I approach the topic of race relations, particularly in our nation's current political climate. Nevertheless, I feel it's an important topic to address, because despite the inescapable fact that we as individuals and as a country have a great deal of work still to do in this area, we have made progress. When my Chinese American husband and I first started dating, I believe it was perhaps a surprise to both sides of our family, but it was not an unwelcome surprise. Our budding relationship and subsequent marriage was warmly embraced by both Cheech's family and mine. As my dad once memorably put it, "I don't care if the man you marry has two heads or purple skin or anything else. As long as he loves Jesus and he loves you, he'll be more than welcome." Our three kids, who are sixth-generation Kansans on one side and second-generation Americans on the other side, are a beautiful illustration of the blending of two cultures and a living reminder that "there is neither Jew nor Greek, there is neither slave nor free, there is no male and female, for you are all one in Christ Jesus" (Gal. 3:28 ESV).

But marriages like ours were not always welcome. As recently as 1967, mixed-race marriages were illegal in some states, a reflection of segregation and institutionalized racism in the United States. And even in those states without anti-miscegenation laws, mixed-race marriage was definitely frowned upon. (In the 1950s, public approval of mixed-race marriage was at 5 percent, compared with over 80 percent today.) Two books I read for research, *Marriage Across the Color Line* (ed. Clotye M. Larsson, Johnson Publishing Company, Chicago, 1965) and *Race Mixing: Black-White Marriage in Postwar America* (Renee C. Romano, The University Press of

Florida, Gainesville, 2003), proved very eye opening as to why interracial relationships, particularly those between black and white, were so taboo. Both black and white societies objected to such relationships for very different reasons, and both these books were enormously helpful in unpacking that. In addition, my sensitivity reader, Jayna Breigh, shed some light on her own interracial marriage. This book would not be what it is without her guidance, and I owe her my deepest gratitude. Any mistakes are my own, and for any oversight or inaccuracy, readers have my sincerest apologies.

Race relations have been an integral part of Kansas history since before statehood. In the decade leading up to the Civil War, Kansas was marked with conflict between free-state settlers and pro-slavery Missourians, which ended only when Kansas was admitted to the Union as a free state in 1861, shortly before the secession of the Southern states. Since Kansas was a free state, many African Americans sought refuge here, leading to the creation of a number of all-black towns (Nicodemus, in northwestern Kansas, being the only one still remaining).

Wichita's black community dates back to the city's infancy, including pioneers, cowboys, and business figures, and continued to grow after World War II, when an influx of African Americans, especially from Southern states, moved here to work in the city's growing aviation industry. Though Wichita was relatively integrated at first, the intervening decades saw a gradual increase in segregation, which led to the creation of all-black neighborhoods featuring churches, movie theaters, businesses, schools, and civic organizations. Schools were segregated at the elementary and junior high levels, but high schools were integrated. Poring over high school yearbooks from Wichita East and Wichita North (the two high schools in existence at the time) helped shape my understanding of the fictional Roosevelt High School, where Rosie and Ephraim attend. And Wichita launched itself into a key, though relatively unknown, role in the civil rights movement when, in 1958, the Dockum Drug Store downtown became the site of the first successful lunch counter sit-in. Although this would have been fun to portray in my story, I decided to set it just a few years earlier, when neither Rosie nor Ephraim had any concrete reason to believe their relationship would ever be welcomed.

AUTHOR'S NOTE

When attempting to portray history, particularly that involving race relations, it is sometimes necessary as a storyteller to use language and portray attitudes that may be offensive to modern readers. I believe that, rather than erase the ugly parts of our national history, a better way is to expose these attitudes for the sins they are, cast ourselves on the mercy of Jesus, and repent. Only then can we grow. Please know that this is the spirit in which racist words and attitudes are used in this book—it is not my intention to hurt anyone through their use, and I have kept them to the barest minimum. Still, if any aspect of this book causes pain to a reader, please accept my apology.

ACKNOWLEDGMENTS

WRITING AND PUBLISHING a second book, I've found, is easier than the first go-round in many ways, much more difficult in a few other ways, and no less of a team effort. With that in mind, and with my deepest appreciation and gratitude, I'd like to thank:

Cheech, Caleb, Jonathan, and Selah, for your unflagging faithfulness, unrelenting hilarity, and eternal patience with my rants, occasional arguments with fictional characters, and times when Mommy needs to disappear into her writing cave to spend time with people who don't exist. This book would not be here without you, and I hope I've made you proud.

My parents, Jim and Deanna Peterson, for the usual love and encouragement, as well as several repetitions of "When are you going to write another book? I've read your other one four times now," which does wonders for a person's motivation. Thank you also for sharing some of your memories of the 1950s and growing up in small town western Kansas, and to my dad for answering a few aviation-related questions. Most importantly, thank you for welcoming and loving Cheech and our children, and thank you that there was never a single doubt in my mind that you would.

The entire Wen/Lee clan, that large, lovable Chinese bunch who welcomed me as one of their own from day one. The fact that Cheech and I are different races and from different cultures has mattered not at all to you, and I feel loved and supported by every single one of you. I'm so blessed to be part of your wonderful family.

Theresa Romain, Linda Fletcher, and Rachel Scott McDaniel, my critique partners extraordinaire. Thank you for your enthusiasm for my work, your eagle eyes to catch all the things that don't make sense, and your ever-present eagerness for the next chapter.

My rock-star agent, Tamela Hancock Murray, and the dream team of editors, designers, and marketing folks at Kregel Publications. It's a real joy and honor to work together with you all to bring another story to life. Thank you for believing in me.

Jayna Breigh, my wonderful sensitivity reader. Thank you for the reassurance in the spots I needed it and your gentle corrections in places where I needed those.

Janine Rosche and Courtney Walsh, for lending your expertise and experience to various aspects of this story.

My music colleagues and students at Haven High School, both past and present, for inspiring and informing parts of this book and for your general enthusiasm for and encouragement of my rather unusual other job.

My amazing friends Nolan and Angie Banks, for your well-timed texts, your much-needed nights out, your love, your support, and of course, your snark.

The Quotidians, my church family at Riverlawn Christian Church, and my mom's prayer group, for championing my first book and praying me through my second.

God the Father, God the Son, and God the Holy Spirit, for giving me the strength and courage to write what at times has been a difficult story. Any glory this book receives goes directly to you.

Last but most certainly not least, all the readers of *Roots of Wood and Stone*. I have been honored by your glowing reviews, emails, and all the other ways you've reached out to me to let me know how much you loved the story and how eager you were for a sequel. Here it is—I hope it meets your expectations.